Steve Martini, a former trial attorney, has worked as a journalist and capital correspondent in the California State House in Sacramento. He has been engaged in both public and private practice of law. He lives on the US West Coast with his wife and daughter. Steve Martini is the author of the highly acclaimed thrillers *Compelling Evidence*, *The Simeon Chamber*, *Prime Witness*, *Undue Influence*, *The Judge*, *The List*, and *Critical Mass* all of which are available from Headline.

Praise for Steve Martini's electrifying bestsellers:

'The best debut, in my opinion, is *Compelling Evidence*' John Grisham

'Compelling indeed . . . a terrific debut' *Sunday Telegraph*

'Nice insider touches, and a hard-punching climax' *The Times*

'Tense and gripping' *Books*

'Martini's plotting proves ingenious' *Publisher's Weekly*

'Thoroughly absorbing' *Literary Review*

'The courtroom novel of the year' *Kirkus Reviews*

'A rousing climax . . . a brilliant series of trial scenes . . . the characters are sharply drawn . . . the courtroom psychology is laid out vividly . . . readers will find their fingers glued to the pages' *Publisher's Weekly*

Also by Steve Martini

Critical Mass
The List
The Judge
Undue Influence
Prime Witness
The Simeon Chamber
Compelling Evidence

The Attorney

Steve Martini

HEADLINE
FEATURE

First published in Great Britain in 2000
by HEADLINE BOOK PUBLISHING

First published in paperback in 2000
by HEADLINE BOOK PUBLISHING

A HEADLINE FEATURE paperback

10 9 8 7 6 5

This is a work of fiction. The events described are
imaginary and the characters are fictitious and not
intended to represent specific living persons. Even when
settings are referred to by their true names, the incidents
portrayed as taking place there are entirely fictitious;
the reader should not infer that the events set there ever
happened.

ISBN 0 7472 6063 X

Typeset by Palimpsest Book Production Limited,
Polmont, Stirlingshire
Printed and bound in Great Britain by
Mackays of Chatham plc, Chatham, Kent

HEADLINE BOOK PUBLISHING
A division of the Hodder Headline Group
338 Euston Road
LONDON NW1 3BH
www.headline.co.uk
www.hodderheadline.com

To Leah

ACKNOWLEDGMENTS

For the return of Paul Madriani, fans and this writer owe a debt of gratitude to Phyllis Grann, president of Penguin Putnam, who has been steadfast in her determination to return the man to the courtroom. For this I owe her both my thanks and acknowledgment.

For color and geographic authenticity, much of it gleaned in the sparkling seaside city of San Diego, thanks are due to the staff of San Diego district attorney Paul J. Pfingst. In particular I thank Greg Thompson, chief deputy district attorney, and James D. Pippin, chief of the Superior Court Division of that office.

In addition I thank San Diego superior court judge Frank A. Brown for his kindness in allowing me a glimpse behind the scenes of the criminal courts and the San Diego Hall of Justice, as well as for his endearing sense of humor and his fishing stories.

For color and authenticity of location at the sailing mecca that is Shelter Island, and for their encouragement in using San Diego as a new setting for these stories, I owe thanks to Jack and Peggie Dargitz and to the entire staff of the Red Sails Inn.

For her endless patience in putting up with me, and her insights into the female psyche, I thank my wife, Leah.

To each of these, and to others whom I may have omitted to mention, I owe a debt of gratitude for their help and insight that, I hope, have allowed me to craft a story of seeming truth. For any failings that the reader may find in this regard, I am solely responsible.

ACKNOWLEDGMENTS

CHAPTER
ONE

I can trace it back with precision to one of those fitful weeks in August, when the thermometer hit triple digits for the tenth day in a row. Even the humidity was high; unusual for Capital City. The air conditioner in my car had died and at six-fifteen, traffic on the Interstate was stalled behind an overturned truck-and-trailer rig filled with tomatoes on their way to the Campbell's plant. I would be late picking up Sarah from the sitter's.

Even with this as background, it was an impulsive move. Ten minutes after I got home, I called a realtor I knew and asked the fateful question, *How much can I get for the house? Would you come by for an appraisal?* The real estate market was heating up, like the weather, so in this respect my timing was good.

Sarah was out of school, in that awkward gap between fifth grade and middle school, and not looking forward to the switch. Her best friends – twin sisters her same age – were in the southern part of the state. I'd met their mother during a legal seminar in which we were both speakers, almost three years ago now.

Susan McKay and her daughters lived in San Diego. Susan and I had been seeing a lot of each other, between monthly trips to San Diego and meetings at the halfway point in Morro Bay. For some reason that adults will never comprehend, the kids seemed to bond at that very first meeting. In San Diego, the weather was cool and breezy. And it held the promise of family life, something Sarah and I had been missing for nearly four years.

We had spent two weeks visiting in early July. I had become infected with the scent of salt in the air, and the facets of the sun dancing on the surface of the sea at Coronado. In the late afternoon, Susan and I sat on the beach as the girls played in the water. The Pacific appeared as some boundless, undulating crucible of quicksilver.

After fourteen short days, Sarah and I bade farewell and piled info my car. As I looked at my daughter, I could read her mind. *Why are we going back to Capital City? What is there for us?*

It took her an hour in the car to verbalize these thoughts, and when she did, I was prepared with all the cold, adult logic a father can command.

I have a job there. I have to get back.

But you could get another job down here.

It takes a long time for a lawyer to build a practice. It's not that easy.

You started once before. You could do it again. Besides we have money now. You said so yourself.

On this point she had me. I had made a killing in a civil case eight months earlier, a wrongful death that went to the

2

jury. We'd hit a verdict, Harry Hinds and I, like gold bars on the pay line of a slot machine. We'd plucked the insurance company for eight million dollars. It's what happens when a defendant circles the wagons in a bad case. A widow with two children was now financially secure, and Harry and I had been left with a tidy nest egg in fees, even after taxes.

Still, uprooting my practice was risky.

I understand. You're feeling lonely, I told Sarah.

I am lonely, she said.

With that I looked at my daughter sitting in the passenger seat next to me, staring doe-eyed, braces and long brown hair, waiting for an answer that made sense. I didn't have one.

When my wife, Nikki, died, she left a hole in our lives that I have never been able to fill. As we headed back toward Capital City, the nagging question remained: *What is here for us?*

The corrosive politics and blistering summer heat of Capital City held few attractions and a great many painful memories. There had been the year of Nikki's illness that even now I could not blot out. There were places in the house where, when I turned a corner, I still saw her face. Couples, who had been friends, no longer had anything in common with a widower approaching middle age. And now my daughter wanted to put it all behind us.

On a Monday morning, the last week in August, I called Harry into my office. At one time, Harry Hinds had been one of the foremost criminal lawyers in town, trying mostly front-page felonies. Fifteen years ago he lost a death case, and his client lost his life in the state's gas chamber. Harry was never the same. By the time I opened a practice in the same building where Harry had his offices, he was defending drunk drivers and commiserating with them on bar stools after hours.

He came on board to lend a hand with the Talia Potter murder trial, and ever since has been a fixture. Harry's speciality is the mountains of paper produced in any trial. With a mind like a steel trap, Harry refers to his document searches as 'digging through the bullshit to find the flowers.' He is the only man I know who hates losing more than I do.

I didn't have the heart to tell him I was leaving Capital City, so I put it out as just opening a branch office.

He surprised me. His only question was where.

When I told him, his eyes lit up. It seemed Harry was game for the move himself. A new practice in a fresh place, the mellow swells of the Pacific, a few boat drinks along the way, maybe snag another big judgment in a civil case and head for the pastures of semi-retirement. In that instant Harry saw himself sipping piña coladas and surveying the swells on their yachts from the veranda of the Del Coronado. Harry has a fanciful imagination.

We found an associate to keep things together in the Capital City office. Harry and I weren't ready to burn our bridges. We would take turns trekking back to the home office, keeping one foot in both worlds until we could make the jump south for good.

In these months Susan played a pivotal role as surrogate mother for Sarah. I could leave my daughter with her for a week at a time. Even though Susan's house was burglarized in the late winter, I felt confident leaving Sarah with her. I knew she would always care for and protect my daughter as if she were her own. When I called Susan's house on

4

those weeklong trips it was difficult to get Sarah even to come to the phone. When she did, her voice was filled with laughter and the abruptness that tells you that your call is an interruption. For the first time in five years, since Nikki died, our daughter was a carefree child.

Susan is seven years younger than I, a dark-haired beauty, and divorced. She has the fine features and innocent looks of a child, coupled with the mind of a warrior.

For eight years, Susan has been the director of Children's Protective Services in San Diego, an agency that investigates allegations of child abuse and makes recommendations to the DA regarding prosecutions and to the courts regarding child custody. It is a job she has held for eight years, though to call Susan's vocation a job is like calling the Christian Crusades a hobby. She pursues it with the zeal of a true believer. Children are her life. Her training is in early-childhood development where the mantra *Save the kids* has become a battle cry.

We have been seeing each other for more than two years, though even now in San Diego, we do not live together. I moved south to be with her, but – after some discussion – we decided not to move in together. At least not yet.

When I moved south, some unstated law of independence dictated that we maintain separate households. It seems we spend increasing amounts of time in each other's company; that is, when I am not on the road back to Capital City.

That particular Gordian knot will be cut as soon as Harry and I have secured a sufficient client base in the south, which is why today I am renewing an old acquaintance.

Jonah and Mary Hale sit across the desk from me. He has aged since I saw him last. Mary looks the same, different hairdo, but in the ten years she has not changed much. That was before Ben's death and Talia's murder trial. Oceans of water under that bridge.

Jonah was one of my earliest cases in private practice, soon after I left the DA's office where I'd cut my teeth. The firm had directed him down the hall to the new man in the cubicle at the end.

At the time, Jonah was just a working stiff, a married man in his fifties with a daughter in her late teens. He was getting ready to retire – against his will. He worked for the railroad in Capital City, the locomotive works which was in its death throes. Jonah had a chronic bad back and knees, thanks to years of toil on hard concrete lifting machine parts. So when the railroad was looking to downsize, he was an immediate candidate to go. Even now he walks with a cane, though this one is much more ornate than the plain curved-handled wooden stick I had seen him with back then.

'The legs don't get any better with age,' he tells me as he shifts back into his chair to find the point of relative comfort.

'But the smile is as good as ever,' I tell him.

'Only because I've found an old friend. I only hope you can help me.'

Jonah has the good looks of an aging Hemingway, with all the wrinkles in the right places. Even with his infirmities he has not put on weight. His tanned face is framed by a shock of white hair. His beard is close cropped, his eyes deep-set and gray. He is a rugged-looking man, well dressed, with a dark sweater-vest under a cashmere sport coat, and light-colored slacks. On his wrist is a gold watch the size of an oyster, a Rolex he could never have afforded in the old days.

I introduce him to Harry.

'I've heard a lot about you,' says Harry.

Jonah just smiles. He is used to this by now: people coming up, slapping him on the back, cozying to get close.

'It's what happens when your number comes up,' he tells Harry. 'Everybody assumes that you had something to do with it.'

'Well you did buy the ticket,' says Harry.

'Yes. And there have been times when I wish he hadn't,' says Mary.

'Having money can be its own curse,' Jonah tells us. One senses that he means what he says.

Jonah won the largest lottery payout in state history: $87 million. He had purchased the ticket five years after I'd won his case, securing a disability from the railroad that paid him $26,000 a year plus medical benefits for life.

'I couldn't believe it when I saw your name in the phone book. I told Mary when I saw your name it had to be you, or your kid. How many Paul Madrianis could there be? Especially lawyers.'

'One of a kind,' says Harry. 'Broke the mold.'

'So what can we do for you?' I ask.

'It's our daughter,' says Jonah. 'I don't think you've ever met Jessica.'

'I don't think so.'

'I went to the police. But they said it wasn't a criminal matter. Can you believe it? She's kidnapped my grand-daughter, and the police tell me it isn't criminal. They can't get involved.'

'Kidnapped?' I ask.

'I don't know what else to call it. For three weeks now,

7

going on a month, I been runnin' around like a chicken without my head. Going to the police. Following up with the lawyer we hired.'

'There's another lawyer?'

'Yeah, but he can't do anything. Supposedly nobody can.'

'Calm down. Tell me what happened.'

'My granddaughter, Amanda, is eight years old. She's lived with us, Mary and me, almost since the day she was born.'

'She's your daughter's child?'

'Jessica gave birth to her, if that's what you mean,' he says. 'She's not what you would call a good mother. Jessica's had problems with drugs. Been in and out of jail.' He pauses to look at Harry and me. 'The fact is, she spent two years in the women's correctional facility at Corona.'

This is not jail, but state prison. Harry lifts an eyebrow in question and before he can put it to words, Jonah responds.

'For drugs. She was caught transporting a quantity of cocaine across the border for a dealer down in Mexico. God knows where she meets these people. We paid for her attorney. He made some kind of a deal with the federal government so that she could serve her time in a state facility rather than a federal penitentiary, supposedly so she could be closer to Amanda. The fact is, she's never really shown much interest in Mandy. That's what we call her, Mary and I.'

He reaches into the inside of his coat and pulls out a small leather container. It looks as if it is designed to hold expensive fountain pens. He opens it, and I see cigars.

'Do you mind?'

Mary shoots him a disapproving look.

Ordinarily my office is a smoke-free zone, but I make an exception. He offers me one, but I decline. Harry accepts.

'My doctor says I shouldn't smoke. My only vice, besides the boat and fishing. Do you ever go out?' he asks. 'Sport fishing?'

I shake my head. Jonah is wandering now, trying to avoid a painful subject.

'You should try it sometime. Soothes the soul. I'll take you out on the *Amanda*.' The words stick in his throat for a second. 'I named it after my granddaughter. She used to love to go out.'

'Enough with the boat,' says Mary. 'Our daughter wanted money. She always wanted money. That ticket was a curse. Without it she would have left Amanda alone. Left her with us and gone about her life, such as it was. But with all that money . . . It was its own kind of narcotic.'

'She came to me for money when she got out. Said she wanted to start a business. I said I wouldn't give her any. I knew the money would go into her arm, or up her nose, for drugs. Or to one of those bums she's habitually shacked up with. My daughter's taste in men leaves a lot to be desired. She is too attractive for her own good.'

He pulls his wallet out of an inside coat pocket, and from it he plucks a photograph. He hands it across the desk to me.

'She had her hair cut like Meg Ryan, the movie star. Everybody kept telling her she looked like her.'

I look at the photo. Her friends weren't lying. Jessica is blonde, cute in a sexy kind of way. Her short hair is cut in a pixie. The most endearing feature is her smile, which, if you stopped there, would mark her as the kid next door. Her jeans look like they had been molded to her body, and a tank top leaves little to the imagination. Slumped over her, hugging her from behind is a guy in a leather vest and no shirt. I can see a tattoo on one arm and, though the picture is too indistinct, I can imagine needle tracks below the elbow.

'Jessica always seemed to collect the losers,' says Jonah. 'Tattoos up the ass. Worthless men living on the backs of motorcycles. You know the kind.' He looks at me through a smoke veil and takes a puff.

'This is Mandy.' Jonah hands me another snapshot. Mandy in a school uniform. Her hair is tied in a neat ponytail with wisps escaping at the sides.

'Mandy's hair is a little longer now,' says Mary. 'At least I think it is. Unless they cut it.'

'The police told us they sometimes do that. And dress 'em up to look like boys. So a picture in the paper, on a milk carton doesn't do any good,' adds Jonah.

Harry looks at the photo of Jessica, an appraising eye. 'How old is she?'

'Jessica's twenty-eight. She survives to be thirty, it'll be a miracle. That's why we gotta get Mandy back. Different man with her mother every night. Some of them pretty bad.'

'What about the girl's father?' says Harry.

'Your guess is as good as mine,' says Jonah. 'Nobody ever came forward, and Jessica wasn't talking.'

'Who has legal custody?' I ask.

'We had temporary custody when Jess went to prison. Now it's permanent. Not that it does a damn bit of good.'

10

'Jessica only got interested in Mandy after I won the lotto. Her message was clear. When she got out, she wanted money, and the collateral was Mandy. Unless I paid, she would be taking her back as soon as she got out. I offered to buy her a house. Of course I wouldn't put it in her name. I wasn't that foolish. She would have sold it first chance, pocketed the money and run off. But just the same, I offered to put her up in a good home in the neighborhood where we live. To support her. But she didn't want any part of that. Too many strings attached, she said.'

'So you filed a petition for permanent custody?' says Harry.

'Right. We went to court. By that time there were a number of letters from Jessica in Corona. She hadn't been too smart. In the letters she threatened to take the child back unless we paid. This didn't put her in a very good light with the court. Though she had the legal right to take Amanda back, the court saw what was happening. Mandy had become like a piece of property in a pawnshop. Her mother would take money in return for leaving her with us, and when that was gone she'd come back for more.'

'I take it Jessica's out of prison?' Harry asks.

'She got out six months ago,' says Jonah. 'Twenty-third of October. I remember the day exactly, because she came to the house. She was different. She looked different.'

'Prison has a way of doing that,' I tell him.

'No. It wasn't that. In fact, she was cleaned up. She looked better than I'd seen her in years.'

'Prison life must have agreed with her,' says Harry.

'I think it gave her some discipline. Focus in her life. Only she directed it in all the wrong ways,' says Jonah. 'She was well dressed. Nothing fancy, mind you. Pair of slacks and a sweater. Wore these new glasses, wire-rims that made her look almost intellectual. She wanted to see Mandy. What could we do?'

'You let them visit?'

'In the living room of our home,' he says. 'Mandy's seen so little of her mother I didn't know how she'd react. When Jessica walked into the room, Mandy sort of collapsed, like someone had let all the air out of her.' Jonah sighs.

'In the living room that day, I felt like someone was ripping the heart out of my chest. Mandy's stomach hurt for days afterward, just from the stress of her mother's visit, the fact that she was back in her life. Mary and I thought it might be good for them both if they could spend a little time together, get to know each other, ease in.

'But Jessica fell into old habits. She started to manipulate the child. Wanted to take her home. Wherever the hell that was.'

'Probably some halfway house,' says Harry. 'That's where they usually go out of the joint.'

'We said no. There was no way we could allow it.'

'Jessica looked me dead in the eye. Told me she was gonna get her child back come hell or high water. That I had no right to take her. This, after she'd abandoned the kid for the better part of eight years. She said she was going to fight me. In court if necessary. Outside the court if she had to.'

'Did she?' I ask.

'She went to court. Got an order of visitation. That's when the trouble started.'

'What kind of trouble?' says Harry.

'Jessica was allowed to take Mandy on weekends. Two

weekends a month. She would pick her up on Friday night and return her Sunday afternoon. It went fine for the first month. Then in early December, they didn't come back until late Sunday night. Close to midnight. Each weekend she'd come back a little later than the weekend before. Like she was testing me.'

'Why didn't you go back to court?'

'Because the lawyer I had told me that unless we had something substantial, a serious violation of the terms of visitation, the court wasn't likely to do anything except warn her. He said it would only make matters worse.'

Jonah's lawyer had a point.

'Then, finally, three weeks ago, she didn't bring Mandy back at all. We were frantic. I called the number where Jessica was supposed to be living. We were told she'd moved. They didn't know where. We called the police. They told us they couldn't do a thing – not unless we had evidence that some crime had been committed. We told them we had a court order of custody. They told us we'd have to go to court, ask the judge to hold Jessica in contempt for violating the order.'

'But she brought her back?' says Harry.

Jonah nods. 'Monday morning, ten o'clock Mandy comes through the front door, Jessica right behind her as if nothing had happened. And they weren't alone.'

'One of Jessica's boyfriends?' says Harry.

Jonah shakes his head. 'A woman.'

'What woman?' I ask.

Jonah fishes in his pocket, pulls out a business card and hands it to me. On the card in bold italic are the words:

13

Underneath it in letters larger than the organization's is the name:

Zolanda 'Zo' Suade
Director

'Without so much as a how do you do, she's in my face,' says Jonah. 'This other woman. She tells me she knows all about me. That because I have a lot of money, won the lottery, I think I can do whatever I want, that I can steal my daughter's child.

'I tell her I have a court order.

'She tells me that it's worthless. That the courts are all run by men for men, that she doesn't recognize court orders, and that if I know what's good for me I'll simply turn Mandy back over to her mother.

'By this time I'm about ready to deck this broad.' Jonah looks at Harry. 'Excuse my language,' he says. 'But I was ready to kill.

'I told her to leave. She refused. She said they'd leave when they were good and ready. Finally, I told her I was gonna call the cops, and Mary, she starts moving toward the phone. That's when this Zolanda . . .' Jonah makes the name sound like the word should have four letters. 'That's when she decides it's time to leave. But not before she tells me I have a choice. I can either give Mandy up willingly, or we can lose her. Either way, she says, Jessica's gonna get her child back.'

'Did she leave?'

'Yeah. She and Jessica both. I was shaking like a leaf. If I'd had this in my hand at that moment' – he holds up the cane – 'I think I'd'a hit her. I would'a crushed her head like a walnut. Luckily I didn't. Amanda was crying. She was standing there listening to all of this. She doesn't like friction, arguments. She can't deal with it. It gives her stomach pains. And here I am shouting with some stranger who's threatening to take her away.

'First thing I do is call my lawyer. I tell ya, this guy's not half the lawyer you are, Paul.

'Anyway I tell the lawyer what's going on, and the minute I mention this woman's name, this Zolanda, he asks me where my granddaughter is. I tell him she's standing right beside me. He doesn't say a thing, but I can hear the sigh of relief over the phone, like somebody who just woke up from a bad dream in flop sweat. I ask him who the hell she is, the devil?

'"She may not be the devil," he says, "but as far as you're concerned, she's got the keys to hell." He tells me we've got to get back to court fast, before the weekend. And no matter what happens, he says, I am not to turn Amanda over to my daughter for visitation. Even if the sheriff shows up with a court order, he says. Just stall him until I can get Amanda away from the house.

'By this time we're really gettin' worried. Mary's frantic. You can imagine.'

'I can,' I tell him.

'Have you ever heard of this woman?' he asks.

I shake my head. 'But then I'm new to town.'

'Apparently she has a reputation beyond San Diego,' he tells me. 'There's been national publicity.'

'I haven't seen it. But then I don't work in the field. Family law.'

'What the lawyer told me turned out to be . . . whaddaya call it?' Jonah searches for the word, can't come up with it.

'Prophetic?' says Harry.

Jonah snaps his fingers, the hand propped on the cane. 'That's it. We were doing everything to take precautions. We were taking Mandy to school and picking her up afterward. Driving her everywhere. We told her teachers that she was not to leave the school grounds with anyone but Mary or me.

'What we didn't figure was that it would happen in our own house. Four days ago I have a doctor's appointment. Mary takes me there.'

'Where was Amanda?' says Harry.

'We left Amanda home with a sitter, a young woman in her early twenties. She's sat for us many times. I figure, what could happen? We were scheduled to go back to court on Friday. The lawyer told me there was a good chance we could get the visitation order amended to require Jessica to see Amanda only in our home, under our supervision.

'My daughter must have been outside, watching. Ten minutes after we leave she shows up at the front door. She's alone and wants to see Mandy. The sitter told her she had strict instructions.

'My daughter is a practiced con artist. She tells you noon is midnight, smiles that cute little smile, and nine times out of ten you'd believe her. She's calm, reasonable, well dressed. She tells the sitter she's driven all way across town to tell Amanda something about a surprise present for her

16

grandma. Mary's birthday is eight months off. Still it's a hot secret between mother and daughter.

'Baby-sitter doesn't know what to do. She tells Jessica she's got instructions.

'Jessica gets all reasonable and understanding. You know the rap,' says Jonah. '"Last thing I'd want to do is get you in any trouble. Walked on hot coals to get here, but you want me to do it again? Sure, no problem."'

'So the girl lets her in. Jessica asks for a cup of coffee. The sitter goes to make it in the kitchen. She was gone three minutes.' He holds up three fingers. 'That's all it took. When she came back to the living room, they were gone. Jessica and Amanda both. She looked through the front window just in time to see the car backing down the driveway, tires screeching. A man was driving. Another man was in the passenger seat. There were two figures in the back.'

'Jessica and Amanda,' says Harry.

Jonah nods. 'We haven't seen them since.'

'Did the sitter get a license plate off the car?' I ask.

He shakes his head. 'Just a description. Late-model sedan, a two-door, dark in color.'

'No description of the driver?'

'She couldn't see well enough. It happened so quickly. But I know this woman's involved. This Zolanda Suade.'

'Let me guess,' I say. 'The sitter didn't see her the day they disappeared?'

'No. But who else could it be? She as much as told us she was gonna take Mandy. And there's more. My lawyer says that's what she does. Suade has an organization that specializes in this.'

'What? Kidnapping children?' says Harry.

17

'Yes. She's done it in other cases. The FBI. The police. Nobody can stop her.'

'Why the hell not?' says Harry.

I answer the question before Jonah can: 'Because she uses a parent in the abduction.'

He points at me with his finger as if to say *Just so*. 'It's why they won't get involved. They say technically it's not kidnapping. Violation of the court order of custody, maybe.'

'But that's a civil matter,' I say.

'Right. And it gets worse,' says Jonah. 'They've taken her across the border. Somewhere into Mexico.'

'How do you know that?'

'Cuz that's what the lawyer told me. He says she's taken others across. Somewhere down in Baja, but he doesn't know where.'

'Why does she do it?' says Harry. 'What's in it for her?'

'She's a feminist nut,' says Jonah. 'Has a problem with men. She has this organization to help wayward women and their children. Self-appointed crusader,' says Jonah. 'Only this time she's chewed off more than she can swallow. I'll bury the bitch.' As he says this, I can see the vein in the side of his head bulge. For a moment I'm afraid he will blow a major vessel in his brain, keel over on my desk.

'But how can I help you?' I ask.

'I want you to find out where my granddaughter is.'

'You need an investigator, not a lawyer.'

'Fine. Hire one. Hire the best,' he tells me. 'But I want you to be in charge. I trust you.'

'You'd be paying me, and there isn't much I can do. You

18

need information, and an investigator is the one to get that. You don't hire an electrician to do plumbing.'

'You do if there are sizzling wires in the water,' says Jonah. 'I've already talked to the other lawyer about hiring an investigator. He says I'd be wasting my time. Suade's too careful. She covers her tracks. Calls from pay phones. Never visits the places where she has the mothers and children holed up. She uses middlemen. It's like an underground railroad.'

'If that's what she's doing, what can I do?'

'I need somebody to take her organization apart. Get her into court. Sue her if you have to. She's created these shell corporations. This is one of them.' He holds up the business card with her name on it. 'She has several others. She takes donations from people who believe in her cause. Go after some of them. Dry up her funds. Put pressure on the cops and the courts to force her to talk. I'll pay,' he says. 'I'll pay whatever you want. Money is no obstacle. All I want is my granddaughter back.'

I look at Harry. My principal concern at the moment is whether I would be taking the man's money on false pretenses.

'I can't make a commitment,' I tell him. 'There really is no legal case. Other than the violation of the court order of custody.'

'Then start with that,' he says.

'We have no direct evidence that this woman, this Zolanda Suade, was involved.'

'You know she was. I know she was.'

'That's not evidence,' I tell him.

'She came to his house. She made threats,' says Harry.

'That might be evidence,' I concede. 'Still it's Jonah's word against hers.'

'I was there,' says Mary.

'Yeah. Don't forget Mary,' says Harry. Now they're double-teaming me. 'We can look into it,' Harry adds. 'We can at least do that much.'

Jonah is desperate, and now he's found an ally. Anyone not knowing Harry might be tempted to say that he is merely greedy. But I know him better. He's a soft touch. He sees Jonah's problem as one with merit. Even if Jonah were financially destitute, Harry would be pitching me to get involved, to tilt at this windmill. The fact that Jonah has money makes it that much easier. 'We can look into it,' I finally say. There are smiles all around, puffing, and a lot of cigar smoke.

CHAPTER

TWO

It is Saturday, a quiet afternoon, and I am doing up a few dishes in the sink. Through the window I can see Susan and the girls on the patio around the pool.

Coronado is an island only in the collective yearning of its inhabitants. It is connected to the city of San Diego by a huge arching bridge, which the locals fought for years, and which now spans the harbor to the east. To the south there is a seven-mile strip of sand known as the Silver Strand that wends its way along the Pacific to the communities of the South Bay and beyond them to the Mexican border.

Sarah and I have joined these refugees from the twenty-first century.

Our house is not large. It sits on J Avenue not far from Alameda, a small white cottage, single story with a quaint roof and white plaster walls, little-pane windows all around. It's a place that says 'home' to both Sarah and me. A feeling we are trying to rebuild in a strange new city and without Nikki.

The house is set back from the street behind a high grape-stake fence. There is a white flagpole with an American flag. This caught Sarah's eye. The privacy of the fence caught mine.

To the south the houses are larger, more expensive, some of them bordering on estates, until you reach Ocean Boulevard, where the houses are mansions. Just a few blocks farther on is the Del Coronado Hotel, a place made famous by Marilyn Monroe as a Florida resort in *Some Like It Hot*. The place is still hot, and very expensive.

We bought the bungalow because Sarah thought it was cute, something out of the Black Forest, and because she loved the swimming pool. It is a lap design and small.

The only thing smaller today is Susan's bikini, almost enough material for a pirate's eye patch. She is lying on a chaise at the far end of the pool, occasionally sipping iced tea from a tall glass, and reading. She is a voracious reader. She ravaged the morning paper over lunch, and now she is poring through some files from work. Susan is married to her job.

I drop a glass in the sink. Fortunately, the water keeps it from breaking. My mind is not on the dishes. At the moment my gaze is fixed on Susan. She is athletic, her body tempered like fine steel and tanned, long, sinuous legs and not an ounce of fat. This she beats from herself with a monk's dedication at the gym nearly every day. Though Susan McKay is nothing if not feminine, she could excel at professional bodybuilding. I have visions of myself on the beach being saved by her from some goon who wants to kick sand in my face.

She is tall, just a couple of inches shorter than I, with a

swanlike neck, high cheekbones, and dark hair cut dramatically short and parted on the left in the style of a fashion model.

I have learned from sorry experience that she also possesses the fiery disposition of a Latin that belies the name McKay. The name is the only thing left from her marriage of thirteen years, except for her two daughters. She did not discard the surname out of deference to the kids.

Her maiden name is Montoya. Susan was born in San Diego. Her family goes back here enough generations that they have lost count. I am told that a distant ancestor once held a land grant from the king of Spain.

Susan looks over the top of a sheaf of papers and spies me looking at her through the window. She waves, beckoning me to come out.

I make a sign, as if to say *in a moment*.

She smiles, an infectious flash of even white teeth.

I can hear the giggling kids in the pool. I take the dish towel off my shoulder and lay it on the sink next to the wet dishes draining in one of those metal racks, and head for the living room and the French doors leading out onto the patio. As I open the door the volume explodes, laughing children and splashing water.

'Daddy, are you coming in?' Sarah is hugging the edge of the pool, her hair shimmering and wet, beads of water running over the freckles around her nose.

'No. He's going to put some lotion on my back,' says Susan. She is already lowering the top of the chaise longue and positioning herself to lie facedown.

'Then are you going to come swimming? Pleeease.' Sarah is persistent.

23

'In a minute,' I tell her. 'You guys have fun. Right now there is something I have to do for Susan.'

'Don't make it sound like such a chore.' Susan gives me a wicked smile, and pulls on the string holding up the top of her bikini from behind her back. She holds it in place with one hand as she lies facedown.

Her body has a golden tone to it that is only partly genetic. We are in the balmy latitudes, above the tropics, not far from perpetual sun.

I sit on the edge of the chaise near her knees, spread some Australian Gold on my hands and warm it with friction. Then I begin to apply it to her shoulders and the upper part of her back.

'Mmm.' She offers some sensuous moves, pressing the front of her body into the soft cushion of the chaise. 'I thought you were never going to come out. I come over to play and you hide in the house.'

'I wanted to get the dishes done.'

'The dishes can wait. Your current assignment is to do this for the rest of the day.' She gives me a little hip bump as she says it.

Susan and I met through a mutual friend three years ago. I had been tagged by the Capital City Bar Association to coordinate a criminal law symposium, two hundred sweating lawyers in a hot hotel ballroom eking out continuing-education credits in order to keep their tickets punched to practice law: a program that has since died under the heel of judicial review.

One of the items on the symposium's agenda was child abuse, its prevention and detection. Susan was the speaker. Another lawyer, an associate in my office, introduced me to her, and the rest, as they say, is history.

She was in the capital testifying on some legislation, fighting with lawmakers to get more money for kids. That night we met over dinner to discuss the symposium's agenda, and somewhere between cocktails and salad I found myself lost in the depth of her gaze and the music of her voice. I was smitten as I have not been since my days of youthful dalliance.

There was something in the chemistry that defied definition, as if I'd been sapped by some sensuous blackjack, candlelight and the deep sparkle of those Latin eyes, the passion with which she spoke of her job, a quest to save children abandoned and abused. It gave purpose to her life, focus and commitment that make those of us who are floaters, mere survivors, envious.

Susan is first and foremost a woman who knows what she is about. She is direct and at times can be intimidating. My initial reaction was a kind of affection born of admiration, with a component of sexual energy that loomed just under the surface.

She gives me a sideways glance through heavy-lidded eyes as if she is drifting off. I spread the lotion down her back.

'That's wonderful. You have magical fingers.'

'What are you reading?' I ask.

'Documents in the Patterson case. What else?'

Susan's job has been made markedly more difficult in the last few months by a burgeoning scandal within her office. Politicians are taking a close look at some of the practices used by her investigators to question young children in cases of alleged abuse.

'They want to tie our hands behind our backs,' says Susan.

The use of anatomically correct dolls and suggestive questions to five-year-olds, some of them on videotape, has opened a Pandora's box of political and legal problems.

A dozen criminal defendants, some of them now in prison, have mounted a defense grounded on the charge that Children's Protective Services, CPS, has engaged in a witch-hunt, that it has tampered with the testimony of children to create public hysteria, this to justify budget increases and the public's perception of the department as a law-enforcement agency. Butch Patterson, a twice-convicted molester, is the lead defendant in these appeals. Susan is livid.

'This WAPUS, short for "walking piece of human sewage,"' says Susan, 'has a record the length of the Milky Way.'

She slaps the folder on the chaise beneath her head. 'I'd kill to be able to show it to you,' she tells me.

She cannot, because the file contains confidential criminal history information that is protected by law. For a public official charged with possession of the documents to reveal them is a felony under state law. She could lose her job in a heartbeat, and probably face jail.

'Can you believe,' she says, 'that there are courses taught at the university, paid for by taxpapers, in which the likes of Patterson are referred to as political prisoners. Phi Beta Kappas telling us they should be released, turned loose so they molest again.'

'Constitutional right. Pursuit of happiness,' I tell her.

'Don't joke about this.'

'Sorry.'

'Now the state attorney general wants to get involved,' she says. 'He's supposed to be representing us. Instead he wants to see documents and videotapes from my office. This is *not* why I got into child welfare,' she says.

'You got into it to work with kids.'

'So why am I spending all my time on my knees pleading with politicians who want to grandstand? Show up at the scene of every tragedy and wring their hands.'

'That's just like working with children,' I tell her.

She laughs. 'You're right. Oh, right there,' she says as she wiggles her bottom and the small of her back.

I press my fingers into the desired area and massage. 'There are other jobs, you know.'

'No.' Susan doesn't say another word, but turns her head on the chaise to the other side, away from me, a signal that this line of conversation is at an end.

I am spreading Australian Gold toward the line of her bikini bottom in the narrow hollow of her back, tawny skin like brown satin.

'Nice bathing suit,' I tell her.

'You like it?'

'Uh-huh.'

'I had to buy a new one,' she says. 'Two of my spare suits got ripped off in the house thing.' Susan is talking about the burglary of her home two months ago.

'I think it was kids,' she says. 'Who else would take Fredrick's of Hollywood lingerie and two bathing suits?'

'Some horny male burglar who likes to cross-dress,' I tell her.

'One of your clients?' she asks.

'I'll check around.'

27

She laughs.

Susan is also missing a television set, a laptop computer that she used for work, some other electronics, and credit cards. We are still battling with her insurance company, filing claims though Susan has insisted on dealing with the credit cards and the credit-reporting agencies herself, a sign of her independence. I told her she was lucky. There are people who will clean out your house and end up stealing your identity. You can spend the rest of your days fending off bench warrants for arrests on traffic tickets they get using your name, then failing to appear in court.

'I've wanted to talk to you for a couple of days,' I tell her.

'What about?'

'I have a problem. Maybe you could help me with it.'

Deftly, without looking or moving her body off the chaise, she slides her hand along my thigh, scraping her fingernails gently on my flesh moving toward the open pant-leg of my bathing suit.

'That's not it,' I say.

'Too bad.'

'It's work related.'

'Are you sure?' She slips just the tips of her fingers, long delicate nails like talons, under the material of my suit and scratches gently on my inner thigh.

'Yes. Though if you keep that up I'm gonna have a growing problem on another front.'

She removes her hand. 'Killjoy.'

'I really could use your help.'

'I tried.'

'Could we get serious for a moment?'

'I'd love to.' She starts to roll over, closed eyes, moist lips, a sensual grin spreading.

I press on her back so that she cannot complete the turn and continue the massage. She gives up.

'I need some information in a case I'm working on. Someone you might know.'

'Fine, who is it?' She sounds frustrated.

'Have you ever heard of a woman named Zolanda Suade?'

With the mention of the name the muscles in her back tense and her head arches off the cushion of the chaise. She is now looking at me as best she can from this position, my hands pressing deep into the small of her back, spreading slick white cream. I squeeze a little more from the bottle onto my hands and warm it as she studies me in silence.

'How in the world did you get involved with Suade?'

'Then you do know her?'

'Yes,' says Susan. 'Unfortunately, I do.' Her head goes back down on the cushion.

'I thought you might have run across her, given her activities and your job.'

'Activities?' Susan is interested, but playing it cool. 'What might those be?'

'Child abduction,' I tell her.

There is a long pause. I can feel the sigh of breath as it escapes her body. 'Yes. That would be Zolanda's stock-in-trade.'

'First-name basis. You must be more familiar with her than I thought.'

'It's a small town,' she tells me.

'Have you ever met her?'

'Oh, yes. You might say we were once friends,' says Susan. 'But that was in another life.'

'Friends?'

'*Emm.*'

'Tell me about it?'

'What's to tell? It's been a long time.'

I allow the fingers of my hands to slip beneath the band of her bikini bottom toward the firm, round globes of her ass. She sucks in a deep breath.

'You're getting a little red around the shoulders,' I tell her.

'You should see my face. Keep that up, and we're going to have to send the children inside.'

'Tell me about Suade?'

'She's not someone you want to tangle with,' says Susan. 'Why do you want to know?'

'I have a client. He has a problem.'

'Let me guess. His child is missing?'

'Granddaughter,' I tell her.

'Now that's a novelty. Usually her victims are fathers with joint custody.'

'Then you've seen this before?'

'Oh, yes.'

'How do you know her? Through your department?'

'That and other places. I've known her for – ten years, I guess. Since some graduate courses at the U. Early-childhood development. She came to speak one night.'

When my hands stop, she knows I'm interested.

'Child protection. It's a small universe. We ran in some of the same circles.'

'What else do you know about her?' I start with the fingers again.

'I heard she had a bad marriage. In another life, before coming to town.'

'Sounds like half the people I know,' I tell her.

'No. I mean a *bad* marriage,' says Susan. 'Her husband had money, and a mean streak. He beat her, tortured her, damn near killed her. The man had a weird edge. He was heavily into kink. Manacles and chains. Not the kind you see in novelty shops with cotton padding and phony locks. Word is he chained her in a room in their basement for almost a month. Tortured her. Rape, sodomy – the whole nine yards. The only reason she got out alive is some neighbor heard her screaming and called the cops. The experience touched her personality.'

'I can understand that.'

'She does not like men,' says Susan.

'An experience like that is likely to put you off them for some time.'

'Fact is, she hates men.'

'All of them?'

'Pretty much.'

'That's a little unreasonable.' I massage Susan's behind, this time through the cloth of her bathing suit with fingers like feathers.

'Of course, she's never felt the tingle of your fingertips on her ass,' says Susan.

'How can you be so sure?'

She giggles. 'Because you still have your fingers.'

'How did she get involved with runaway mothers and their kids?'

'Call it revenge,' says Susan. 'Her way of striking back at the male establishment. Courts with men in black robes.

Law-enforcement agencies that discount claims of spousal abuse. Of course she's gone around the bend,' says Susan. 'For a while she had her supporters. Even some people in high places, a few legislators, city councilwoman or two. But she went too far. Abused the privilege. Her answer is not a solution. Turning kids into fugitives is like slitting a man's throat to put him on a diet. A cure worse than the disease. There have been a few cases – very few, mind you – where mothers she has taken into hiding have been caught and jailed. That's an entirely new bundle of misery for the children. But you're not going to tell Zo that. She won't hear of it.'

'My client is convinced that Suade is involved. She came to his house with the mother and told him either give the granddaughter up or lose her.'

'Sounds about right. She wasn't always like that,' says Susan. 'Not when she started. She formed a women's advocacy group. Did a lot of lobbying, mostly local stuff, appearances on TV. She tried to intervene in some high-profile custody cases, though the courts slapped her down, wouldn't let her appear. She's not a lawyer. Since she wasn't a party, she didn't have standing.'

'I see.'

'The judges ruled that whatever she had to say was irrelevant. They wanted nothing to do with her. That was like waving a red flag under Zolanda's nose. They may as well have painted a bull's-eye on their own ass. The one thing you don't do with Zo is ignore her. Somewhere along the way she decided that the courts were irrelevant. She set up her own procedures for enforcing custody.'

'Abduction.'

'She refers to it as protective action,' says Susan. 'Her organization is called Vanishing Victims. It's part self-help, part social services agency – with no accountability and no appeals. If somebody makes a mistake, and Zo has made plenty, there's nowhere to go to complain. From what I hear, Zo's gotten pretty sloppy over the years. She's actually had a few abusers in hiding. Mothers who complained about fathers who were themselves putting cigarettes out on their kids' arms and getting a little carried away with corporal punishment.'

'Why haven't the courts held Suade in contempt?'

'She's certainly held them in contempt,' says Susan. 'Problem is, you have to prove she's involved. Zolanda operates like the godfather in the mob, the president in the Oval Office; she's always just one step outside the loop of incrimination. If she and her organization have taken this girl, you won't find any witnesses placing Zo at the scene. She's very careful.'

'Who does the snatching?'

'People in her organization. Volunteers. Guys who, no doubt, go to church on Sunday and aren't bothered by the fact they're going to grab some kid out of the school lunch line on Monday. Cuz Zo's told 'em it's a mission from God.'

'What you're saying is, fanatics?'

'Let's just say misguided.'

'And prosecutors haven't been able to charge her?'

'No. The FBI's turned her and her organization upside down, at least that's what I've heard. She always uses one of the parents for cover, so it's not a straight-up kidnapping case, and there's a reason Suade is set up on the border.

Mexico's not a bad place to lose people.'

'You think that's where my client's granddaughter is?'

'If I had to guess. To Zo, the Baja is just like one big half-way house. Move them down to Ensenada, maybe Rosarita for a while, until they can find someplace more permanent. Tell me about the mother.'

'Mom was in the joint, a troubled past, mostly drugs. The grandparents got a custody order from the court. When the mother got out of jail, she showed up at the house with Suade making threats to get the kid back. A week later mom came back alone, under the guise of an on-site visit. Only there was nobody home but the granddaughter and a baby-sitter.'

'Convenient,' says Susan.

'Mother and granddaughter disappeared.'

'And let me guess,' says Susan. 'Nobody saw Zolanda anywhere near the house during the visitation.'

I nod. 'And mom and daughter haven't been seen since.'

'And they won't be,' says Susan. 'At least not under the same names, and not in this city. If Suade could take them to another planet, she would. You can be sure the mother's hair will change color and length a dozen times in the next year. Your client's granddaughter may end up looking like a little boy. No one's going to recognize either of them when Zolanda's done doing her magic.'

'You'd think Suade would have checked the mother out,' I tell her. 'Jessica Hale had a prison record. A history of drug abuse that stretches back to her teen years.'

Susan is silent.

'Your client, does he have a name?' she asks at last. 'Is he somebody anyone's ever heard of? A celebrity?'

34

'Not really. Why?'

'Zo's made a big thing of celebrities lately. Word is she's become afflicted by the need for publicity. It scratches some itch deep down inside. She's gone after a few well-known locals, the PJ of the local court.'

'You're kidding?'

'No. His son and his ex have been missing for over a year, along with nearly half a million dollars from a joint savings and investment account.'

'You'd think he would have thrown Suade's ass in the slammer on sheer principle.'

'He did,' says Susan. 'She's got some good lawyers. And as I said, the judge couldn't connect enough dots to make a picture involving Zo. She seems to be gravitating in the direction of money and power.'

'My guy's just a working stiff who's won a lot of money.'

'How?'

'The state lottery.'

'You're kidding.'

'No, I'm not.'

'You actually know somebody who won that thing? I thought they just called those numbers to keep the mobs happy, government equivalent of the bloody games of ancient Rome.'

'I knew him before he won, but he remembered me. Fondly, as it turns out.'

'How much did he win?' she asks.

'Eighty-seven million dollars.'

'God!' She laughs. 'That's obscene. You'll have to introduce me. Is he married?'

'Going on forty years.'

'Why are all the good ones taken?'

I press a little with one of my thumbs into her side just above the hip.

'*Aow!* That hurts.' She giggles a little. 'This client of yours. What does he want you to do?'

'He's desperate. He wants me to throw a legal hammerlock on Suade. Force her to tell us where the child is. And hire a PI to find his grandkid.'

Susan laughs. Shakes her head. 'He doesn't understand what he's dealing with.'

'He has a lot of resources. And he's willing to spend every dime to get his granddaughter back.'

'He'll need it. Let me give you some advice.' She rolls up onto one hip so that she can look me in the eye. 'Don't get involved.'

'Why not?'

'Because you're asking for a lot of heartache, and in the end you're going to come up empty. Zo has a reputation for winning in these things. She's never been tagged yet, not by the courts, not law enforcement. Some of the best private investigators in the country have tried to trail her people to find the kids who have disappeared under Zolanda's wing. They haven't succeeded yet.'

'Thanks for the vote of confidence.'

'You asked me if I knew the woman. I'm just telling you like it is. She loves what she does. She gets off on it. She has no use for the courts, and she hates lawyers. Her ex hired a good one. He had lots of money, too. The lawyer got him off on charges of assault, kidnapping, and attempted murder. Walked him right out of the courtroom, then turned around and made a pitch for custody of their little boy.'

'Suade has a child?'

'Had,' says Susan. 'He was four years old. The court saw no problem in granting joint custody to the father. After all, he had no criminal record. A year later the little boy was dead. A broken neck. He fell off a balcony while visiting with Dad.'

Susan rolls over on her back so that she is now looking up directly at me, one hand shading her eyes from the setting sun. 'It makes you understand just a little,' she says, 'why Zo Suade is on a mission.'

CHAPTER
THREE

This morning Harry and I meet at the law office on Orange Street, behind the Brigantine Restaurant and the Hotel Cordova. The façade on the street is white plaster in the style of a colonial Spanish hacienda. A green neon sign hisses and flickers over the arched gate leading to the courtyard. It reads:

MIGUEL'S CACTUS RESTAURANT

Inside, and surrounding the open-air restaurant, are boutiques, small shops, and a styling salon connected by a maze of narrow walkways and paths, all of them under a canopy of shade trees and banana plants.

Our office is in the rear among these shops, a two-suite affair with a small wooden porch outside and two steps leading up to the door, a scene from the jungles of World War II.

Inside, it is not palatial. There are no oil paintings or

39

metal sculptures, trappings of lawyerly affluence or corporate opulence. There is a small library that doubles as a conference room, an even smaller reception area, and a larger room that we have divided into two offices.

We have refrained from posting a sign out front or on the door for a reason. Harry and I are not looking for walk-in traffic. So far, we have made it on word of mouth, a few referrals from lawyers up in Capital City who have legal matters pending in San Diego and from the growing number of friends and acquaintances we have made in this city.

The restaurant, hotel, and courtyard are situated at a Y-intersection where Orange Street, the main drag in Coronado, forks, just before passing in front of the Del Coronado Hotel across the street, and Glorietta Bay farther on. A half mile south is the northern edge of the Silver Strand. Our neighbor in that direction is the US Navy, which uses part of the beach for its Amphibious Training Base. At the other end of the peninsula is the North Island Naval Air Station.

From the Ocean Terrace Restaurant of the Del Coronado, overlooking the tennis courts and the beach, the screaming A-4s on approach come close enough to drop their landing gear in your coffee.

From the look of his face this morning, Harry hasn't shaved in two days. During that period he has been on a mission to find out whatever he can about Jessica Hale, the friends she ran with, her background, perhaps leads as to where she might be. He has dredged up information from the parole board in Capital City, an old friend on staff. He has also copied whatever he could find from the court files in Jessica's drug conviction.

Harry sits perched on the corner of my desk perusing a good stack of paper, some of it filmy, thermofax documents.

'She's a troubled young lady,' he says. 'From all indications, an addict with a serious habit.'

'Cocaine?'

'Methamphetamines. Lately, she's moved up the food chain to Black Tar.'

It is one of the two types of heroin on the streets of America; the other being White China, from the poppy fields in Asia. Black Tar streams across the southern border from Mexico and has been on the rise as the drug of choice for the last several years. Police agencies will tell you it is a growing epidemic on the streets of the inner cities, and is acquiring a foothold among more affluent users.

'She may have been clean in the joint,' says Harry, 'but she had a habit that was running up a tab like the national defense budget when she went in. She had the crimes to go along with it.'

I look at him.

'Mostly burglaries to support her habit. She's was on probation when they nailed her with the drugs.'

'Any evidence that she might have been using inside?'

'Not from the parole reports. And she got out in the minimum, which leads me to believe that they had no indication that she was doing drugs while incarcerated.'

'Still,' says Harry, 'she could have fallen back into the habit when she got out.'

We are looking for a thread here, and Harry knows it. If Jessica was still using drugs, it would present us with

41

a more immediate problem. Mother with a needle in her arm, on the run with a child. But it would also offer the possibility of a lead.

'What are the terms and conditions of parole? Any drug testing?'

Harry looks at the documents in his hand. 'Full supervision. Weekly meetings with her parole office, and drug screening – every two weeks.' He licks a thumb and forefinger, presses the faxed documents onto my desk and quickly rifles through them looking for the same entry on each one.

'First screening was two weeks out. She was clean. Came back negative.' He flips through a few more pages, passes one, then quickly turns back to it. 'She missed the second screening.' A few more pages. 'And the third.' He looks some more. 'Nothing after that.'

'So she could be using again?' I say.

'I would say that's a probability,' says Harry. 'Why would she fail to comply with probation, unless she had a reason? Something to hide.'

'That's one possibility. By the same token, why comply with probation if you already know you're going to run?'

'True.'

'Still, it's an angle,' I tell him. 'Do we know who her supplier was, before she went to prison?'

'I'm still working on that one,' says Harry.

'It could be a lead if she's using, and if she's still in the area.' I am figuring the addiction would lead her back to her supplier.

'If she buys off the street and is known to have frequented

the same location on a regular basis, we could have some-body stake it out, watch for her and try to follow her back to the child,' says Harry.

He makes a note to push her dealer up higher on his list of priorities.

'According to Jonah, she was transporting for somebody when the feds picked her up.'

'At San Ysidro,' Harry fills in the blank.

I pick up the parole sheet that he's placed on my desk, and I study it. The statutory code numbers on the document show convictions based on entry of a plea.

'These are state charges,' I tell him. 'Transporting across an international border, that would be federal.'

'If they chose to prosecute,' says Harry. 'I am told they did not.'

'Why?'

Harry shrugs a shoulder, like he doesn't know.

'I've never known a federal prosecutor to turn up his nose at a case like that.'

'You think they rolled her for some information?' he asks.

'It's what I'm thinking. Is there anything from the court file as to who she was carrying for when they nailed her?'

'No. I looked. The feds handed it over to the state, and the prosecutor dealt that away. Jessica copped a plea to counts of possession and possession for sale.'

'Why were they so generous?' I ask.

Harry looks at me. 'She had something they wanted?'

'Let's see if we can find out what.'

He makes another note.

'Also, do we know if they've violated her on probation

yet? Issued a bench warrant? Jessica has missed at least two meetings with her parole officer and has failed to perform required drug screening. Sooner or later the state will catch up with her, at least in the judicial process, by scheduling a hearing to revoke probation.'

'They'll be a month getting around to that,' says Harry.

'So in the interim, if they stop her on a speeding ticket, assuming she's using her own license, they wouldn't even haul her in.'

'Not yet, anyway,' says Harry.

'Wonderful system,' I tell him.

'Our clients don't usually complain,' says Harry.

On this I can't argue with him. 'What about friends? Anybody she was close to, who she might have kept in contact with?'

'I'm checking to see what I can find. Only thing I've come up with so far is a name in the court files.' Harry looks at his notes. 'A guy named Jason Crow. Apparently he's got a long record. He and Jessica were an item for a while. Crow went down on state charges for burglary about the same time that Jessica got nailed on the drug thing.'

'So he wasn't a character witness?'

'Not hardly,' says Harry.

'He has a history. Reaches back to the juvenile side. I don't know what that was for. It's sealed. But as an adult he has convictions for assault, petty theft, and burglary. The biggest beef was a child-endangerment rap. He put the kid in a zipped-up sleeping bag and sat on the open end until the child passed out from lack of oxygen. Apparently it stemmed from a dispute with an ex whom he routinely used as a punching bag.'

'Crow was married?'

'*Was* is the operative word,' says Harry.

'Maybe we can find him through his ex-wife?'

'I doubt she'd keep in touch.'

'What do we know about this Crow's relationship with Jessica?'

'They lived together for a while. Crow worked at the airport. He was a luggage handler. Jessica was waitressing at a bar on one of the concourses.'

'This was all in the court file?'

'The judge was picking up story lines for *The Young and the Restless*. What do I know? He left notes at sentencing, half a legal pad with chicken scratches all over it. Apparently, from what I could read, Jessica's lawyer tried to make the argument that Crow was a bad influence on her.'

'Is there any indication he was involved in the drug thing?'

'What I was thinking,' says Harry. 'Given his job at the airport. Stuff a few bags with heroin and have your friendly baggage handler remove 'em before customs gets a sniff. But there's nothing in the notes to indicate,' says Harry.

'Where is he now – this Crow?'

'He's on parole, but I don't have an address. I can probably get it.'

'See if you can get a lead on him. What else have we got?'

'That's about it. She didn't have a lot of friends. No women she ran with. I'm still looking. But I could use some help.' Harry's thinking a private investigator.

'I'm working on that, but for the time being, we're it. See if you can find an address on this guy, Crow. Maybe he knows where she is.'

'We could go get an order to show cause,' says Harry. 'Go to the family-law judge on the custody thing and try to get an order for contempt. See if we can draw Suade in.'

'It's a good thought,' I tell him, 'but not likely to produce results. I mean, there's no problem getting an order of contempt on Jessica. The problem is how to find her for service.'

'If we could do that we wouldn't need the order. Just steal the kid back,' says Harry.

'Jessica'd be in no position to complain. But as for Suade, we've got a bigger problem.'

'What's that?'

'How do we make Suade a party? How do we get the judge to issue a contempt citation against Suade and her organization?'

Harry thinks for a moment. 'She did make threats to the old man. Didn't she tell Jonah that unless he gave the child back to the mother, he was going to lose the kid?'

'Yes. But you see the problem,' I tell Harry. 'Is that a threat?'

'I'd say so.'

'Yes, but you're not the one wearing the black robes. Even if she admits that she was there, Suade is going to say her words were merely a prediction. That what she meant was that hostile actions toward Jessica by Jonah, taking custody away, was ultimately going to alienate the child. That that's what she meant by *lose the child*.'

'And you believe that?'

'No. But a judge might. Particularly where there's no hard evidence, no witnesses to put her at the scene, and

46

the alternative is a harsh jail sentence for contempt.' Harry knows I am right.

'Most judges I know, while seeing through Suade's lie, would look for some artful way to avoid a contempt citation. In this case there are plenty of them, including the issue of whether the court even had jurisdiction over Suade as she was not a party in the original custody proceeding. We would have to prove that she acted as Jessica's agent in abducting the child. Without witnesses to put her there, it would be a tough sell. Unless I'm wrong, Suade would simply tell the court that she was trying to bring harmony to the family.'

'Like Hitler in Czechoslovakia,' says Harry.

'Maybe so, but right now I'm not even sure we could get Suade into a courtroom. No. Before we apply salt, we'd be advised to try a little sugar.'

Harry looks at me with raised eyebrows.

'I think it's time to meet with Zo Suade. Try to reason with her.'

CHAPTER
FOUR

A month after moving south I purchased an old CJ-5, an early eighties vintage Jeep that Harry calls Leaping Lena. I got it from a kid, good at mechanics, who had babied the machine so that it ran like a clock. Its short wheelbase in two-wheel drive made it turn on a dime. I bought it, not for off-roading, but because it was easy to park in tight spaces, a valuable commodity in a crowded, car-happy state.

In the warmer months I keep the top up, but zip out the side and back-window panels, allowing the wind to run through my hair. This helps me to forget that there are now some wisps of gray also running with the wind. Maybe it's a second childhood. Who knows? But the wheels turn and the motor runs.

It has been four days since my conference with Harry, and this morning I bounce along the Silver Strand headed south toward Imperial Beach.

My mission this morning is one of those futile exercises that seem to defy better judgment, but is required

49

in the grand scheme of crossing the *t*'s and dotting the *i*'s.

I pull into a strip mall on Palm Avenue and make a sharp turn into one of the parking spaces facing the street. The object of my attention is a small building across the street, a rundown, stucco-sided commercial rental that fronts on Palm and backs up onto an alley.

From behind the wheel of Leaping Lena I can see the small parking lot behind the Copy Shop. Near the building's rear iron-shuttered door are three spaces for employee parking. An alley runs the length of the block and comes out on the next side street. There is a large dumpster positioned haphazardly in the alley, one corner jutting out, an obstacle on a course, with a lot of trash around it like the owners of this business have bad aim. The shop is the universe of Zolanda Suade.

It is one of those places with machines that can kick out copies like ticker tape over a parade, where, for a fee, you can also rent a private mailbox. It's an interesting sideline for a woman with her own version of the witness-protection program.

I am sipping coffee from a paper cup, reclining in the driver's seat, feeling foolish even to be making this attempt. From everything I have heard, 'rational' and 'objective' are not terms that come to mind when considering Zo Suade.

Still, it is one of the things you learn in the law: that if you don't ask, some judge will surely look you in the eye and ask why not. Suade may be the most virulent, male-hating feminist on the continent, but if I draw her into a courtroom before making an effort to reason with her, I will surely face the question from her lawyer, find myself on the defensive:

Why didn't you give her the courtesy of inquiring before filing and serving papers, wasting the court's time?

There are a few people on the street, cars whizzing by on Palm. Some rummy, wearing rags, pushes a shopping cart filled with his possessions heading up the street along the side of the Copy Shop. He proceeds at no particular speed, with no apparent purpose other than to vacate one space and occupy another, living in that realm where moving is not so much a journey as an occupation.

He is midway across the entrance to the parking lot behind Suade's, at the point of no return, moving like a snail, when out of nowhere this boat, a large dark town car gleaming blackness, makes the turn off of Palm, rubber protesting on the road as it swings over the curb and into the driveway.

The driver makes not even a pretense of braking; there's not the slightest glimmer of red from the taillights. The car nearly spears the man who moves only at the last instant.

Instead, the vehicle separates him from his belongings. A glancing blow sends the cart careening in one direction onto its side, the man sprawling in the other.

Plastic bags filled with private treasures spill over the sidewalk. The guy disappears and for an instant I wonder if he's under the car. Then I hear the rum-soothed voice from the other side: 'Whydunya just run me over?'

'Okay.' The voice is sharp, clear as crystal from the half-open driver's window as she rolls into the parking lot and swerves into the slip directly behind the shop.

For a fleeting moment there is the stillness of a framed picture, the car motionless in its stall, the man prostrate on

51

the sidewalk, his belongings strewn, the image like some painting in a postmodern gallery – *Chaos Frozen*.

It lasts for only an instant, and is broken by the motion of the driver's door as it opens. She steps out and slams the door, then moves to the rear of the vehicle. There is not an ounce of hesitation, no remorse or compassion, no concern that the man might be injured or dying. He is, after all, still capable of crawling.

She is an image off the pages of *Vogue*, sporting a broad-brimmed hat: lady of the hacienda. Her black pants are as tight as a toreador's. A fitted jacket is zipped up over her ample bosom; as she peers across the trunk of the car she is the picture of the matador, sans sword.

She surveys her handiwork on the sidewalk. Her figure is shapely; curves in all the right places. Her gold jewelry, earrings and a bracelet, glimmer in the sunlight. I cannot tell her age from this distance, but she certainly appears fit.

The man is now on his hands and knees, working up some venom, mumbling expletives, mostly to himself. He's having difficulty getting to his feet. What I have witnessed is as close to a hit-and-no-run as I am ever likely to get.

He crawls on hands and knees. There are a lot of slurred words here, feeble attempts at foul language, but nothing that could be called threatening, except perhaps to the demented, alcohol-sodden mind of another drunk.

He stops crawling long enough to raise one hand, a finger in the air for emphasis, his motions failing to synchronize with his words. Jack Daniel's sense of timing.

Her right hand is now lost in the main pocket of a large purse that hangs from a strap on her shoulder. It stays there, making me wonder what's inside.

He's talking trash. 'Bitch' is every other word. Those that I can understand.

'Come on. Get up. You can do it,' she says.

Her body language almost wills him onto his feet. She beckons him with the curved fingers of her other hand, the one not buried in her purse.

He struggles to get up.

'Sure. That's it. Get up. Come on over here and kick my ass. You're the man. You can do it.'

He is up, stooped, wobbling and unsure, a stumbling lexicon of slurred epithets. Moment of truth, her elbow begins to flex.

It happens in the flash of an eye, a marked instant of sobriety. The trash talk ceases, a reckoning which reveals that even to a booze-burned brain there can be a near-death experience. The pins go out from under him. He is again sitting on his ass on the ground, thirty feet from her, looking up in wonderment as if asking the silent question – 'How'd I get down here?'

She shakes her head more in disappointment than contempt, then fishes in her purse and comes up with keys. She strides to the back door of the building, not even taking notice of him now, and works the locks like a jailer, first the steel bars and then the wooden door behind them. An instant later, señorita of your darkest dreams disappears into the shadows of her shop.

If there was any doubt as to my quarry, it is resolved by the plates on her car: blue letters on a white background – the word ZOLAND – not so much a place as a state of mind, an empire of attitude as dark as her attire.

I figure there's no sense waiting. Hit her while she's

on a psychic high. I put my coffee on the floor in the passenger-side well and step out, slamming the door of the Jeep. I walk as I wonder. Did she have a piece in her purse? Would she have used it? I'll never know. Maybe if she'd gotten the chance to shoot the drunk, she might have been sufficiently giddy with euphoria to give up the whereabouts of Amanda Hale? Maybe. It certainly would have made me a witness with leverage – make my day.

I head down the side street, around the corner, toward the front of the building, taking my time, so as to give her a chance to open up. When I get there the door is still locked, lights off in the front of the shop though I can see her moving in the shadows behind the counter inside.

She appears to be reading mail, slitting open envelopes. I tap on the glass and she looks up.

'I'm closed.' She dismisses me. Her gaze returns to the mail.

'Sign says you're open.' I shout through the door, where the hours are posted: '8:00 A.M. to 5:00 P.M.' It is now nearly nine o'clock. I point to my watch and to the sign on the door.

'I told you I'm closed.'

I knock again.

She looks at me, this time with real irritation, studying me, then takes her purse from the counter, slings it over her shoulder, one hand buried inside.

With a look of exasperation she comes around the counter, turns the lock on the inside and opens the door just a crack, the security chain still on.

'What part of closed don't you understand?' she says. Her hand is still buried deep in the dark recesses of her purse. At

54

the moment, I suspect I am living more dangerously than I want to know.

I slip a business card through the crack. 'I could tell you I represent the man you just ran down on the street, but that would be a lie.' I give her my best smile.

She reads my card. 'What's that to me?'

'I'd like to talk to you.'

'What about?'

'I'd rather not do it while standing in the street.'

'I'm afraid that's as good as it's going to get,' she says. 'Which one of the molesting deviants do you represent?'

'None. I just want some information.'

'Come back some other time. Or better yet, don't bother.' She starts to close the door.

'It's possible we have something in common.'

'And what could that be?'

'Bailey,' I tell her. The single word seems to freeze her in place. The door is still open, just a sliver. She studies me searching for some point of recognition but fails to find it, then hesitates for a moment. Indecision. What to do? One hand is still buried in the purse, the other on the lock.

'What do you know about Bailey?'

'I know he was your son.'

'Anybody could have told you my son's name.'

'I know he died under suspicious circumstances, probably as a result of abuse by your former husband.' This has never been reported in the press, even though she screamed and ranted at the time. Susan had told me the rest of the story.

'There's no *probably* about it,' says Suade.

There was never a conviction, though I sense that now is not the time to debate the point.

'I want to stop it from happening again,' I tell her. The magic words, like open sesame. She assesses me for a long moment, an expression that says, 'What the hell. Talk is cheap.' She slides her hand up the door, catches the chain and slides it off.

'Come in.'

I know that if I tell her why I'm here, mention Jonah's name, I would never get through the door. Besides, it's only a little white lie, a matter of degrees. There is little question in my mind that one or more of Jessica's live-in lovers possess the same proclivities as Suade's former husband, and present the same dangers to Amanda Hale.

She steps outside and checks the street, first in one direction, then the other. Then she bolts the door behind us.

'So what do you know about Gerald?' she says. Her hand is still in the purse, resting languidly in the bottom I suspect, like a coiled snake.

'Rumor has it he's responsible for the death of your little boy.'

'Is that what you've come to tell me? Rumors?'

'Your son died twelve years ago.'

'There's no statute of limitations on murder,' she says. And apparently none for revenge.

Gerald Langly is Suade's ex. He is currently in prison.

'I know that he beat you. That he brutalized your son. That the boy died under highly suspicious circumstances.'

'And how do you know all this?'

'Let's just say we have a mutual acquaintance.'

She looks me up and down, then finally motions me deeper into the shop. Finally she lifts her hand from the purse.

The overhead lights are still out. The large copying machine behind the counter is as cold as a frozen brick. There are envelopes on the counter, some of them opened, others waiting for the edge of a needle-sharp stiletto opener that lies on the counter next to them. She lays the purse on the counter and picks up the letter opener, trading one weapon for another.

'Who's this mutual acquaintance?' she asks.

'I'm not at liberty to say.'

She's clearly interested, racking her brain, trying to figure who would know the intimate details of her life, or for that matter care enough to tell some stranger.

'What do you want?'

'As I said, to talk. Just a little help.'

Her gaze comes up, her expression suddenly filled with an afterthought.

'Stop. Are you wearing a wire?'

'What?'

'It's a simple question. Are you wired?'

'Why would I be wired?'

'Three little letters,' she says. 'FBI. You don't mind if I look?'

She doesn't wait for a reply, but comes around the counter and starts to feel me up, around the waist in the cleft at the center of my back, and at the belt line. She's still holding the needle-sharp letter opener in her hand.

She steps away, wearing a look of suspicion, wary eyes.

'You're clean.' She says it as if I don't know this. Like some aliens might have planted a bug on my body without my knowledge. Suade obviously lives in a world of her own invention.

'The fibbies would love to bust me,' she says. 'They park out front. Watch me with field glasses. Try to read my lips.'

I'm wondering if she has a rich fantasy life, or if the feds really are onto her.

'I'm not working for the FBI. My sole concern is a little girl. At the present time I think she's in danger. I think you can help and I think once you hear all the facts you will want to.'

She looks at me as if this is nine-to-five work. Another hour, another child to save. It's a story that puts me squarely in the fold of followers, like a welfare applicant crying for relief.

'You have a client?'

'I do.'

'Tell me about her?'

The first problem.

I'm saved by the tap of metal on the glass door behind her. I see some guy standing there, a file of paper under his arm. He's looking intently at Suade, tapping on the glass with his keys.

'What do you want?' She doesn't turn but shouts at him through the closed door. Hers is a voice with multiple personalities. This one is a candidate for exorcism.

'I need some copies.' Muted voice from outside.

'Try Kinko's.'

'Just take a minute,' he says.

'How do you know how long it'll take? Machine's not warmed up. Read the sign. We're closed.'

He looks at the closed sign, and the hours posted next to it on the door. 'It's after eight,' he says.

'Excuse me.' She turns around, brim of her hat like a cutting edge. 'What is this? Nobody can read.' She's still holding the letter opener with its tip like a stiletto. 'Maybe if I stick this up your ass, you'll get the point,' she says.

By the time she gets to the door, the guy's already backing up, staring at her wide-eyed, wondering if somehow he's wandered through the portal to hell.

She turns the lock on the door. In less than an hour, she's run one man down on the street and now she's threatening to stab another. Discretion tells me I should end my conversation while I'm ahead.

'No need to get abusive, lady. All I wanted was some papers copied.'

'You think this is abuse?' she says. 'You want abuse? I'll show you abuse.'

The guy's staring at the needle-sharp point. By the time the door is open, he's out in the middle of the sidewalk, pedding in reverse like some back judge in a football game.

Suade picks up a newspaper that's in front of the door and throws it at him, classifieds flying in the breeze.

He turns and starts to run.

'Like I said, try Kinko's,' she says.

'Well, the hell with you.' He tries to reclaim a little pride as he scurries down the street.

'Yeah, right. Another hero,' she says and steps back through the door. Almost in the same breath: 'You say your client's child is in danger.'

'Yes. I think that's safe to say.'

'This child. Boy? Girl? How old?'

'A girl. Eight. My biggest problem is I've got to find her.'

'What are you talking about, find her? Where is she?'

'I don't know.'

'Who's the mother?'

'The mother's got some problems.'

'Who doesn't,' she says.

'She has a serious criminal record.'

'Is that how you came to represent her?'

'Not exactly.'

'Listen. I don't have time for twenty questions,' says Suade. 'Why don't you just tell me your story so we can cut to the chase.'

'I don't represent the mother,' I tell her.

This stops her in her tracks. 'Don't tell me. You represent the father?'

'No.'

An instant of relief.

'The grandfather,' I say.

She looks at me and laughs. I can't tell if I'm about to get the point.

'I knew it. Have you got a subpoena? If so, hand it here and get out,' she says.

'I don't serve subpoenas. I have a process server who does that.'

'Fine, then just get out. Or would you like me to call the cops?'

'No need for that. What are you afraid of?'

'Not you,' she says. She's reaching for her purse, pulling it closer.

'Fine. I just want to talk. Easier here than in a courtroom.'

'For who? Not for me,' she says. She's giving me a look

60

I've seen in barrooms from guys with broken bottles in their hands, offering the business end to somebody else.

'There's no reason for hostility,' I tell her.

But the look in her eyes tells me that's my opinion. Some of us get off on it.

'I have a client . . .'

'Good for you.'

'His only interest is in finding his granddaughter.'

She doesn't say a word and is no longer looking at me. She's back to her envelopes.

'For some strange reason, he thinks you might know where she is.'

Suade is a stone idol of contempt, an expression that says if I had anything, I'd be here with the sheriff and a summons.

'He's led to this belief by the fact that you met with him once. At his home. In the presence of his daughter and granddaughter. That you made certain statements, and that both his daughter and granddaughter disappeared shortly after that meeting.'

'Life is just a simmering pot of coincidences,' she says. 'Tell me. Did your client see me take this child?'

'What he saw or didn't see is for a court of law. I was hoping that could be avoided.'

'I'll bet you were. Now for me, I love going to court,' she says. 'All that pomp and ceremony. All that lying. Proof by the preponderence of perjury. Lawyers tripping over their tongues. Notice how they can always come up with some excuse for why their clients did it or didn't do it. Or why it doesn't matter even if they did do it. Should I tell you how many times I've been to court in the last year?'

When I don't ask, she volunteers.

'So many times I've lost count. And no matter how many times I go, it always ends the same way. Like a movie you've seen too many times, with a bad ending. You keep hoping for a happy one, but you never get it. They always get it wrong. That's why I do what I do. If they knew what they were doing, if they cared, they wouldn't be giving custody to child molesters, and abusive husbands. Of course that assumes they want to get it right.'

'Have it your way,' I tell her. 'But it's going to get very messy. My client is what you might call well-off. Deep pockets. And he's willing to spare no expense to make your life hell if you want to force the issue.'

'Hell. He's going to make my life hell!' Her eyes light up like two glowing coals. 'You tell your client I've been there and back and got the burns to prove it. Trust me, he couldn't find the place with a map and a flashlight if all the road signs pointed up his ass and he had the devil as a guide. But you tell him, he screws with me, and I'll be happy to show him the way.'

Then he would indeed have the devil as a guide, I am thinking.

'You can leave now,' she says. 'And don't let the door hit you in the ass on the way out.' She reaches for her purse and buries her hand deep inside.

'Are you threatening me?'

'Do I look like I'm threatening you?'

'I don't know.' Which is the way she wants it.

Then curiosity gets the better. 'You never told me your client's name?'

'His granddaughter's name is Amanda.'

'That doesn't help me.' Like she doesn't keep track of the kids. They're incidental to the process, the war between Zolanda and American justice.

'Jonah Hale is my client.'

She lights up like a lantern. 'Mr Lotto. Why didn't you say so?' The hand comes out of the bag. The purse is back under the counter. She's suddenly all smiles. The fact that she takes such pleasure in this information has me worried.

'I was just getting ready to do something special for him,' she says. 'I hope he likes publicity.'

I don't bite.

She drops behind the counter like a jack-in-the-box on the rebound. I'm wondering if she's going back into her purse. Visions of me running for the door and getting shot in the ass. But instead she's talking to herself all jovial, fussing with boxes and papers as I hear them clunking and shuffling under the counter.

'Where did I put that? Just had it,' she says. 'Damn. Oh here it is.' She emerges from the other side holding a letter box, heavy with papers.

'Copied these just yesterday,' she says. 'I was gonna wait and surprise him tomorrow. But since you came all this way, why wait?' She hands me one of the packets, two pages stapled together.

In inch-high letters across the top the words – PRESS RELEASE – so everybody knows what it is. Contact: Zolanda Suade, and her phone number.

Vanishing Victims, a self-help organization for abused women and their children, today announced that it is bringing charges of child molestation and rape against

63

a man who won one of the largest payouts in the history of the state lottery.

'I want the taxpayers to know what they're supporting,' she says.

I continue reading:

Jonah S. Hale, a resident of the wealthy seaside community of Del Mar in San Diego County, has been charged by the organization with the forcible rape of his daughter, Jessica. On at least three separate occasions, Hale is alleged to have sexually assaulted his daughter who at the time was a minor. In addition, Hale is charged with having molested his granddaughter, a minor who had been placed in his care under a formal custody order entered by the San Diego Superior Court more than a year ago. The child's name is being withheld.

In her all-knowing arrogance Suade has written it not in the style of a press release but with the tone of a news story, an accomplished fact, as if Vanishing Victims were a public agency and her libel of Jonah were a grand jury indictment.

'You've got to be kidding.'

'Hardly,' she says.

'What evidence have you got?'

'Jessica's testimony in a sworn affidavit.'

'A pack of lies from a jealous and vindictive daughter,' I tell her. 'You know she tried to get money from her father and that he turned her down. Jessica's engaged in extortion and now you're helping her.'

'What I would expect from you,' she says. 'A mouthpiece for the male establishment. How much is your client paying you?'

'And I could call you a self-appointed vigilante. We can call each other names, but it doesn't address the issue of evidence.'

'It's the truth,' says Suade. She raises one hand as if in a mock oath. 'Though I wouldn't expect someone like you to believe it. Read on. It gets better,' she says.

'Besides the rantings of a convicted felon, a drug addict, what else have you got?'

'Former drug addict,' she says. 'She's rehabilitated herself.'

'She tell you that? Fine, for the moment, former drug addict who wants money. Did she tell you that she offered to leave Amanda with her grandparents if they paid her enough?'

Suade doesn't answer, but her eyes don't lie.

'She didn't did she?'

'That's an easy thing to say.'

'Just like allegations of rape and child molestation. Put it this way, I'd believe Jonah and Mary Hale before I believed their daughter on virtually any subject.'

'I know the woman's background,' she says. 'I'll tell you what else I know. I know that agencies in this county have been carrying water and providing cover for people like Jonah Hale for years. Men of influence with money,' she says. 'The old boys' club.'

'You don't know anything about Jonah Hale other than

the fact that he won the lottery and that his daughter likes to tell lies.'

'I know that the authorities wouldn't have listened to Jessica Hale if she'd gone to the cops with a videotape of the evidence. Well, it's all going to come out now. Read it,' she says. 'Go ahead.'

I look down at the sheet again.

'No, not there,' she says. 'The next page.' She rips it from my hand and flips the sheet over. 'There. Read right there.' The pressure of her fingernail on the paper actually leaves an impression under the words.

Charges against Hale were known to county officials, and a number of public agencies, including the Department of Children's Protective Services, did nothing in response. Instead, they assisted Hale in his attempts to obtain formal custody of the child in question. The failure to act on the part of the county is part of a much larger and more serious scandal, involving public corruption and criminal wrongdoing on the part of county officials. These officials will be named and further details concerning their activities will be disclosed during a press conference on Wednesday morning, April 19th, at 9:30 A.M. on the steps of the Hall of Justice.

'Tell me you didn't know that she brought these charges to the cops eight months ago, to Children's Protective Services, to that Judas, McKay.'

Suade dropping Susan's name stops me cold. For a moment I wonder if she knows about Susan and me. She couldn't.

'That pack of whores,' she says. 'They're in the pocket of people like your client. They're worse than worthless. They lead people to think that something's being done when it's not. You can read all about in the morning papers. After the news conference. Two days,' she says. 'Read it and weep.'

This is the first I am hearing that Jessica made charges against Jonah, that is, if Suade's telling the truth. I am not surprised that the cops didn't do anything. No doubt if Jessica went to them, they took one look at her record, made a few inquiries, and without any evidence closed the matter. It wouldn't take a genius to figure that a woman right out of prison, locked in a death struggle over the custody of her daughter, might say anything that came into her head in order to gain an edge. But she made the charges, I'm wondering why Jonah didn't tell me.

'Jessica Hale is a drug addict with the basest of motives to lie,' I tell Suade. 'All she's ever wanted from her parents is money. That's what this is all about.'

'Well, it looks like he's found other recipients for that,' she says.

'What are you talking about?'

'I'm talking about the old man sprinkling money in all the right places, to sweeten the judgment of judges, to have cops look the other way. That is the way it's done.'

'Jessica told you this?'

'She didn't have to. I know how the system works, how they discard the rules when it suits their purposes. And I have evidence,' she says. 'You can tell them that.'

'Tell who what?'

'Read about it,' she says. 'In the paper.'

I look back at the press release as if there is something I've missed.

'No, not there,' she says. 'The morning papers. What do you think, I'm going to put it all in the press release? Turn it over to some stupid reporters to blow by asking all the wrong questions? I have documents to prove it. All of it,' she says.

'What? Documents to prove that Jonah Hale molested his granddaughter? That's not something anyone would reduce to writing unless he were demented.'

'Never mind,' she says, as if we are talking on two different levels.

'Oh, I do mind. Jonah Hale has nothing to do with any of this. If you're engaged in a war with the county, that's between you and them. Don't drag an innocent man into it.'

'Innocent man!' she says. 'You can take that copy of the release to your innocent man and watch him sweat.' She points to the press release. 'And tell him to wear his asbestos galoshes. Cuz he's about to step in it.'

I give her a quizzical look.

'Hell,' she says. 'Now get out.' She dismisses me with a flick of the back of her hand. 'I have work to do. Envelopes to address.'

I am feeling heat out to the tips of my ears, anger that I cannot repress.

She looks up. I'm still there, beet red. 'Go,' she says. 'Get out. And close the door.' She turns her back on me and disappears into the shadows at the back of the shop. I look for the box of releases on the counter. She has taken them with her.

CHAPTER
FIVE

The language is littered with proverbs on justice. *It is a sword with no scabbard; a blade that is double-edged; the other edge of justice is revenge.* For Zo Suade it seems this is the only edge that cuts.

On leaving her shop I waste no time. The cell phone is locked in Leaping Lena's glove box. I pull it out, plug the adapter into the cigarette lighter, and start punching numbers.

Heading down Palm Avenue I am driving with one hand, shifting with the other and punching buttons on the phone in between gears.

A feminine voice on the other end: 'Hello.' I can hear the hiss of a speaker phone. Anybody in earshot at the other end can now hear our conversation.

'Susan. Paul here. Can you pick up the receiver?' I've dialed around her secretary to a direct line in her office.

The hiss goes away as she picks up the receiver.

'You caught me at a bad time.' I can now hear her voice

clearly. 'I'm in a staff meeting. We're pretty busy.' I can see the picture: a half dozen drones huddled around her desk taking notes as Susan micromanages their divisions. My woman is a control freak.

'No. I'm afraid it can't wait,' I tell her.

'What's wrong?' Susan's good at detecting problems from the tone in a voice. 'Where are you?'

'On the road. About to head onto the freeway. So we won't be able to talk for long.' The wind at high speed makes it impossible to hear in the open vehicle.

'I just came out of a meeting with your friend Suade.'

'I take it she wasn't helpful?'

'Like a viper in your jockey shorts.'

'I did warn you,' she says.

'Don't remind me.'

'Listen, Paul, I really am busy. Can't it wait till tonight?'

'Unfortunately, it can't. She's getting ready to stick a pike in Jonah.' No last names. Not on an open cell phone.

'How so?'

'Suade's making wild charges, accusations that he molested the child. Had relations with his own daughter.'

'That sounds like . . .' She almost says Suade's name, then remembers she's not alone in her office. 'Our friend,' she says. 'If you remember, I warned you not to get involved.'

'I know. But it's too late for that now. I can't leave Jonah twisting in the wind.'

'The question is, what you can do for him?'

When I don't respond, she allows my silence to provide the answer. 'Cut your losses,' she says. 'You can't fight Suade. She plays by a set of rules that were never provided in your book. Believe me. You don't know what you're up

70

against. She's got a machine, and it's well oiled.' Her voice goes down a full octave, and from the sound I can tell she's cupped a hand over the mouthpiece so no one else in her office can hear.

'She can lay down lies the way a paving machine does asphalt,' says Susan. 'Reputations don't mean a thing. Not Jonah's. Not yours. Trust me. You get in her way, you're going to find yourself on your back, covered with tar wondering what it was that rolled over you. I really would like to help.' Susan can be hard-nosed. Suddenly her voice is back to pitch, up to volume. 'But I'm in the middle of a meeting. We'll just have to discuss it tonight.'

'There is something else,' I tell her.

'What?'

'She said some things about your department. She mentioned you by name.'

There's silence on the phone, as if someone's dropped an anvil on her. I wonder if I've lost the connection, or if she's hung up.

'You there?' I ask.

'I'm here.' Her voice is back in the nether regions. I can visualize the high back of her executive leather chair being swiveled so that it faces the drones across her desk. Makeshift privacy. 'What did she say?' she asks.

'Took your name in vain,' I tell her.

'You didn't mention me?'

'Never. But it did make me wonder if she was mind-reading.'

'I'll bet.' For a moment I'm left to ponder whether Susan believes me.

'What exactly did she say about me?'

71

'Called you "Judas". She thinks your department's sold out to the honky male establishment. She seems to think the county's been covering up crimes in custody cases, selling favoritism. She's making vague claims about scandals. Wouldn't tell me the details. I've got the press release with me if you want to see it.'

'Press release?'

'She's sending it out today. As we speak.'

There's silence while she thinks. At this moment, I can tell Susan would like to suppress free speech. 'What does it say, this press release?'

'I can't read while I'm driving,' I tell her. 'But it's heavy on accusations, light on the details. Says she's holding those for the press conference in two days.'

More rubber burning on Susan's end, silence as she thinks. I hear some conversations, distant voices. 'We'll have to continue this later.' But now she's not talking to me. 'Catch the door on the way out. Thanks.'

Then she's back, mouth to the receiver. 'Read me the press release.'

'I'm not going to get in an accident. I'm two blocks from the freeway at a light.'

'Where do you want to meet?' No whys, whats, or wherefores. Suddenly, I have her undivided attention. Threats to Susan's realm have a way of focusing her in ways that no argument can.

'My office. In an hour. I've got to try to find Jonah Can you get ahold of Harry? I'm not sure he's still in the office. You might try his apartment. Do you have the number?'

She doesn't, so I give it to her over the phone.

72

'You may want to consider bringing one of your investigators,' I tell her.

'Why?'

'Because we may need help. We don't have much time.' What I always wanted, a woman with her own private police force.

'Let me think about that one,' she says.

'Your call,' I tell her. 'As I say, we don't have much time. See you in an hour.'

I don't wait for an answer but press the 'End' button. Seconds later, I'm up to speed heading north on I-5, trying to get above the traffic to a place where I can pull off.

At this hour I'm guessing that Jonah is in one of two places – what a man does with nothing but time on his hands and eighty mil in the bank: at his house up in Del Mar a good twenty minutes north, or at the docks with his boat. I'm hoping he hasn't disappeared out onto the bounding main chasing bonita or yellowtail.

I take one of the off-ramps downtown, find a quiet street and pull over to the curb. I check Jonah's home number in my Palm Pilot, dial and on the second ring it's answered.

'Hello.'

'Mary?'

'Yes.'

'This is Paul Madriani.'

'Have you found Amanda?'

'Not yet. Is Jonah there?'

'No, I haven't seen him this morning. When I got up he was gone.'

'Do you know where?'

'Has something happened?'

73

'I just need to talk to him. Do you know where he is?'

'If I had to guess, I'd say he's probably at the boat.' She gives me directions.

'Are you sure there's nothing wrong?' she asks.

'Nothing to worry about,' I lie.

'Is there a way to reach him there?'

'Cell phone,' she says. 'But I think he left it on the nightstand this morning. Just a second.' She checks and is back to the phone a couple of seconds later. 'Yes. He must have forgotten it.'

'Listen, Mary, if Jonah comes back, if I don't catch him at the docks, tell him I need to meet with him. Tell him to call my office. I'll be there in an hour, and I'd like to see him then. It's important.'

'What's it about?'

'I can't talk right now.'

'He has your number?'

'Yes.' Just in case, I give it to her again, along with the cell number in the car.

'In one hour?' she says.

'Yes. One more question. If he's out on the boat, is there any way to reach him?'

'There's a radio. UHF or VHF. Something like that. But I don't know how to reach him on it. Coast Guard probably could in an emergency.' She waits for me to reply. When I don't: 'Is it an emergency?'

'No. Don't worry about it. Just give him the message if you see him.' I say good-bye and press the 'End' button again.

Instead of heading back to the freeway I cut through town, down Market Street, then jog my way through the Gaslight

District. On Broadway I hang a left and head toward the water, across the Santa Fe tracks and onto North Harbor Drive. I move at speed catching most of the lights along the waterfront, past the piers and the Navy Supply Center, and work my way toward the north end of the bay.

Spanish Landing is situated on a long spit, part of the fill used to construct Harbor Island back in the sixties. It is separated from the harbor's main channel by a peninsula that is now crowded with hotels and restaurants. The taller of these loom into sight as I pass the Coast Guard Air Station. Less than a mile west I take the traffic circle and come out on Harbor Island Drive.

To the landward side is a park popular with the jogging set. This morning there is more congestion on the sidewalk than in the street. Two women in white walking shoes and spandex shorts hustling buns of steel are passed by a young girl, a rocket on Rollerblades, showing a little skill and a lot of skin in her thong bikini. A guy in baggy-surfers on a skateboard strutting his stuff jumps some steps and rides the crest of a stair rail until he loses it. The board purls out from under him, and in my rearview mirror I see it embed itself in the side of a car going the other way. Circus maximus.

History has it that the old Spaniards in their galleons first set foot in California on or near this spot, not on the spit of land, but on the beach across from it – soldiers, Jesuit missionaries, and a handful of horses. One gets the sense that they might have turned around and reboarded their boats for home if they could have glimpsed four hundred years of Western progress. There is little doubt that the natives wore more clothes and had more sense than some of the current inhabitants.

A half mile down is the marina. I pull into the parking lot and bring Lena to a jolting stop against the concrete curb. Mary had given me vague directions. There are several main docks running perpendicular to the island. Jutting out from these like fingers are slips for the smaller, more maneuverable boats. The bigger vessels like Jonah's are moored at the end of the large docks, on the outside, at least that's what Mary told me.

From the parking lot the marina is a forest of aluminum, masts from sailboats, and radar antennas in containers like hatboxes hoisted on sticks. There is the occasional work boat, and a good fleet of sport fishers, more activity on the dock than I would have credited to the middle of the week; crews and charters either coming in or on their way out. There are people on the docks pushing carts with gear and supplies.

The *Amanda* would be low and fair sized, according to Jonah, forty-two feet with a flying bridge. I step from the car and use one hand to shade my eyes like a visor and scan the end of the docks. Within a minute I identify at least a half dozen boats that fit the bill. Near one of them there is a lot of activity – a fish the size of a small car is being hoisted on heavy gear out of the back of the boat. It's drawing a small crowd, though from this distance I can't make out faces.

I take a chance and head in that direction, down the angled metal bridge that connects the floating dock to the parking lot. It's low tide and I drop ten feet down the ramp. Once there I lose my vantage point, though I can still see the fish's tail, like a delta wing, hanging from the hoist.

I work my way in that direction, passing a gray-haired couple living out their dreams pushing groceries to their boat.

76

Another guy is hosing down the side of his vessel.

'I'm looking for Jonah Hale.'

He looks at me, shrugs his shoulders. Shakes his head.

'Don't know him,' he says. 'Looking for a charter?'

'No, thanks. Another time.'

I pick up my pace and reach the end of the dock where it dead-ends in a long 'T'. The larger vessels are tied up here, on the outside. As soon as I clear the steel pilings that anchor the dock, I see her. Stenciled in black letters across the stern, the name:

AMANDA

There's a small crowd milling on the dock next to the vessel. The center of attention is the fish on its rolling hoist, and the man standing in front of it, posing for pictures. Around him, fishermen hoist cans and bottles of beer, toasting their friend's success. Jonah doesn't see me. He's standing next to the fish.

They're trying to weigh it and having trouble. The hoist doesn't seem big enough. It's the biggest marlin, or swordfish (or maybe they're both the same) I've ever seen. What I know about fish you couldn't cook.

Jonah's wearing fishing togs, an old shirt and suspendered pants stained with the remnants of the giant fish. He has started to gut it with a knife the size of a machete, enduring a lot of backslapping and kudos from the men on the dock. Somebody hands him a beer still foaming out of the long neck of the cold bottle. It is only mid-morning, early for a beer, but these guys have probably been out on the water since dawn.

It's not until Jonah turns to take the bottle that he sees me. He points to the fish and makes big eyes, then realizes I'm not here for sport.

He hands the knife to somebody else and steps away, working through the crowd of backslapping men like a politician, shaking hands, accepting felicitations with grace from some fairly drunk men. Jonah's gaze never leaves me as he works his way through the crowd. He's trying to read any message in my expression, wondering if I've found Amanda.

When he reaches me, he doesn't waste time. 'You've got some news?' he says. 'You found Amanda?'

'No, but we need to talk.'

'What's wrong? Has something happened to her?'

'No. At least not that I know of. We're still looking. It's something else.'

This brings a palpable sigh of relief, like an electrical charge leaving his body. He takes a swig from the bottle in his hand, then realizes I don't have one.

'Charlie, get a beer for my friend here.' One of the crew members on the stern is into a cooler before I can stop him.

'No, thanks.'

'Forget it, Charlie.'

'I've just come from a meeting with Zolanda Suade.'

His expression turns dark. 'What did she tell you? Did she admit coming to my house?'

'She didn't deny it.'

'Good. I think that's good, don't you?' He takes another drink.

'She's on the warpath. Making some very ugly charges.'

78

He looks at the bottle, at the boat, at everything on the dock except me.

'She's a crazy woman. Certifiable,' he says. He's not interested in what she had to say. 'I'm glad you could make it down here. You sure you don't want something to drink?'

'No.'

'Got all kinds of pop. Root beer.'

'Nothing.'

'Would you like to see the boat?' Suddenly he wants to take a tour.

'Jonah, we need to talk.'

'Did you ever see a fish that big?'

I shake my head.

'Neither have I, before today,' he says. 'It's El Niño. The warm water's pushed everything north. Hell, last year I woulda' had to go down to Cabo to even have a chance at anything like that. Gonna have it mounted,' he says. 'Hang it on the wall. Gonna need a bigger wall.' He laughs, a kind of nervous chuckle as if he knows where I'm going.

'Why didn't you tell me that Jessica had accused you of rape?'

The jovial expression on Jonah's face fades. He offers a deep sigh, looks at me sheepishly. 'It's not something you want to talk about. Not with anybody. Besides, there was nothing to it. More lies from my daughter. The cops knew that. They didn't bring any charges. Hell, they didn't even investigate.'

'Still, it would have helped to know about it. If you want my help, I need to know everything.'

'It was a lie. I just didn't think it was important.'

'Did the cops open a file?'

He looks at me as if he doesn't have a clue.

'Did they conduct any kind of investigation?'

'What? Investigation? They talked to me. They talked to Mary. I imagine they looked at Jessica's record.'

'Did they question Amanda?'

'No.' His expression makes it clear that the mere thought that his granddaughter could be questioned about such things is offensive.

'What did you tell them? The cops.'

'The truth. That it was a lie. Jessica brought the charges after the custody case. It was clear what she was trying to do. The cops knew it. There was not a shred of evidence.'

'Did they question anybody else? Anybody besides Jessica, you and Mary?'

'I don't know. What does this have to do with anything?'

'Suade is using it as justification,' I tell him. 'Stirring the embers.'

'What do you mean?'

'I mean she's about to go public with everything Jessica told her. She's getting ready to issue press releases telling the world you committed incest with your daughter . . .'

'And?'

'Claiming that you molested Amanda.'

He's looking straight at me as I say it. No flinching. 'It's a lie. I swear.' He raises his right hand as if taking an oath. 'Should I burn in the fires of hell for eternity if I'm not telling the truth. My daughter is lying. She had friends in prison telling her to do this. I know it. I guess they give you a lot of time to think up bitter lies in a place like that. No doubt she was inspired by other inmates.'

'Do you have evidence that they talked about this?'

'No. But I can see her now sitting at a table or in a cell getting pointers from some other loser on how to incriminate her old man. Well, the cops didn't buy it. Neither did the court.'

'She made the charge in the custody proceedings?'

'Through her lawyer,' he says. 'The court said there was no evidence and cut him off. Wanted to know why she didn't file formal charges. They came up with that same old lame crap,' says Jonah. 'Most women don't report it. The humiliation is too much. She was young. The court didn't believe her or her lawyer.'

'Suade does. Or at least that's what she's getting ready to tell the world. That's what the press release says.'

He thinks for a moment. Darting eyes. Looking everywhere, and then back to me. 'The press won't believe her.'

I laugh. 'Believe her! When you win eighty million bucks and somebody levels these kinds of charges, it's national news. Talk-show heaven on the tube,' I tell him. 'Belief has nothing to do with it. Where have you been for the last decade? You must be the only man in America who's never heard of tabloid television.'

'I don't watch it,' he says.

'You should. Your name's about to be spattered all over it like roadkill. "Big bucks lotto winner accused in child rape".'

The dour expression on Jonah's face tells me that even in his darkest dreams, he has never considered this.

'Why would she do it?'

81

'Suade?'

'I can understand Jessica,' he says. 'But Suade. What's in it for her? There's no evidence.'

'It justifies her cause, validates what she does. And besides, the best defense is a good offense. She had to assume you had the resources to come after her. Of all the people she's screwed over in the past few years you've got one of the bigger bankrolls. She's guessing you'd be hip deep in lawyers. What the rich do when they have a problem.'

'Damn right,' he says.

'Your greatest strength is your biggest weakness. Now she has the offensive. It puts us back on our heels trying to fend off charges. How do we prove you didn't rape someone or molest a child.'

'I don't have to prove anything. I'm not on trial.'

'You will be if you sue Suade for defamation.'

'You're the only lawyer I've talked to, except for the custody guy. And he wouldn't get involved.'

'Because he knows Suade. That's what you told me.'

'Right.'

'Maybe the man's smarter than you thought.' What that makes me is uncertain, at the moment.

'Suade is betting that she can destroy your reputation before you can get her to court. And once you get in court, she's gambling that you have more to lose than she does. It gives her a chance to argue that the only reason you're pursuing her is because she speaks the truth. She's not afraid of you. It's the kind of image Suade craves. Joan of Arc slaying evil.'

A somber look falls on his face. He never saw the battle

being waged in quite this way. Jonah's sense of justice pictured lawyers arguing the law and the facts in a courtroom before an evenhanded judge, not a propaganda machine spinning lies and pumping poison before he got there.

'We need to go to my office and talk.'

'Of course,' he says. 'When?'

'Right now.'

He looks down at his clothes, soiled with the aftermath of the huge fish.

'Don't worry about it. My digs aren't that formal.'

He looks at the mob on the dock. Bottles of beer and cameras. Blood all over and under the fish.

'What do I tell them?'

'Nothing. Tell 'em you've got a meeting. You've got to leave right now.'

'Sure. Now,' he says. Jonah sounds like an echo. Man in a daze.

One of his buddies who's been hanging on the fringe just out of earshot seizes the moment and edges in closer.

He puts a hand on Jonah's shoulder, face of wisdom flushed by booze. 'Hey, buddy, I gotta get one more picture,' he says. 'You and that monster fish.' The man's jingling ice in a tumbler with something harder than beer. 'Except that's no fish. That's a damned whale,' he says. 'Jonah and the whale.' He laughs at his own joke. The kind of friends you get when you have eighty million on account.

He pulls Jonah by the arm, hauls him away. Jonah's still lost in inner thoughts, his face like a death mask.

'Come on, man. Take holda the lead and gimme a smile for *crysake*.' A drunk's impression of photo composition.

The man with the iced tumbler is giving directions while his buddies try to hold their cameras still.

Jonah hunkers down, on his haunches, takes the shank of the large steel hook that protrudes through the fish's gill and grips it in one hand so that the phosphorescent lure can be seen dangling just out of the marlin's mouth. At the moment he is looking past all the cameras at me, blood running across his arm and onto his shirt and pants. He doesn't even notice. Instead, he offers up a queasy smile as shutters click, and a couple of strobes in the shadows flicker like stars from the tiny thirty-five-millimeter point-and-shoots.

As Jonah starts to rise he stumbles and falls toward the fish. He grabs the marlin in a death grip around the gills to avoid going flat on the dock.

'Be careful there, big guy.' The man with the tumbler staggers out of the crowd to offer assistance – only one hand because the other is full. 'Give that man another beer.' He laughs. Jonah's front is covered with blood and whatever else is expelled in the after-death of the deep. He steps away from the huge fish, and wipes his hands on the seat of his pants.

For a moment I watch Jonah poised next to the giant marlin with the barbed steel hook lancing its gill, and wonder which one of them looks more dead.

CHAPTER
SIX

W ithin ten minutes I've talked myself out, covered the options, few as they are.

Harry thinks the best thing we can do is ignore it. Don't give Suade the satisfaction. Bring suit afterward if Jonah still has the desire.

'It's a damn joke.' Jonah's face is flushed. His blood is up. He's had time to think on the way over to the office, and now he wants answers.

'You're telling me there's nothing you can do? That I've wasted my time and money hiring myself a lawyer.'

'What I'm telling you is there is no way we can stop her from going public.'

'Not even with malicious lies?'

'Why don't you sit down.' I gesture toward one of the client chairs.

'I don't want to sit down. Besides, I'll get your furniture dirty.' He's covered in muck from the docks, dried blood and whatever else. The office is beginning to reek.

'Can't we sue her now? Get an injunction?'

'No.' Harry is looking professorial, with his arms folded as he leans against my credenza. 'Doctrine called prior restraint,' says Harry. 'Welcome to the First Amendment. Until she publishes, we can't do a thing.'

'What do you mean, "publishes"?'

'I mean, until she formally relays the information . . .'

'Vicious lies,' says Jonah.

'I know,' says Harry. 'Calm down. It's not gonna do any good if you pop a vessel. Until she communicates it to some third party, in this case the press, we can't touch her. After that, we can sue her for slander, libel, invasion of privacy, assuming you have a right to any.'

'Lotta good that does.' Jonah turns on Harry.

'Could be worse,' says Harry. 'You could be a public figure.'

'What do you mean, "public figure"?'

'Let's not get into all that,' I tell Harry.

'No. I wanna know,' says Jonah. 'What's this "public figure"? What's he talking about?'

'He has a right to know,' says Harry. 'You won the lottery, accepted the money. Courts could find that this makes you a public figure. If you voluntarily put yourself in the public eye, people are allowed to make fair comment about your character.'

Jonah's eyes light up like somebody's fired a roman candle into his pants. 'What are you saying, "fair comment"? False charges that I raped my daughter, molested my granddaughter. How can that be fair comment?' Jonah looks at me, then back to Harry.

'It's not,' says Harry. 'I know that. So does Paul. The

problem is that if a court should find that you're a public figure, it makes the case more difficult. We would have to prove certain elements before we could sustain a lawsuit against Suade.'

I remind Harry that false charges of criminal wrongdoing are defamatory per se. 'Besides,' I tell him, 'winning the lottery doesn't make you a public figure. So she can't claim fair comment.'

'Could be,' says Harry. 'There's no case law on the subject. I checked.' Harry gives me one of those looks he does so well, the kind he offers up just before I step into some pit.

'Of course we could end up making case law,' he says. 'Three or four years on appeal.' He arches an eyebrow in my direction as much as to say – 'Do you really want to get into that?'

I'm convinced that Suade has no evidence. That makes her charges either knowingly false, or at very least made with reckless disregard for the truth. Either way they're defamatory, and actionable. Whether it would be worth suing her is another question. We're back to where we started.

'What difference does it make?' says Jonah. 'I didn't come here for money. I don't care about damages. I care about getting my granddaughter back.'

'Any leads on that front?' says Harry. 'Did Suade give you any hint?'

I shake my head.

'I just thought maybe somebody could do something.'

Harry and I look at each other. Jonah wants the one thing we can't give him, and now he's about to be keelhauled through Zolanda Suade's private cesspool.

During all this we have a silent audience, his head swiveling toward Harry, Jonah, and back to me like the net judge at Wimbledon. John Brower is one of Susan's investigators, bald and beady-eyed, he sits in a client chair across from my desk, a leather folder closed, resting in his lap, ready to take notes should lightning strike.

As for Susan, she is pacing slowly in the open area of my office, running her eyes over a copy of Suade's press release as if an answer to our problems will rise like vapor off the page.

She hasn't said a word since I handed her the press release, though I have seen signs, the kind of body language I have come to read from the woman I know – a subtle shrug of the shoulders, wag of the head – as if it is all Greek to her. These are not aimed at me but lofted telepathically, like encrypted code, to Brower.

Apparently Susan thought better than to come alone. I take this as a sign that she views Suade's threats as serious, even if not credible.

Finally, she turns and looks at me. Bolt of lightning. 'The press release only nibbles at the edges of the department,' she says. 'No details.'

'I know.'

'She didn't tell you anything more?'

'Apparently she's saving that for the press conference. She wants us to twist in the wind for a few days. Get a few sleepless nights. I have the feeling that inflicting pain is one of her private pleasures.'

'She didn't give a hint what she's talking about? What exactly did she say?'

'She went into a rage about Jonah . . .'

'No, I mean about the department?' It's clear that Susan wouldn't be here except for the threat that Suade is about to kick up dirt, and that some of it may land on Children's Protective Services. She is a woman who defends her own with the tenacity of a cougar protecting its young.

'What did she say exactly, about the department?'

'I wasn't taking notes,' I tell her. 'She said she had documents.'

'What kind of documents?' says Susan.

'I asked her. She wouldn't say. She said the documents would prove everything.'

I look at Jonah. 'There wasn't anything that you wrote to your daughter when she was in prison that could be misconstrued? Used against you?'

He thinks for a second. Shakes his head. 'No.'

'Did we help Mr Hale get custody of the child?' Susan's question is for Brower. 'That's what Suade seems to be saying here in the press release. The innuendo is that we did something wrong.'

Brower opens his notebook and looks at something inside. I can't see what it is. The leather folder is tilted up away from me.

'Lemme see. We filed a report with the family law court. We did make a recommendation – for the grandfather.' He looks over at his boss and senses that this is not helpful. 'But it wasn't based on anything we did.' Brower makes it sound as if he's apologizing.

'Did we initiate the findings?'

'No. No. We based our recommendation on a probation report,' he says. 'The mother had an extensive record.' He's reading whatever it is in the folder with a finger on the page. 'Drug use. There was evidence that the child had been abandoned. Pretty routine. Nothing wrong with that. I don't see how we could have recommended anything else.'

'Would our recommendation be in the court files?'

Brower nods.

'So Suade would have been able to see it, if she went down to the courthouse and pulled the case file?'

'Probably.'

'Did we investigate the case?'

Brower flips a few pages in the folder, then slowly shakes his head. 'Doesn't look like it.'

'So we had no contact with Mr Hale?'

Brower is still reading. 'Not that I can see.'

'Did you ever come to our department?' Susan is now directing questions to Jonah.

'Hold on a second. You weren't asked to come down here so that you could interrogate our client.' Harry interrupts her.

'Am I on trial?' says Jonah. 'Did I do something wrong?' He looks at me.

'I don't know. Did you?' says Susan.

'No, you didn't.' Harry answers before I can.

'All I want is to find out what Suade has,' says Susan. 'Your client may be the only one who knows.' She makes this appeal to me.

'This isn't gonna happen,' says Harry. 'Not on my watch. You don't come into the office and question a client.'

'I have nothing to hide,' says Jonah.

'I don't care. Don't say a damn thing,' says Harry.

'I think it's safe to assume,' says Susan, 'that we, the department, and your client are being victimized by Suade's lies. She's got some plan. What it is, I don't know. But we need to find out.'

Harry gives her an expression like maybe yes, maybe no.

'Suade may have nothing to base these charges on. But it would help if we knew whatever details there were. Such as whether your client ever had contact with my department?' Susan's back to what she wants.

'I never came to your department,' says Jonah. 'We've never met.'

'You wouldn't have dealt with me,' she tells him. 'One of my investigators? A caseworker, perhaps?'

Jonah shakes his head. 'We went to court. I had a lawyer. He took care of everything.'

'What was your lawyer's name?'

'You gonna let her do this?' Harry asks me.

I nod. 'For the moment.'

Jonah gives her the name. Susan looks at Brower, who peruses his folder one more time and shakes his head. 'No contact with the lawyer.'

'So we didn't even have communication with the petitioner,' says Susan. 'I'd like to see her make a scandal out of that.'

'I'm glad you're satisfied,' says Jonah. 'Meanwhile, my granddaughter has been ripped from the only family she's known, held hostage by a drug-dealing mother. I'd like to know what you're going to do about it?'

Susan shakes her head, shrugs her shoulders. No answers here. 'If she's in the county we'll make every effort,' she says.

'Not good enough,' says Jonah. 'And what if she's in another state? What if she's in Mexico?'

'We'll do what we can.'

Jonah sees this for what it is, the government tango, you lead, we'll follow.

'Do you have any idea how many children are snatched by disgruntled parents every year in this country?' Before Jonah can answer: 'More than a hundred and sixty thousand,' she says. 'Most of them used like battering rams for revenge against a spouse. And sometimes an occasional grandparent. And the numbers are exploding.'

'Do you ever get any of them back?' he asks.

'Sometimes.' A statistic Susan would rather not offer, even if she had it on the tip of her tongue.

'Sometimes?' He turns around, palms up, looking at the ceiling. 'Sometimes? That's as good as it gets? You'll do what you can? Sometimes you get them back? I thought I had custody. I thought the law was worth something. I took the time. Went to court. I could have just as easily taken the child. Disappeared. I guess I should have. Knowing what I know now. I could have taken Amanda to the back side of the moon. Where Jessica and this – this Zolanda Suade would never have found us. But I didn't.'

'And you did the right thing,' says Susan.

'I didn't because I thought the law protected people who were in the right.' Jonah ignores her. 'But obviously it doesn't.'

'That's not true,' says Susan.

'Then why aren't you over there, at Suade's office, pounding her head against a rock right now to find out where Mandy is?'

'Because that's not how the law works.'

'The law doesn't work. That's the problem,' says Jonah.

92

'I'll tell you what I'd do. I'd go over there and wring that bitch's neck. I'd find out,' he says, 'if I had to . . .'

'Jonah!'

'Kill her.' He's looking directly at me as he says the words, an expression that only lends emphasis. 'The last thing she'd ever tell anybody on this planet is where Mandy is. There are ways to get information,' he says. 'Maybe I hired the wrong people. Why the hell don't you go after her?' Jonah looks at Brower, who shrugs a shoulder – as if to say, Don't look at me, I'm only the hired help. Then to Susan.

'We've tried. Believe me.'

'What have you tried? Talking to her?' He gestures toward me, the last fool to converse with Suade.

Jonah's been chomping on a dry cigar, now he lights it. 'Hope you don't mind?' he asks after the fact.

I shake my head. It's the only satisfaction he's likely to get here. At the moment he could probably burn the place down and I would be the last to object.

He reaches into the breast pocket of his shirt, now a rusty hue of dried fish blood, and comes out with a handful of cigars, each in its own small aluminum cylinder.

'Would you like one?' He starts to hand them around.

I shake my head.

He offers one to Harry, who takes it, then to Brower, who looks, raises an eyebrow and smiles, then puts it in his pocket. Save it for later. Jonah is not of the generation who would think to offer such a thing to Susan, but now she is looking, and finally he does. She takes it and puts it in her purse, probably planning to use its fiery end on my ass tonight in order to refresh my recollection of details from my meeting with Suade. I am in for the third degree.

93

Harry lights up and pretty soon my office looks like some alderman's pit of public corruption; a blue haze everywhere.

'There's one thing I am wondering?' I direct this to Susan.

'What's that?'

'We've established that Jonah never came to your department in the original custody case. What does your department know about Jessica's criminal allegations against Jonah?'

'What do you mean?' says Susan.

'Did you investigate them?' I'm shopping for information.

'The DA would have done that,' says Susan.

'But I'll bet your little form in there' – I'm pointing to Brower's folder, now closed and back in his lap – 'would tell us if the investigation is closed. For lack of evidence, say.'

She looks at Brower.

'We can't discuss that,' he says.

'Why not?'

'Criminal investigations, pending or closed, are confidential, unless charges are brought,' says Brower.

'So you *did* investigate the charges?'

'Can't say,' he says. 'We would like to help you, but that's off-limits.'

'So my client lives under a permanent cloud. Suade goes before the cameras, and he can't even obtain information from the county as to whether he's been cleared?'

Brower looks at Susan, who is a stone idol, then turns back to me.

'That's the way it is,' he says. 'There's nothing we can do about it.' It is now clear why Susan brought her conscience

94

to the meeting. Alone in this room she knows she would have difficulty not disclosing what she knows about this, at least to me. With Brower present she is safe, for now.

'So where do we go from here?' she says.

'Looks like Jonah goes to the public pillory. Where you and your department end up, I'm not sure. I guess we'll have to wait for the news conference.'

'I'd like to know why nobody can do anything when this woman came to my house and literally threatened to kidnap my granddaughter?' says Jonah.

'When did she do that?' asks Susan.

'Few weeks ago. When my daughter came back late from visitation.'

'You never told me this.' Susan looks at me.

'Suade will deny it,' I tell her. 'She may admit she was there, but as for the words, she will deny that they were ever intended as a threat.'

'What did she say, exactly?' says Susan.

'That unless I gave Mandy back to my daughter, I would lose her. Bold as brass she stood there in my kitchen and told me I was about to lose my granddaughter.'

Susan looks at Brower. 'What do you think?'

'How soon before the child went missing?' he asks.

'Few days. Maybe a week.'

'It could be useful,' he says. 'It could show agency, that she acted as an agent in the abduction. At least it's arguable.'

'You said she didn't deny being there,' says Jonah. 'When you met with Suade.'

'We didn't debate the subject. Didn't get into the details. But she didn't deny it.'

95

'There.' Jonah looks at Susan as if having won the point.

'Admitting she was at your house for a conversation and proving that she was part of an abduction are two different things,' I remind him.

'Still, we could use an affidavit,' says Susan. 'Would you be willing to come to my office and provide a statement under oath?'

'Absolutely,' says Jonah. 'My wife, too, if you need her.'

'Your wife heard Suade make the statement?'

He nods.

'Gets better and better,' says Brower.

'Her lawyers will shred it,' I tell them. 'Two grandparents whose granddaughter is abducted by their mother. Suade's lawyers will paint Jonah and Mary as being mad at the world. Ready to make wild accusations against anyone who happened to be standing around. And you have no real evidence.'

'If it were anybody else standing in that house making threats, maybe,' says Susan. 'But the courts know about Suade. We take the affidavit to Family Law,' says Susan, 'and ask the court for an order to show cause why Suade shouldn't be held in contempt if she doesn't tell where the child is.'

'You forget Suade's already got a lawsuit pending against the county for abuse of process. There's no way a judge is going to take the chance without solid, slam-dunk evidence of her involvement.'

'I don't like the idea of a client going down to her office alone.' Harry's talking about Susan's office.

'Then you come with us.' She calls his bluff. 'Protect his rights.'

'Fine by me,' he says.

I can see blood all over the county carpets.

'What about you?' Harry looks at me.

'I've got a meeting. I'm not sure this is such a great idea. If it doesn't work, it only serves to strengthen Suade's hand.'

'How so?' says Susan.

'It'll make it more difficult to pursue her later if better evidence develops. If we try to take her back into court later, it's going to look like harassment.'

'Do you have any suggestions?' Susan looks at me.

Reluctantly I shake my head.

'When can we do it?' says Jonah.

'Right now. Can you come down to my office?'

'Before he signs any affidavit I want to see it,' I tell Susan.

She agrees.

Brower has another appointment. He looks at his watch. He's already late. Susan snagged Brower on the run on his pager, so he came here separately. Harry has some phone calls to return.

'I can take Mr Hale down to the office in my car,' says Susan. 'Get everything set up.'

'No talking till I get there,' says Harry. He pulls Jonah aside and whispers something into his ear, no doubt telling Jonah not to say a thing until he gets there. Harry signals me, subtle palms-down, like it's all cool. Nothing to worry about.

I'm not so sure.

'Good.' Susan's all smiles. 'Then it's settled.'

Brower's out of his chair. Jonah's halfway to the door, the seat of his pants still covered with muck from the docks.

Susan's got a hand on his shoulder, talking in his ear. 'We get an order to show cause, I'll get my press people working. We'll take the edge off of Suade's press conference. Hit her with contempt and take that smile off her face.'

'Not unless I miss my guess,' I say.

Susan turns to look at me.

'That one thrives on threats.'

CHAPTER
SEVEN

Harry makes his phone calls while Jonah and Susan head downtown, for her office.

Susan is inspired by nothing but contempt for Suade, another reason for concern on my part.

Five minutes later I'm behind the wheel in Lena bouncing over the Coronado Bridge and north on I-5. I drop off the freeway and work my way down toward the airport. At the intersection of Pacific Highway I am stopped at a light. I can hear the screaming engines of a jet and see its large tail assembly over the steel baffles that line the fence as the plane revs for takeoff, the vibration rattling the teeth in my head.

The light changes and I move through the intersection away from the noise now descending down the runway. I head toward Harbor Drive. In the distance I can see Harbor Island with its high-rise hotels.

Rumbling at speed toward Rosecrans, I merge with traffic, go a few more blocks, catch the light and do a left, heading out onto Shelter Island.

A forest of aluminum masts and steel-cabled riggings, this is the world of sailing and regattas, the place where the America's Cup last touched US soil.

A few blocks down I stop and back into a tight space at the curb, just enough room for half of a car, or a stub-backed Jeep. I look over at the slip of paper pinned under my coffee cup on the seat next to me, and then back to the sign over the street on the other side – Red Sails Inn. I'd scrawled the name in pencil a few days before, after making a half dozen phone calls.

With open windows there is nothing to lock, so I step out, slam the half door, and make my way across the street around a few slow-moving vehicles.

The Red Sails Inn is a landmark, a restaurant and bar that has been a San Diego fixture since before Lindbergh came to town to pick up the *Spirit of St Louis*. The restaurant moved from its original digs near the waterfront out to Shelter Island when that landfill was created back in the sixties, so once again, it is nestled by a sea of boats. There are large boats and small boats, all tied up in slips out back. Some of these could easily be classed as yachts. These are generally defined as a large hole in the water into which one pours money. Fortunately, I have never had the inclination to find out. What I know is that these gleaming, white palaces of floating fiberglass look expensive.

There are a few pedestrians ambling along the street: a guy window-shopping pricy property through the glass front of a real estate office, a delivery truck driver off-loading supplies, signs of commercial life in the afternoon.

I open the door and enter the Red Sails, lifting the dark glasses from my eyes so that I can see. I've landed here at the meal hour, and the place is crowded. There are a few locals sitting on bar stools and a line forming for tables in the dining room. The bartender is mixing drinks and taking orders, talking to another man in a sport coat and open collar who has the look of management about him.

In another minute, the man in the sport coat escorts two couples in front of me to their table and comes back. 'Smoking or nonsmoking?' he says.

'Actually, I'm looking for Joaquin Murphy.'

The guy looks around and doesn't see him. 'Murph was expecting you?'

'Supposed to meet me here for lunch.'

'Jimmie. Have you seen Murph this morning?'

'Not yet.'

'My guess is he's out back. On the *Money Pit*.'

I give him a blind stare.

'His boat.'

'Ah.'

'Lemme see if I can get ahold of him. What's your name?'

I give him a business card from my pocket.

The guy disappears behind the bar and a second later he's on the phone, talking to somebody. I can see his lips moving. It's a quick conversation and he hangs up.

'He got busy with some chores. Forgot the time. He'll be over in a minute. Go ahead and sit down. Can I get you a drink?'

It's a little early, so I order a Virgin Mary. 'Easy on the Tabasco,' I tell him.

I sit and study the decor. It's rustic contemporary, lots of wood on the interior, tables set with sturdy wooden chairs in the lounge. The restaurant is to the rear, where a large wall of windows and a sliding glass door frame a deck for outdoor dining. This merges with the dock and the slips beyond. Outside umbrellaed tables are full of people extending the lunch hour, enjoying the bobbing masts and cool breezes off the harbor. A waitress returns with my drink. Just then I see a figure moving like a comet leaving a tail, dropping socks and then a shoe as he hops between tables out on the deck. He still has one shoe in his hand when he reaches the sliding door.

He is short and stubby, more than a little overweight, in Bermuda shorts that reach halfway to his ankles so that he has the look of a comic pirate. He wears a wrinkled polo shirt that does little to disguise his bulging Buddha belly. From the look of his tousled dark hair, I judge he has only moments before pulled it over his head.

As he comes through the sliding door he leans against the frame. Still fighting with the one wayward shoe, he surveys the people inside. It takes him only a second to figure I'm the one he's looking for. By the time he makes it to my table, the only thing amiss is the shoelaces dragging in his wake.

'Mr Madriani.' His smile struggles to be disarming, and instead he comes off looking like an elf who slept with Santa's wife on Christmas Eve. His teeth are a little uneven, flashing white set against a deep tan and an even darker five-o'clock shadow. 'Sorry,' he says. 'I got tied up.'

'So I gathered. Name's Paul.' I offer my hand and he shakes it, a firm grip.

'Joaquin Murphy,' he says. 'You can call me Murph. Everybody else does.'

'Murph it is. Have a seat.'

He's a bucket of sweat.

'I thought we'd go to my place. Out back,' he says. 'Little more privacy there.'

'Whatever. Can I get you something to drink?' The waitress has now joined us.

'Corona,' he says. 'And Rosie, make it to go.' He has one foot on the chair next to mine trying to tie his shoelace. There are smudges of grease and oil on his forearms, and his fingernails look as if he has been using them to plow the back forty.

'Been waiting long?'

'No.'

He notices me looking at his arms.

'You own a boat, you get like this,' he says. 'I was workin' on a bilge pump. Time got away from me. If it isn't one thing, it's another. Ever owned one? A boat?'

'I've missed that pleasure,' I tell him.

'Unless you're handy, into maintenance, you don't want one. Either do it yourself, or pay through the nose. When it's floating, maintenance isn't something you can let go. Not like a house. Spring a leak in your plumbing at home, you get a little dry rot. Do it on a boat, and you find yourself at the bottom of the slip.' He's now wiping grease off the back of one of his hands with one of the linen napkins from the table.

The waitress arrives. He takes the chilled bottle of beer from the girl. We order sandwiches. 'They'll deliver,' he says. I peel off some bills from my money clip and we walk.

I follow Murphy, drinks in hand, out the back through the sliding door, across the deck and down the dock. He is three slips down, in the direction of the boatyard, which I can now see jutting out into the marina, some sparks flying from an arc welder in the shadows.

He grabs a line to balance himself as he walks cleanly under the bowsprit of a large sailboat, twin masted. If I had to guess, I'd say at least forty feet.

I have to duck to join him.

The *Money Pit* is larger than I'd imagined, a wood hull, shiplap, a vintage vessel. In the stern I can see a large teak wheel in the cockpit under a green canvas bimini. The boat is painted Kelly green with dark trim and a teak deck. It is meticulously outfitted, brass fittings and neatly coiled white sheets, lines to work the sails. The brightwork gleams so that I can nearly see my image in the marine varnish.

'My office,' says Murph.

'Investigations must pay well.'

'That, some investments, and a rich uncle,' he says. 'This is mostly the uncle.' He takes a sip from the bottle as we stand on the dock and admire.

'She was built in the early thirties for some bootlegger. When I found her, she was in bad shape. Fortunately, there wasn't enough metal to justify the salvage yard. The only reason she survived,' he says.

'Labor of love,' I tell him. 'It's beautiful.'

'She is gorgeous, even if I say so myself.' He talks as if the boat were alive, then leads me up the gangway onto the deck and along the side of the house that juts up in the center of the boat like a miniature cottage with a pitched roof. This has six round portholes running the length to provide light down into what I imagine is the salon and cabins below.

Murphy turns the corner and sidles through the sliding

hatch door, then skips down a ladder. For a short, fat man, still dragging a loose shoestring, he possesses a degree of agility that is deceptive. I follow him into the spacious interior.

The salon is paneled in dark mahogany, the floor polished teak, and above it all is a low curving ceiling, a grid work of varnished beams beneath the open canopy of the house where shafts of light stream in through the portholes overhead.

'Sit down. Get comfortable.' He nods toward one of the benches that line the inside of the hull as he searches and finds a small notebook and pencil at a built-in desk.

I sit and put my drink in a cup holder.

Murphy takes the desk and places the bottle of beer on top of an unfurled chart where the chilled glass deposits a round watermark.

'Like I told you on the phone,' he says. 'I don't do much domestic stuff. Wouldn't have taken the case except Fred Hawkins referred you. I do a lot of personal injury for Fred.'

'I would think divorces would be a PI's life's blood.'

'Not this one. It's a good way to get shot. Angry husbands kill more people than the mob.'

'I'll put your mind at ease. There's no husband involved in this one. I don't do family law work myself.'

'So what got you involved?'

'A friend with a problem.'

'Not the money?'

'A rich friend.'

This news has a leavening effect on Murphy. It generates some interest in note taking. He sweeps papers off his desk and sharpens his pencil, jamming it into the little hole in the electric device until I can barely see the eraser.

'Tell me about your client.'

I had sent Murphy a check for a thousand dollars, drawn against my client trust account, a retainer from Jonah. Murphy is working at two hundred dollars an hour plus expenses, mileage and meals if he has to travel, hotels if he is overnight.

'As far as you're concerned. I'm your client.'

'Fine by me,' he says. 'I'll work against the retainer. Bill you after that.'

This gives me the argument that whatever Murphy does is sheltered, privileged as attorney work-product, and not subject to discovery if I have to get into a courtroom with Suade.

I had decided long before this moment to share information about Jonah only on a need-to-know basis. When you have the prospect of eighty million dollars sitting in timed accounts, friends and benefactors tend to crop up like mold on rancid cheese.

'Have you had a chance to check into the woman I told you about on the phone?'

'Some,' he says. 'Made a few inquiries. Very discreet regarding this Zolanda Suade. Pulled what I could from Lexis-Nexis, the internet. Whether what she does is legal or not I'll leave to the lawyers. One thing's certain: She doesn't shrink from talking about it in the press.'

'You found a lot of news stories?'

'Enough newsprint to take out the Black Forest.'

'Anything of interest? Let's start with background.'

'According to my information, she's been in the area about twelve years. Out of Ohio originally, result of a bad marriage and a pissed-off husband who threatened to kill her – after he gets out of prison.'

'He may have to get in line,' I tell Murphy.

'Yeah, people tend to get angry when you steal their kids,' he says. 'Anyway, the husband's doing twelve to twenty for rape and child molestation. Apparently that all happened after she divorced him. She was not the rapee, though she claims he used force to have his way with her during the marriage on more than a few occasions.'

'Any children?'

He thumbs through his notes. 'Not that turned up in any of the reports.'

So far he's batting 900. I can only assume that the death of her son is a sore point and the one thing that Suade does not talk about to the press.

'According to Suade, she filed complaints with the cops about his beating on her. They did nothing. This appears to have built up more than a little resentment toward the authorities on Suade's part.'

He looks at me as if to see whether this is the kind of stuff I am looking for.

'I'd heard that she has little use for the courts and the customary processes of the law. Which brings me to another subject. Has she ever done jail time?' Something I am thinking that might not be on Lexis-Nexis.

'No record of convictions, if that's what you mean. Closest she came, she did a few nights for contempt, before her lawyer sprang her. She wouldn't have done that except the kid she snatched belonged to a judge.'

107

'Davidson?'

'You knew about that?' His expression sags like a child with a secret that everybody knows. 'You could be wasting your money hiring me.'

'The devil's in the details,' I tell him with a smile.

Brad Davidson is the presiding judge of the San Diego Superior Court. Two years ago he was on the bench hearing criminal cases when his estranged wife disappeared with his son and a pile of cash that was waiting to be divvied up in a divorce proceeding. He hasn't seen the kid, his wife, or the money since.

'I had heard he held Suade in contempt.'

'He did more than that,' says Murphy. 'He issued a bench warrant. Had her arrested and summarily hauled off the street into his courtroom where he did everything but wire her nipples to electrodes. All in front of his bailiff, who had a gun strapped on his hip.

'When Suade didn't blink, he had her put in the bucket and played hide the pea for about three days, moving her from one facility to another so her lawyers couldn't find her. Each move was a new experience in cavity searches. Even put her in the federal metro lockup for twenty-four hours before her lawyer figured it out and sprung her on a writ. The county is still trying to deal with the fall-out.'

'What fallout?'

'A twenty-million-dollar lawsuit for false imprisonment. Davidson had no jurisdiction for anything. The warrant was based on a lot of surmise, no witnesses who saw Suade take the kid. It's like your kid disappears and, knowing Suade's reputation, you check her house first.'

'I understand the judge's attitude. What happened to Davidson?'

'According to the reports, he came close to losing his judicial wings. The commission that reviews such things considered his long service on the bench and the fact that his son had been kidnapped. They let him off with a formal reprimand and a few hundred hours of community service. Word is he's still doing penance at some women's shelter in South Bay two nights a week.

'As for Suade, she still has her claws into the county with a team of lawyers working on contigency to push local government into bankruptcy. According to the reports, she has the rapt attention of the county council.'

'They're worried about the suit?'

'You could say that. They're self-insured. May have to take a loan from the state if she nails 'em. The board of supervisors has been doing belly dances up in the capitol to keep the lines of credit open.

'Funny thing is, Suade doesn't seem to be motivated by money. I checked her credit rating. There are people living in cardboard boxes using racing forms for wallpaper I'd sooner make a loan to.'

'She's broke?'

'She's got a dozen judgments outstanding. None of 'em satisfied, all of them by pissed-off husbands and their lawyers. Infliction of emotional distress. Conversion of personal property. You name it. Most of them taken by default. She doesn't show up in court. Not to defend anyway. Everything she owns is in her husband's name.'

'She's married?' Murph's batting average is back to a thousand. Something Susan omitted to tell me.

109

'You sound surprised?'

'I am. From everything I'd heard, I just assumed she hated men.'

'Apparently not this one. New addition to her life. Three years ago.' Murphy looks at his notes. 'His name is Harold Morgan. She kept her maiden name, at least for publicity purposes. He's a mortgage banker. Conservative. Christian right. Good at business. His credit report shows some considerable net worth. Heavily into real estate development. According to the reports – of course this is Suade telling the reporters,' he says, 'new hubby saved her from a life of bitterness after her first marriage failed.'

'Apparently he's not a total success,' I tell him.

'Can't win 'em all,' says Murphy.

'What does he think of his wife's activities?'

'Oh, he supports her. Thinks she's doing God's work. Saving neglected children and their abused mothers from a corrupt court system. But his support, according to the stories, is limited to the moral variety, having his picture taken with his arm around her. So far, none of the lawyers chasing his wife has been able to tag any of his assets to satisfy the judgments against her. They can't show any involvement on his part in her *business*. And the business is always veiled behind a corporate shield. She operates three of these at present, all in the red. She's had as many as eight going at one time. When they get too messy, when lawyers start climbing through the window and coming up the stairs, she chloroforms the corporation and moves on.'

'So the plaintiffs get a bag of bones.'

'Bleached and baked,' says Murphy. 'Even the filing cabinet is rented. She only has one. She advertises the fact

110

that she doesn't keep many business records on paper. Sort of a disclaimer to anybody who might be looking.'

'I've seen her office,' I tell him. 'I can vouch for the single filing cabinet.'

'If you're planning on suing the lady, you'd get more satisfaction falling out of bed during a wet dream. Money is not what makes Suade run. And the threat of losing it doesn't even register on her list of a hundred worst fears.'

'Do you think there's any benefit in talking to Davidson?' I ask him.

'He might give you a lot of sympathy,' says Murphy.

'But no help?'

He shakes his head. 'If you find the key to Zolanda, there's gonna be a long line forming to use it. According to everything I've read, she hasn't made a lot of friends in this town.'

There's a tap on the wooden house up by the open hatch: the waitress with our sandwiches. We take a break, talk while we're eating.

Murphy takes a deep swig from the bottle of Corona, like he's sucking air from a vacuum, swallows slowly and looks at me. With the last bob of his Adam's apple he finally pops the question: 'So who is it you want that Suade's holding?'

'A child. Little girl.'

'Kid's with her mother?'

'We think so.'

'I could set up on her. Suade,' he says. 'Do some surveillance. There's an outside chance she might lead us . . .'

'No. Not yet. From everything I've heard she's been surveilled by the best.'

'The FBI?'

I look at him. 'You've heard the same thing?'

'According to her, anyway. She takes delight in advertising the fact. Like a badge of honor. She's talked about it to the press. Claims they camp outside her door morning, noon, and night. Public enemy number one. But she's too smart. She's snookered 'em.'

'You don't believe it?'

'I don't know. All I know is they've never hauled her in for questioning. Never even interviewed her.'

'Sounds like you have sources?'

'Some people talk,' he says.

'FBI?'

He's not saying.

'If you have contacts like that, it could be helpful.'

'How's that?'

'There's another facet to the case.' I tell him about Jessica, and the fact that she apparently cut some deal with the feds for a reduced sentence on state time. 'She's the mother in hiding,' I tell him. 'I'm retained by the child's grandfather. Jessica's dad. He had legal custody at the time the kid disappeared.'

'What's the child's name?'

'Amanda Hale.'

'Mother go by the same surname?'

I nod.

He makes a note.

'Maybe your sources could enlighten us as to the specifics of the deal the feds cut with Jessica?'

'Why do you want to know?'

'It could provide some leads. Her arrest was drug related.

112

She may be running in those circles again, going places, seeing people.'

Murphy smiles. A widening of the commercial horizon. The old revolving retainer. He makes a few more notes, the fact that it was probably heroin or cocaine she was carrying across the Mexican border.

'Left to her own devices, she shouldn't be too hard to find,' says Murphy.

'That's what I'm afraid of.'

He lifts a questioning eyebrow.

'That she may not have been left to her own devices.'

'Suade?'

'Her connections will no doubt make Jessica and the child a lot harder to find. If her group's providing cover, moving them around. Possibly down in Mexico. They may have helped in the abduction, but we don't have any hard evidence. Anything you could turn up in that connection would be helpful.'

'What's Suade's interest in all of this?'

'Self-proclaimed do-gooder with a warped sense of justice,' I tell him.

'No, I mean why did she take this particular kid? Mother's a loser. Done time. What's in it for her?'

'Publicity. Jessica's father gets her press.'

'How?'

'Read the papers. Next few days. Suade's adding to her scrapbook,' I tell him.

'Is he a politician? Some celebrity?'

'In his own way. Whatever you do, don't go near Suade. I've already met with her. It's a waste of time and may cause more problems. It may be difficult for me to move freely for a while. If the press bites, I may be emitting a tail of reporters like a comet.'

He laughs. 'I understand. How old is the drug case involving the daughter?'

'Two, two and a half years,' I tell him.

'Pretty cold trail.'

'It's why we should just take it in little pieces.' Rather than waste his time and Jonah's money drilling holes that are likely to come up dry, I want to use Murphy where he might do some good; with his federal sources.

'I'm told the feds pitched her to the state for prosecution on the Mexican drug thing. Made a deal for a lighter sentence and easier time. But it was never clear why.'

He looks up from his notepad. 'And you wanna know what she had that they wanted?' Murphy's looks are misleading. He's a quick study.

'That. And whether she gave it to them. If you can find out. Without attracting too much attention. Or giving anything up.'

'Like what?'

'Like my identity. The last thing I need are FBI agents visiting my office. It tends to make clients nervous. Like the IRS doing house calls with your accountant.'

'Why would you think the feds might come looking for you?' No sooner does he ask the question than the answer dawns on him. 'You think they're looking for this Jessica?'

'It's a possibility.'

'Why?'

'We don't know. We're not sure. It's possible that whatever she offered them for the deal she failed to produce.'

'What? You think they may want to revoke parole?'

'Anything's possible. Listen to whatever they have to say. See what you can find out. Maybe we'll know more after you talk to your sources.'

'Your name will not pass my lips,' he says. 'What if I stumble over her? This Jessica. It could happen. They might have a lead on her.'

'Listen, as far as I'm concerned, they can arrest her. I'd give 'em a big kiss. It would solve all my problems.' If Jessica were taken we could enforce the custody order, get the child back and deal with Suade after the fact.

'And if I do find her, this Jessica?'

'Don't approach her. Keep her under surveillance and call me immediately.'

'You make it sound like she's dangerous.' He has a look as if this could be a surcharge.

'No, I don't think so. Just very skittish. She wouldn't be easy to find a second time.'

'I see.'

'If you find her, call me.' I give him my card. 'If I'm not there, leave an urgent message on voice mail and they'll page me immediately, night or day.'

CHAPTER
EIGHT

It was after six by the time I finished at the office, some paperwork that had stacked up, and phone calls to return. The sun had dipped behind the giant palms surrounding the Del Coronado so that it looked like a blinding orange beach ball tethered on the horizon.

Traffic heading home had thickened in both directions on Orange Avenue. I took some back streets home, a five minute drive.

The sitter had picked up Sarah, and her car was still parked out front as I swung into the driveway. My daughter is eleven, but I am not yet ready to turn her into a latch-key kid. I half expected to see Susan's blue Ford parked there too, but it wasn't. I wondered if she'd finished up with Jonah.

Before I could get the car door open, Sarah was bounding down the front steps and toward the car, the sitter behind her, purse in hand.

'You're home early.' She greets me with a big smile

and a hug, soft cheek against the stubble of my after-noon beard.

'Thought maybe we could take in a show tonight.'

'Really?' Her eyes light up.

'It is Friday.'

She's jumping up and down, crying yippees.

'What would you like to see?' I ask.

'Oh, I don't know. There's supposed to be a very funny movie at the mall.'

Sarah is still heavily into slapstick. I am left to wonder when this phase passes, and at times shudder to think what may follow. I relish the dreams of childhood that in these moments seem to reside in the sparkle of her eyes. It seems that each age is a new adventure, one in which I have often thought I would like to freeze her, only to be enchanted by the next as she grows up. I have friends who tell me they would not trade places, the terrors of a teenage daughter still ahead of me. I suppose ignorance is bliss. Take each day at a time.

'Why don't you look at the paper while I change,' I tell her.

'Are you going to ask Susan?'

'I don't know. Do you want me to?'

'It's up to you.'

'I thought tonight maybe just you and me.'

Sarah smiles, dimples in the cheeks and spaces between the teeth. A date with Dad.

I grab the newspaper, an afternoon throwaway, and the mail from the box in front of the house, and thumb through the stack of mostly bills.

Peggie Connelly is on the front step waiting for me.

Twenty-seven going on fifty, Peggie is a graduate student in early-childhood development at the university, someone Susan put me onto. She sits for a couple of families during the week and picks Sarah up after school for pocket change while she works on her studies. Peggie is the closest thing Sarah has to a surrogate mother. They spend the afternoons together, sharing quality time, something that I don't often give her.

'See you on Monday, same time?'

'You bet. You'll pick her up.'

She nods, smiles and heads to her car.

It takes me less than a minute to check the messages on the phone. The first is a guy trying to sell aluminum siding; the second is a message from Harry telling me to call him as soon as I get home. It sounds as if there is traffic in the background, as if Harry had to call me from a pay phone. I have told him many times to get a cellular, but Harry resists technology.

I dial his number. There's no answer.

A few minutes later I try him again. This time I leave a message on his answering machine.

'It's Paul. I got your message. Sorry I missed you. Should be home about ten o'clock tonight. Taking Sarah to see a flick at the mall. Wish you could join us.' I laugh. 'I'll call you when I get home.' Then I hang up.

Ten minutes later I'm changed, polo shirt, slacks, and loafers.

Sarah comes into my room with the newspaper in her hand. 'I thought we could do the mall, have dinner there. Catch the movie at the cineplex.'

'You did, did you?'

'You said we could get dinner out.'

'Cheese pizza and Coke, my favorites.'

Sarah smiles and gives me one of those looks. Well, you promised.

'How was school?'

'Good.'

'What did you do today?' I run a comb through my hair as I stand in front of the vanity mirror and look at Sarah in the reflection. She's lying on the bed, chin propped on elbowed hands.

'Oh, nothing.'

Like pulling teeth. 'You spent six hours there. You must have done something.'

'Had a math test.'

'How did you do?'

'Got an A.' She says this matter-of-factly, no big deal. A year ago she was drawing down D's until I started taking some time with her, teaching her not so much the elements of mathematics, but that she had a brain and that if she applied it she could succeed.

'Well, that's good.'

Sarah has finally reached that plateau where she has discovered the correlation between studying and grades, that there is a reward for work. Some kids never do. Others just assume that they don't have it, can't compete. They sell themselves short, give up before they have a chance.

I curl the comb so that my hair does a teardrop over my forehead, throwback to the fifties. I turn and model it for her. She laughs. Sarah is always an easy touch when it comes to comics.

'It's you,' she says.

I comb it back into shape.

'Let's get out of here before the phone rings,' she says.

'You got it.' We're out the door.

The food fair is not my idea of fine dining. My father would never have done this. He was of an age before fast food. But tonight Sarah and I sit at a table under the sprawling mall roof, next to a hundred other parents and kids, cutting cheese pizza with plastic knives. Sarah likes hers with nothing on it, just string cheese that looks like white rubber and doesn't taste much better. No green stuff. Not even parsley. The green stuff is poison.

Dinner takes all of ten minutes. We spend the next twenty negotiating the line for tickets, forking over our savings to gain admittance and going into deep debt for popcorn. We sit through an hour of trailers, enough close-up action to give you motion sickness, with sound effects delivered at a level to raise the dead. For the price, they should hand out earplugs and eyepatches.

Finally, we settle into fantasy. Sarah's chomping on popcorn. I slump down, head against the back of the seat, my knees against the seat in front of me. I'm as engrossed as Sarah by the time I feel a hand on my shoulder. I straighten up in my seat, and suddenly there's the hot breath of a whisper next to my ear. 'Paul.'

I turn. It's Harry.

'Please, mister. I'm trying to watch the movie.' The woman behind me is giving Harry irritated looks.

He's standing in front of her, probably on her toes, pressed between the row of seats.

'Excuse me, madam. This is an emergency.'

'Why don't you take it outside?'

'I'm trying.' Harry appears breathless. 'We've gotta talk.' He motions me outside.

Sarah gives me a look, rolls her eyes, as if she knew it was too good to be true.

I pat her knee. 'Relax, sweetie. I'll be right back.'

'Sure.'

I step over people, making my way to the aisle, and follow Harry toward the exit. Outside the door, he doesn't stop but continues walking, heading toward the lobby.

'Why can't we talk here?'

''Cause I'm not alone. We've got a problem. The cops found Suade. A few hours ago,' says Harry.

'What are you talking about?'

'She's dead,' says Harry.

'What? How?'

'Don't know the details. But I'd be willing to bet it wasn't a heart attack,' says Harry.

'When did it happen?'

'I don't know. Late this afternoon. Early this evening. They're not sure. They found the body a few hours ago. But it gets worse.'

'What do you mean?'

'I don't know where Jonah is.'

'He was with you. At Susan's office.'

'I'm afraid not. It's why I tried to call you at the house. Jonah stormed out of McKay's office a few minutes after we got there. One of McKay's lawyers agreed with you that Jonah's information was not enough to warrant an OSC, an order to show cause to bring Suade up on charges of contempt. He told Jonah there was nothing the department could do.

'Jonah got pissed off. Said a lotta things he shouldn't have. That's when he left. Walked out in a rage.'

'Damn it.'

'I'm sorry.'

'It's not your fault. I should have gone with you.'

'Wouldn't have done any good,' says Harry. 'Believe me. When that old man gets up a head of steam there's not much, short of a two-by-four up about the back of his head, that's gonna slow him By the time I got outside, he was gone. Got into a cab and disappeared.'

'What time was this?'

Harry scratches the back of his head. Thinks for a moment. 'About two. Maybe two-fifteen. When I got home, I called his wife. She hadn't seen him. That's when I started to get worried. He said some pretty provocative things. You heard him in the office this morning.'

'Did you try his boat?'

'I did. He wasn't there. No sign of his car, either.'

'That means he must have picked it up,' I tell him. 'I took Jonah to the office this morning. He left his car in the parking lot at the marina. I was going to take him back out there after our meeting. Forgot all about it.'

As we reach the lobby, I see why we have come here. Susan is standing just the other side of the ticket taker with the investigator Brower. She's wringing her hands, bundle of nerves.

'Did Harry tell you?' she says as soon as she sees me.

'Yes.'

'I tried to talk to him. He wouldn't see reason. The lawyer told him . . .'

123

'Yes I know. Harry told me. How did you find out about Suade?'

'It came over the car radio,' Brower answers for her. 'Police band. I heard it in my car.'

'When was it? What time?'

'Jeeze, I don't know.' Brower looks at Susan. 'I was heading back in from that interview out in the east county. Five-thirty. Maybe six o'clock. I called the office from the cell phone in the car. Talked to Susan, Ms McKay. Asked her if she'd heard. She hadn't.'

'I don't know if anything's moving on the news yet,' says Susan.

I can tell from their collective expressions they're all thinking the same thing I am. Where was Jonah?

'Was there any information on cause of death?' I ask Brower.

'At the time, they didn't know if she was dead,' says Brower. 'They were calling in the paramedics. According to the reports, it looked like a possible gunshot.'

'I called your house,' says Susan. 'You were out. So I called Harry. He'd just collected his messages, said you were at the show. Where's Sarah?'

'She's inside.'

'Do you want me to stay with her? Take her home?' says Susan.

I think for a moment. Sarah is going to be disappointed, but under the circumstances I have no choice.

'That would be great.' I pull Harry off to one side where Susan and Brower can't hear us. 'Go to Jonah's boat and sit tight. If he shows up, call me on my cell phone.' I make sure Harry has the number. 'Don't go near him.'

Harry looks at me. 'You don't think . . . ?'

'I don't know what to think right now. I'll call Mary at the house and see if he got back.'

'Save your nickel,' says Harry. 'I tried five minutes ago from the pay phone out front. He wasn't there. She hasn't seen him all day.'

'Wonderful. Did you tell her what happened?'

'No. I figured no sense worrying her.'

I stop for a moment and think.

'She had a million enemies. Why settle on our client?'

'Tell that to Brower. You saw the look on his face. Besides, if Jonah's done something truly stupid, a conversation with Suade that turned ugly, what if he goes home? If he's berserk, panicked, no telling what could happen.' Harry knows what I'm thinking. Murder, then suicide, is not beyond the pale.

'So what do you want me to do?'

'Forget the boat,' I tell him. 'Try his house again. If he's come home, call me on the cell line. I'll be with Brower. If he's not there, tell Mary we need to talk to her, a meeting at the office.'

'At this hour?' says Harry.

'We've got to get her out of that house until we know what's going on. Offer to pick her up. If you're sure Jonah's not there, ring the doorbell. Any pretext. Get her out of the house. Do it quickly. Take her to the office and sit tight. Tell her anything. Tell her I'm going to meet you there. If there are any questions, I'll explain to Jonah later.'

'Where are you going?' asks Harry.

'Since we don't know where our client is, I'm gonna see if

I can get Brower to escort me down to Suade's office. Maybe get me through the police lines.'

'What for?'

'To find out what the hell's goin' on.'

'Can we help?' Susan's moved closer, to a point where she might be able to hear.

I smack Harry on the back. 'Go.'

I turn to Susan and Brower. 'You can,' I tell her. I fish for the theater ticket stub in my pocket and give it to Susan. Her hands are trembling. She gives me a hug, a kiss on the cheek. 'I hope it's okay, Mr Hale I mean. I'm sure he had nothing to do with it. I'll take Sarah to my place when the movie's over. The girls are there with a sitter. They can play for a while.'

I thank her, check my watch. It's now eight-twenty. I prevail on Brower. Any hesitation is quickly crushed by Susan who directs him to do whatever he can to assist. It's nice having a woman with a private police force.

Twenty minutes later, I'm sitting in the passenger seat of Brower's county car as we pull into the same parking lot where earlier in the day I'd sat and watched Suade play hit-and-run with the homeless.

So much has happened that it seems as if a month has passed since witnessing those events.

Cops seem to have a sixth sense, a traction beam that carries them to the scene of violent death, like iron filings drawn to a magnet. If it is anywhere within fifty miles, they will find their way there. The place looks like a motorcycle convention. Cops in leather jackets and riding boots, black-and-whites everywhere.

It has an otherworldly appearance about it. The parking lot at the strip mall across the street from Suade's shop is filled with emergency vehicles, flashing lights from patrol cars and paramedic units, a fire truck, cops controlling traffic on Palm at the cross streets. People are slowing down to rubberneck. Kids cruising, seeing where the action is.

Across the street the entire building that houses the Copy Shop, from the corner on Palm to the neighbor's fence behind the rear parking lot of Suade's office, is quarantined behind yellow police tape. Cops, some in uniform, others in plainclothes, are milling everywhere, most of them outside the tape.

'You let me do the talking,' says Brower.

'You got it.'

'This is crazy,' he whispers under his breath as he shakes his head and gets out of the car. Brower is not a happy camper playing safari guide to a defense lawyer, escorting the enemy into the cops' camp. I exit from the passenger side and together we walk through the crush of cops and media, cam crews with their vans, satellite dishes aimed skyward. We cross the street.

A large blue van with white letters a foot high emblazoned on the side

SDCSID

is parked just outside the tape. Its two rear doors, guarded by a cop in uniform, are open.

'County's Scientific Investigation Division,' Brower whispers under his breath.

'I see 'em.'

'If they're here, you can be sure she didn't die of natural causes,' he says.

They are gathering trace evidence as we approach.

The large blue town car, the one I'd seen Suade driving that morning, is parked in the same place I had seen it earlier. Near its left rear fender, several figures, a woman and two men, seem to be crouching under bright lights. One of them is videotaping. I can see a single foot: the sole of a shoe, what appears to be a woman's high heel, protruding just beyond the rear wheel of the town car. The rest of the body I cannot see.

'Johnnie Brower. What brings you out on a night like this?' The husky voice comes from a uniformed cop, a big man with a beefy smile, shoulders like a bull, with sergeant's stripes on them. He is standing at the tape offering a ready hand to Brower, who seizes it.

I stand in close, riding on coattails so that I can follow Brower under the tape if he makes his move.

'Just makin' sure you guys don't step in the evidence,' says Brower. 'Sam, meet Paul. Paul Madriani, Sam Jenson, one of San Diego's finest.'

Sam shakes my hand and gives me the once-over, one eyebrow raised as if Brower's okay, but he's not so sure about me.

'We were just drivin' by. What's goin' on?' says Brower.

'They're gettin' ready to put the body in the bag,' says Jenson. 'As for me, it can't happen soon enough.' He rolls his toes in his shoes and rocks back on his heels. 'Feet are starting to go flat,' he says.

'You just noticed?' says Brower.

'Yeah, well, us real cops gotta work for a living. Not like

128

some truant officers I know. Please, Mr Policeman, don't slap me with that ruler!' Jenson looks at Brower, then winks at me and offers up a beefy laugh.

'I'll have to remember that next time I get called to a domestic dispute,' says Brower. 'Be sure to let one of you real cops go through the door first.'

'That's us, fuckin' bullet fodder with flat feet,' says Jenson.

'So, what happened here?' says Brower.

'Looks like she bought it as she was gettin' ready to go home from work. Just outside the back to her shop there.'

'Not a good way to end your day,' says Brower.

'No.'

'So, what are they thinking?'

'Probably a robbery,' says Jenson. 'SID's working the area over pretty good. Still can't find no weapon, though. At least not so far.'

'How'd she get it?' says Brower.

'Gunshot. Small caliber. That's what the paramedics said who got here before us, anyway. They probably kicked the fuckin' gun down the alley into the next block. You know the EMTs with all that shit,' he says. 'Tramp through the evidence. By the time we get on the scene, you can't tell what the hell was where. You're looking for a bullet hole, they got a fucking tracheotomy in it.'

'Sounds like a vote against first aid,' says Brower.

'That's a thought. All the good it did her,' says Jenson.

'Who called it in?'

'Do-gooder citizen with a cell phone,' says the cop. 'Some rummy stepped out in front of her car, flagged her down. God knows why she stopped. You should get a load of this guy.' Jenson's got a big grin on his face, looks around, first one way, then the other, sees what he's looking for off behind us, in the back of one of the parked squad cars.

'Over there.' He points. 'Guy looks like an escapee from Father Damien's leper farm. I'm afraid to look under the rags. His nose might fall off. I had him put in the back of Jackson's cruiser, cuz he ain't gettin' in mine.'

'Ranks gotta have some kinda privilege,' says Brower.

'Damn right.'

Jenson and Brower continue kibitzing as I study the figure in the back of the patrol car. The shadows are deep, and all I can see is a silhouette. But if there was any doubt, it is resolved by the shopping cart parked near the rear fender of the patrol vehicle. There can't be two with the same arrangement of plastic bags and wobbly third wheel not quite reaching the ground, the bundled treasures I'd seen scattered all over the sidewalk that morning.

'Did he see anything?' asks Brower.

Jenson gives him a shrug of the shoulders. 'Let me put it this way. If I was the fuckin' shooter, I'd want him as the witness,' says Jenson.

'Any chance he coulda done it?' I ask.

'Only if somebody showed him where to find the trigger and kept the muzzle out of his mouth cuz it looked like the business end of a bottle. I don't think he's high on our list. Two of the guys had to carry him to the car. Walking him was taking too long.'

'No other witnesses?' says Brower.

Jenson shakes his head. 'Not that we found so far, though the evening is young.'

While we are talking, another man, in shirtsleeves, tie loosened, the knot part way down his chest, approaches the yellow tape. He's wearing white surgical gloves, and Jenson lifts the tape so the guy can slip underneath without bending too low. He's holding one small paper bag, in one hand, and a plastic evidence bag in the other.

'Whatcha got there, Vic?' Jenson's all eyes.

'A spent one.' Vic, the tech, holds up the Baggie. There is a small bullet cartridge inside, tiny, almost invisible at this distance.

'Three-eighty,' he says. 'Enough to do the job. Close range. Found it right by the body. We think it got caught up in her clothing. When he dumped her, it fell out on the pavement.'

'What do you mean, "dumped"?' says Brower.

'We think she was in a car, parked there facing the alley with whoever killed her. Whoever did her, shot her inside the vehicle, dumped the body and drove off. Down the alley.' He points back in the general direction with the hand holding the paper bag.

'How did you come to that?' says Jenson.

'Cuz we found what appears to be stuff from the ashtray of the car, dumped on top of the body.'

'What kind of stuff?'

Vic opens the paper bag, gingerly puts his gloved hand inside and carefully removes two cigarette butts.

'Got a little lipstick on 'em,' says the tech. 'You can see it right there. Looks like it matches the color of the gloss in the victim's purse. Also her brand of cigarettes.'

'Her purse was there?'

'And her wallet with almost two hundred dollars in cash, and her keys, and enough credit cards to give the average junkie one hell of a shopping holiday.'

'There goes the robbery theory,' says Jenson.

'I'd say so. But he also left something else,' says the tech. He drops the cigarettes back into the bag, looks inside and reaches in once more. This time he comes up with something larger, brown and cylindrical – the stubbed-out remains of a good-sized cigar.

'Maybe they'll find some chompers on it,' he says. He's talking about tooth impressions that a forensic dentist might be able to cast to match the cigar with its owner.

I suspect that the crime lab will be working overtime on this. I can tell that this thought is also running through Brower's mind.

For the moment he is simply staring at me, a portrait of angst. He is feeling around, inside his coat to the breast pocket of his polo shirt, where he finds what he is searching for: the cigar given to him earlier in the day by Jonah, at the meeting in my office.

CHAPTER
NINE

The county is a patchwork quilt of law enforcement. The larger cities within it have their own police departments. Imperial Beach is not one of these. It contracts with the county sheriff for most aspects of high-end enforcement and investigation, including homicide.

At three in the morning, I am wiping sleep from my eyes as I steer Lena into one of the parking spaces marked VISITOR outside the sheriff's Imperial Beach station.

In law school I savored the notion that only emergency room physicians kept hours like this, an illusion that twenty years of criminal law practice has crushed.

According to Jonah, he has not been arrested, only detained. Still, they allowed him to make one phone call, and he placed it to my pager. In turn, I called Mary and told her I would try to bring him home. She is worried sick. I then called Harry. I decided not to wake Susan. Fortunately, she has taken Sarah for the night.

From my conversation with Jonah, he required two things:

legal advice and clothes. I asked him about the second, and he told me he would explain when I got here.

For a Saturday morning the place is quiet, a drunk being hauled out of the back of a squad car for his turn on the intoxalizer. I grab the shopping bag on the front seat next to me and move quickly through the parking lot to the entry and under the bright florescent lights of the lobby. Here the walls are an antiseptic shade of white, functional linoleum tiles on the floor, and bulletproof glass. The cops are on the other side.

A big black woman in a halter top and shorts that fit her like a glove is arguing with the booking sergeant at a counter inside. I can see them through the glass. Her voice is muted by the thick wall of acrylic. Still she makes herself heard, insisting she was just looking for a ride when the cops happened on her at the curb. Every other word out of her mouth is 'entrapment'. She looks at me through the glass and says it one more time, in my face as if maybe she's not pronouncing the word right – like 'open, sesame'. She says it a couple of more times, and they haul her away, through a door that opens electronically and leads to the bowels of the building and the holding cells.

The cop gives a quick shove with his feet, and his chair wheels from the booking desk to the public counter where I am standing.

'What can I do for you?'

I slip a business card into the sliver of an opening in the stainless-steel frame around the glass. I speak into the small microphone embedded in two inches of bulletproof acrylic.

'I represent Mr Jonah Hale. He's being detained. I'd like to see him.'

The cop on the other side picks up my business card and looks at it, then at me. 'You got a bar card?'

I fish it out of my wallet and the sergeant takes it, my passport to the nether regions, then writes my name, bar number, and time on the log in front of him.

'Have a seat,' he tells me.

'I'd like to see Mr Hale now.'

'I'll convey the message,' he says. 'Have a seat.'

I hit the hard bench across the room, check the time, and start counting floor tiles. It is then that I notice I have slipped my feet into my loafers sans socks; white ankles beneath the cuff of my pants. I cool my heels for several minutes and wonder if I am going to get any sleep this night.

'Mr Madriani.'

When I look up there's a tall man standing there, suit and tie, close-cropped hair, and slender build. He has a pleasant smile, though his dark face has business written all over it.

'I'm Lieutenant Avery.' He hands me a business card:

Floyd Avery, Detective Lieutenant
Homicide/Robbery Division

I take his card and introduce myself.

'I understand you're here to collect Mr Hale. He's in the back,' he says.

'Is he free to go?'

'I thought we could talk for a minute,' says Avery. Never-never land: not under arrest, but not exactly free either.

Avery leads the way. By the time his hand hits the knob on the door, the buzzer erupts, triggered by the cop behind the glass, and we are through. He takes me down a short corridor, stops at a door and opens it.

Inside I can see Jonah sitting at a table. As soon as he sees me, he's on his feet, a look of relief. He's dressed in an orange jumpsuit with large black letters stenciled across the front as if he were the property of the county jail.

As I enter the room, I see another man lurking in the corner, a mirror centered in the far wall, the distinct impression there are other eyes watching us: one-way glass.

'This is Sergeant Greely,' says Avery. 'Bob, this is Attorney Madriani.'

I nod. We don't shake hands. It isn't that cordial.

'Is my client under arrest?' I ask.

'No.' There is no hesitation from Avery.

'May I ask where his clothes are? Why the jail jumper?'

'We sent them to trace evidence.' Greely is more direct. The aggressive one.

I give him a questioning look. 'I take it you have a search warrant?'

'We don't need one to search what he's wearing,' says Greely.

'Really? If you're searching his pockets for weapons, for evidence of contraband, maybe,' I tell him. 'But if you're vacuuming his clothes for trace evidence, hair and fibers, I beg to differ.'

'Your client volunteered.' Avery rescues his partner.

Until this moment I hadn't been paying much attention to Jonah, who is still standing behind the table, two hands planted firmly on the edge.

'Are you all right?' I ask him.

'Fine.'

'Have you taken a statement from him?'

'Nothing you could call formal,' says Greely.

'What does that mean?'

'We haven't taken any statement,' says Avery.

'How long have you been here?' I turn back to Jonah.

He looks to his wrist, then realizes his watch is gone. He shrugs his shoulders. 'I'm not sure.'

'Are you analyzing his watch as well?'

'We'll give him his valuables when he leaves,' says Greely.

'You better get 'em ready, because unless he's under arrest, we're leaving now.'

'Why the hurry?' says Greely. 'We're just trying to get some information.'

'Did you read my client his rights?'

'We didn't think it was necessary,' says Avery. 'We haven't asked him any questions.'

'And you're going to tell me next that he doesn't fall within your scope of suspicion?'

Avery makes a face as if he might argue the point.

Jonah actually smiles. 'I let them take my clothes. They said it might help to clear me. I didn't think there was anything wrong.'

'Clear him of what?' I turn this on Avery.

I hand Jonah the brown paper shopping bag. Inside is a gray cotton sweatsuit, large, one size fits all, something I grabbed from the back of my closet.

'We're investigating the death of Zolanda Suade. You're not going to tell me you haven't heard?'

137

I shake my head, as if this doesn't compute, the best I can do under the circumstances. 'If you have evidence against my client, maybe you can enlighten me.'

'We might be able to clear your client and move on,' says Avery. 'That is, if he's willing to cooperate.'

'Sounds like he already has.'

'We'd like to ask him a few questions.'

'I'll bet you would. It's not going to happen tonight.' I have no idea what Jonah would say, or where he's been.

'We picked your client up out on the Strand,' says Avery. 'Sitting on the beach, looking at the water.'

This is a stone's throw from the scene of the crime. Avery lets this information settle on me for effect, measuring how I react. I don't.

'It was a nice night,' I tell him. 'Maybe he wanted to look at the stars.'

'His car was parked illegally,' says Greely. 'Partway on the road. He's lucky it didn't get nailed. Traffic out there moves at a clip,' he says.

'I'm sure my client appreciates your help. Where is his car?'

'Sheriff's impound. Maybe you'd like to talk to your client alone for a moment,' says Avery. 'Perhaps he would like to make a statement.'

'If I talk to my client, it won't be here.' I look at the one-way glass and wonder if there's a lip-reader on the other side.

'Sounds like your client has something to hide, Counselor.' Greely would like to get into it with me.

'Bob.' Avery stops him.

'Well, he shouldn't object to a gunshot residue test.'

Greely debates this with Avery as if it were a question between the two of them.

'You're not conducting any tests unless you have a search warrant, or you want to arrest my client.' They don't have enough evidence for an arrest, that much is clear. If they did, Jonah would be in a cell.

'Take about two minutes,' says Greely. 'A few squares of cotton wipes on his hands. No pain. If he's got nothing to hide, he can't object to that.'

Jonah offers an expression as if it might be okay with him.

'He can, and he does,' I tell Greely.

I glance at Jonah's hands. They appear soiled. I don't know what's on them any more than Greely does. But consenting to anything the cops want in a case like this is against a lawyer's religion. The fact is that at this moment I'm working from the same assumption as Avery and Greely. Jonah may have done it.

There's a tap on the door. Avery gets it. He opens it just a crack. Whoever is on the other side passes him a slip of paper. Quickly he reads the note, then folds it in a neat little square and puts it in his pocket.

'Is there a place where my client can change?'

'Sure,' says Avery. He opens the door wide this time. 'Bathroom's right down the hall. You can leave the jumpsuit on the hook behind the door.'

Jonah heads down the hall to change.

'I'd like his valuables, perhaps his shoes?'

'Valuables you can have. His shoes already went to trace evidence,' says Avery.

'At three in the morning?'

'We're a full-service agency,' he says.

'Right. And I assume you wouldn't have tried to take residue off his watch?'

The look on Greely's face tells me he has not thought of this. I can sense the gears turning. Before Avery can stop him, Greely is whispering in his ear, wondering, I am sure, if the consent they extracted from Jonah would cover the watch. Avery's shaking his head, coming down on the side of caution. When the lawyer is in place, you don't play games. It's a good way to draw a motion to suppress, which I'll no doubt file in any event. But games with the watch at this late a stage would add fuel to the fire. Avery calls the desk sergeant and a couple of minutes later just as Jonah returns with the empty paper bag, in bare feet, a uniformed cop delivers a good-sized manila envelope. Avery takes it and hands it to me.

I open it on the desk and Jonah does inventory, taking out his watch and ring. He puts them on.

'Where are the keys to my car?'

'Those we will keep,' says Avery. 'Until we're finished with the vehicle.'

'What do you mean finished?' I ask.

'We have a search warrant for the car. We just obtained it. As we were standing here talking,' he tells me. He has this in his hand, brought to him by the desk sergeant when he delivered the envelope. He shows it to me.

'Based on what?'

'Where're my cigars?' says Jonah.

Before Avery can respond, I have my answer.

'The cigars in question appear to match one we found at the scene,' says Avery. 'That, coupled with your client's name all over some press releases at the victim's office, was enough for the judge to allow us to look in his car.'

'I'll give you a lift home,' I tell Jonah.

'I understand you were at the scene tonight.' Avery's talking to me. He says this as we are heading to the door. 'With John Brower. Nice of him to show you around.'

I don't respond.

'What exactly is your connection?'

'Just an acquaintance,' I tell him.

'And I suppose he knew you were representing Mr Hale at the time?'

'I don't know if he did or not.' I'm trying to keep Brower out of trouble.

'He also gave us a cigar,' says Avery. 'Says your client gave it to him. And some information about threats Mr Hale made against the victim, at a meeting in your office.'

This is not looking good. Jonah and I are moving swiftly now down the short corridor, his naked feet padding along on the hard linoleum behind me.

As my hand reaches for the knob on the door leading into the lobby, Avery issues his last shot. 'I wouldn't want Mr Hale to be taking any long trips for a while.'

'We'll keep it in mind.'

CHAPTER
TEN

This morning I don't get into the office until ten. I called Susan from the house before I left, filled her in, what little I knew, and told her to stay away from Brower until we could talk. The last thing I need is Susan browbeating one of her investigators for assisting the cops. It's a short walk to tampering with a witness, and I'm trying to keep Susan out of it. We had to cut it short as she had to get the kids to soccer practice, Sarah included. Fortunately, the girls are the same size and can wear clothes interchangeably.

When I get to the office, the lights are on, the receptionist is there, but Harry is not. He is baby-sitting, out in Del Mar, seeing if perhaps Jonah will tell him something he has not told me. I still haven't gotten straight answers from him as to where he was last night. We talked until nearly five in the morning at his house. He says he was depressed, angry, so that when he left Susan's office after the failed attempt to go after Suade for contempt, he drove aimlessly for hours until he found himself on the beach sitting in the sand, where the cops picked him up. He doesn't recall meeting anyone, talking to anybody. It is a story that is likely to light a fire of enthusiasm under the cops.

When I get to my desk, messages are stacked neatly near the phone. I paw through them. One catches my eye. Joaquin Murphy wants to see me for lunch. I look at the time. He called a little after nine. I dial his number, I am assuming on the boat.

It rings several times, and I'm about to hang up when he finally answers. 'Hello.'

'Murphy. This is Paul Madriani.'

'You got my message,' he says.

'Do you have some information?'

'Better than that. My source wants a meeting.'

Twenty minutes later, Murphy picks me up at the curb out front near the entrance to the Brigantine. It is just before eleven, and I am operating on adrenaline, fighting off sleep deprivation.

I get in, and he looks at me from the driver's side. He is hunched over the wheel, wearing a Hawaiian shirt, printed flowers the size of basketballs, and Bermuda shorts.

'You look wiped,' he says.

'Where's the luau?' I ask.

'It's a business meeting. I thought I'd go conservative.'

'Just so long as we don't end up pig in the pit,' I tell him.

I get in and he drives, north on Orange through downtown Coronado.

'I take it you had a busy night?' he says.

'Why's that?'

'I saw the news on TV about Suade.' He checks me for effect. 'They're calling it a drive-by. Must be a new gang. Tell me,' he says, 'what kind of graffiti do angry white husbands use?' He's smiling.

'Not exactly a drive-by. That is, if the cops are guessing right. More of a sit-in.'

He looks at me as if he's not sure what I'm talking about.

'They think she was sitting in the perp's car when she got it.'

'Ah. Is your client in any difficulty?'

'Depends who you want to believe. Him or me. The cops have the carpet of his car under a microscope as we speak.'

'Optimistic sort, is he?'

'Sees a doughnut where the hole is,' I tell him.

'You do have a few things going for you.'

'Name one?'

'A hundred enemies who wanted to kill the woman,' he says.

'I'll give you that.'

'And right now I'll bet you're trying to identify them all.'

'Something like that.'

The newspapers and local media are speculating that the police have a lead, a possible suspect in Suade's murder. So far, Jonah's name has not surfaced.

'I figured you might be getting busy,' says Murphy, 'so I thought I should get this information to you sooner rather than later. My source thought a face-to-face meeting would be best. Outside your office.'

'What does he have?'

'He'll have to tell you that himself. But I do have some stuff on your gal. Jessica. Mostly background,' he says. 'She had a dozen misdemeanor convictions before they sent her to Corona. Mostly small stuff. Petty theft.'

'Tell me something I don't know.'

'She tried her hand at a little forgery, but the checks were small. Has a list of real colorful friends as well. Their latest kick was household burglaries and washing checks. That was before the drug charge sent her away.'

'What about her friends? Any names?' So far Harry has not been able to come up with much.

'One in particular keeps cropping up,' says Murphy. 'Jason Crow.'

I've heard the name, but I can't place it.

'He worked at the airport,' says Murph. 'A baggage handler.'

'Ah. I remember.' The guy Harry told me about.

'Word is he and Jessica lived together for a while. He's also reputed to have been her local pharmacist. Pills, pot, coke – you name it, Crow could get it. He put her in touch with people higher up on the chemical food chain.'

'Is that how she got nailed on the drug thing?'

'Probably. The man you're going to talk to may have more on that.'

'Tell me about him. Why all the secrecy?'

'The nature of his job,' says Murphy. 'He and his partner cross over into Mexico like birds in migration, only more frequently. I'm led to believe he works for the government – undercover.'

'Ours or theirs?'

'Ours. I think.'

'Wonderful.'

'It's what you call a high-risk occupation. He's not gonna tell you his name, or what agency.'

'Do you know his name?'

Murphy shakes his head.

'Then how do you know you can trust his information?'

'Because he's given me stuff in the past, and it's always proved out. If I had to guess, I'd say he works for DEA. I've seen him with another man driving a large car with Mexican plates. Automatic weapons in the trunk,' he says.

'Maybe they hunt.'

'Heckler and Koch MP-5s, fully silenced?' He looks at me as if this is supposed to mean something.

'If you saw the assault on the Branch Davidians, you saw the FBI packing these. It'd cost you a couple of grand for one in mint condition. One silenced on full automatic could cost you five-to-fifteen at Terminal Island. I went with them once, down to Mexico. These guys were able to cruise back and forth through customs with a wink and a nod.'

'Where are we going?'

'To a restaurant,' he says.

'Why is it I feel like a character in *The Godfather*?' I ask him.

'Don't worry,' he says. 'There're no pistols in the toilet.'

'That's what I'm worried about.'

He laughs. 'Anyway. Back to your friend Jessica,' he says. 'She and this guy, Crow, worked a scam together for a short time, out of the airport. He checked bags and gleaned information on addresses from the luggage tags. Then she and a few friends would stake out the houses, see if anybody was home. Newspapers in the driveway, mail being picked up by neighbors – if a place looked empty, they'd hit it. Clean it out. It's how he went down, Crow. Nosy neighbor called the cops.'

'What's interesting about this is the cops found evidence implicating Jessica when they arrested her. Property in possession tying her to Crow and the burglaries. But the authorities didn't press it.'

'Maybe it wasn't big enough.'

'Three hundred grand in stolen property?'

I whistle long and low through my two front teeth.

'Why would they let it go?'

'You might want to ask the man when you see him,' he says.

Seaport Village is Disneyland on the water, without the rides. A lot of shops. People milling in an out, licking ice-cream cones and periodically looking for a bench on which to rest their weary feet along the meandering boardwalk that fronts the bay.

Today it is not very crowded. A few school groups on what pass for field trips, and tourists shopping in the traps for something to take home.

We climb a flight of stairs to a landing that spans the walkway below and makes like a bridge over two small shops. We arrive at the entrance to a restaurant. It's closed.

'You're sure he said to meet him here?'

Murphy doesn't answer, but taps on the door with a

set of keys. A couple of seconds later, a man wearing a dark sport coat, pleated slacks that hang on him like an oversized flag, and a dark turtleneck sweater opens up.

'How ya doin', my friend?' He's talking to Murphy. 'Come on in.' The man must be about six-nine, not just tall, but big. His clothes come from Omar the tentmaker. He's wearing a pair of dark glasses that cover half of his face, wraparounds like the windshield on a sixties Cadillac. On his left wrist is a gold watch, a Rolex the size of the mirror on the Hubble telescope. He shakes Murphy's hand, then looks at me.

'Ha ya doin'?'

I get the quick treatment, the kind that tells me I'm being studied from behind all that glass. What hair he has left is dark brown and slicked back forming a ponytail at the rear of his head.

'Bob's waitin' for ya out on the deck.' He nods toward Murphy, who leads the way.

I can feel the bigger man's hot breath on the back of my neck as we walk through the empty restaurant and out onto the deck that overlooks the water. When I get there, I see his partner. He is almost as big, leaning against the railing, smiling in our direction.

'Hey, Murph. Been a long time. How's business?' The entire time he's talking to Murphy, he is looking at me.

'It's good,' says Murphy.

'This must be your man.'

The guy leaning against the railing is the size of your average mountain. Shoulders and hindquarters like a sumo wrestler, with dark glasses just slightly smaller than his companion's. He has curly blond hair, receding at the sides like a glacial retreat, and forearms like Popeye, well tanned.

'Bob. This is Paul,' says Murph.

My hand goes out and gets lost in his grip – evoking memories of holding my father's hand when I was six.

'Paul . . . ?' He leans toward me, his voice on an audible quest for my last name. 'Paul what?' he says.

'My friends just call me Paul, Bob.' I smile and lift my dark glasses out of the breast pocket of my coat, then slip them on. We stand on the deck looking like the Blues Brothers.

Bob has a face like the lunar surface, pockmarked with craters you could get lost in.

'Have a seat,' he says.

Murphy has kept the faith. Apparently he hasn't told them my last name or the reason I am asking questions about Jessica Hale.

We pull up chairs and sit around a table that looks as if it hasn't been wiped down since Christmas. Bob looks at his elbows after resting them on the glass surface.

'I think this is what the EPA calls particulate matter,' he says. He laughs it off and wipes the back of each arm with the opposite hand.

'Gonna have to get after the tax boys,' he says. 'You'd think they'd take better care of their property. You met Jack?' says Bob.

'We've met,' I tell him.

'IRS shut this place down a few months ago,' he tells me. 'Nonpayment. We got a few places like this around town. We don't like to get rid of 'em too quickly. They come in handy – for gatherings like this,' he says.

'Where we gonna get lunch?' says Murphy.

'We thought you were bringing it.' Bob laughs big and broad. He doesn't have the look of a man who's missed many meals.

'I can have Jack there beat around behind the bar and see if he can find a bottle. On second thought. Don't bother. This shouldn't take that long. Maybe Paul here will spring for lunch down the way after we're finished.' He looks at me as if I'm going to open my wallet and give him a peek at my credit card.

'I understand you're looking for Jessica Hale?' he says. 'Can I ask why?' Right to the point. No beating around.

'You can ask,' I tell him.

Our eyes lock behind dark glasses.

'I thought we would be exchanging information,' he says.

'You first.'

'What do you want to know?'

'Why the federal government turned her loose on major drug charges.'

'Why do you think?' he says.

'Because you wanted something from her in return.'

He makes with the fingers of his right hand like a gun and lets his thumb drop like a hammer.

'What was it the government wanted?'

'That's two questions,' he says.

'Yes, but you never answered the first one.'

'Why do you want to know?'

'Now you answer a question with a question. Fine. I'm assuming that if the woman was on drugs at one time, she may have slid off the wagon, if she was ever on it.

151

Old habits, old friends, whoever supplied her might know where she is. You might know who that is. That might provide a lead.'

'It won't.'

'How can you be so sure?'

'Because we're lookin' for her, too. She owes us some information. Part of a deal that she didn't deliver on. We've checked her old haunts. She hasn't been to any of 'em. We know. We've squeezed the people who are there. If they'd seen her, they woulda told us.'

'Why do you want her?' I ask.

'Have you ever heard of a man named Esteban Ontaveroz?'

'No.'

'Also known as El Chico, Jefe, Enfermo de Armor. The last one means love stick.'

'Man don't suffer from low self-esteem,' says Jack.

'He's believed to have been involved in the killing of eighteen people in a little town north of Ensenada about a year ago. You may have read about it. They shot kids, women. One of 'em was pregnant. Took 'em out on a patio and laid 'em facedown, then did 'em with machine guns, execution style.'

Bob picks up an envelope from the chair next to him and pulls out a picture, four-by-six glossy, and lays it on the table in front of me. It shows a tall, swarthy man, hollow cheeks, talking to another guy across the top of a car. The other man's back is to the camera, but the ponytail and the size of the body, shoulders like a bull, bear a striking resemblance to his partner, the one he calls Jack. The picture possesses the grainy character of having been taken from some distance, magnified and cropped.

I look, shrug my shoulders. Shake my head. 'Never seen him.'

'Deals drugs. Supplier up out of Chiapas. A businessman. You might call him a transporter.'

'No, he'd probably call him a client,' says Jack.

'Be nice.' Bob looks up at his partner, then back to me. 'Mexicans tell us that Ontaveroz has a fleet of planes to make FedEx jealous. And a motto.'

'And it ain't "Fly the fuckin' friendly skies",' says Jack.

'*Plata o plomo*,' says Bob. He looks at me to see if I get it. 'No?'

I shake my head.

'Silver or lead. Bribes or bullets. You either take his money or you better have your funeral plan prepaid. He used to work the middle between suppliers farther south, Guatemala, Colombia, Costa Rica, but he's been coming north lately, spending more time, expanding into the States. He has connections with the Tiajuana Cartel. They control half the US-Mexican border. Juarez Cartel has the other half. They say they're ten times more powerful than the American Mafia at its height. They spend more money on bribes each year than the Mexican government spends on law enforcement.'

'About twice as much,' says Jack.

The way he says it makes it sound as though he's tasted their money, a thought I keep to myself with this bull standing behind my chair.

'We've had him, this Ontaveroz, under surveillance, on and off, for better than five years,' says Bob. 'One of our major breaks was Jessica Hale. She and Ontaveroz lived together for more than a year. She spent some time down in Mexico with him, living the high life, Acapulco, Cancun, Cosamel. She did provide some transportation. Moving product from Mexico across the border.'

'But we think that was incidental to their relationship,' says Jack.

'Sounds like you were in the bedroom taking pictures,' I tell him.

'We got solid information. You want pictures, we can get 'em,' says Jack.

'I'll bet you can.'

'Jessica knew intimate details about his operation,' says Bob. 'The one source who could connect Ontaveroz with some major deals.'

'She also knows where some bodies are buried,' says Jack. 'And I'm not speaking metaphorically. She has enough to put him away for a long time, maybe life over there.' He's talking about Mexico. 'On this side, a couple of states I can think of would like to inject him with something besides his own product. That's what she had to offer.'

'You say she didn't deliver?'

'Not to match the proffer she gave to get the deal,' says Bob. 'She fed us some information, testified in a few cases – trickle here, trickle there, allowed us to nail some small fry. We took a couple of Ontaveroz's buyers down, crippled his organization for a short time. But the big enchilada slipped off the platter when she disappeared.'

'In view of the people who cut the deal,' says Jack, 'the lawyers at Justice, Jessica didn't fulfill her obligations. They'd like her back. Now tell us,' he says, 'what's your interest?'

'I'm not particularly interested in Jessica, only as a means to an end. It's her little girl I want. She's eight years old. Legal custody reposes in the grandparents.'

'And you work for them?' he asks.

I nod.

'Tell me, are you a lawyer? An investigator?'

'I'll tell you after you tell me who you work for.'

He just smiles, trying to read my eyes through polarized glass.

'Her parents, Jessica's, do they know anything? About her friends? Her dealings? Where she might be?'

'If they knew anything, I wouldn't be talking to you.'

'They knew about Zolanda Suade,' he says.

I look at Murphy. A man with this many connections has to feed them something to keep the channels open. But he puts his hands up in protest.

'They already knew,' he says.

'We had her under surveillance a month ago, right after Jessica disappeared,' says Bob. 'Which begs the question: Why didn't you tell us about her?'

'Client confidence,' I tell him.

Bob reaches over on the chair next to him, picks up a newspaper and flops it on the table in front of me. The headline blaring across the top two columns:

ADVOCATE FOR BATTERED WOMEN MURDERED

'I guess you could say that source has dried up,' he says. 'So you figure Suade helped Jessica and the child disappear?'

'That's the theory,' I tell him. 'What led you to Suade?' I ask.

'We knew Jessica had made contact.'

'Letters from prison,' says Bob. 'Their mail is censored. When she got out, Suade was already on the list of her contacts.'

'Who else?' I ask him.

'Now you're getting personal.' He smiles as if this is out of bounds. 'You don't have any idea where she is?'

'I was hoping you could tell me.'

'If we knew that, we'd go pick her up,' says Bob.

'While there's still something to pick up,' says Jack.

'What do you mean?'

'We're not the only ones looking for her.'

'Ontaveroz?'

Bob hesitates just a beat. 'It'd be wise if we cooperated,' he says. 'Kept in touch.'

'Why is that?'

'We have a mutual interest. You want the little girl. We want her mother. Ontaveroz doesn't like the idea of Jessica walking the streets knowing what she knows.'

'Even though she hasn't given him up? If what you're saying is true, she did two years and never mentioned his name.'

'That was then. This is now,' says Jack. 'There's a certain sense of insecurity that runs through these people. Comes with the turf,' he says. 'We also have information that before she went down she stashed some cash. Probably what she's living on now – purchase money belonging to the man and his friends for stuff she'd transported across the border a few weeks before her arrest. They want it back.'

'But mostly, they just want her dead,' says Jack. 'Which,

according to my calculations, could be a serious compli-
cation for the little girl.'

CHAPTER
ELEVEN

This morning we are headed downtown, away from the substation at Imperial Beach. This to avoid the media, which have now grown to the usual circus. Suade's murder is taking on a dangerous dynamic.

She may have had a checkered past in life, but in death she is beginning to take on the proportions of a mythic figure. There has already been one piece on national news, not the cables, but the networks, featuring her murder. It was billed as the latest high-profile crime against women.

Feminist groups are on the tube beating their drums. They are calling it a gender crime, and trying to fit it into a hate category.

It seems lately that every crime of any note is a national crime. Welcome to the electronic village. If your death garners enough pixel images on the million or so cable channels that now bless the airwaves, your demise runs a chance of entering the lottery to become the 'crime of the century'.

The assumption is that Suade's death is the work of a demented spouse, some middle-aged angry white male, a husband of one of the women being shielded by her organization.

But unfortunately for us, the cops are about to shatter this theory. The call every lawyer dreads came this morning. 'Are you prepared to surrender your client?'

It was a courtesy from Floyd Avery, lieutenant at homicide. The alternative was that they would arrest Jonah at his home in front of all his neighbors with video vans parked out front.

Jonah has been under close surveillance for more than a week. The obvious unmarked cars parked in front of his home, a rolling sheriff's escort every time he went near his boat, which has been lashed to the dock by court order under a search warrant since the morning after the murder.

If he had set foot on another boat, set sail with one of his now-diminishing group of buds, I am certain that the Coast Guard would have stopped them before they cleared the harbor.

Mary is in the backseat with Jonah. Harry is driving. We are using Jonah's Cadillac for the occasion since neither Harry's car nor mine fits the bill. His sport utility, a dark green Explorer, Eddie Bauer package, has been seized by the cops and hauled to the city's impound for analysis. They'll be vacuuming the seats looking for the other bullet, the one they didn't find at the scene.

'Maybe if I talked to the police they wouldn't do this,' says Jonah.

'Don't believe it,' I tell him.

'Why are they arresting me? Because I made statements I didn't mean?'

'I don't know. But talking to investigators isn't going to help. Making further statements is not the thing to do. Not until we know what the evidence is.'

'And we may not know that until trial,' says Harry.

'What evidence could they have? He didn't do it,' says Mary.

The stony silence that follows this endorsement causes Jonah's gaze to fall on me. 'I'm not sure Paul believes us, hon. I didn't kill her.' He leans forward and says it with conviction, then settles back against the cushioned leather. 'She deserved to die, but I didn't do it.'

'Oh, that's great,' says Harry. 'Tell that to the cops.'

'What? I didn't do it?'

'No. The "deserved to die" part,' he says. 'Take the DA about two seconds flat; he'd turn that into an admission.'

'I would never say it to the DA,' says Jonah.

'That's comforting,' says Harry.

'Will they let him out on bail?' asks Mary.

'I don't know. We'll ask for a hearing.' But I tell her that it's up to the judge. I am guessing that because of the proximity to the border, Jonah's considerable financial resources, and the fact that it is a capital crime, the answer may be no. I don't burden her with this at the moment.

'There must have been somebody you saw that night,' she asks him. 'Think. Try to remember.'

'We've gone over and over it,' says Jonah. He is weary, growing lines of stress etched on his face, looking every inch his age, and then some.

'I didn't see anybody. I didn't stop for gasoline. I didn't get anything to eat.'

'Not even coffee?' she asks.

'Nothing. I just drove.'

'But if you had an alibi?'

'If,' he says, 'but I don't.'

Mary is no shrinking violet, a good ten years younger than Jonah, blonde hair that I am sure has been colored, and makeup to cover the aging creases. She is a strong woman, about five-eight, a hefty build.

'I could say he was with me at the time of the murder.' She shifts forward so that her hands are gripping the back of my chair, slender white knuckles. The expression on her face says it all – desperation.

'That's not a good idea,' I tell her.

'They haven't asked me that question, you know. That I wasn't with him.'

'They did ask him how long he'd been on the beach.'

'Maybe he got it wrong. Maybe he was confused,' she says.

'They may wonder why you waited so long to volunteer this alibi,' says Harry.

'I was in shock. I wasn't able to think clearly,' she says.

'Right,' says Harry. 'That'll work.' He looks at me out of the corner of one eye.

'If he was with you, what time did he leave to go for his ride, the one that took him to the beach?' I turn to look at her. Arched eyebrows over the back of my seat.

'I don't know. I can't remember.'

'And what were the two of you doing at the house just before he left?'

No answer.

'Where did he tell you he was going when he left? Why did he go?'

She's beginning to look at me now with eyes that are mean little slits. Not fair asking questions she can't answer.

'Was he with you?'

She hesitates.

'This is *me* asking you. Was he with you?'

'No.'

I turn back around and settle in my seat. The police and the jury would see it for what it was: a desperate attempt by a woman to save her husband. The fact that Mary felt it necessary to perjure herself would allow prosecutors to float the inference that a woman doesn't lie unless she thinks her husband is guilty.

'Besides,' I tell her, 'we don't know precisely when Suade died. That's a problem with any alibi.'

'Good point,' says Harry. 'You may have been her last visitor before the bullet festival.' He's looking at me, one eye on the road.

The thought has crossed my mind more than once that the sheriff's techs may have found my fingerprints in Suade's shop. I have been practicing my own answer if they ask. I am prepared to tell them that I met with Suade and talked to her that morning. I am not so sure I am prepared to discuss the subject matter, as this may get into motive – Jonah's – and I would argue it is covered by attorney-client privilege.

'We don't have a lot of time to talk,' I tell them. 'There is one thing. Some information. Did either of you ever hear Jessica mention a man named Esteban Ontaveroz?'

163

Mary looks at Jonah. I can see her in the mirror on the back of the sun visor that I have flipped down.

He offers up a face of puzzlement and shakes his head. 'One of her boyfriends?' says Jonah.

'Could be.'

'I didn't know any of the men she ran with,' he says. 'God knows there were enough of them.'

'This is not someone she is likely to have brought to your house,' I tell them.

'Who is he?' asks Mary.

'It's nothing you need to concern yourself with right now. But you're sure you never heard his name?'

Both of them shake their heads.

The trip becomes more somber as we approach the center of the city, like a ride in a tumbrel with the shadow of the guillotine looming ever closer. Harry turns onto Front Street, a block from the courthouse, and stops in front of the new county jail. He lets us out at the curb and goes to park the car.

Jonah takes a deep breath as he looks at the steel door framing thick glass that is the entrance.

'Are you all right?' I ask.

He looks withered and beaten, shoulders drooping, back hunched, thinning wisps of hair dancing in the stiffening breeze.

He nods. 'I'm okay.' Then he leans closer and whispers in my ear, 'Get her home.' For a moment I think he's talking about his granddaughter, Amanda. Then I realize he's talking about Mary.

'Get her out of this as quickly as you can.'

I nod.

'There's a woman next door who'll look after her,' he says.

'I don't need any looking after,' says Mary. She's overheard him. 'I can take care of myself.'

'I know you can,' he says. He turns from her, his gaze fixed on the stainless-steel door. I can read in his eyes the dread of the unknown inside.

I lead the way, open the door and step inside, offering myself first as a kind of psychic shield. Mary follows me, Jonah taking up the rear.

When I turn, I notice Jonah has hesitated just inside the door. For an instant I think he's going to stumble, or bolt. I step back and take his elbow to stiffen his resolve.

'It's okay,' he says. 'I'm fine.'

The public lobby is antiseptic, bathed in bright lights, one wall a thick bulletproof partition, behind which the sheriff's minions scurry about on their mission of confinement.

Avery is waiting for us. He sees us through the glass, and the jail guards buzz him through a kind of airlock, a small chamber not much larger than a phone booth with steel doors on each side. One is closed and locked before the other is opened.

When Avery emerges on our side, his expression is serious.

'Mr Madriani.'

I nod.

'Mr Hale, we can step in here.' He motions that Mary and I can follow.

By now Harry has caught up with us, and we pass through the lock two at a time, Avery and Jonah, Mary and I, with

Harry the odd man out. He sets off a buzzer and ends up trapped in the airlock.

'What have you got in your pockets?' A guard's voice on the PA.

Harry reaches deep in his pockets, and pulls out a set of keys and a small pocket knife.

'Put 'em in the tray,' says the PA.

A stainless-steel tray slides out and Harry deposits them inside. The tray closes just as quickly. He tries the door again, and this time he's buzzed through.

Like the death-house walk, we stroll down the corridor under the gaze of guards behind glass with Avery leading the way, around a corner to the booking area. Here we are met by a burly man, middle-aged and bald, in sheriff's overalls and boots with the pant legs tucked in, keys jangling from a web belt around his waist. He moves on Jonah.

'Just lean forward, hands against the wall.'

Jonah looks at me. I am powerless to stop it.

'I'll read him his rights in a minute,' says Avery.

The guard eases Jonah into the position. Separates his feet, going through his pockets. Everything he finds is dropped into an envelope.

'That's his blood pressure medicine,' says Mary. 'He needs that.'

'We'll see that he gets it,' says Avery.

The guard eases Jonah back onto his feet and cuffs his hands behind his back.

'Is that necessary?' I ask.

'Jail policy,' says the guard.

They will strip him and search him, probably the full

cavity number when we leave, put him in the shower whether he needs it or not, and give him a jail jumpsuit.

'Can we talk for a moment before you take him in?'

The guard looks to Avery for the answer.

'You can go in here.' Avery points to one of the holding cells, a concrete room with a thick plate-glass window and a steel door.

'Harry, why don't you take Mary to the car.'

'No, I want to stay.'

'I think it's best if you go,' I tell her.

She starts to argue. Jonah cuts her off. 'We agreed,' he says. 'Remember? You weren't going to make a scene.'

She starts to cry, steps forward, arms around him. He cannot hug her back, but he kisses her on the cheek, nuzzles her with his chin on the neck. Her grip is like a death lock around him. She nearly pulls him off his feet, so that the guard has to take an elbow to steady him. Harry steps in and takes her by the arm. Jonah whispers in her ear, but the words carry. 'I'll be all right,' he says. Tears now running down his face. I can't tell if they are his or hers.

Harry gently peels her arm off him and finally gains separation. The words, 'I love you' come from her tear-stained mouth as he tugs her toward the door. Her body moving in one direction, her head turned in the other, she waves the one free hand in her wake, as if motioning for Jonah to follow as he stands there in shackles.

A guard behind the glass in the control booth hits the buzzer, and when I look back, she and Harry are gone.

Avery motions the guard to open the door to the small lockup, and Jonah and I step inside. The door closes behind us.

'Are you sure you're okay?'

He nods.

I'm worried. Jonah has high blood pressure. He's had at least two episodes of hospitalization to get it under control. It's one of the arguments I will make to the court, that his health is better preserved at home than here.

'Just one final word,' I tell him. I look closely at his face. He is dazed. I'm not sure he's listening.

'Sit down.' I help him down onto the hard stainless-steel bench that is bolted to the floor.

'Don't talk to anybody, or answer any questions. The sheriff. The DA. They have no right to question you. Do you understand?'

He nods.

'More important than the DA or the sheriff,' I tell him, 'don't say anything to any of the other inmates. They may put you in a cell with somebody else. Keep your distance. Don't get too friendly. An offhand remark can be misinterpreted, misconstrued, used against you at trial. Don't say anything except hello and good-bye. Pass the time of day,' I tell him, 'but don't discuss your case or any of the details with anyone but myself or Harry. Am I clear?'

'Yes.'

'Good. I'll try to set a hearing for bail as soon as possible.'

'Do you think there's a chance?'

'I don't know. Is there anything you need?'

'My medicine,' he says. 'Something to read, maybe.'

'I'll take care of it.'

'Thanks,' he says. 'I guess that's it. Will you be back?'

'I'll come back tomorrow. Check and see how you are.'

Thirty seconds later the guard has him at the booking counter, and Avery leads me out.

'A tragic situation,' he says. 'I'm sorry it had to come to this.' Standing in the lobby, car keys in his hand, Avery looks at me with the cop's businesslike expression. All in a day's work. Still I suspect that on the scale of perps, one to ten, bad guys being high, Jonah hardly registers.

'Nice old man,' he says. 'Too bad he did it.'

'You seem pretty sure.'

'We don't make an arrest unless we are.'

'You can try to sell that to the jury,' I tell him. 'I'm not buying.'

'We will. The evidence is solid.'

I give him a questioning look.

'You don't deny he made threats a few hours before Suade was killed?'

'Half the people in town were sticking pins in dolls with Suade's name on them.'

'He has no alibi. He can't account for where he was at the time. And the cigar. The one from the scene. It matched the one Brower gave us. Said he got it from your client. Hale was handing these out at your office?'

'A lot of other people smoke cigars.'

'Not this kind,' says Avery. 'Very rare. A Cuban blend. Contraband,' he says. 'Sold only on the black market. Your client, when he won the lottery, should have formed cheaper habits. We found a box of these cigars in his house, on the desk in his study, and a receipt from the shop where he bought them. We've been talkin' to the owner. He seems real nervous. Doesn't want any trouble with Customs. Mr Hale was the only one who ordered that particular brand,'

169

says Avery. 'When the analysts at the lab get through, we'll be able to tell you which field in Cuba they grew the tobacco in.' He gives me a satisfied grin, like Morgan Freeman in a scene where he has the last word.

'You want more?' He's having fun ruining my day.

'Trace evidence,' he says, 'found blood and some other stuff on your client's clothes, in his car. Matches what we found on the victim. You want some advice?' He doesn't wait for me to say yes or no.

'You should cut a deal, fast as you can. He's a likeable old man,' says Avery. 'I wouldn't want to see him spend the rest of his life behind bars – or worse.'

CHAPTER
TWELVE

'I feel like I've been violated.'

'Not by me, I hope.'

'Don't get cute.' Susan's fishing in the drawer of the bureau in her bedroom, second one down, the one she keeps her panties and bras in. She's wearing my white dress shirt, tails halfway down her thighs, morning attire when the kids are asleep in the other room and the door is closed.

'What are you looking for?'

'My camera. The little thirty-five millimeter with the pop-out zoom.'

'I've got a pop-out zoom,' I tell her. I point down in the direction of my midsection with the sheet pulled up to my chin. 'Maybe I could be of service? Much more fun than a camera.'

She laughs. 'I want to take a picture. The girls are piled in there like cordwood. All in one bed. Laid out so cute I wanted to get a quick shot before they wake up. All you can see is long hair and pillows.'

'If you're worried about Sarah, you can relax. She won't stir 'til noon. Not unless we go shake her out. And then it'll take her four hours to wake up. Walk around like a zombie waiting for breakfast to magically appear on the table and the room fairies to make her bed.'

'Damn it.' Susan's talking to herself, under her breath, ignoring me as she pushes things to one side, then the other in the drawer.

'You remember the one? Little Olympus with the lens cover that looked like chrome. Case looked like leather?'

'I remember seeing it.'

'It looks as though they got that, too,' she says. Susan has been filling out insurance forms for what seems like forever. An item here, an item there. Going through tax records and old credit card bills, finding receipts to prove she owned things that are now missing. It's the stuff you don't use all the time, she can't find. In a fire or a flood you do it all in one fell swoop. Try to remember what was there and write it down, close your eyes and do a mental walk through every room, psychically rifling drawers in your mind's eye. But a burglary, unless they back a truck up to your front door, it's different.

One afternoon she went in her closet looking for something to wear. A formal dinner we'd been invited to attend. She had her black sequined gown laid out on the bed. Ten minutes later she came out spitting vinegar, angry as a March hare. A black lace-fringed teddy, not something she wore every day, the only thing she could wear underneath the dress, except skin, was gone.

'It's got to be kids. Who else steals something like that?' She half expected to see it show up hanging from a street sign in the neighborhood. She was too embarrassed to claim it on insurance. Give the adjuster a thrill.

Susan gives up on the camera.

'Guess you'll just have to draw a picture,' I tell her.

'That's what I like about you. You're so sympathetic.' The thing about Susan. She has a knack for misdirected anger.

'What do you want me to do?'

'I want you to throw that sheet off.' Her dark eyes flashing toward the sheet at the bottom of the bed, she telegraphs it just an instant before she moves. My hands are a half second too quick as I grip the top and she can't pull it off. Still she is tugging.

'You want a drawing, you gotta take off the sheet,' she's laughing at me. Giggling like a schoolgirl. 'What's the matter?' she says. 'Never did any posing in college for the art classes? I thought all the good-looking studs did that.'

'You must have gone to a different school,' I tell her.

'Either that, or you weren't one of the studs.'

'Complaining, are you?'

'No.' She gives up on the sheet. I find my boxers.

'About time you got your bones out of the sack,' she says. 'Talk about your daughter.'

'What time was it we crashed?' I ask her.

'I don't know. Twelve-thirty?'

'That's the earliest I hit the sheets in a week.'

'What, you want me to feel sorry for you?' She makes with her thumb and forefinger like a miniature violin, then before I can react she's back to the sheet, and rips it off the bed.

'Too late.' I've got my boxers on.

'That can be remedied,' she says.

'Another time.' I look at my watch on the bedside stand.

'I didn't realize it was this late.' In two seconds I'm rummaging around in her closet searching out a pair of jeans I left hanging on a hook the last time I was over, and a plaid flannel shirt sharing the same spot. We see enough of each other that we have now assembled a casual wardrobe at the other's house. I gather up a pair of running shoes on the floor of the closet, each with a white cotton sock tucked inside. It is Saturday morning.

'I've got to go downtown,' I tell her.

'What, the office?'

'The jail. I have to talk to Jonah.'

'Are you sure?' She's starting to do a dance for me, hoochie-coochie at the foot of the bed, toying with the top button as she sways her hips and sashays. 'You want your shirt back?'

'Sooner or later, but I don't need it right now.'

Her shoulders droop and her head cocks at a forty-five. 'You know how to kill a girl's act,' she says. 'I thought we were going to spend the day together.'

'I'll only take an hour or so. I've got to talk to Jonah.'

'Maybe you should move in with him,' she says. 'He certainly sees more of you than I do.'

'I don't think they'd let us double-bunk,' I tell her. 'Besides, my shirts wouldn't look nearly as good on him.'

She gathers up her bra and a pair of pants, a slip-over top and heads for the master bath. 'How is he holding up?' she asks. The door is half closed, so our voices go up a few decibels.

'All right, I suppose. His wife's worried about his health.'

'Is he sick?'

'Bad ticker,' I tell her. 'High blood pressure.'

'On top of everything else,' she says. 'Must be tough for both of them.'

'It is.'

'Sorry about the cigar with Brower,' she says. 'If I'd known he was going to volunteer, turn it over like that, I would have at least given you a heads-up.'

'Doesn't much matter,' I tell her. 'They found a box of them on Jonah's desk at the house. He wasn't exactly looking to hide 'em.'

'I should never have brought him that day,' she says. 'At your office. Now he's a witness. I mean, if he hadn't heard Jonah say the things he did . . .'

'You heard him,' I say.

She steps out from behind the door. 'Yes, but I'm me.'

'What's that supposed to mean? You wouldn't testify if you were subpoenaed?'

'If Brower hadn't been there, nobody would have known I was there, except you, your partner, and the defendant. They can't make the defendant testify, and unless I misunderstand the rules,' she says, 'a lawyer can't be forced to provide evidence against his client. So who's to tell them I was there, except Brower?'

Susan has it all figured out. As it is now, she is likely to draw a summons to appear, to testify as to what she heard.

'Have the investigators talked to you yet?'

She shakes her head, running a brush through her hair, standing in front of the vanity. 'But I've been expecting them any day. Sooner or later,' she says, 'they're gonna come knocking. Especially the way Brower's been looking at me. He's been very nervous, keeping his distance. He knows I'm angry at him.'

'You shouldn't take it so personally,' I tell her.

'He should have asked me first before running to the cops with the cigar. He was only at the meeting because I invited him.'

'And what would you have told him, to smoke it? The cigar, I mean.'

'No.' She lays the brush down, turns and looks at me. 'I would have told him to turn it over. But I would have been the one telling him. Now it looks like I might have been trying to cover things up.'

'Not on my account, I hope.'

'People downtown know about us. They talk. I have enough problems in the department right now,' she says. 'Attorney general breathing down our neck. Newspapers claiming we're fabricating evidence, suggesting horror stories to little children. God knows, they don't need us to invent them. Brower should have been more sensitive to the bigger picture.'

'*Sensitive* is not a word that comes to mind when thinking of Brower.'

'Exactly,' she says.

I am thinking that the man's future is now limited. She returns to the brush and the mirror, rapid strokes through hair of thick silk.

'Maybe *I* should have been more sensitive,' I tell her. 'Maybe I was the one who shouldn't have asked you to come to the office that morning.'

'I was there for a legitimate reason,' she says. 'After all, you had reason to believe Suade took Jonah's granddaughter.'

'Yeah. Talk about a motive for murder.'

176

'Tell me,' she says, 'what happened to the theory it was a drive-by?'

It was the story, printed early in the papers, when the cops threw a blanket over things, before there was anything else to report.

'Shooting in an alley. That's the obvious assumption,' I tell her. 'I don't think the cops ever bought into it. Doesn't square with the physical evidence.'

'Like what?'

'Like the fact that they found two cigarettes belonging to Suade dumped out on her body. One of 'em actually burned part of her outfit. They're thinking remnants from the killer's ashtray.'

'Like the cigar?'

'Right.'

'So she smoked? So what?'

'If Suade had time to smoke two cigarettes and stub them out in the car's ashtray, she and whoever shot her spent some time talking in the car. It's the kind of evidence causes the reconstruction experts to think it's a more calculated act.'

'Ah.' I can see Susan's head nodding slowly in the mirror as she takes it in, the evidence and where it leads.

'Have they found the gun?'

'Not yet. At least if they have, they haven't disclosed it to us.'

'Did Jonah own one?'

'He says he didn't.'

'But you don't believe him.'

'I don't know. I've got a man trying to check it out.'

'It's the difficult thing when you're outside the loop,' I

177

tell her. 'Agencies that record such things, like who owns guns, aren't falling all over themselves to share this with you when they find out you're defending a homicide. It's against their religion.'

'What kind of bullet was it? What caliber?'

'What is this? Some sudden morbid interest in ballistics?'

'Humor me.'

'She was shot twice. Three-eighty caliber. It would be a little semiautomatic.'

'The kind of gun a woman would use,' she says. 'Might keep in her handbag.'

'Yes.'

'She owned one.'

'Who?'

'Suade.' She looks at me. Inscrutable reflections. 'What can I say? Some of us are inside the loop.' She can't keep from smiling. 'I had somebody check. Not Brower,' she says. 'Somebody I can trust.'

I am thinking Brower's replacement. Tiberius has a new Sejanus.

'I wasn't going to say anything unless the caliber was the same,' she says. 'Why get your hopes up? But Alcohol, Firearms and Tobacco . . .'

'Alcohol, Tobacco and Firearms,' I say. 'ATF.'

'That's what I said. Alcohol, Tobacco and Firearms. They show that Suade owned a pistol. And I think it was the same kind.'

She can tell she has caught me flat-footed, staring at her in the glass. She gets up and walks across the room to her purse that is hanging over one of the head posts of the bed. She pulls out a note and reads a serial number.

'Yes. It says a Walther three-eight-oh. PPK. I don't know what that is.'

'The model,' I tell her.

She hands me the scrap of paper.

'That is it, isn't it? The same caliber?'

I look at the note. 'That's it.'

'Maybe she was shot with her own gun,' says Susan. 'Could be a case of self-defense. Even an accident. Just do me a favor,' she says. 'Don't tell anybody where you got that.'

I nod. 'I wonder where it is?'

'What?'

'Suade's gun?' I say.

Susan shrugs, as if to say, 'Who knows?'

CHAPTER
THIRTEEN

It is a popular myth that courts of law are immune to politics. In this state, judges run for reelection and generally break out in a cold sweat every six years wondering whether they'll draw opposition on the ballot.

Judges on television have become a growth industry, an army of ambition in robes looking for face time on the tube: the next Judge Judy or Joe Wapner. In a notorious trial, they can become celebrities overnight with a new career in the offing: dishing out justice for ratings.

For a number of reasons, some of them perhaps even logical, Jonah has been denied bail. The prosecutors have prevailed in their argument that a man with the kind of financial resources my client has may suddenly develop a yen for the balmy beaches of Mexico, or maybe Rio, where the word *extradition* isn't even in the dictionary, rather than face charges on a capital crime.

Jonah is now reconciled to spending time behind bars pending trial. I can only pray that this is all he does.

Each day it seems the mountain to be climbed is steeper. Women's groups have gotten their hands on damaging evidence, the press release that Suade never had time to send out, the one charging Jonah with the sexual assault of his daughter and granddaughter. They have been making the most of it on the airwaves, effectively poisoning the jury pool. Jonah is rapidly becoming the poster boy for abuse of women, even though Mary has faced down the cameras in her front yard telling the press that the charges are untrue.

Two days ago she was forced to come forward, with Harry at her side on the front lawn. 'My husband has never laid a hand on me in anger. He has never sexually assaulted our daughter.' When she was not quick enough making similar disclaimers for her granddaughter, they pounced on it like an admission, drowning out her repeated denials with a million innuendo-laden questions until Harry was forced to step forward, hands raised to quell the mob, explaining: 'Mrs Hale's statement goes for her granddaughter, as well.' As expected, the oversight became the lead on every newscast that carried the story. They are now calling it the *Lotto Lust Case*, and getting smirks and winks from their twenty-mil-a-year anchormen who offer this up as a teaser on the nightly news.

It is the reason I am here this morning, at the DA's office in an attempt to put out the fire, before it turns into a barn burning. The DA's office has called. I think they are worried; the publicity, the kind that can lead to appeals, is getting out of control.

Ruben Ryan sits behind his desk, fingers interlocked, hands clasped behind his head as he sways in the black leather high-back chair. Ryan is a career prosecutor, one of three in the DA's office who try the high-profile murders in this county. He has twenty years with the office, the grim countenance that goes with the experience, and a bottle of antacid tablets the size of a mayonnaise jar to prove it.

'You expect me to believe your office had nothing to do with the release?'

'I don't care what you believe,' he says. 'I'm telling you what I know. We're investigating,' says Ryan.

'Who else besides you and your investigators had access to those press releases Suade printed?' I ask him.

'I understand you had one.' Which begs the question of how I got it, though he doesn't get into this.

'Why would I give it to the media? Turn them loose on my own client?'

'Adverse pretrial publicity? Open the door on appeal?' he says. 'Some defense lawyers have been known to do that, you know. Maybe you want a change of venue?'

'Right. Mojave in August,' I tell Ryan. As if we could get away from the fallout. We'd have to go to the moon.

He concedes the point with an expression of disinterest.

'You come to town, you learn how it's done down here. Maybe a little different from what you're used to.' He says it as if the Constitution doesn't apply south of the Tehachipis.

'Do you want to hear what we have to offer or not?'

'I'm listening.'

It is our first meeting, and although it is cordial, there is a clear agenda. Ryan wants to stay ahead of the curve of public perception. He is assuming that within a month, because of leaks and intense publicity, the public numbers will show that most of the voters think Jonah is guilty. Once this view takes hold, in a high-profile case, you don't want to lose it in a jury trial. It can have a bad effect on reelection which, when an incumbent is thrown out, can turn an entire office on its ear. One way to avoid the risk is to deal early.

Ryan jacks up the expression on his face a little, what you see from some actors on the screen getting ready to make a pitch.

'Your client is old,' he says. 'He's gonna die in the joint – that is, if we don't do it for him first.'

'You're telling me you think you've got a death case here?'

'I'm telling you we can make special circumstances if you wanna press the issue.'

'Press away,' I tell him.

'We will. It's also possible,' he says, 'she was shot outside the car, maybe leaning in the window.'

This is one of the finer points of the law. The statute on first-degree murder in this state was amended a few years ago to deal with the rash of drive-bys, defining it as first-degree murder whenever the shooter shoots to kill from inside a car and the victim is outside. Such facts would make the death penalty available.

'Maybe you can explain to the jury how she got her cigarette butts inside the killer's ashtray. Long arms? And the powder burns on her clothes?'

'You want to run it up the flagpole and find out?' he says. 'There's a lot of angles here. Your client is not gonna be well loved. An eighty-million-dollar winner in the lottery. There's a lotta people spend their hard-earned money and don't win.'

'Is that what this is about?'

'I'm just telling you the dynamics,' says Ryan.

What he's trying to do is hammer me with everything he has, blast from a shotgun to see what penetrates and what doesn't. This before he gets to his offer, making it look like some sweet deal.

'We believe there's a chance we could show she was a witness with information of criminal wrongdoing,' he says.

'What are you talking about?'

'We're talking about the murder of a witness. Another separate special circumstance under the code,' he says. 'Grounds for the death penalty.'

Now he's more than reaching. He's dreaming. 'That requires a witness in judicial proceedings. I don't recall anything Suade was talking about having been filed on by your office or anybody else. In fact, the allegations against my client were investigated and dropped. If that's your case,' I tell him, 'let's go to trial, and I'm not waiving time. Not to speak ill of the dead,' I say, 'but your victim was publishing a lot of lies.'

'Maybe that's why he killed her?' says Ryan. 'Couldn't control his rage.'

He allows the thought to settle on me for a moment, that a lie will work just as well as the truth for motivation.

'That's a good theory, but in case you haven't noticed, Suade had a lot of enemies. There was a lot of rage out there, and not all of it belonged to my client. I think there was a lawsuit she had against the county. Unless I'm wrong, the cause of action died with her. Maybe you should be looking for some angry taxpayer.'

I can tell this has an effect. Something Ryan would not like to have to explain to a jury, how the victim came to be suing the county for twenty million dollars over false imprisonment by the presiding judge.

He clears his throat, sits up in his chair, runs a hand through shiny black tresses. 'It's why we're talking,' he says. 'If I thought your man was a stone-cold killer, I wouldn't have you in. But as it is, I'm not anxious to put the old man in the death chamber. That is, if he wants to be reasonable. Cop a plea,' he says.

'To what?'

He thinks for a second, more for effect, as if he hasn't given the matter thought before this moment, worn a rut in the linoleum between here and the plush-carpeted confines of his boss's office upstairs.

'Second degree,' he says. 'Your guy avoids lethal injection, does fifteen to life.'

For Jonah Hale, fifteen years is life. I tell him this. 'Besides, you're never going to do better than second degree no matter who your suspect is. That's not a deal; that's your pitch for a vacation. You want the month off, you should ask your boss.'

He shifts in his chair, a little uncomfortable knowing he hasn't made a sale, or even come close.

'You can't prove lying in wait,' I tell him. 'Not unless you've got a witness who saw the car at the scene. You know and I know, there's no such witness.'

'Are you sure of that?'

I shrug. He's bluffing. I can feel it. 'The rest of it,' I tell him, 'is crap. You want to play with the physical evidence? Was she inside the car? Was she outside the car? When did the bullets start flying? Maybe it was a blind date went bad. Take your best shot. But I've seen your forensics report, and it's not a theory you're gonna be able to leap on and ride.'

'Maybe we just put your man at the scene and let the jury fill in the blanks,' says Ryan. 'There's plenty of premeditation and deliberation to go around.' Another theory for first-degree murder. 'After all,' he says, 'a man doesn't come to a party with favors unless he plans to pop somebody.'

'The gun?'

He nods.

'How do you know it belonged to the killer?'

'Who else?' he says.

'I know you can't pick and choose your victims, but you ought to at least try to learn a little bit about them.'

He looks at me, not exactly sure what it is I am trying to say. Then it dawns: 'You're telling me she was killed with her own gun?' I can see the eyes, windows to the mind, venturing the next guess, but not stating it, that perhaps this is something Jonah has shared with me.

'I'm not telling you anything. You're forming conclusions. But I wouldn't discourage the thought. You may want to do some homework.'

Suddenly Ryan's eyes are scanning the desk, looking at the closed file with Jonah's name on it, wondering if anything is in there that he's missed.

'How did you know she owned a gun?' he asks.

'You don't really expect me to tell you that.'

This puts him deeper in the hole, wondering if I'm just shoveling against the tide, making it up as I go.

'So what do you want? Short of dismissal?'

'I don't know that my client would take anything. I'm

187

not sure I'd be prepared to recommend he take anything.'

Nothing like bargaining from strength.

'That could be a big mistake.'

'For who? Him or you?' I offer an expression, make a face, like maybe this is the best we can do.

Ryan is silent. Then, slowly, he says, 'It's against my better judgment. The only reason I would even consider it is your client has no prior record. No history of violence. And he's old.'

'Spare me the justifications,' I tell him.

'And it would depend on whether I can confirm that she owned a gun that matches the ballistics, that that weapon is unaccounted for,' he says. This is a big problem for him, wondering where I got this, assuming my client has knowledge.

'What would depend?' I say.

He hesitates for a second to demonstrate how painful this is. 'We might be willing to do voluntary manslaughter,' he says at last.

It is obvious he has already cleared this with higher-ups.

'And?'

'And your man does six years.'

I shake my head. 'Not a chance. Maybe three years, out in two, and I still have to sell it to my client.'

'I can't do that,' he says.

'Then it looks like we tried and failed.' I start to get out of my chair.

'You shouldn't be hasty,' he says. 'Your client could end up spending his golden years eating off a stainless-steel tray, wearing prison blues – or worse, wondering how he came to be strapped to a gurney with his arms exposed. We've got him tied to the scene four ways from Sunday.'

'Yeah, I know about the cigars.'

'There's more,' he says. 'For your information, we haven't finished dotting all the *i*'s, crossing all the *t*'s in our report. There are things you don't know.'

'Then why are we talking? Seems to me you're taking advantage, trying to get me to deal when I don't know all the facts.'

He stares at me, his mouth slowly melting into a smirk. I smile back. The mutual recognition of bullshit.

'Why don't you talk to your client?' he says. 'There's no sense you and me sitting here talking if he won't deal.'

'Talk to him about what?'

'His state of mind,' says Ryan. 'Maybe whether he's feeling guilty.'

An hour later I'm in the office trying it out on Harry.

'I don't know. I don't think he'll go,' he says. 'He's adamant he didn't do it.'

'Do you believe him?'

'I don't think he's that good a liar,' says Harry. 'It's the thing about people who live ordinary lives. Takes practice to learn how to lie about something like that. A career criminal,' he says, 'I wouldn't be able to tell one way or the other. So he's either pathologic, or he's telling the truth.'

'What about this witness?' I ask him. 'You seen anything in their reports?'

Harry has become our master of evidence, digesting every scrap of paper coming in on the case, which has now become a deluge.

'Nothing I've seen,' he says. 'It's too early for a witness

list, so they wouldn't have to divulge it yet. But there's no witness statement in the materials they've turned over yet. Did he give you any clue as to what they saw?'

'The car in the alley for a long time before she came out.'

'Jonah's car?'

'Ryan wasn't that specific. Just enough to make me worry. He was definitely planting the seed, though, telling me there was more we didn't have.'

Harry's dipping into the jar of pistachios on my desk. He is addicted. He went on the wagon ten days ago, swore off the things after he put on ten pounds. Then a week ago he came back from the store with pistachios in a bag the size of Santa's. Told me they were a present. Since then, he's been camped in my office cleaning out the jar faster than I can fill it, and reminding me whenever it's empty, as if this way he can eat them and the pounds end up hanging from *my* gut.

'You want some beer to go with those?'

'You got some?'

I give him a look and he laughs, closes the lid on the jar.

'So what do we do now?' he says.

'We go talk to our client. Moment of truth,' I tell him. 'If he's lying to us, he has to know now that he's taking a risk.'

'You never told me how you found out about the gun,' says Harry. 'Suade's.'

'My lips are sealed.'

'But you're sure about it?'

'Got the serial number in my pocket,' I tell him. 'What's more, I am reasonably confident from the look on Ryan's face that the cops didn't find it in Suade's purse at the scene or in her office. If they had, he wouldn't have been sitting there with egg all over him when I told him.'

'So Suade's gun is missing.'

'It would appear so.'

I have never told Harry about my suspicions the day I met her, about Suade's hand in her purse. If she had only pulled it out that morning, on me or the drunk lying on the sidewalk, I wouldn't be Jonah's lawyer. I would be his best witness. Or maybe I would be dead. As it is, it is all surmise.

'So what are you thinking? Suade came out to the car with the gun on her? She climbs inside. They smoke and talk. Maybe she loses it somewhere during the conversation and pulls the pistol from her handbag. They struggle over it. It goes off. Twice,' says Harry. He looks at me as if this could be a problem. 'Killer panics, dumps the body, dumps the ashtray. But why take the gun if it belongs to Suade?'

I don't have an answer.

'Still, maybe we can make a case for self-defense,' he says.

'Only if Jonah leads the way.'

CHAPTER
FOURTEEN

'I won't do it. No way. You can't make me.' Jonah won't sit at the table any longer. He paces the room in front of the door like a caged cat, causing the guard outside to shoot nervous glances every few seconds through the glass.

'We're not trying to make you *do* anything,' says Harry. 'But we do have to tell you what they're offering. It's one of the rules,' he says. 'We get our asses disbarred if we don't communicate the offer.'

'And so what are you saying?' Jonah turns to me.

'The court won't take a plea unless it's satisfied there's a factual basis,' I tell him. 'So it's your call. You're going to have to tell us.'

'Then it's easy. The answer's no.'

'Listen to what it is first, before you say no,' says Harry.

Jonah starts to shake his head.

The worst thing going is a criminal client with a closed mind, one who can't appreciate the options, and doesn't want to look at the risks.

'The cops are telling us they have you nailed to the scene four ways,' I tell him. 'Hard physical evidence putting you there.'

'Yeah, I know, the cigars. Harry told me. So what? I offered you one. Gave one to that cop, Brower. I thought he was supposed to be helping us find Amanda; instead he's playing boy detective.'

'Anybody else you gave them to?' says Harry.

'I don't know. I don't keep a list who I give cigars to.'

'They tell me it's a rare brand,' I say.

Jonah makes a face. 'Montecristo A's. I don't know how rare.'

'Contraband out of Cuba?'

'What is that supposed to mean? Like I was buyin' dope?'

'It means they were imported into the country illegally. In violation of a trade embargo,' I tell him.

'They wanna put me in jail for that, too?'

'No,' says Harry. 'But it does make the cigars easier to trace. Not a lot of people could afford them. They find a crushed box of Dutch Masters at the scene, it opens a larger realm of possibilities when it comes to suspects,' says Harry.

'All I know is they tasted good,' says Jonah. 'I go to this guy's shop, he takes me in the back room, pulls a box out from under the counter. I tried one, and liked it, so I bought two boxes.'

'How much?' says Harry.

'I can't remember the exact price.'

'Guess? Round it off,' says Harry.

'Maybe a thousand dollars, a box of twenty-five,' says Jonah.

194

'That's pretty round,' says Harry. 'At that price you shouldn'ta been givin' 'em away, at least not without collateral.'

Harry turns to me. 'You can expect Ryan's gonna get into this big time in front of the jury. Conjure up images of Jonah standing over the body, lighting up with hundred-dollar bills,' he says.

'According to the prosecutor, the cigar is not the only thing tying you to the scene,' I tell Jonah. 'He says they've got more, but he's not saying what it is. Not yet, anyway.'

'I don't know what they could have, because I wasn't there. Unless somebody's planting evidence,' he says.

'Why would they do that?'

'I don't know.'

'They're offering manslaughter,' says Harry. 'Paul thinks he might be able to get them down to two years.'

Jonah shoots him a look to kill, then turns it on me. 'And you want me to take it?'

'I didn't say that.'

'But you want me to think about it.'

'Thinking would be nice,' says Harry.

'In two years I'd die in this place,' he says.

'They wouldn't keep you here,' says Harry. 'State prison.'

'Oh, well. Wonderful. So I'm in prison when Amanda comes back.'

Harry and I look at each other.

Jonah catches the glance.

'You *are* gonna get her back?'

'We're trying,' I tell him.

'I can't take the deal,' he says. 'Let 'em kill me. Put

me to death,' he says. He's rolling up his sleeves. Clearly he's already given some thought to the way in which they do this.

'You're being dramatic,' I tell him. 'No one's talking about the death penalty.'

'You said earlier the prosecutor was.'

'He was being dramatic. They don't have a case.'

'I'm not confessing to something I didn't do,' he says.

'There is a chance,' says Harry, 'that we could argue self-defense.' Harry looks to see if there's some change in Jonah's attitude or an alteration in his story.

The old man merely knits his eyebrows in question, furrowed gray crescents.

'We have reason to believe that the gun that killed Suade may have belonged to her,' I tell him.

Jonah cocks his head.

'I don't understand. How did the killer get her gun?' he asks.

Harry and I look at each other, eyes meeting in the middle distance. It's not likely Jonah would be asking this if he was there that night, unless he's a more practiced liar than we think.

'Our guess is she brought it, probably in her purse. She may have carried the gun as a matter of course.'

'They found this gun? The police?'

'No. But we have a record of it. A serial number in her name, the same caliber as the murder weapon.'

'So,' says Harry. He's sitting on the edge of the table starting to speak with his hands, like maybe he has some Italian in him. 'If Suade brought the gun into the car, and she pulls this thing out of her purse, maybe in the middle of an argument, whoever killed her might have grabbed the gun in self-defense. If it went off in the struggle, the whole thing could be viewed as an accident. Even justifiable homicide. We could make out a case. Maybe walk that person out of here.' He looks at Jonah with hopeful eyes, seeing if he'll bite.

'That's a good argument,' says Jonah. 'For whoever did it. But I can't help you. Because I don't know what happened that night. You keep forgetting, I wasn't there.' He says it with emphasis, and finally sits down. Jonah's last word on the subject.

Harry sighs deeply, then turns his attention to me. 'We could still argue it as a theory,' he says. 'Some unknown perpetrator shot her in self-defense with her own gun. Not nearly as effective, I grant you, but at least it takes the sympathetic edge off the victim. What do we care we end up acquitting somebody else,' says Harry. 'It could drive a stake through the state's case.'

'If we can even get it in,' I tell him. 'There's no witness putting her gun at the scene. From what we know, it's just missing.'

'Yeah, I know. One of those matters of evidence,' says Harry, 'sound discretion of the trial court judge. And so far we don't know who that is.'

'Frank Peltro,' I say.

'When did you hear that?'

'Yesterday. Outside Ryan's office. Checked it with the court this morning. Peltro's the man. He drew the assignment from the presiding judge.'

'Davidson?'

I nod.

Harry rolls his eyes. 'Not doing us any favors, is he? You'd think given his history with Suade, the suit against the county and all, Davidson woulda stayed out of it, let the Judicial Council appoint the judge or something.'

'You'd think.'

'What do you know about him?' says Jonah. 'This judge?'

'Peltro?'

'Yeah.'

'Former cop,' says Harry. 'Fourteen years on the force. Went to law school at night. Ten years with the DA's office. Won his place on the bench by election.'

'He is well-thought-of,' I tell Harry.

'So was Judge Parker, by everybody except the people he hanged. I grant you, he's the only man in this county wearing a robe who doesn't owe the governor squat,' says Harry. 'So we have an independent judge pulled himself up by the bootstraps is gonna make the arrangements on behalf of our client with the state's version of Dr Kevorkian. You'll have to excuse me, but I don't see the benefit.'

'He runs a tight ship in court. Not exactly what I would have hoped for,' I tell him. 'But there could be some benefits.'

'Name one,' says Harry.

'He knows where he came from. He also knows everybody else knows. A man that independent doesn't like to be predictable. Likely he's going to be leaning backwards just a little to make the playing field tilt away from his old friends. He also knows the games they play. How stuff leaks when it shouldn't.'

'You're thinking Ryan's gonna try and run us into a ditch with publicity,' says Harry.

'Wouldn't you?'

'The prosecutors aren't likely to be able to pull the wool on Peltro. He knitted the stuff when he was there. Or, for that matter, bully him. It's not like he's gonna run scared in the next election. There's something to be said for rugged individualism,' I tell Harry. 'Especially in a case like this.'

'I'd just as soon take my chances with a judge who worked for the ACLU, thank you,' says Harry. 'Maybe we should affidavit him. Just to be safe.'

'And draw what?'

Harry gives me a shrug. The unknown.

'What's this affidavit?' says Jonah.

'We could bump the judge,' says Harry. 'We get one free shot. We don't have to state any cause. We can remove him from the case.'

'The downside,' I tell him. 'You may draw the wrath from the rest of the team. Whoever replaces him may take it out on us.'

'The proverbial *us*,' says Harry. 'Meaning *you*.' He's looking at Jonah.

I look at him, too. Once again, he's slumped at the table, his color not looking good, the pallor of a piece of faded parchment, his head on propped elbows. The doctor at the county medical center, the one who does jail rounds, has doubled the dosage of Jonah's blood pressure meds.

'Is there any way we can find out if Suade had run-ins with the law?' says Harry. 'Maybe pulled the gun on somebody else? An arrest for brandishing – that would be nice,' he says. Harry's thinking this could help wedge the door open to get Suade's gun into evidence.

'I already checked,' I tell him. 'There's nothing.'

'I was going there,' says Jonah.

He catches Harry and me musing about the law and the tactics of evidence as he says it, Harry stopping in mid-sentence.

'Going where?' I ask.

'To Suade's office,' says Jonah. This is the first he has ever said about it.

'But I never got there. I stopped on the Strand to think. To clear my head. Ended up sitting there for three hours, staring at the ocean. Wondering where Amanda was. If she was alive.' His eyes come back to me. 'You haven't heard anything?' he says.

'No.'

'You gotta find her.'

'We're looking,' says Harry.

We haven't told Jonah that Ontaveroz may be looking as well.

'Mary can take care of her. Be good for the two of 'em,' he says. 'Specially if I'm not there.'

By the time we get outside, it's dark except for a few yellow streetlamps and some traffic shooting beams of light. Harry is parked around the corner in another lot. His apartment is up on the hill, above Old Town, overlooking the freeway and Mission Bay.

'Heard my share of lying clients,' he says, 'but this doesn't sound like one of 'em. He never even took a whiff at the deal they offered. And the theory she was killed with her own gun. That's a get-outta-jail-free card. You notice he didn't blink.'

'I noticed.'

200

'So you believe him?'

I don't answer.

'Thing that makes me believe him is the lame story,' says Harry. 'Sitting on the beach looking at the ocean for three hours. Who in the hell's gonna shoot somebody, drive two miles, then sit in the sand and wait for the cops?'

'Somebody in shock,' I tell him.

Harry chews on this for a second, dead silence.

'I think we play on her packin' a pistol for all it's worth,' he says. 'Let the jury dwell on the notion she got what she deserved.' Harry's sold on the theory of self-defense, whether Jonah did it or not. 'What do you think?'

'I think I'll have to call Ryan. Tell him it looks like we're gonna have to do the trial. I may wait a day or two.'

'What? Make it look like Jonah considered it a little longer?'

'That, and try to slow the government steamroller from running up to speed.'

'The minute they find out, they're gonna go for the jugular.'

'At least we'll get the rest of their evidence.'

'Yeah, probably dropped on us like bricks off a building,' he says. 'Unless I miss my bet, we may have to read about it in the newspapers first.' Harry's fishing in his pocket for his keys. 'Wanna stop for a quick one? There's a little bar down in the gas lamp. A few blocks away.'

'I can't. Got an early-morning arraignment, and the sitter's home with Sarah.'

'We'll have to talk in the morning. Till then,' he says, 'keep a good thought.' Harry strikes out for his car, while I head toward the corner, walking past the county law library toward the trolley tracks on C Street.

I wouldn't have noticed, except there is little or no traffic on Front Street at this time of night, and the car's engine starts almost on the precise beat of Harry's farewell. I hear the engine, a low rumble, panther growl in the night a half block behind me. The wheels rolling slowly at a walking pace, grinding gravel under tires a hundred feet before the driver turns on his lights.

For a second, I think maybe it's the Bob and Jack Show, Murphy's federal sources come to follow me to see where I might lead them. But as I pass a car parked at the left-hand curb, one-way in this direction, I can see the reflection in its driver-side mirror. One of the headlights of the moving vehicle is either burned out or broken. The car's exterior has the look of a rolling wreck: it's not one of the dark sedans – Crown Victorias and big Buicks – favored by the federal motor pool. Still, its engine sounds souped, not like some junker.

I continue walking as if I'm oblivious. The feeling is that any glance, no matter how furtive, may force a hand. I cross the trolley tracks at a clip and saunter on along Front Street, up by the Greyhound bus depot.

Now at least there's more light, some activity at the corner. Broadway has four lanes, two in each direction, and stoplights. Here the traffic is heavier. I stop at the light with a few characters milling around on the corner, and consider my options, go right toward the lot where my car is parked, which will put me in front of their vehicle as I cross toward the old courthouse or go left. Left has more possibilities, the added advantage of forcing them to cross traffic to make a left turn up Broadway. This would put two lanes of opposing traffic on a busy street between us.

I hear the engine idling somewhere well back of the limit line. Whoever is there is still behind me. Awkward to turn and look so I don't, but peripheral senses and the hair on the back of my neck tell me that the driver is boring holes through me with his eyes.

I stand at the light. A guy with a grizzled beard in a moth-eaten coat comes up. 'Spare change?' he says. His palm, open and extended, looks as if it hasn't been washed in a month.

By now there are a half dozen people standing at the light. Even at this hour, Broadway is busy. I use the opportunity, maneuver so that I am facing the man as I poke around in my pocket and come up with several quarters, sneaking one quick glance at the car. The driver I don't recognize: dark-complected pockmarked face, maybe Mexican or Middle Eastern. Next to him in the passenger seat is another man, a hulking shadow I cannot make out. The rear windows are tinted, so I can't see in. The car is a Mercedes, maybe ten years old with a good deal of wear. There's no license plate on the front.

The light changes. The guy hustling change lumbers toward the bus depot. Two young kids, hand in hand, start across Broadway like they're shot from a cannon, the girl skipping to keep up. An old man with a cane starts the sojourn. Another guy, just drifting in the crosswalk, gets around him and fills in the middle.

At the last second I don't go. Instead, I turn left on the sidewalk and head up Broadway away from the corner. I can almost feel the agitation inside the car. It is palpable, like boom-box music and lifters, as if the car were bouncing around in place. Suddenly they have to make a left, through pedestrians crossing in front of them.

I move as fast as I can without breaking into a run. I cover a third of the block and end up in front of windows to the Greyhound bus depot, with doors set back off the street. I step into one of these, place my back against the edge of the building and peek around the corner, just a sliver of my head, enough for one eye.

The driver is in the middle of the intersection, gesturing with his hands. The car *is* in fact bouncing up and down, but not from any lifters. Whoever is in the back seat is shouting at the driver, who keeps looking over his shoulder into the back, then this way. He's lost me. His passenger is turned sideways, trying to act as spotter, but the driver's got him blocked.

I look at the shops down the way, the next block. At this hour everything is closed. Only the depot with a few people milling inside is well lit, its interior visible from the street, like a glass box.

I step inside, away from the door. The traffic outside heading west on Broadway starts to pile up at the light.

I make for a bench a few feet away, just inside the depot. Its back is to the windows on Broadway. In about as much time as it takes to fall, I sprawl facedown on the seat so that from the outside it looks like an empty bench. I lie there.

A woman sitting across the way facing me, is giving me strange looks, the kind you see being flashed at people who talk to themselves on the street.

I smile at her. She looks the other way. With one eye I

study my watch, feeling my heart pounding as the seconds tick away – thirty, forty-five – wondering if they've pulled up at the curb across the street to sit and wait or – worse – if they're coming inside.

Finally, I lift my head, take a peek over the back of the bench. I don't see the car. I scan the street: traffic moving at a clip, nothing parked across the street.

I turn my head to look at the woman. It's then I see them. Not out on Broadway, but on First Avenue. The car with the single headlight has made the turn, taking a left up First, trolling slowly, the driver's head halfway out the window looking at the bus depot from the other side, scanning the windows. I drop back down on the bench, hoping he doesn't see me. When I look up again the car is gone.

First Avenue is one-way. He'll have to go two blocks, cross the trolley tracks at C Street, come back on B to get onto Front Street in order to make the slow loop back around onto Broadway for another pass. Unless he's setting land speed records I've got maybe a minute, ninety seconds at the outside.

Jack Flash, I'm out the front door. I don't go to the light at the corner, but instead cut across the street, dodging traffic to the other side of Broadway, then west at a full run to the corner of Front, across from the bus depot.

I move down Front Street maybe thirty yards into the shadows of an alcove that forms the entrance of a small photo shop; its lights are out. There are cars parked on the street, providing cover. A good place to sit and watch.

I wait a few seconds, looking north on Front across Broadway, up toward the jail two blocks away. By now

Harry should have had plenty of time to get to his car. I wait, watching in the distance, looking at the luminous sweep hand on my watch, timing their lap.

Fifty seconds and I start to borrow problems. Maybe Harry stopped for that drink along the way. Their route would take them directly in front of the lot where his car was parked. If they saw us together on the street, talking in front of the jail . . . My brain starts to fill in the blanks.

I step out of the alcove onto the sidewalk, start walking, then a slow jog toward the corner, not sure exactly what to do. Maybe the jail. There are cops there on duty.

I'm ten feet from the corner when the sweep of the cyclops nails me dead in my tracks. The ominous single headlight swings around the corner two blocks away. It barrels toward me down Front Street at full bore, bouncing across the tracks on C.

I find myself backpedaling toward the shadows, out of the light, wondering if the driver's seen me. Within seconds I'm crouched in the alcove again, nowhere to run. The car makes the stop at the corner across Broadway. I can't see anybody inside, glare on the windshield. The vehicle has only a single headlamp, but this is on high beam.

The traffic light changes. The car doesn't move right away but sits at the intersection, nothing behind them, the driver considering his options, probably getting instructions, like a rudder being jerked with wires from the backseat.

Finally, the Mercedes slides forward across the intersection, the beam of its light rising then falling with the crown at the center of the road until the shaft of light slides down the sidewalk like a snake stopping a foot from where I am huddled. They start the turn onto Broadway, taking it wide so that by the time they finish, they end up at the curb on the corner, the Mercedes stops.

It sits there motionless for several seconds, its engine a low grumble, tail end sticking out just a little into the right traffic lane on Broadway.

Finally the passenger door opens and a guy gets out. He's short, stocky, dark-skinned, with hair cut long on the sides, short on top. What is left of it is orange, something from a bottle that didn't work right.

'You wan me check ova there? Ova here?' The guy's shrugging, leaning into the car as he talks.

'*La estación*.' The command voice comes from the backseat.

The car doesn't move. The hulk does. He slams the door, skips the crosswalk, and heads instead toward the front of the vehicle where I lose him, line of sight behind the buildings on the block.

I am now trapped in the alcove. All I can see is the tinted rear window of the Mercedes, wondering if its occupant is looking my way. It seems to take forever, probably three or four minutes. The car parked at the corner, its motor running. The orange-haired hulk finally comes back, opens the passenger door and gets in. But he leaves the door open.

'Old lady inside sez she saw him. He run out this way. Cross the street. You wan I look for him?'

'No.'

Hulk slams the door and the car starts to ease its way out into traffic, a sharp left into the slow lane so that for a half second both taillights are visible, along with the license plate, green numbers on a white background. One of the states, I don't know which one, but not from here. The plate is Mexican. I kill five minutes huddled in the shadows, praying they don't come back.

CHAPTER
FIFTEEN

'Can you take Sarah for a while?' I'm talking to Susan on the phone, sweeping graphite dust off the surface of my desk with a sheet of paper, like shoveling black snow. 'No, I can't tell you why right now.'

Floyd Avery is standing in the doorway to my office watching Harry as he wades through paper on the floor up to his knees, and steps around the splintered wood splayed all over the floor from one of the drawers of my credenza.

'Trust me on this one. Right now it would be best if she wasn't around the house for a few days. I'll explain tonight. Can you pick her up at school? Great. I owe you one,' I tell her.

She tells me I owe her more than one, then gives me a smooch of a kiss for a good-bye. I don't return the gesture with Avery watching. Instead I just hang up.

'Should at least tell the girl you love her,' he says. 'Kiss like that.'

I can only hope he didn't hear her voice enough to recognize it.

'Remind me not to hire your janitor,' he says. 'Fortunately, it's not my jurisdiction. But if you want my advice I wouldn't be touching things. Not if you want any chance of getting prints.'

'They dusted already,' says Harry.

Avery looks at one of the windowsills. 'Thought it was ant shit,' he says.

'Yeah, I suppose your guys would save that to use in law-office break-ins,' says Harry. 'They didn't bother doing the front door. Guess they figured that's the way they came in, seeing as the wood's splintered all around it.'

'Probably figured you don't get much off the bottom of a boot that kicks your door in,' says Avery.

'All I know is it's gonna take the cleaners a month to get all that black crap off the windows that were locked.' Harry picking through papers on the floor.

'Missing anything?' asks Avery.

'Yeah. We're gonna give you an inventory,' says Harry. 'Soon as we're done counting up the missing confessions to murder, notes on current drug deals, and the list of who did JFK. Hell, you could just dip into the pile and close all the pending cases in your department.'

'I wouldn't mind,' says Avery.

'I'll bet you wouldn't. Man's wading through our claim and he wants to get his pan in the water,' says Harry.

'Your partner has a hair trigger,' Avery tells me.

'What brings you this way?' I ask him.

'I heard 'bout the break-in. Thought I'd come by. See what happened.'

'What you thought is that it had something to do with Jonah Hale.'

'Did it?'

'You should learn to trust your instincts. If you'd followed them earlier, you would never have arrested Jonah for Suade's murder.'

'Other people callin' those shots,' says Avery.

'So you're not committed to the case?'

'Fortunately, I don't have to lay odds. But I wouldn't be feelin' too comfortable if I was your client.'

Harry's still grumbling. 'Only prints they're gonna find are yours and mine,' he says.

'We could get lucky. Nail one of your clients,' says Avery. 'Maybe one who's got a history of burglary. You should look at it as a horizon-building experience. You get to see things from the victim's point of view.'

Harry gives him the expressive equivalent of spit.

'You got any ideas might narrow down who broke in? Or why?' says Avery.

'Probably the same people who followed Paul from the jail last night.'

Avery gives Harry a look, then says, 'Bad people hang out there. Though most of 'em are inside.'

'No, it wasn't jail guards followed him,' says Harry. 'Car full of Mexicans. At least the car had Mexican plates.'

'What kinda car?'

'Older-model Mercedes, SL. I think. You'd have to ask a German mechanic. Those things confuse me. Too many different letters.'

'Maybe it was a disgruntled client,' says Avery. 'You know. A felon with a consumer complaint.'

211

'Nobody I know,' I tell him.

'You tellin' me all your campers are happy?'

'I didn't say that. But it wasn't a client, present or former. Still, there may be a connection.'

'What's that?'

'With Hale.'

Now he perks up.

'Not the father. The daughter,' I tell him.

Avery's in the doorway leaning against the jamb, wondering if he really wants to ask. 'Why is it I smell the simmering aroma of a cooking defense?' he says. 'I know I'm gonna regret it. But I'll bite. What do these people following you have to do with Hale's daughter?'

'They're looking for her.'

'Everybody's looking for her,' says Harry. 'The woman's a virtual map to buried bodies.'

'She see her old man kill Suade?' says Avery.

'Only if she was hallucinating,' I tell him.

'Then we're not looking for her,' he says.

'Maybe you should be.'

'And why is that?'

'Because I think maybe she knows more about this thing with Suade than you or I.'

'What exactly?'

'Perhaps if I knew, my client wouldn't be in jail.'

'Did you get a look at these guys? The ones in the car with the Mexican plates?'

I can't be sure whether he believes these people exist or not.

'Two of them.'

'And?'

'One of them had a stocky build. Mexican. Bottle-blond hair turned orange. Hired muscle. The driver had a mustache, dark hair.'

'Why would they want the daughter?' He may not believe the story, but he's hooked.

'For the same reason the feds are beating the bushes as we speak. You should talk to them,' I say.

'And which feds might these be?' He takes his notebook out, waiting for a name.

'Bob.'

He writes it down. Looks up.

'His friend's name's Jack.'

'These people saving space on their business cards?'

'That's all they gave me. But I would check with DEA.'

He raises an eyebrow. 'Your client running drugs?'

'No. But I couldn't give the same testimonial for his daughter.'

'I know she has a record. Checked it out,' says Avery. 'But even if all of what you're tellin' me is true, you got a problem,' says Avery. 'What's it have to do with Suade's murder?'

'These people are desperate to find Jonah's daughter; they might go visit Suade.' .

'Might. Coulda. Maybe. Interesting theory,' he says, 'but where's the evidence? Let me guess. The man, this Ontaveroz, he wants to whack her because she knows all about his business.'

'How'd you know that?' says Harry.

'Saw it on TV. Old rerun of *Ironside*,' says Avery. 'What I can't figure is why these people come looking in your office to find Hale's daughter.'

213

'I don't know. Maybe they think we know where she is.'

'Maybe Ontaveroz doesn't know she and her father are on the outs,' says Harry. 'They think Jonah knows where the girl is, he might share that with his lawyers.'

'Does he? Know where she is?'

'That's why he hired us,' I tell him. 'To find her.'

'Why hire a lawyer to find somebody?'

'Same question we asked him. He wanted to put the legal squeeze on Suade.'

'He found another way of doing that,' says Avery.

'Why kill her if he wanted to find his daughter? Doesn't make any sense you kill your only source of information,' says Harry. 'Your man Ryan's a little obtuse if he hasn't seen that.'

'Maybe Hale went to see her, when he got there just lost it,' says Avery. 'Or maybe he wasn't as interested in finding his daughter as he was in keeping Suade quiet. She was making a lotta noise about incest.'

'He had no reason to talk to her. That's why he hired me.'

'Yeah. But you didn't fare too well,' says Avery. 'By the way, you left your prints in Suade's office.'

'I was wondering when you were going to get around to that.'

'We knew, the day after the murder, that you were there,' says Avery. 'Brower told us. Why didn't you mention it?'

'I knew sooner or later he'd get around to it, or you'd figure it out.'

'What did you talk about? You and Suade.'

'What do you think?'

'Did she know where the daughter and the kid are?'

'If she did, she wasn't telling me.'

'I suppose that's when you got your glimpse of Suade's press release. Did she give you a copy, or did you steal it?'

When I don't answer, he says, 'We know you had it. We know you shared it with Hale in your office. Brower told us. Next time you hold a meeting with one of your clients, you'll have to remember to keep all the cops out.'

'That's before somebody did Suade.'

'*Somebody?* I'm guessing she gave you the release,' he says. 'Strikes me as the kind who might get off twisting a knife into Hale. Show it to him and let him stew for a day, knowing he couldn't do a thing to stop it. 'Course, in retrospect, it was a mistake. Some might call it fatal. Excuse the pun,' says Avery. 'Still you shouldn't blame yourself, and you oughta thank Brower. You'd be a suspect in a murder case, except he puts you at the scene earlier in the day, before other people saw her alive.'

'Man's a prince,' I tell him.

'And it's a real interesting concept,' says Avery. He's turning for the door now. 'This Mexican drug dealer. Just one problem.'

'What's that?'

'How you gonna prove he even knew about Suade?'

CHAPTER
SIXTEEN

It's the biggest problem we have, and the only available defense other than the bald denial that Jonah did it – the information from seemingly reliable sources that the drug dealer Ontaveroz had been looking for Jessica.

This morning Harry and I are in court. Over our objections, Jonah has waived his right to a preliminary hearing. This allows the state to go to trial by way of a grand jury indictment.

Still Jonah is adamant. He is insisting on his right to a speedy trial, to take his chances.

We've warned him that he may not like the result. What is driving him is the obsession to be out of jail, so that he can look for Amanda. He doesn't have a clue as to where he would start, but for some reason, in his mind, the four walls of his cell are now keeping him from Mandy. To make things worse, the judge has denied a rehearing on bail. Harry and I are beginning to feel like oranges in a squeezer.

The business before us is a pretrial motion. Jonah's not

here. Such motions do not require the attendance of the defendant.

Murphy is now our investigator of record on the case. He has acquired three articles from Mexican newspapers, all of them in Spanish that at least allude to the existence of Ontaveroz by name. There are no photographs, but the articles, retyped in English by a qualified translator and attached to our brief, provide details on a man you wouldn't want to meet across an ocean, with God on your shoulder, in a two-minute dream.

Most of the pieces deal with attempts by the Mexican Judicial Police to find him. So far, he is believed to have killed at least three of their agents.

Ontaveroz is believed to have participated in the murder of a number of business competitors, and at least two political assassinations. Harry says these were probably business, too, like motor-voter laws, only down there they lean out the window – ballots by bullet.

Harry has prepared subpoenas for the DEA, FBI, and Justice demanding that they produce information, notes, records, anything in writing regarding Jessica's plea bargain that sent her away to state prison. We are hoping that these may lead to Ontaveroz, at least some reference to the man by name. If Ontaveroz knew about me, my guess is he knew about Suade. The problem is, how do we prove it?

'So d'ya bring the doughnuts, Mr Madriani?' Frank Peltro is looking down at me from the bench, face like an Irish bartender, made-to-order smile, everybody's best friend. The only things that give him away are the eagle eyes under heavy, gray, hooded brows.

'Not me, Your Honor.'

'You were supposed to bring the doughnuts,' he says. 'I gotta cageful of angry people back there waiting for arraignment. Gotta deal with 'em in ten minutes. No doughnuts, there's gonna be hell to pay.' All of this with a smile on his face. 'So what am I supposed to do?' he asks.

'Have the guards pass out Quaaludes,' I tell him.

'That's no answer,' he says. 'They already got those. They want doughnuts.'

The court reporter is obviously not taking any of this down, not until Peltro gives her the okay. He's been on the bench long enough to know how to stay out of trouble with the humorless tight asses on the Commission for Judicial Performance.

'Can I tell 'em you'll bring doughnuts for lunch?' he says.

'That depends.'

'On what?'

'On how enlightened and reasonable the court is in the matter pending.'

'Sounds like a felony to me,' says Peltro. He looks at the DA. Avery is laughing. Ryan is ignoring him.

'I think you're in trouble, Mr Ryan. I need doughnuts for an angry mob. What are you offering?'

'Nothing,' says Ryan. 'I'm fine. I've been taping all of this.'

Peltro laughs deeply, something from the belly. Santa Claus on the bench. 'Now I *am* in trouble. Mr Bailiff, you can put Mr Ryan there in the cage. And tell them that *he* ate their doughnuts.'

The bailiff doesn't move, but is laughing, his gut bouncing up and down above his gunbelt.

Peltro takes one last look at Harry's brief, points and authorities, now that the fun is over. Then looks down at Harry and me and says, 'Who's gonna argue this mess?'

I rise, and step to the podium, front and center.

Peltro nods to the court reporter.

'I read your brief,' he says. 'There's no need to go through all the arguments. Maybe we should just focus on the problems.'

This is not a good beginning.

'As I see it,' he says, 'you want to bring in evidence, but you've got no evidence.'

'That's not exactly true, Your Honor. We do have two federal agents.'

'Did I miss something?' he says. The judge flipping pages. Looking at the motion, tracing lines of print with his finger. 'I thought you couldn't identify them,' says Peltro.

'We can't right now. We're working on it.'

'Can you produce them?'

'Given time, I believe we can.'

'Your Honor, they've refused to waive time. The case is scheduled for trial.' Ryan is on his feet, sensing where I'm going, demanding a speedy trial and requesting a continuance at the same time.

'DA makes a point,' says Peltro. 'Are you asking for a delay in the start of trial?'

'Not at this moment, Your Honor.'

'That doesn't sound good to me,' says the judge.

'No,' I tell him.

'That sounds better. Unless your client waives time, I'm not gonna be allowing any continuances.' He looks down at the bench blotter in front of him, the one with a slice of acetate over it the size of an army blanket. He holds up some pages on the giant calendar underneath it so I can no longer see him. 'My next opening . . .' Voice lost behind a wall of paper. 'My next, ah, available date for trial's not till late September,' he says. 'And I'm not available then on account of I'm going down to La Paz. Gonna be on the back of a friend's Grady White with my pole over the stern searching for yellowtail. That means your man's in the bucket at least five months, maybe more, pending trial.' He drops his calendar, raises those bushy eyebrows. Looks at me over the top of half-moon cheaters. The spectacles make him look even more judicial.

'My client would reconsider waiving time,' I say, 'if we could come to some accommodation on bail.'

'Why? So's he could meet me in La Paz?' says Peltro.

'No, Your Honor.'

Now Ryan is laughing.

'We've already been through all that,' says the judge. 'I don't think under the circumstances the court can take the risk. Your client wants to look for his granddaughter. I'm sympathetic,' he says. 'Got two of 'em myself,' he says. 'Don't know what I'd do if somebody took 'em. But you, yourself, acknowledge there's a good chance the child could be down in Mexico. So you know where he's gonna go if I let him out.'

'He could have gone down there before he was arrested. He didn't.'

'He may have second thoughts now,' says Peltro.

'I'll guarantee that my client won't leave the county.'

'You gonna tie yourself to his leg?' he says.

'You could take his passport,' I tell him.

'He doesn't need a passport to cross into Mexico,' says Ryan. 'Not at the border.'

'I am aware, Mr Ryan. Let's get back to issues more germane,' he says. 'I appreciate your good-faith effort to assure your client's appearance, Mr Madriani. And I'm sure you would try. But there are compelling forces,' he says, 'stronger than you and me. And I'm not sure in the end that they would not overtake us in this case, notwithstanding your intentions. My ruling on bail stands.'

'What else is here?' he says.

'Witness list, Your Honor. We'll need some accommodation in getting our evidence together,' I tell him.

'I hope you're not asking latitude to argue facts not in evidence. Cuz that's not gonna be happening.'

'No, Your Honor.'

Ryan is wheeling back in his chair, enjoying it as I twist on the spit, savoring the aroma as the judge roasts me and the state gets ready to barbeque my client.

'Then what are you asking?' says Peltro.

'Some relaxation of the time for the defense to file its witness list.'

'What he's asking for is trial by ambush.' Ryan kicking back in his chair, casual, feeling he has a colleague on the bench gonna do his fighting for him.

'No, we're not, Your Honor.'

'Mr Ryan, you'll be given your opportunity.' He nods toward me to go ahead.

'The defense is at a severe disadvantage,' I tell him. 'My client has a right to a speedy trial, but no opportunity to develop a defense. There is evidence that we have good reason to believe exists, but that we cannot get before the trial starts.'

'That's their problem, Your Honor. Then they should waive time.'

'Mr Ryan!'

'Sorry, Your Honor.'

The judge starts pawing through the pages of our motion, points and authorities by the pound. Harry has done his usual stellar job.

'You want to be able to argue this man, Ontaveroz?' he says.

'That's correct, Your Honor.'

'Where's the nexus? What's the connection with your case?' says Peltro.

'My declaration. Another affidavit from my investigator,' I tell him. 'Attached there to the motion.'

Peltro starts to read.

'Your Honor, even if this is true, this is the defendant's own lawyer, his own investigator, telling us secondhand what they were told by a witness whose credibility we have no way of testing.'

The judge's hand is in the air, telling Ryan to shut up.

Ryan's rolling his eyes toward the ceiling, like maybe we're gonna argue the man on the grassy knoll next.

'Tell me again how you found these people. These two agents,' says Peltro.

'Through my investigator.'

'Has he dealt with them before?'

'He has. And he's found their information to be reliable.'

'Can he testify from firsthand knowledge that they are agents of the federal government?'

'Your Honor.'

'Mr Ryan.' He looks down at the prosecutor, an expression that says he is no longer joshing.

'How do you define firsthand?' I ask the court.

'Has your investigator seen some credentials with their pictures and names?'

'I don't know. But he's dealt with them before, and they've given him information that I believe could only come from federal law enforcement sources.'

'Or somebody with a fertile imagination,' says Ryan. He's now testing the outer limits.

'They showed me a picture of the man they called Ontaveroz.'

'How do you know that's who it was, aside from what they told you?' says Ryan.

I don't answer.

'Do you have this picture?' he says.

Peltro looks up but doesn't stop Ryan from doing his work.

'No, Your Honor.' I ignore Ryan. 'They showed it to me. They didn't allow me to keep it.'

'That's very convenient, Your Honor, but it ignores the real issue.' Ryan squares himself to the bench and closes the center button on his coat, girding himself for forensic combat, or jail if he's not careful.

'Your Honor, being charitable' – he says it as if the word might curdle in his mouth – 'even assuming that these two mythic figures exist, these federal agents, and assuming that what's contained in counsel declarations is accurate, that this man Ontaveroz exists, and that he knew Jessica Hale . . .'

'It's more than the fact that he knew her.' I'm not going to allow him to understate what little evidence we have. 'She carried drugs. That was the basis for her arrest and incarceration. Possession of drugs. Transportation. *That* is verifiable,' I tell the court.

'Fine,' says Ryan. 'She carried drugs. Let's assume it was for him. There's still no evidence he was ever involved with Suade. Or that he even knew about her.'

Ryan has just made a critical mistake. I can read it in Peltro's face. If Ontaveroz exists. If he and Jessica dealt drugs, it's a short skip to the news articles about the Mexican's violent past. If he was looking for Jessica, he might find Suade.

'Are you saying, Mr Ryan, that there's no evidence Suade helped Jessica Hale disappear?' says the judge.

'We don't know that, Your Honor.' Ryan now sees the problem he's created for himself, a little too late. He starts to backpedal. If Suade didn't help Jessica disappear, where's Jonah's motive for murder?

'Then what are all these accusations regarding Mr Hale doing in Suade's press release?' says the judge. 'Are you saying Suade didn't have a dog in this fight?'

'No. Obviously she had some connection,' says Ryan.

'They can't have it both ways, Your Honor,' I cut in on him. 'If Jessica had a history of drugs, and she did, we must be allowed to explore that history.'

The judge is now nodding in agreement.

'They're looking to take a field trip into the irrelevant,' says Ryan. 'Where's the evidence?'

'So what do you want?' Peltro's looking at me. Ignoring Ryan.

'An opportunity to identify the witnesses we need as the trial progresses,' I tell him.

'Your Honor!' Ryan's voice rises a complete octave. 'What they want is to see our case, then dream up a defense that fits.'

Sounds fair to me, but I don't say this to Peltro.

'All we're asking is a little latitude, Your Honor.'

Peltro looks at me, then at Ryan. He thinks for a moment. 'How do you intend to deal with this in your opening?' he asks me.

'You mean Ontaveroz?'

'Yes.'

'I'd like to mention him.' I'd like to do more than that, put some clothes on him, show his picture, trot him out in front of the jury. Who do you want to convict: behind door number one, my client, grandpa in suspenders and a cardigan, or door number two, king of a major drug cartel?

'You'd like to mention him by name?'

'I would, Your Honor.'

'How can he do that . . . ?' Ryan sputters.

'I don't think so,' says the judge. 'What do we do if you can't produce evidence during the trial? How do we erase the thought from the jury's mind?' he says.

In actuality, this would do more damage to us than the prosecution. It's a risk mentioning Ontaveroz in my opening statement unless I can close with him in my argument. Jurors have a tendency to remember such failures, and to punish for them.

'I don't think I can allow you to mention the man unless

226

there's some evidentiary nexus,' says Peltro. 'Something linking him in some way to the victim.'

'You expect me to put him at the scene?'

'That would be fair,' says Ryan. Now he's smiling.

'Do I have to put the gun in his hand, too?' I'm looking over at the prosecutor, who makes a gesture with his hands, like suit yourself.

'I don't know that I'd require that much,' says Peltro, 'but some reasonable basis to believe this man Ontaveroz was pursuing Jessica Hale. Perhaps some evidence that he knew or at least could be aware that Suade might have information. Obviously, the better your evidence, the more persuasive it'll be to the jury,' he says. 'But I won't be letting you argue Ontaveroz at close unless you have some basis in the evidence. Do we understand each other?'

'What about the witness list?' I ask him.

'I'll give you some latitude. Your final witness list will be due when you open your case in chief for the defense, but only in this one area,' he says.

'Your Honor!' Ryan is now sensing his punishment for not having listened to the judge earlier.

'Your other witnesses. You gotta disclose those under the rules,' he says. 'Do you understand?'

'I do, Your Honor.' It's the best I'm likely to get.

'You can prepare the order. My clerk will provide the minutes by way of transcript. Any questions?'

Ryan doesn't like it. 'Your Honor, he should at least be required to give us some clue as to his witnesses. Is he gonna produce Ontaveroz?'

'Not unless I got my gun under my robes,' says Peltro. 'We're off the record.'

I'm packing up my briefcase, leaning toward Harry, trying to make sense of what we won and lost.

'Mr Madriani.'

I turn to look up at the judge as he says my name.

'You owe me some doughnuts.'

CHAPTER
SEVENTEEN

'I haven't asked you a lot of questions about what's going on,' says Susan. 'I know you're busy. But I also know there's something happening you're not telling me about.'

We're having coffee this morning, bagels and some fruit.

I have papers from work spread out in front of me on Susan's kitchen table, trying to avoid the questions I knew were coming.

'Earth to Paul,' she says.

I'm forced to look up. *'Hmm?'*

'I know you're busy.'

'Sorry.' I stack the papers, turn them over on the table facedown.

'You're always busy,' she says.

'I know. When this is over, we'll have more time. I promise.'

'Tell it to your daughter,' says Susan.

'Is there something wrong?'

'Nothing, except for the fact that she's been living here

now for almost a month and she doesn't know why. Neither do I.'

'I'm sorry to impose.'

'It's not an imposition,' she says. 'But there is something wrong, isn't there?'

'Has Sarah asked?'

'Not in so many words. You come over. You sleep at the house a few nights a week. The rest of the time you disappear. We don't see you. The child is beginning to wonder where home is.'

'I know. You've been great,' I tell her.

'And I don't mind,' she says. 'I'd just like to know what's going on.'

For a moment, I think she suspects I'm seeing someone else.

'It's just that I'm buried. Burning the candle at both ends.'

'You've tried cases before. You've never been like this.'

I take a deep breath, sip some coffee, pick up a bagel and start to break it. Her hand comes across the table to stop me: no more distractions, eyes staring through me like two lasers.

I put the bagel back in the basket.

'The day I called you. Asked you to take Sarah.'

'Yes.'

'The night before, I was followed by some people in a car. I can't be sure who they were. But I have reason to believe that it would be better, at least for the time being, if Sarah stayed here.'

'These people are dangerous?'

'I don't know, but I couldn't afford to take the chance,

leaving Sarah in the house when I'm gone so much of the time.'

'Are these the same people who trashed your office?'

'I don't know for sure. But there's a chance.'

'Why didn't you tell me?'

'I didn't want you to worry.'

I have mentioned Ontaveroz to her once or twice, but as a vague theory of defense only. Now I give her the rest of the story. She listens, looks at me across the table as I fill in the details.

'If they know where my law office is, they probably know where I live. It's why I didn't want Sarah at the house.'

She looks off into the distance, an anxious expression on her face. 'I understand.' I can read her mind.

'I've been very careful about coming over here,' I tell her. 'I take a cab from the office to the sheriff's station downtown. I figure if they are tracking me, they're not likely to follow me in there. There's a detective. Not a friend exactly. But he came by the office that morning after the burglary. He lets me go out the back way. Harry picks me up at a spot a couple of blocks away. Brings me over here. Picks me up the next morning, takes me to the office.'

'You told me your car was in the shop.'

'White lie,' I tell her. 'Lena's in the driveway at the house. Hasn't been started in a week. Probably has a dead battery by now. I'm gonna rent a car this afternoon – something they won't recognize – and keep it away from the office and the house.'

'You think they're still following you?'

'I don't know. If so, they've gotten better, because I haven't seen them.'

'You told your detective friend about this man, Ontaveroz?'

'The detective is no friend. He's the man who arrested Jonah. But, yes, I told him. Though I doubt it'll show up in any of their reports. If it does, it'll be carefully couched. The cops don't want to be put on the stand having to admit they're investigating the man because he was following me, or because he's a suspect in the break-in at my office. That might lend credence to our theory on Suade. Unless I miss my bet, they think that's why I told them. Lawyer tricks. Force it into their reports, then use it at trial.'

'And of course, you're not that devious,' she says.

'Honest. You think I would go to all this trouble coming over here? Let Lena languish in the driveway and take a cab?'

'Looking at your car, it's a possibility,' she says. 'But I know you're telling the truth, because you wouldn't do this to Sarah. You think Ontaveroz could actually have killed Suade?'

'It's certainly possible. More plausible than Jonah's having done it. Ontaveroz has a violent past. He's killed before. If you believe the news articles and the federal agents I talked to at the restaurant.'

'Any lead on them? The federal agents?'

I shake my head. 'Vanished. I've called Murphy. Pounded on him to find them. He's come up empty. Says they do that. Disappear for months. According to Murph, they're probably undercover down in Mexico someplace.'

'While this man Ontaveroz is looking for Jonah's daughter,' says Susan.

'And likely to find his granddaughter,' I add.

'You don't think they'd hurt her, do you?'

'I don't think they care who gets in their way. It's why I've taken such precautions for Sarah,' I tell her. 'I haven't been sleeping all that well at night.'

'And you haven't told Jonah?' she says.

'How can I? The old man's locked up, already going crazy. I can't make it worse. What he doesn't know . . .' I tell her.

'Sooner or later, he's going to have to know your theory of defense. You don't want him sitting at the table in the courtroom with his mouth hanging open when you casually mention the Mexican drug dealer who wants to kill his daughter.'

'The court may solve that one for me,' I tell her. 'The judge may not let me get into it at all unless I can come up with witnesses or official records putting Jessica and Ontaveroz together.'

Susan stares down into her cup of coffee slowly cooling on the table. 'One thing's for sure. You're not going back to your house,' she says. 'Not until this is over.'

'I'm gonna run out of underwear pretty quick.'

'You can go around in the buff,' she says. 'At least you'll be alive. And besides, I like men who wear nothing underneath.'

'Yeah, but you're kinky,' I tell her.

She laughs. 'You ever get the urge to just run away?' she says. 'Some desert island.'

'All the time.'

'Me, too. Lately it's been getting stronger,' she says. 'I've got a meeting Tuesday morning with the board of supervisors. Executive session,' says Susan.

This means it's behind closed doors, away from the press and public.

'The papers haven't picked it up yet. The board's calling it a personnel matter,' she tells me.

I sit silent, looking at her across the table. Short dark hair, fiery Latin eyes, a face like Isabella Rossellini's. Apart from her two daughters, the only thing Susan cares about in life is her job, and now that is in jeopardy.

'It doesn't have anything to do with the gun, Suade's pistol?' I ask.

She shakes her head vigorously. 'Not directly,' she says. 'They're claiming there was an internal report containing evidence that some of my investigators were using improper tactics when questioning children. That we deep-sixed the report to keep it away from defense attorneys in some cases.'

I look at her.

'There was no report,' she says. 'Ordinarily I'd have cover. The prosecutor's office wouldn't let them beat me up. But I think they know where the information on Suade's handgun came from.'

'I didn't tell them.'

'I know. Process of elimination,' she says. 'And I think Brower probably found out. He knows he's crossed me. The man is not stupid. He knows it's do or die. He either gets me, or I get him.'

'Can't you talk to him?'

'About what? When you have disloyalty in a small office, there's nothing to talk about. He knows that. There're only two ways for Mr Brower to go. Either up or out.'

'You think he's after your job?'

'I wouldn't put it past him.'

'I'm sorry to have put you in this situation.'

'You didn't,' she says. 'The die was cast a long time ago.'

When I look at her for an explanation she just shakes her head, gets up from the table, doesn't want to get into it, nothing to talk about.

'What are you going to do about Jonah's granddaughter?' she asks.

'What can I do? Keep trying to find her. I've got Murphy looking.'

'Do you think he'll be able to get a lead?'

'Maybe through the two federal agents. They're looking for Jessica. They know she's in trouble with Ontaveroz. I'm hoping that'll lead to something. In the meantime, I've got a case to try. Which leads me to another question,' I tell her. 'What do you know about Brad Davidson? The presiding judge.'

'Former,' she says. 'Former PJ. He was removed on Friday afternoon.'

This surprises me. Susan can tell by the look on my face as she turns back toward the table.

'You hadn't heard?'

I shake my head.

'They'll announce it publicly on Monday,' she says. 'The judges voted behind closed doors, secret ballot, so they could all tell him how much they supported him. I'm told that, technically he'll resign. He'll remain on the bench,' she says. 'The question is, for how long. He'll definitely draw opposition in the next election. Somebody from the prosecutor's office, no doubt. You don't involve the county in a twenty-million-dollar lawsuit and escape unscathed,' says Susan. She speaks like a woman about to find out.

'Davidson might have walked away, except for the public fallout from Suade's murder. That revived the thing.'

'But the lawsuit died with her.'

'The controversy didn't,' says Susan.

'What do you know about Davidson, the man?'

Susan mulls over the subject for a moment in silence, then sits across the table from me again.

'Former Marine. I think he's still in the reserves. A certified hard-ass,' says Susan. 'Family was largely dysfunctional. Wife was kind of frizzy. The boy kept changing the color of his hair every other day – orange, pink, Day-Glo purple. The child was into counterculture. You can imagine this didn't go over big with his father, who probably provoked it. Rebellion works that way,' she says. 'It put the child in a fix. A squeeze between the mother and the father when they split. Weekends with the old man doing bivouac, then back to Mom who coddled him. The father would buzz-cut the colored hair every chance he got.'

'Sounds like a nightmare.'

'For a fourteen-year-old boy,' she says, 'it couldn't be anything but.'

'This action the judges took. Is there some suspicion Davidson could be involved?'

'In Suade's murder?'

I nod.

She shakes her head, doesn't know. 'With a bunch of judges, who could tell what's on their minds? The original secret clan,' says Susan. 'Never anything on their lips but a million views on every subject in their heads. And Davidson violated the cardinal rule. He brought controversy on the

236

court. But why are you asking about Davidson if Ontaveroz is your man?'

'One thing about the practice of criminal law,' I tell her. 'You never want to shun a good alternative theory.'

Like the chasm that divides rich from poor, criminal cases in this county are tried on the other side of the divide, across the fourth-story bridge in the antiquated criminal courts building. Growth in crime is invariably the justification for expanding justice budgets in this state as well as others, though the money always seems to be split in other ways when it finally arrives.

The county's Hall of Justice is reserved for civil cases, silk-socked lawyers with their rolling brief-boxes full of documents, and corporate clients in worsted pinstripes, with escalators to carry them to the upper floors.

Here there are stained-glass windows honoring various states, something discovered in a county basement at the start of construction a few years ago. These have been installed at the head of each escalator as you rise through the first four floors. They are mounted in decorative wood moldings and surrounded by old photos of county judges, some of them in stayed collars, and long since departed, not only from the court, but from this world.

This morning I have a sense that I am about to visit one of these relics-in-the-making.

The corridor outside Davidson's office is a barricade of furniture. A cordovan leather sofa on a piano dolly blocks the hall on one side, while two leather office chairs stacked one atop the other finish off the labyrinth on the other. I have to squeeze sideways between them to get through.

Beyond the door, down the hall is a table, and on top of it are two round files, office trash cans of teak, and cardboard boxes with no tops, an assortment of personal objects inside of each, ashtrays and a commemorative gavel sticking out of one of them. There is a stack of framed degrees and licenses, the remnants from a wall of respect next to the boxes.

The door is partway open, the frosted glass panel on the top is lettered on the inside in gold paint, the words PRESIDING JUDGE. Underneath, the letters *idson* are being scraped off the glass by a man in white overalls.

I stick my head through the door. There's no one at the clerk's desk, so I look at the guy on his knees behind the door.

'Is the judge in?'

The workman doesn't answer, but gestures with his head toward chambers down a little corridor in back of the clerk's desk.

There's no one stopping me, so I walk in. I can hear a voice inside. I wander in that direction. As I round the clerk's station, I can see the door to the judge's chamber is open. I stop at the open door and look in.

A tall man, graying close-cropped hair, his head well above the high back of the executive leather chair, is seated facing away from me talking on the phone as I stand in the doorway.

'Jim, listen, I don't blame anybody. I know you are. I know. I know. There's no need to explain. They did what they had to do. And I appreciate your call. I do. Yes, we'll have to get together for a drink . . . Tonight I'm busy . . . When this settles down.'

Behind him a cardboard box, half full of items, is the only

thing on the otherwise-bare surface of the desk. There's a signed baseball on a trophy pedestal sticking out of the top. The rough lettering on the white baseball makes it look as if it might have been signed by kids.

Except for a set of codes on the shelves to my left, and a single item in an ornate framed walnut case on the far wall, the room feels naked, stripped down.

'I don't know for sure. They're supposed to tell me this afternoon. I think they're putting me in department fourteen. But it's probably temporary. From there, I don't know.'

I don't want to be eavesdropping, so I rap the back of my knuckles down low on the surface of the open door.

He spins around in the chair to look at me. Thin gray eyebrows, hollow cheeks, and a long face, punctuated by a pencil-thin mustache, the Great Santini, only taller and leaner. It's a face with character, most of it stern. He holds up a hand as if to beckon me to hold on a second.

'Jim, listen, I'm gonna have to go. Somebody just walked in. No, listen, there's no need to talk to anybody. But I'm glad you called. And say hello to Joyce for me. Take care.' He hangs up, turns his attention to me.

'Can I help you?'

'Sorry to bother you. Your clerk wasn't outside. The man at the door said you were in.'

'I'm sort of between clerks right now,' he says. 'You look familiar. I've seen you around the courthouse.'

'My name's Paul Madriani. I do criminal defense. You might say I'm new to town. From up north.'

'Where up north?'

'Capital City.'

'I used to testify on a lot of legislation up there,' he says.

'No need to stand in the doorway,' he says. 'Come on in. I'd offer you a chair, but they're both out in the hall along with my couch.'

'I noticed.'

'Usually this doesn't happen until election time.' He's busy in one of the drawers of the desk, until he looks up and sees my questioning expression.

'Musical chairs,' he says. 'You don't want to be the one with furniture out in the hall when the tune stops. They're moving me to one of the closets downstairs. As soon as they find one small enough, with a naked lightbulb.' He looks at his watch. 'The movers were supposed to be here at ten. They're running late. I have a feeling everything's gonna be running late with the new regime,' he says.

'I won't take much of your time. I wanted to introduce myself.'

'Last week that might have done you some good,' he says. 'As of today, I'm just one of the drone bees.'

'It's the drones that hear the cases,' I tell him.

'A criminal lawyer with diplomacy,' he says. 'You'll go far.'

He starts working through one of the open drawers on the other side of his desk. A stapler, a little plastic tray of paper clips and pencils. He lifts these out and carefully sets them into the open box so as not to spill anything.

'You don't mind if I work while we talk?' he says. 'I'd like to be out of here before noon. The new tenant is coming in, and I'd like to be gone. Judge Mosher. Do you know her?'

'I can't say that I've had the pleasure.'

'You could stick around, kiss her ring,' he says. 'I'd

240

introduce you, but I'm not sure I'd be doing you any favors.'

'Actually, it's you I wanted to see.'

His brow furrows.

'I represent Jonah Hale.'

He is poker-faced, says nothing, but I can tell by the eyes that the brain has shifted into another gear.

'So you got a piece of the Suade murder?' he says. 'I heard there were two lawyers.'

'My partner and I.'

'Why do you want to see me?'

I try to edge into it as delicately as I can.

'It's the task of every lawyer in a case,' I tell him. 'Investigating the facts, gathering information.'

'What kind of information?' He stops fishing in the drawer for a moment and gives me his undivided attention.

'I'm told you're one of the few members on the court with firsthand knowledge of Zolanda Suade.'

He says nothing, simply stares at me, a wicked smile under the hairy pencil.

'If you mean I threw her ass in jail?'

'That's what I mean.'

'You should learn to be more direct,' says Davidson. 'On the subject of Zolanda Suade I have no comment. In case you haven't noticed, there's pending litigation.'

'I'm told she provided cover that allowed your wife to disappear with your son.'

He gives me a quizzical look. Something sideways, an animal hearing a strange sound.

'Just being direct,' I tell him.

He gets out of his chair to see if there's anyone in

241

the corridor outside, like a stenographer taking notes or his successor with a tape recorder. Then he quietly closes the door.

He stands ten inches from my face, then lifts one flap of my coat. I realize he's looking to see if I'm wired.

Satisfied, he steps back a few inches, studies me a second, weighing if he should speak. Venom gets the better of him.

'You can talk to anybody who knows me. They'll tell you I have a good number of faults,' he says. 'I suffer from arrogance, a bad temper, and impatience, but hypocrisy is not numbered among my character flaws. I shed no tears when Suade was killed. The woman was pathologic. She had absolute contempt for the law and everything and anyone associated with it. As far as she was concerned, she *was* the law, judge, jury, and jailer. And if your client shot her, he did the world an immeasurable favor. Now that's all I have to say on the subject, and if you repeat it to anyone, I'll deny it.'

'It sounds like you knew her well.'

He looks at me. Our eyes lock. 'I wish I'd never met her,' he says, then turns his back and walks to the desk.

There's a knock on the door. A second later it opens, some guy in overalls pushing a furniture dolly.

I step across the room, out of the way. Davidson reaches his chair and turns to catch me gazing at the object in the walnut case, hanging on the wall.

'It's a commemorative gold cup,' he says. 'Forty-five automatic. A gift from my officers when I left the Corps. And in case you're wondering, it's the wrong caliber.'

'I know.' He can't help but notice the disappointment in my voice.

Two movers now picking up boxes, stacking them on the dolly, eunuchs to a cryptic conversation.

'It was good to meet you.' I'm headed for the door, almost there when he pipes up.

'By the way,' he says. 'I wouldn't want you wasting your time. That evening, I had a speaking engagement. A group of lawyers up in Orange County.' He's talking about the day Suade was murdered. 'I left court early, in the middle of the afternoon, to beat the traffic,' he says, 'and I had a passenger. A deputy district attorney.' He arches his eyebrows as he says this. 'Stan Chased. You might want to check with him.'

'I'm sure there's no need to do that.'

Davidson has told me what I needed to know. He is hot, has a temper, a mountain of motive, and what appears to be a titanium-clad alibi.

CHAPTER
EIGHTEEN

Courtrooms in America are laid out with an eye toward turning defendants into furniture. The counsel table for the prosecution is parked, as it is today, right next to the jury box so that the DA can pass winks and nods to jurors without fear of getting a kink in his neck.

Harry and I, with Jonah at the far end, are seated at the defense table, ten yards away, clear on the other side of the room. Between the two sets of lawyers is a rostrum nearly as tall as a man and twice as wide. Erected in the gap between the two contending teams of lawyers, this podium stands directly in line with the judge's bench so that even if Jonah wanted to look down the line to make eye contact with jurors, he couldn't.

It's like seats under the bleachers at a basketball game, except that here, Harry says you can't even grab an occasional glance up a passing skirt. While Jonah may have a jury of his peers, in this setting so would the chair he is sitting in.

The panel of twelve, tried and true, has already been

seated, with five alternates down from six. One of them begged off two days after opening arguments for reasons of health.

We have nine women, three men. Two of them work for the phone company, which seems to be disproportionately represented on nearly every jury I have ever seen. Whether it's civic pride, or that they get paid time-and-a-half for jury service I've never figured out.

Several of the jurors are older. This could be an advantage, given the facts. There is no way that prosecutors can avoid the issue of Amanda, Jonah's granddaughter, and the inference that Suade played a part in her disappearance. This is key to their theory of motive in the murder.

On the other side, behind the prosecution table, directly behind the railing, sits the widower Harold Morgan, Suade's husband. He is tall, slender, urbane, with gray hair parted on the left and a bow tie. He looks the part of some Ivy League think-tanker, only here he has the explosive potential of cordite, sitting as he does in a sea of reporters. I have seen him outside in the hall, holding forth in front of the cameras, calmly intoning that all he seeks is justice.

When asked whether he would favor the death penalty if Jonah is convicted, Morgan looked at the reporter, and said he would have to defer judgment on the question until he sees the evidence.

Mary Hale sits one row behind us, up close to the railing on our side so that on occasion Jonah can turn and talk to her during breaks. She is worried about his health. There have been some spikes in his blood pressure over the last week.

The doctor is now seeing him nearly every day, monitoring his pressure and his medication.

Though Jonah is depressed, we have one advantage in the social skirmish to win empathy with the jury. It is Jonah's affable nature. He tends to smile at the world, all the jurors as they come and go from the jury box, at the older women, and the young checkout girl from Vons, the car salesman from auto row, and the school teacher from the South Bay as well as the man who does bookkeeping for a large commercial nursery out in La Mesa. Some of them actually smile back.

This last, the bookkeeper, is a concern. Ryan fought hard to keep him on the panel, and by the time the accountant popped up we had used up our peremptory challenges and were shooting blanks.

People with ledgerlike minds can be a problem when it comes to weighing evidence. They like things that add up at the bottom of every column. Unfortunately, the facts in a criminal trial, like most of the true mysteries of life, are seldom that neat. When chaos happens meticulous minds tend to impose their own sense of order, filling in gaps of reasonable doubt with assumptions based on probability. Scientists, engineers, and mathematicians are seen to be high risks for the defense. Give them a problem and they are trained to solve it, sometimes bending jury instructions along the way.

It is just that kind of reach that Ruben Ryan is hoping for. His case is entirely circumstantial, the kind that put most defendants in prison blues, and fills the cells of death row at Quentin.

Today Ryan works the angle of death. The medical examiner, a beady-eyed little man wearing round horn-rims with glass as thick as a telescope lens. His name is Howard Morris. He is telling us how it happened, making sure the jury understands that Suade didn't die of old age.

'You autopsied the body?' says Ryan. He works from the podium.

'I did.'

'Can you tell us the cause of death?'

'Two bullet wounds, one of which was fatal,' he says. 'The fatal round entered the victim at the mid-thoracic region on the left side. About here.' Morris points to his own chest with a finger just below the left breast pocket of his shirt, opening his coat for the jury to see.

'It passed through the intercostal muscles missing the ribs, perforating the left lung, and severing the aorta.'

'And that was what caused death, the severing of the aorta?'

'Yes. I would estimate that she died within thirty seconds. Certainly less than a minute after receiving this wound.'

'The other bullet. You say that the wound from that round was not fatal?'

'That's correct. It passed through the right chest wall at an oblique angle, fracturing two ribs, exiting the chest and entering the right arm where it lodged in the area around the elbow.'

'But that would not have been fatal?'

'No. Not with proper treatment.'

'Did you recover that bullet as well?'

'I did.'

'And was it the same as the first in terms of type and caliber?'

'It was. Nine-millimeter pistol round,' he says.

'Do you have any opinion as to the distance these bullets may have traveled before they struck the victim?'

Morris thinks for a moment, makes a face as if in judgment, then says, 'Close range.'

'Were they contact wounds? Do you know what I mean by that?' says Ryan. 'Maybe you should explain for the jury,' he says.

'A contact wound is generally one in which the muzzle of the weapon is held against the body at the time it is discharged, fired.'

'And were either of these wounds contact wounds?'

'I would say probably not. If they were, they were incomplete.'

'What do you mean by incomplete?'

'What I mean is that the muzzle was not completely pressed against the victim. What you would call a hard-contact wound.'

'And how did you determine this?'

'In a hard- or direct-contact wound there would be soot and metallic particles, vaporized metal from the bullet and the cartridge case, maybe some primer residue and powder particles driven into the wound track along with the bullet.'

'And was there any of this residue in either of the wound tracks you found in the victim? Ms Suade?'

'Not that I could detect.'

'So would you say that the muzzle of the murder weapon was not held directly against the body of the victim?'

'That would be the conclusion I would draw,' says Morris.

Ryan mulls this over for a moment, thinks, looks at the ceiling.

'Let me give you a hypothetical,' he says. 'Let's suppose that the assailant was seated in the driver's seat of a medium-sized vehicle, and that the victim was seated in the passenger seat of that same car. A distance of say two, two and a half feet. And let us suppose that the assailant fired two rounds at that distance into the body of the victim. Would the wounds in this case be consistent with those facts.'

'I would say so. Yes,' says Morris.

It's clear where Ryan is headed; cold-blooded, all the signs of an execution except that here the bullets were not pumped into the back of the victim's head. He collects his papers and steps away from the podium.

'That's all I have, Your Honor.'

I get up, take a yellow notepad with me, and another sheaf of papers, typed forms stapled together.

'Doctor, you said there were two items you would look for in determining whether there was a contact wound involved in this shooting. Residue in the wound tract is one of them?'

'That's correct.'

'And you say you found none of that?'

'That's right.'

'Did you examine the victim's clothing?'

He nods.

'Is that a yes?'

'Yes.'

'Did you find any powder tattooing on the victim's clothing? You know what that is, don't you?'

Morris handles it well, doesn't display any lapse of thought or judgment here. Just a simple, straight 'Yes.'

'Could you tell the jury what tattooing is?'

'Generally lesions, reddish-brown or orange-red around the entrance wound of a bullet.'

'That's if they're on the skin of the victim, right?'

'Correct.'

'But they could also be masked by heavy clothing if the victim were wearing such garments? I mean to say, isn't it a fact that in such a situation evidence of tattooing might appear on the clothing, not on the skin?'

'I've seen that,' he says.

'Did you find any evidence of tattooing on the victim's clothing in this case?'

'There was some,' he says. 'But that can occur out as far as eighteen to twenty-four inches.'

'I'm not asking you that. I'm asking you if you found evidence of tattooing, hot particles of powder and escaping gas from a firearm's discharge on or near the entrance wounds or point of bullet impact on the victim's clothing?'

'I found some,' he says.

'Thank you. Now this would indicate that the muzzle of the firearm that fired the two shots was close enough to leave these marks from hot powder residue, correct?'

'As I say, eighteen to twenty-four inches,' says Morris.

'You're saying that the muzzle of the firearm when fired was that far away?'

'It could have been,' says Morris. He's looking at Ryan now.

'That's for a thirty-eight caliber, isn't it, Doctor? Aren't we talking a smaller round here? Less powder in the cartridge?'

'I don't know,' he says.

'Isn't it a fact, Doctor, that the two bullets in question were not nine-millimeter rounds, but three-eighty caliber, what's known as a nine-millimeter kurz, or short, round?'

'They were nine millimeter in diameter,' he says. Morris trying to make it clear that he didn't deceive the jury, just misled it a little.

'You know what a kurz round is, don't you?'

'Yes.'

'And do you know the difference between that type of round and the nine-millimeter luger round?'

'It's *shorter*?' Morris says it with a little rise in the voice on the word *shorter*, as if it's a question, then smiles as he looks at the jury. Gets a few chuckles.

'Doctor, isn't it normal procedure in an autopsy to weigh bullets removed from a body to determine the grain weight of those bullets?'

'Yes.'

'And did you weigh these bullets?'

'I did.'

'Do you recall the grain weight of the two rounds in question?'

'I'd have to look at my report,' he says.

'May I approach the witness?' I ask Peltro.

He nods. I have the stapled sheaf of paper in my hand. I show it to Morris.

'Page five of the autopsy report,' I tell the court. Ryan flipping pages.

'Looks like ninety-four point three grains on one, and the other was fragmented. Hit the bone,' he says. 'That one was only eighty-two, with fragments.'

'Let's concentrate on the bullet weighing ninety-four point

252

three grains for the moment.' I turn, heading back toward the rostrum. 'Is that the usual grain weight for a nine-millimeter bullet?'

'Your Honor, this goes beyond the size and caliber of the round,' says Ryan.

'If the witness knows, he can answer the question,' says Peltro.

'I'm not sure,' says Morris. He's looking for a way out, taking the judge's lead.

'Doctor, isn't it a fact that the normal weight for a nine-millimeter bullet, the usual store-bought round, is a hundred and fifteen grains?'

'A hundred and fifteen sounds right,' he says.

'And yet both of these bullets are well under that weight.'

He says nothing, just nods.

'Do you know the grain weight of a three-eighty or short nine-millimeter bullet?'

He makes a face, a dozen expressions of concession, then comes up with it off the top of his head. 'Ninety-five grains?' He says it like a question, but it's clear he knows the answer.

'Right. So isn't it likely these were three-eighty rounds.'

'Probably,' he says. 'Still nine millimeter in terms of caliber.' He won't give up on the point.

'But in a smaller cartridge, right?'

'Probably.'

'And less powder in that cartridge?'

'I would say so.'

'So your estimates of the distance, the maximum distance, I might add, for tattooing aren't correct at eighteen to twenty-four inches, are they?'

'That's approximate,' he says.

'Isn't it more likely that the maximum range is closer to twelve inches?'

'It's possible,' he says.

All I'm going to get from the witness, little victories composed of possibilities.

'Now that's the farthest distance we're talking about, isn't it?' I start to bear down.

'Perhaps.'

I look up at him.

'Yes,' he says.

'Wasn't there scorching on her vest?'

'There was some scorching.'

'Wouldn't this point to a much closer shot than your previous testimony would indicate?'

'As I said, these are estimates of range. Of the distance.'

'Isn't it possible that the victim could have struggled for the weapon in question?'

'What do you mean, struggled?' he says.

'Doctor, did you find powder residue on the victim's hands?'

'Defensive wounds,' he says. 'This would be expected if she had raised her hands in a defensive gesture as the gun was being fired.'

I begin paging through his report as he studies me from the witness box through spectacled Coke-bottle bottoms.

'Doctor, did you bag the hands of the victim at the scene.'

'No.'

'Why not?'

'I didn't think it was necessary.'

'Isn't it usual procedure in most homicides to place a victim's hands in paper bags, tie them off around the wrist to preserve trace evidence under the fingernails?'

'Sometimes,' says Morris. 'Depends on the crime.'

'I see. And for what kind of crime would you bag the defendant's hands?'

He thinks for a second. 'A rape where the victim was killed,' he says. 'You might find skin or hair under the fingernails.'

'What else?'

He looks around, searching his mind. 'A stabbing where there might have been a scuffle. Fight for the weapon.'

'What else?'

He shakes his head, not sure, run out of answers.

'Isn't it a fact, Doctor, that proper procedure calls for the bagging of the victim's hands in virtually every homicide to prevent cross contamination.'

'Some people might do it,' he says. 'It's a matter of judgment.'

'Is that right? Your judgment?'

He nods.

'And yet your report shows gunpowder residue on the victim's hands?'

'As I said, evidence of defensive movements on her part,' says Morris.

'On the back of the victim's right hand?' I say.

This stops him.

'Is it usual for a victim to extend her hand with the palm facing herself in a defensive gesture?'

'It's possible if she didn't have time,' he says.

I slap his report on the podium. 'Isn't it a fact, Doctor, that the powder residue you found on the victim's right hand is consistent with her holding the gun? That, in fact, you found residue on her other hand as well, and that both hands were on this weapon when it was fired?

'Objection, Your Honor. There's no evidence that the victim shot herself.' Ryan's on his feet.

'I didn't say that.'

Ryan has planted the seed. I make the most of it. 'But now that counsel mentions it, there may be as much evidence for suicide in this case as for murder.'

'I object.' Ryan pounding on the table now.

'The jury will disregard the last comment,' says Peltro. 'Mr Madriani, we'll have no more of that.'

'Yes, Your Honor.'

'I ask that the question be stricken,' says Ryan.

'What was the question?' says the judge.

'I asked the witness whether the gunpowder residue found on the victim's hands was consistent with her holding the gun.'

'And I object,' says Ryan. 'The question contains an inference unsupported by the evidence.'

'What inference is that?' I ask.

He looks at me, refusing to explain in front of the jury, maybe dig himself in deeper. He knows I'm headed toward Suade's little gun.

Peltro's waving us toward the bench, telling the jury to take a break. They file out, one of the bailiffs right behind them.

'What's this about?' Peltro looking at Ryan down from the bench. He doesn't have a clue as to where I'm going because we have deferred our opening until the start of our case. I had to do this in order to preserve comment on Ontaveroz, in hopes that I can find the evidence.

'He's trying to make my witness put the gun in the victim's hand. There's no evidence she shot herself,' says Ryan.

Two reporters from the front row start edging forward, leaning toward the railing, seeing if they can catch what's happening.

Peltro sees them, gestures with a forefinger. 'Maybe you'd like to get some coffee outside,' he says. And lose their seats to the horde in line? They sit back down.

Peltro looks at me. 'There is evidence,' I tell him, 'that the victim owned a gun. A three-eighty caliber pistol.'

With this, his eyebrows arch. He looks at Ryan.

'There's absolutely no evidence she had it at the scene,' says Ryan.

'There's no evidence she didn't,' I say. 'You didn't find the weapon,' I remind him.

'Are you arguing that this is the murder weapon?' Peltro's asking me.

'We're saying it's a possibility, Your Honor.'

'Do you dispute that she owned a gun?' He's back to Ryan.

'No, Your Honor.'

'Have you found that gun? The one she owned?'

Ryan shakes his head.

Peltro's heard enough. He leans back in his chair. 'I'm gonna allow the question,' he says, and motions us back. They bring the jury back in. Like calisthenics, jack-in-the-box, these people may get more exercise than they want.

'Doctor Morris. I ask you again, isn't it a fact that the

evidence of gunpowder residue found on the victim's hands is wholly consistent with her holding the gun?'

'It's possible,' he says. 'It's not entirely clear.'

'Fine. Let's concentrate on the right hand,' I tell him. 'Are you familiar with the concept of blow back as it relates to the discharge of a firearm?'

'I think so,' he says.

'And what is your understanding of that concept?'

'That somebody holds a gun and fires it, that some residue floats back over the hand of the shooter.'

'And where does it float? Over the palm?'

'No.'

'Because the palm is closed, holding the gun, right?'

'Yes.'

'So where do you find this residue, Doctor?'

'Over the back of the hand,' he says. He touches the crotch of his right hand between the forefinger and thumb, brushing toward the wrist.

'And where did you find the gunshot residue on the victim's right hand? Wasn't it in precisely this area?'

'Some of it,' he says.

'Thank you, Doctor.'

CHAPTER
NINETEEN

This evening Murphy is waiting for us, sitting on the stoop out in front of the office when Harry and I get back from court. I'm toting my briefcase full of papers. Harry's behind me with a rolling dolly, one of those fold-up contraptions people used to carry luggage on at the airport. He's carting two large sample cases full of documents and an open cardboard box on top, documents of evidence in the state's case along with items we may use ourselves to cross their expert witnesses.

'Why the hell don't you return your messages?' says Murphy. 'I've been tryin' to reach you for two days.' He's up on his feet as he sees us rolling past Miguel's, the hot sounds of salsa coming from the jukebox inside.

'You find Bob and Jack?' I ask him.

'Next best thing,' he says. 'I located Jason Crow. Jessica's old boyfriend.' The luggage handler from the airport.

Twenty minutes later, I'm sitting in the passenger seat as Murphy guns his beat-up Chevy Blazer past the Gaslight

District and up Golden Hill. Contrary to the name, the area is anything but. The neighborhood sits above downtown, south of Balboa Park. It's on the edges of aging light industry: here there are mostly apartments, run-down old homes carved into flats.

Murphy turns down one of the side streets south of Market, goes two blocks, looking for an address, a piece of paper in his hand as he steers.

'There,' he says. He pulls over to the curb in front of a large three-story wood-framed house. In its time it might have been part of doctors' row, but its time is long gone. The white clapboard siding is badly in need of paint. Hanging over the edge of one of the gutters on the roof, off the side, is an old television antenna, a relic from the fifties. It's clinging to a single frayed remnant of wire that probably hasn't carried a signal in thirty years. One of the windows in the front is punched out, the pane replaced by a piece of plywood weathered enough to look as if it's been there at least a decade.

There are lights on upstairs, in the front and along the side. Two naked bulbs lighting up the porch.

Murphy's looking out the other way, off to his left now, checking something written on the scrap of paper in his hand.

'Little Datsun over there,' he says. 'That's Crow's. I got the license from DMV. He bought it about a week ago, paid cash. But the seller filled out the papers. Guess he was afraid Crow'd hit somebody and he'd get sued. It's how I got the address.'

'Sounds like Crow's come into some money,' I say.

'Probably somebody else's,' says Murphy.

We get out. Close the doors quietly and climb the wooden front steps.

Murphy checks the gang of nameplates next to the line of bell buttons on the wall by the front door. One of them I can see is a name penned in block letters, ballpoint ink on paper a little cleaner than the rest.

Murphy turns to me and holds up three fingers, then finds the button that corresponds and presses it. Doesn't wait, presses it again. Punching it fast like the key on a telegraph. We can hear it buzzing somewhere upstairs.

'Whaddaya want?' Not a friendly tone, a voice like it's coming from a tin can on a string. It pours from a squawk box over the door, round cover with vents cut in it.

'Some kids beat the shit out of a car across the street,' says Murphy. 'Gray Datsun. Somebody said it belonged to you.'

'What the fuck? Who is this?'

'A neighbor,' says Murphy.

'Gimme a second.'

We wait, maybe ten seconds, then the sound of boots on the wooden stairs inside. Counting the cadence of steps, vision of hands on the banisters, skipping two steps at a time, sailor on a ladder. Shadow on the glass of the front door. He turns the lock and opens it up, throws the screen door out, like fuck whoever happens to be standing there.

But Murphy's already stepped aside. He's standing between me and Crow, so that Crow, when he steps out the door, walks right into Murphy's fist, shot from a cannon at crotch level.

There's a groan, a good octave higher than the average male's range. Crow doubles over onto his knees on the wooden porch, both hands going for the jewels, but a beat too late.

'Jeeze! Did ya hurt yourself?' Murphy's over him now, grabbing one arm, forcing it up behind Crow's back, turning the fingers and wrist for maximum effect. He's like a gnome, little man with magical powers, as he lifts Crow off the floor.

'Ohhh, shit.' Crow's face is a shade of purple I've not seen on human skin before.

'Matter of leverage,' says Murphy as he looks at me over his shoulder, pushing Crow ahead of him up the stairs. 'All depends what hurts more,' he says. For the moment it's Crow's wrist, arm, and elbow, though his testicles aren't doing too well either. Bent legs shuttling up the stairs, stumbling as they go, one hand twisted up nearly making it to the back of his head, the other buried between his legs. 'What do they say about idle hands?' says Murphy. 'Devil's workshop.'

Two minutes later we're inside Crow's apartment, the door bolted and the shades drawn.

The place is like a rat's nest. Part of a hamburger with fuzz growing on it sits on its gold foil wrapper on a card table. Around it I count at least six open beer cans, two of them on their sides. More on the floor. There's a fold-out sofa for a bed, no sheets, just a blanket that looks as though it hasn't been washed since it was purchased.

Magazines with pictures of nude women on the covers, most of them in obscene positions with strategic private parts blacked out, are strewn over the floor. There's a broken-down chair in one corner. Murphy plops onto this.

'Oh shit.' It's becoming Crow's mantra. He's doubled over on the mattress pulled out of the couch, lying on his side, cupping his crotch with one hand, making sure everything's still there, trying to make his other elbow bend again in the right direction.

His face is now regaining some of the color from the shades of deep blue I'd seen while he was on his knees on the front porch.

'What the *fuck*?'

'I think the door got ya,' says Murphy. 'Gotta watch out for those knobs.'

'My car.' It's like Crow's in a fog. Last thing he heard.

'Don't worry about it,' says Murphy. 'We chased 'em off. You are Jason Crow?'

'Who's asking?'

'The same Jason Crow dated Jessica Hale?' says Murphy.

'Ohhh.' Too much pain to answer.

'Is that a yes?' Murphy's up out of the chair, moving toward Crow on the couch.

'Yesss.'

Murphy nods toward me, like my witness. Then strolls toward the window, all five-foot-five of him, and peeks at the edge of the shade, out along the side of the house toward the street.

'Have you seen her recently?' I ask Crow

'Who?'

'Jessica Hale.'

'No. Why do you want to know?'

'When's the last time you saw her?'

'I don't know. Been a while.'

'Try to remember,' I tell him.

'Maybe I can help him,' says Murphy.

'I haven't seen her in two years. Not since I went in.'

263

'Prison?' I say.

He nods. He's probably lying.

'Bitch hung me out to dry. Gave the cops some of the stuff.'

'Drugs.'

'No. The stuff we took.' He's talking about stolen property, the burglaries that sent him up. 'She turned tail on me. When they caught her.' Slowly rolling onto his back now, trying to stretch out, one leg then the other.

'Just stay down there,' says Murphy. 'Let's not get frisky.'

'Do you know a man named Esteban Ontaveroz?' I ask.

Crow looks at me, beady eyes, deep set, a face that would grow a beard if it could, a few long straggly hairs on the chin. Hair on his head looks like it's been cut with a butcher knife.

'Do you know him?'

He nods. 'What do you want with him?'

'I'm told that Jessica lived with him a while back?'

'They knew each other.'

'When was the last time you saw Ontaveroz?'

He makes a face. 'Down in Mexico,' he says. 'I don't know. Maybe three years ago.'

'Was he with Jessica then?'

'Yeah. They had a place together. Outside La Paz. In the hills. She told me about it. I never saw it. They used to skip over, spend time in Mazatlán together. Fuckin' skiing behind cigarette boats. They'd pick up some blow. Do some business,' he says.

'Cocaine?'

He nods. 'She'd carry it for him, then take a cut.'

'Money?'

He shakes his head. 'She'd take it in drugs. Never had a fuckin' dime in her pocket. He had to give her tickets to get back. She'd fly in, bring the shit with her in suitcases. That's what she told me, anyway.'

'You never saw any of it?'

He makes a face. 'Once or twice,' he says.

'But you saw Ontaveroz and Jessica together?'

He nods. 'Sure.'

'You know any reason why Ontaveroz would want Jessica dead?'

Suddenly his eyes go from me, over to Murphy and back again, all in a heartbeat. 'Is she dead?'

'Do you know why Ontaveroz might want to kill her? Why he might want to find her?'

'I heard stories,' he says. 'But I don't know.'

'What kind of stories?'

'That she took some money. But it may be just rumors,' he says.

'Who did you hear this from?'

'Some guy. Con up at Folsom,' he says. 'He knew her. Told me he met her in Mexico. But I don't know if he was tellin' me the truth.'

'What was his name?'

'Eddie. Eddie something.'

'Is he still inside?'

'Unless they're givin' out passes to lifers,' he says. 'He's still there.'

'But you can't remember his last name?'

He thinks for a moment, then shakes his head. 'If I think about it maybe.'

'If you remember it, write it down.'

He nods.

'You ever work for Ontaveroz?'

'Me? No. No way. Never dealt drugs,' he says. Like his high sense of morals wouldn't permit it.

'He just let you hang around, is that it?'

'Sometimes,' he says. 'I did some things for him. But never drugs.'

'Like what?'

'You know,' he says.

'No, I don't.'

'I'd sell him stuff. Cheap,' he says. He looks over at Murphy, wondering how this guy, like a bull without legs, got the better of him, not sure he wants to find out again.

'What kind of stuff?'

'The good stuff. Televisions. Cameras. Four-foot Sony. The big screens. He liked those.'

'And you, of course, found these in other people's homes?'

He nods.

'How long did you know Jessica?'

'Few years,' he says. 'We met down in Florida. She was workin' a club.'

'She ever roll over on Ontaveroz? Give him up, maybe to the feds?'

'I don't know nothin' about that.' He's working his sore elbow with the other hand. His legs still propped up on the bed, bent at the knees. 'All I know's Ontaveroz had more to offer.'

I raise an eyebrow in question.

'Jessica was heavy into lines,' says Crow. 'Face was always bent over looking in somebody else's mirror with a straw up her nose. Mexican had more snow than a fuckin' avalanche,' he says. 'She told me bein' with him was like bein' in a blizzard. Anytime she wanted it, it was there,' he says. 'We saw each other once in a while, but once she met Ontaveroz, got a taste of his blow, that was it.'

'But you saw her when she came north? When she brought the drugs up?'

Now his eyes become little slits. 'I don't know,' he says. 'Like I say, I just saw her once or twice after that. But I don't know what she was into.'

'Apparently she was into other people's houses with you,' I tell him.

'That,' he says. 'That was just a sideline.'

'For her, or for you?'

'Her. Jessie could be a fuckin' freak. Specially when she got high. She liked being on the edge. Takin' risks. For her it was just entertainment. Ya know what I mean?'

'Why don't you tell me?'

'She wanted to do some places,' he says. 'You know, cat burglar shit. Dark T-shirts and knives, break in at night, people still inside. That's a good way to get shot,' he says. 'They think it's wetbacks crossin' over to kill 'em in their beds.'

'And instead it's just you and some hophead with butcher knives,' I tell him.

'Yeah. She wanted to crawl around in the dark with the fuckin' owner snorin' in the sack. She got off on that kinda crap.'

'She took some of the stuff, didn't she?'

He looks at me as if he's not sure what I'm talking about.

'The stuff you stole.'

267

'Sure. Some of it. Mostly the stuff hard to unload,' he says. 'Clothes. Few computers. She liked the kinky shit. Give her a thong bikini with sequins, ya'd think she died and went to heaven. Be giddy for an hour.'

'I'm hearing that some of the things she took had a high value,' I say.

'Cops always overvalue that shit,' he says. 'So they can jam ya in the joint forever, piss off the judge when they catch ya. She got crap,' he says.

'Then you went down on the burglaries?'

He nods.

'She went away for drugs?'

'Yeah.'

'And you haven't seen her since?'

'I told you. No.'

'And you haven't seen Ontaveroz?'

'Why do you keep asking?'

'Just want to make sure you got your story straight,' I tell him.

I look at Murphy and nod.

He reaches into the inside pocket of his sport coat, pulls out a folded piece of paper, walks over and slaps Crow on the shoulder with it. 'You've been served,' says Murphy.

'With what?' Crow recoils from the folded paper, doesn't want to touch it.

'With a subpoena to appear in court, day after tomorrow,' I tell him. 'Nine o'clock in the morning. Location's on the subpoena.'

'What for?'

'Just be there,' I tell him. 'If you're not, we'll report it to your parole officer. It's a summons to appear. You don't

268

show up, you'll get your ass picked up, thrown in the slammer. Do you understand?'

He nods.

'It's a lawful order of the court,' I tell him. 'You don't show up, your parole could be violated. And believe me, I'll make every effort.'

Murphy flips a business card onto him on the bed. 'You have any problems, you call me at that number,' he says.

He picks it up, looks at it, then at me. 'Who are you?'

'You don't need to know who I am. You just report to the courthouse every day, same time, nine o'clock, until you're called to testify. You understand?'

'I don't know nothin' about the drugs,' he says.

'Do you understand?'

'Yeah.' Beady eyes filled with resentment, but scared.

Crow's testimony may not be worth much, a convicted felon. Ryan may have him for lunch. But he can make my case in an offer of proof, to put Jessica and Ontaveroz together, the first link in the chain that I need to build the Mexican into my defense.

CHAPTER
TWENTY

Having laid the medical basis for Suade's murder, and been burned in the process, Ryan now turns his attention to more solid ground, the evidence tending to tie Jonah to the killing. The state seems to have regrouped, and learned a lesson: keep it simple and direct.

'Could you state your name for the record?' says Ryan.

'John Brower.'

'And what is it you do for a living Mr Brower?'

'I'm an Investigator Three with the county of San Diego, Department of Children's Protective Services.'

'And in that capacity could you describe generally your duties?'

'I supervise, or did until recently.' He looks at me as he says this. 'I do mostly field work now. Cases involving crimes against children. Injury cases, some deaths. We respond to complaints of child abuse and neglect.'

'So you're a sworn law enforcement officer with powers to arrest?

'That's right.' Brower puffs out his chest a little, looks over at the jury.

'Officer Brower . . .'

'Investigator's my title,' he says.

'Sorry. Investigator Brower, I want you to direct your attention to earlier this year, around the seventeenth of April. Did you have occasion on or about that date to visit the law offices of Paul Madriani, the defense attorney in this case?'

'Objection.' I'm on my feet. 'Anything this witness heard or saw in my office when I was consulting with my client is privileged.'

'Not so,' says Ryan. 'The witness was invited to the office by Mr Madriani. Counsel made no objection to Mr Brower's presence, nor did the defendant, Mr Hale. In fact they wanted him there.'

'Enough,' says Peltro. 'Not another word.' The judge is shaking his head, angry at Ryan for getting into the details before the court's had a chance to determine whether it's something the jury should hear. He beckons us toward the bench. We have a brief conference, whispers off to the side at the edge of the bench farthest from the jury box. Finally he lifts his head, swivels toward the jury in his chair.

'I'm gonna excuse the jury,' says Peltro. 'Let you get some coffee,' he says.

They've been in the box a total of an hour, and now they're heading out for coffee. The second break this morning because of arguments and sessions in the judge's chambers with counsel. By the time we get to a verdict, they'll all have the jitters from caffeine, and the ones who smoke will be climbing the walls with nicotine withdrawal.

The bailiff clears the box. The door leading to the jury room closes.

'Now what's this all about?'

'What Mr Ryan says is not true. I did not specifically ask for him or invite Mr Brower to my office. I asked his boss to attend a meeting to pursue official matters pertaining to child-protective services. She brought him along.'

'She told us you asked for an investigator.'

I don't respond. I'm not going to allow Ryan to cross-examine me.

'I'll make an offer of proof,' says Ryan, 'if the court will allow the witness to explain how he came to be in Mr Madriani's office.'

'Any objection?' Peltro looks at me.

'I don't think it matters how he came to be there.'

'If you and your client talked in front of him, waived the privilege, I might disagree,' says the judge. He nods to Ryan. 'Ask the witness your questions.'

Ryan's all smiles. 'Investigator Brower, did you speak directly to Mr Madriani before arriving at his office on April seventeenth?'

'No. I was asked to attend the meeting by my boss.'

'And who is that?'

'Susan McKay. She's the director of the Department of Children's Protective Services.

'And do you know whether Ms McKay had spoken directly with Mr Madriani?'

'She said she had. That he wanted her to attend a meeting at his office. She mentioned that he asked for an investigator, and that she wanted me to go with her.'

'That's all hearsay,' I tell Peltro.

'Maybe you'd like us to bring on Susan McKay?' says Ryan. He looks at me as if he's holding a cocked pistol. He'd love this, get into the fact that Susan and I are lovers, that she turned over the dirt on Suade's pistol and has been assisting the defense. Even if he can't get it all before the jury, he could work on poisoning the judge.

'Move along, Mr Ryan.'

'So you attended the meeting at Ms McKay's request?' says Ryan.

'That's right,' says Brower.

'And was Mr Madriani told that you were a law-enforcement officer?'

'He was.'

'And was the defendant, Jonah Hale, in the office at the time?'

'He was.'

'And he was told you were an investigator with the department?'

'That's right.'

'So there was no mystery as to who you were, or what you were doing there?'

'None.'

'And after these introductions, did Mr Madriani and Mr Hale speak openly and freely about the reason why you and Ms McKay were present at the meeting?'

'They did.'

'And what was that reason?'

'They wanted help from the department in locating Mr Hale's granddaughter, who was missing.'

'Missing!' I'm out of my chair now. 'The child was kidnapped by Zolanda Suade.' The jury's out of the box, but

274

the pencils in the front rows are now cutting grooves in paper pads.

'The defendant, Mr Hale, made some allegation to that effect,' says Brower.

'But they made no attempt to maintain confidentiality, to hold side conferences, to speak outside your presence, isn't that so?' says Ryan.

'That's true.'

'That's all,' says Ryan. 'Unless of course Mr Madriani wants us to bring on Ms McKay to testify as to what was said between the two of them leading up to this meeting.' Ryan looks at me as he says this, leaving me to wonder if Susan is waiting outside in the wings under subpoena.

It's the problem we have. There was no confidence to protect at the time of the meeting, only Jonah's indiscretions and wild threats, which I had not foreseen. When we met, there was no crime. Suade was still alive.

'I'm not sure there's a need for more witnesses,' says the judge. 'Mr Madriani. Do you want to cross-examine the witness?'

'No, Your Honor.' There's nothing I could ask Brower that would unring the bell, undo the damage.

'Your Honor, I would submit the offer of proof,' says Ryan. 'And request that I be allowed to inquire as to the conversations that took place in front of Mr Brower in counsel's office.'

Peltro looks down at me from the bench. 'I'm sorry, Mr Madriani, but I see no basis for a privilege as to these conversations,' he says. 'I'll overrule the objection.'

'Your Honor, I'd like a ruling as to the scope. That

this doesn't constitute a wholesale waiver of the entire attorney-client privilege?'

'Mr Ryan, you're not suggesting a complete waiver, are you?'

Ryan hesitates, arches his eyebrows, shrugs a shoulder as if to say, *Why not*? Nothing verbal on the record; it's an open question.

'Then I'll resolve the issue for you,' says Peltro. 'My ruling applies only as to the meeting at which Mr Brower and Ms McKay were present. Anything else,' he says, 'is off-limits. Do you understand?'

'Of course,' says Ryan.

The jury comes back in.

'Investigator Brower, I'd like to refresh the jury's recollection. You say you attended a meeting with Susan McKay at Mr Madriani's office on April seventeenth of this year?'

'That's right.'

'Wasn't that the day that the victim, Zolanda Suade, was killed?'

'It was. She was murdered, I think it was in the early evening.'

'Objection. Assumes facts not in evidence, beyond the scope of any expertise of this witness, and outside of his knowledge, unless he knows more than he's saying.'

The state hasn't determined a time of death, not with any precision, and so Brower is trying to fill one in.

'Strike the last part of the witness's answer,' says Peltro. 'The jury will disregard any suggestions as to the time of death, or the fact that it was a murder. That's what we're here to determine,' says the judge. 'Mr Brower.' Peltro turns his attention toward the witness, knitted eyebrows like Cecil

B. DeMille's vision of God. 'Do us all a favor. Listen to the question, and just answer what's asked. You got it?'

'Yes. Sure. Sorry, Your Honor.' Brower's wearing a heavy sport coat, and starting to sweat.

'Is it safe to say that the meeting occurred on the same day as the victim's death?' Ryan tries to dig him out.

'Yes. I think that's safe.' Brower looks up at the judge for approval. All he gets is a stone idol.

'And what time did you arrive at Mr Madriani's office?'

Now Brower's thinking, not wanting to step in it again. 'It was probably about eleven A.M.'

'And did you arrive with Ms McKay?'

'No. We came separately. I was in the field, and she paged me. We talked by phone. She gave me the address and told me to meet her there.'

'So she took her own car?'

'Right.'

'What time did she get to Mr Madriani's office?'

'About ten minutes after I did.'

'That would make it about ten minutes after eleven?'

'About,' says Brower.

'And was Mr Madriani there when you arrived?'

'No, but his partner was,' says Brower.

'Let the record reflect that the witness has identified Mr Hinds.'

'Was the defendant, Jonah Hale, at the office when you arrived?'

'No.'

'Where was Mr Madriani when you got there?' says Ryan.

'We were told he was . . .'

'Objection, hearsay.'

'Sustained.'

'When did Mr Madriani arrive for the meeting?' says Ryan.

'About, ahh.' Brower thinks for a second. 'About forty-five minutes after I got there.'

'That would make it about eleven forty-five?'

'Sounds right.'

'And was the defendant, Jonah Hale, with him when he arrived?'

'Yes. They came in together.'

'So by eleven forty-five in the morning on the day the victim died, Ms McKay was present, Mr Hale, Mr Madriani, Mr Hinds, and yourself, all present in Mr Madriani's law office.' Ryan makes it sound like a conspiracy. 'Did Mr Madriani tell you why he was late?'

'No.'

'Did he tell you where he'd been – that morning?'

Brower's looking at the prosecutor now, not sure what Ryan wants him to say, whether he's trying to get at where I was just before the meeting, the reason I was late, or something else.

Rather than have his witness step in it, Ryan says, 'Let me rephrase that. At this meeting, did Mr Madriani relate to you and the others present the details of another meeting he'd had earlier that same morning?'

'Oh, that,' he says, 'yeah. He did,' says Brower. Now it's clear. 'He said he'd been to see Zolanda Suade, at her office down in Imperial Beach.'

'Where the victim's body was later found?'

'Objection.'

278

'If he knows, Your Honor. The witness went to the scene later that night,' says Ryan. 'Counsel knows that.' Ryan looks at me. Smiles. He's about to screw me into the wall, and he knows it.

'If the witness has personal knowledge, he can answer the question,' says Peltro.

'Yeah,' says Brower. 'He said he went to her office. It's where they found the body later.'

'And did Mr Madriani say why he went to see the victim?'

'He said he wanted to question her about Mr Hale's granddaughter. Wanted to know what Zolanda Suade knew about the disappearance of the child. Mr Hale's granddaughter.'

'Did Mr Madriani indicate to you whether his meeting with Zolanda Suade that morning was successful?'

'No. It was a disaster,' says Brower.

'How do you define "disaster"?'

'She'd given Madriani a press release she was getting ready to send out to the papers and television stations.'

'What did this press release say?'

'Objection!' I'm on my feet. 'The document speaks for itself.'

'Goes to motive,' says Ryan. 'Let me rephrase the question. Did Mr Madriani describe what was in this press release during the meeting with all of you present?'

'He did.'

'And what did Mr Madriani say the press release said?' Ryan puts the question beyond the pale.

'According to Mr Madriani, Mr Hale was charged with incest with his daughter, as well as child molestation of his granddaughter.' By putting the words in my mouth instead of relating what he read on the press release, Brower gives the accusations more effect.

'And Mr Hale heard all this?'

'He did.'

'And what was his reaction?'

'He was very angry. What you might call ballistic,' says Brower.

'Did Mr Hale ever get to look at the press release in question? In your presence?'

'Sure. It was handed all around. We all saw it.'

'Did Mr Hale say anything?'

'He wanted to know why the law hadn't put a stop to Ms Suade's activities.'

'Did anybody explain this to him?'

'Yeah. Ms McKay told him the department had investigated her several times, but was never able to determine any violations of law. Nothing that we could arrest her on, or get an injunction or a restraining order for.'

'And how did the defendant take this?'

'It seemed to make him even more angry.'

'Did he say anything else?'

'Yes. He said that if the law couldn't deal with Zolanda Suade, there were other ways to deal with her.'

Ryan turns to look at the jury as Brower says this, to make sure they understand the significance, that he's reaching the pinnacle of this testimony. If it were Moses on the mount, the finger of God would be etching the tablets about now.

'Did he explain what he meant by that?' says Ryan.

'He wanted us, meaning the department, to go over and

force the victim, Ms Suade, to tell us what happened to his granddaughter.'

'The defendant wanted you to use force?'

'That's what he said.'

'And what did you tell him?'

'The director, Ms McKay, told him that we couldn't do that. That it wasn't possible under the law.'

'And what did the defendant say to that?'

'Then he said that the law didn't work, something to that effect,' says Brower. 'And then he said he knew exactly what he'd do. He'd go over and wring the bitch's neck. That he'd find out where the child was. And that if he had to, he'd kill her.'

'Kill who?'

'He said he'd kill Zolanda Suade. Those were his words.'

Ryan allows this last point to settle on the jury in silence for a moment while he moves to the counsel table, and rummages in one of the paper bags of evidence.

Next he has Brower identify the cigar given to him by Jonah that day in my office.

'Did anyone try to stop you from turning this evidence over?' asks Ryan.

'Objection.'

'On what ground?' says Peltro.

'Irrelevant,' I tell him. 'There's no charge of evidence tampering.'

Ryan's trying to go after Susan, my guess is to even things up for the information she's given us on Suade's pistol.

'Withdraw the question,' says Ryan. He moves on to later that same evening, when Harry, Susan, and Brower found me at the cineplex. 'What happened then?' he asks.

'Ms McKay . . . We were all standing in the lobby of the theater, and Ms McKay told Mr Madriani what had happened. He wanted to go to the scene.'

'The scene? Where the body of the victim was?'

'Yeah.'

'Did he say why?'

'Not in so many words,' says Brower.

Ryan looks at the jury, does everything but wink.

'What happened next?' he says.

'Ms McKay told me to take him there.'

'Why did she tell *you* to do this?'

'Because I had law enforcement credentials. She knew I could get him through the police lines.'

'And did you?'

'Against my better judgment,' says Brower.

'But you took him there?'

'I was ordered to by my boss,' he says.

'Is Ms McKay a friend of Mr Madriani's?'

'I had heard that,' says Brower.

Peltro's looking down at Ryan from the bench now, wondering how far the prosecutor is going to go with this.

'Did you have any feeling that this request, to take Mr Madriani to the scene of a crime, particularly in light of the meeting earlier that day . . . did you have any sense that this might be inappropriate?'

'Objection. Calls for a conclusion,' I say.

'He's a trained law-enforcement officer,' says Ryan. 'He should know when it's appropriate and when it's not to cross the line into a crime scene, and who should be with him when he does.'

'I'll allow it,' says Peltro.

'Yes. I thought it was inappropriate.' Brower can't wait to answer.

'But you went anyway?'

'Yes. As I said, against my better judgment.'

'Could you see the body?'

'Part of it. It was behind a parked car, but we could see a foot, part of a leg.'

'And were crime scene technicians working the area?'

'They were.'

'Did they find anything at the scene and show it to you, in Mr Madriani's presence?'

'Yes. They said they'd found some stuff close to the body, and then one of them showed me something.'

'And what was that?'

'They found a cigar. Just the remains, smoked and stubbed out,' says Brower.

'Was there anything remarkable about this cigar?' says Ryan.

'Yes. It looked just like the one the defendant gave me earlier in the day, at Madriani's office.'

CHAPTER
TWENTY-ONE

'So you're an expert on cigars?'
'No. I never said that.'
'How often do you smoke them?'
'I don't know.' Brower's not nearly as forthcoming on cross-examination. He's had a night to sleep on it, think about what might be coming. Now he sits in the witness box looking at me with cagey eyes.
'Once a month?' I ask.
'Not that often,' he says.
'Once every other month?'
'Probably less than that.'
'Maybe you smoke them only when you get them for nothing, given to you by somebody else?'
He recoils at the notion of freeloading. 'I buy one once in a while. Smoke it when I get the time.' Now he's getting mean-eyed.
'When was the last time you bought a cigar, Mr Brower?'
'I don't know. Can't remember.' He doesn't try very hard.

'And yet you can tell from one look that the cigar in that bag, the one Mr Ryan showed you yesterday,' I point to the evidence cart. 'That that cigar was the same brand, the same kind as the cigar *stub* you were shown by the evidence tech that night behind Zolanda Suade's office? The night she died.'

'It looked the same to me,' he says.

'Was it dark that night, behind the office?'

'You know it was,' he says.

'How long did you look at that cigar stub. The one the evidence tech showed you?'

'I don't know. A few seconds,' he says.

'Did you touch it? Pick it up?'

'No. It was evidence. You don't touch evidence at a scene,' he says.

Must have seen this on *Columbo*.

'So where was it when you saw it?'

'You were there,' he says. 'You know where it was.'

'I want you to tell the jury.'

'It was in a bag. A paper bag.' He looks at the jury as he says this.

'So, in a dark parking lot, in the span of a few seconds, looking at a cigar stub at the bottom of a paper bag, you could tell with certainly the kind of cigar it was?'

'Objection,' says Ryan. 'Counsel misstates the evidence. The witness never testified as to the kind of cigar it was. He merely said it looked like the cigar that the defendant gave him at Mr Madriani's office.'

'Let me restate the question. Do you know what kind of cigar was in the paper bag that night?'

'It looked the same,' says Brower.

'That's not what I'm asking you. Do you know what kind of cigar was in that bag?'

He flexes the muscles in his face, rubber mask, looks at Ryan, back at me. 'The kind you smoke?' He looks at the jury, but they don't laugh.

'Was it a Panatella? A Corona? Maybe a Petit Corona? Or was it a Double Corona?'

'I don't know. As I said, I'm not an expert.'

'Isn't it a fact, Mr Brower, that you can't say with certainty what kind of cigar it was you saw that night in the evidence bag? Nor can you tell us what kind of cigar Mr Hale gave you in my office?'

'They looked similar, that's all I'm sayin'.'

In terms of evidence, that's all he has to say to hurt us. A nonexpert telling what it looked like to him.

'Answer the question,' I tell him.

'What was the question?' he says.

'Can you tell us precisely the type or kind of cigar it was in the evidence bag outside the victim's office?'

'No.'

'Can you tell us precisely the kind of cigar Mr Hale gave you in my office?'

'No.'

'So the cigar stub you saw that night at the scene could have been an entirely different kind of cigar than the one the defendant Mr Hale gave you at my office that morning, isn't that a fact?'

'It's possible,' he says.

'Now that we've explored your knowledge of cigars, let me turn your attention to the press release, the one you saw at my office that morning. Did you actually read the press release?'

'Most of it. I scanned it,' he says. As if his mind were a vacuum, picking up only the bad parts about my client. The problem here is that Ryan and Brower have now put into play questions of molestation and incest. Poisoned the jury. When they filed in this morning, none of them was willing to look at Jonah. Ryan has left me a hill of rehabilitation to climb that doesn't even deal with the murder. Suade's allegations against Jonah, the charges in the press release, would not even be admissible except that the state's theory is that they go to motivation, part of the reason he killed her, and on that score they are deadly.

'Besides the portions that dealt with my client, Mr Hale, what else did the press release say?' I ask.

He looks at the ceiling, checks Ryan as if he's looking for signals from a third-base coach. A few more seconds pass, some heavy thinking, world-class recollecting going on. 'Can't remember,' he says.

'Didn't it talk about the county?' I ask.

'Oh, yeah. That's right.'

'And what did it say about the county?'

'I'm not sure. It was rambling,' he says.

'It seemed pretty clear yesterday when you were talking about unfounded allegations concerning my client.'

'Objection.' Ryan from the table. 'Counsel's characterizing the evidence.'

'This evidence requires some characterization,' I tell him.

'Sustained. Mr Madriani . . .' Peltro looks at me and shakes his head.

'How is it you could remember the charges about my client from the press release, but nothing else?'

'I don't know. What stuck in my head,' says Brower.

'Let me ask you a question concerning the charges regarding Mr Hale as contained in that release. As far as you know, those were unfounded allegations weren't they?'

Ryan's on his feet objecting. 'How would the witness know that? Beyond the scope,' he says.

'The witness is a law-enforcement officer, works in Children's Protective Services. If there was anything there, I would think he would know.'

'The witness can answer if he knows,' says Peltro.

I look at Brower.

'What charges are you talking about?' He raises his eyebrows, wants me to say them again in front of the jury: the words *incest* and *molestation*.

'The charges made in Zolanda Suade's press release regarding Mr Hale. There's no evidence whatever that my client ever committed any of those acts to your knowledge, is there?'

'I never investigated them,' he says. 'I wouldn't know.'

'Isn't it a fact that if your department had evidence regarding the commission of those acts by my client, he would have been arrested?'

'He was arrested,' says Brower.

'When?'

'It's how he got here,' he says.

'Your Honor?' I look up at the judge.

'Mr Brower, answer the question.'

'What was the question?' he says.

'Isn't it a fact that if the county had evidence regarding

the acts stated in that press release regarding my client, they would have arrested Mr Hale?'

'I assume so,' he says.

'And was he ever arrested on those charges?'

'Not that I know of.'

'And if he had been arrested, you would have known, wouldn't you?'

'I might have,' he says.

'You expect the jury to believe that you would have attended the meeting in my office, read those charges in the press release and never checked after that time as to whether Mr Hale had been arrested or investigated concerning any of those charges?'

Brower doesn't answer, looks at me, thinks for a moment. 'I get busy,' he says.

'Was he arrested on those charges?' I ask him.

'Asked and answered,' says Ryan.

'The witness hasn't answered the question, Your Honor.'

'Overruled. Answer the question,' says Peltro.

'I think I checked. He was never arrested.'

'Was he ever even investigated on those charges?'

'Investigations are confidential,' says Brower. He pounces on this one, happy with the answer because it leaves Jonah twisting in the wind.

'Are you telling us there was an investigation?'

'I'm telling you I can't comment. They're confidential.'

I look up at the judge.

'You can comment in this court,' says Peltro.

'Your Honor, there are state statutes,' says Brower.

'I'm aware,' says the judge. 'Answer the question.'

'There were no open or pending investigations,' he says.

290

'Any closed investigations?' I ask.

'There was a record of the daughter's charges. It was looked at, but no evidence,' he says.

'Now let's go back to where we started,' I tell him. 'The rest of the press release. The portions that didn't involve my client. Those portions talked about the county, didn't they? About a scandal in the county?'

'Something about the county,' he says.

'That's all you can remember?'

'Right now. Yeah.'

'Let me refresh your memory. If I were to show you a copy of that press release, would you be likely to remember what you read that day in my office?'

'I might.'

Harry's fishing in the box, comes up with copies of the release, one for the judge and Ryan, one for me, and another for the witness. The bailiff passes them around.

'I want you to look at that, read it carefully and tell me if that was the document you saw that morning in my office, the so-called Suade press release?'

He studies it, his gaze periodically lifting off the page to check on me, see what I'm doing – as if maybe I'm sneaking up on him, getting ready to nail him with a sap from the blind side.

He flips the page, reads the second, and finishes.

'Is that the document you saw in my office that morning?'

'Looks like it,' he says.

'The one we've been calling the Suade press release?'

'Yeah.'

'Now do you remember seeing the items in the release concerning the county?'

'Sure.'

'Would you say they're true?'

'No.'

'Do you know anything about a scandal in the county? One regarding child-custody proceedings?'

'No.'

'How would you characterize these allegations regarding the county?'

'Objection, Your Honor.' Ryan sees where I'm going. Discredit one part of the release, and undercut it all. The rantings of an unstable woman.

'The witness has already stated that he doesn't know of any scandal in the county. How he might characterize the contents of the press release is irrelevant.'

'Mr Ryan's the one who brought up the subject of the release,' I tell the court. 'He seemed to think it was quite relevant when he was using it to slander my client.'

'It goes to motivation,' says Ryan.

'Right. And that's the only reason you brought it up.'

'Precisely,' says Ryan.

Peltro's on the gavel. 'Gentlemen, if you have anything to say, you direct it to me. I don't want to hear another word.' He thinks for a moment.

'I'm gonna overrule the objection. For the moment.' Peltro says it as if he might take it back in the next breath. The judge has a problem: trying to give the defendant a fair trial. There was no way to keep the contents of the press release, the charges against Jonah, away from the jury. Ryan is right. Even if they aren't true, they go to the very core of motivation. The fact is that they are also highly prejudicial, the kind of charges likely to inflame a jury, cause them to convict the defendant of murder, because they think he might be a molester.

Peltro is busy trying to level the field. 'I'm gonna give you some latitude, Mr Madriani. Try not to abuse it,' he says. He motions me on with the gavel in his hand.

'Mr Brower. Would you say that the contents of Ms Suade's press release are truthful and accurate?'

'How would I know?'

'You just testified that you're unaware of any scandals in the county, and yet her press release is filled with allegations of scandal. Would you say that those are accurate?'

'Not to my knowledge they're not.'

'And you say you're unaware of any investigations ever being launched by your department against my client?'

'Right.'

'And no charges were ever brought against him in connection with any of the allegations contained in that press release, correct?'

'Yes.'

'So would you say those parts of the press release were truthful or accurate?'

'No.'

'Have you ever heard rumors or talk regarding scandals in the county.'

'Your Honor.' Ryan is pleading with the judge.

Peltro waves him off.

'There're always rumors and talk,' says Brower.

'But have you ever heard anything specific?' Now I've got him in a minefield. Brower knows the state attorney general is investigating his own department for alleged abuse by investigators. It's been in the papers.

He's looking at Ryan, and not getting any help. Prosecutor with his head down, looking at the tabletop.

'You mean scandals involving child custody?' says Brower.

'I think that's what the press release is talking about.' I look at him. He knows where I'm headed if he doesn't give me the right answer.

'No. I don't know of anything. No rumors,' he says.

'So in your opinion, given your knowledge, your experience working in the county, would you say this press release is inaccurate, filled with information that is untrue?'

'Probably,' he says.

'Probably?'

'Yes,' says Brower.

'In fact, Investigator Brower, are you able to point to a single piece of information in this release, a single item, whether it relates to the county, or to my client, that is accurate?'

He looks at the document, takes it in both hands. Flips the page and studies it for a second. Finally he shakes his head. 'Maybe the victim's phone number,' he says, 'at the top of the page. But I couldn't swear to it.'

To Jonah it's a high point, major victory, the admission by Brower that he's not a child molester.

'Ryan can still argue it in closing,' I tell him, 'and it's just as devastating, maybe worse.'

We're huddled in the conference room, a tiny closet just off the holding cells outside Peltro's courtroom. Two guards are getting ready to take Jonah back to his cell for the night.

'I don't understand,' says Jonah. 'How could it be worse? He said it wasn't true.'

Harry's leaning, his back against the closed door, looking dour.

'Because if it's false,' says Harry, 'Ryan may argue that the charge is even more infuriating. Don't you understand? The only real issue, in the end,' he says 'as far as the cops are concerned is what wound you up. What sent you over to Suade's to kill her. And that they've got in spades. He's gonna argue that you were enraged by the lies. That you killed her because of it. And that ain't justifiable homicide,' says Harry.

It slowly begins to dawn on Jonah. We've spent the entire day talking about crimes that didn't take place. Trying to extract the poison, that even in death, Suade has been able to inject into the minds of the jury.

CHAPTER
TWENTY-TWO

'What did you *think* you were doing?' Susan's at the table, the dining nook in her kitchen, standing, not sitting, glaring at me over the top of the morning paper.

I'm in my bathrobe, cup of coffee in front of me, an hour from court.

'I was defending my client,' I tell her.

'I'm up to my hips in auditors. Investigators crawling all over my office and you're giving Brower a pistol to play Russian Roulette with my head,' she says.

'What are you saying?'

'Asking him what he knows about scandals in the county in open court. What was going through *your* mind?'

'I couched it very carefully. Brower knew what I was talking about. Made it very clear I was talking about Suade's press release.'

'That's what you were talking about. What if he decided to talk about something else?'

'Like what?'

'Like the investigation going on in our office.'

'Why would he talk about that?'

'To embarrass me,' she says. 'In case you haven't noticed, Mr Brower and I are not exactly on good terms. In some quarters it's being said he wants my job. What would it have taken for him to make wild accusations?' she says. 'Accuse me of shredding documents in my office. The press sitting there,' she says. 'Court reporter taking it down.'

'He didn't.'

'No thanks to you,' she says.

'You make too much of it,' I tell her, though I took a calculated risk when I popped the question with Brower on the stand.

'Did you know I'm on Ryan's witness list?' she says.

'I saw your name,' I tell her. 'You and half the people in the state. It doesn't mean he's going to call you. I've been waiting to see if he puts mine on.'

She gives me a look of surprise. I tell her I'm only kidding. Peltro would never allow it. Case would turn into a mistrial in a heartbeat.

'But I *am* on the list,' she says. 'Why didn't you tell me?'

I'm wondering how she found out.

'Because I didn't want you to worry. You've got a lot on your plate right now.'

'And now I've got this.' She folds the paper and slaps it on the table. 'And what if he does call me? What do I do then?'

'You take the stand and you testify. What can you tell him?'

'What I heard in your office that morning with Jonah.'

298

'Brower's already told them. The damage is done.'

'What if Ryan asks how I found out about Suade's gun? Brower knows I gave you the information,' she says.

'I wouldn't worry about it. You tell him the information came to your attention. We know each other. You happened to share the information with me.'

'Just like that. He's going to wonder just how this information came into my possession, don't you think?'

'You tell him one of your investigators got nosey. There was a case in the news. He came across the information and brought it to you.'

This doesn't allay her fears.

'He's not gonna call you,' I tell her. 'What does he have to gain? He tries to get into our relationship, I'll cut him off at the knees. Peltro's not going to let him explore that. It's irrelevant, prejudicial.'

'It's certainly prejudicial to me.' She's talking about our relationship. 'I wish I'd never given you the information on the gun,' she says.

'Why? So Jonah could be convicted?'

She looks at me, doesn't say anything, emotion welling up in her eyes.

I haven't had time to read the paper, but I'm assuming they didn't pick up on Ryan's question, the inference that somebody pressed Brower not to turn over the cigar to the cops. If she saw that, Susan would be ballistic by now.

'How did we get into this?' she says.

I get up out of the chair. Step around behind her. She's still facing the table, palms spread flat, leaning on it.

'Listen, you're under a lot of pressure.' I rub her shoulders with my hands, kneading the taut muscles like baker's dough. 'When this is over, we'll take a trip. Maybe south, down to Baja. Sit in the sun and relax. The kids can swim. We need a break. All of us. We can't keep doing this.'

She gives up a deep sigh. 'Yes.'

I can feel some of the tension go out of her body.

'In the meantime,' she says, 'I'm going to be fending off the sharks. The ones on the board of supervisors.'

A guy named JerOme Hurly, an eccentric who spells his first name with a big O in the middle, is the owner of a smoke shop downtown, and it turns out is Jonah's supplier of fine cigars. He actually smiles at my client as he takes the stand.

Jonah waves back before I can stop him.

Ryan moves quickly through the preliminaries, the witness's name, the name of his shop, the fact that he's been at the same location for thirty years.

'Do you know the defendant, Jonah Hale?'

'Oh, sure. Good customer,' he says.

'When was the last time you saw him, before today?'

The witness thinks for a second. 'Three months ago, maybe.'

'And where was that?'

'In my shop. He came in to buy cigars,' says Hurly.

'Had he done this before? Purchase cigars from you?'

'Oh, sure.'

'How many times?'

'I don't know. What would you say?' Hurly looking at Jonah, actually trying for consensus on this point. 'Eight or ten times, wouldn't ya say?'

300

Harry knees Jonah under the table, and the old man doesn't respond, total deadpan.

'I suppose eight or ten times,' says Hurly.

'What kind of cigars did he usually buy?'

'Oh, Mr Hale's got good taste. Premium cigars,' he says.

'Expensive?' says Ryan.

'Oh, sure.'

Ryan retreats to the evidence cart off to the side. Takes his time, and finally comes back with two small brown paper bags. 'May I approach the witness, Your Honor?'

Peltro waves him on.

'Mr Hurly, I'm gonna show you a cigar and ask you if you recognize the brand.'

Hurly opens the bag handed to him and looks inside. 'Help if I could take it out,' he says.

Neither Ryan nor I object.

Hurly rolls it in his fingers, smells it, holds it up to the light, and nods. 'Montecristo A,' he says. He could also tell this by simply looking at the container still inside the bag.

'Did you ever sell that kind of cigar, a Montecristo A, to the defendant, Jonah Hale?'

'Oh yes. He bought them generally by the box, but sometimes individually, in the little containers like this,' says Hurly.

'Is that an expensive cigar?' says Ryan.

'A box of twenty-five would cost you nine hundred dollars outside the U.S.' says Hurly. 'But ahh . . . they're a little more than that here,' he says.

'Why is that?'

'They come from my private reserve,' says Hurly. 'Hard to get.'

'Isn't it a fact, Mr Hurly, that these cigars are grown and manufactured in Cuba? Illegal to buy or sell in this country under the Cuban embargo?'

'I'm not sure of that,' he says. 'A lot of suppliers will tell you cigars come out of Cuba. Most of 'em are grown and made in this country. Some in the Dominican Republic,' he says.

'But your supplier for this particular cigar told you it was made in Cuba didn't he?'

'Cigar distributors say a lot of things. I don't know that I always believe them. Half the cigar shops in town claim they keep Cuban cigars under the counter. It's not always true.'

'But you were told these were made in Cuba, right?'

'What I was told,' he says.

'Is that why they're so expensive?'

'Well that's a fine cigar,' says Hurly. He's looking at Jonah, caught on the horns of a dilemma: consumer fraud on one tip, federal customs agents on the other. They will no doubt soon be examining Hurly's private stock in the back room, that is, if he hasn't already buried it or burned it.

'How many of your customers buy that cigar?'

'Oh.' Hurly thinks for a moment. 'You mean a cigar or a box?'

'Let's start with individual cigars.'

'I sell a few of them a month.'

'What's a few?'

'Maybe three or four.'

'All to the same people?'

'Regular customers,' he says.

302

'How many regular customers?'

'Two of them,' he says. 'Three including Mr Hale, there.'

'How many of those customers buy them by the box?'

'Oh. Only Mr Hale.'

'He was the only one who bought them in quantities?'

'Yes.'

'Do you know whether any other shops in the area carry that particular cigar?'

'I don't think so,' he says. 'Not that I know of. Requires a certain kind of clientele to stock that kinda thing,' says Hurly.

'I'm sure,' says Ryan.

'Would you call this cigar, the Montercristo A, a rare cigar?'

'Oh, it's a fine smoke, all right.'

'That's not what I mean. I mean, would you call it rare in the sense that it's not something you find on the street every day?'

'Oh. Yeah. That's true,' he says. 'Few places up past L.A. sell 'em. I've only heard rumors, of course. Place in Brentwood sells 'em to celebrities,' he says.

'Apart from the defendant and your two other customers who bought one cigar at a time, nobody else in the area smoked these cigars, did they?'

'Objection, calls for speculation?'

'Sustained.'

'Nobody else bought them from you, right?'

'Right.'

'And to your knowledge no other shops in this area sold any, right?'

'That's true.'

Now Ryan surprises me. 'That's all I have for this witness,' he says. He never removes the contents from the other evidence bag, the smoked and stubbed-out cigar from the scene.

Harry's in my ear, but I wave him off.

'Mr Madriani. Your witness,' says Peltro.

'Just a few questions, Your Honor.'

'Mr Hurly. Did you have an opportunity to see another cigar, partially smoked and stubbed out . . .'

'Objection,' says Ryan. 'Beyond the scope of direct. If the defense wants to call the witness they can do it in their own case.'

'Sustained,' says the judge.

'I have no other questions,' I tell the court.

'The witness is excused.'

I sit back down, Harry looking at me. 'What do you think?' Whispering in my ear. 'Maybe he couldn't ID the other one? Maybe he said something Ryan didn't like?'

I'm shaking my head, not sure. Maybe it's something worse.

Ten minutes later, and we find out it's worse. It takes Ryan that long to get through the man's credentials.

Lyman Bowler is a plant biologist from a southern university, author of a treatise on tobacco and, according to Ryan, one of the foremost experts on cigars in the country.

He is a tall, slender man, what you would call stately, and speaks with an accent that is not southern. I would guess from somewhere in the northeast.

Ryan has already placed the two evidence bags in front of the witness.

'Dr Bowler, I would ask you to look at the two cigars in

those bags and tell me whether you've had an opportunity to examine trace evidence from either or both of them before today?'

The witness looks at them, checks the markings, not on the cigars but on the bags holding them.

'Yes. There's a lab stamp on the bag, and I've seen pictures that correspond to the two cigars in question.'

'Just pictures?'

'No. We also received samples of the tobacco.'

'And when was that?'

'About a month ago,' says Bowler. 'Samples of both of these cigars were sent to me by your office.'

'Did you render any kind of a written report regarding that examination or your findings?'

'No.'

Ryan doesn't ask why, but the answer's clear: because the prosecutor didn't want a report floating around in his files that he would have to disclose. This makes it easier to sandbag us now.

'And what kind of examination did you perform?' says Ryan.

'Under a stereomicroscope. On slides,' he says. 'I examined both trace samples from the wrapper as well as the filler tobacco in each of the two cigars. The materials that were supplied.'

'So that the jury understands,' says Ryan. 'There are two different kinds of tobacco, wrapper and filler?'

'Yes. The filler is generally a blend of several different kinds of tobacco. The wrapper is what the name implies, a leaf tobacco that is specifically grown to use as the outer wrapper for cigars.'

'Were you able to come to any conclusions following your examination of the samples?'

'Yes.'

'And what were those conclusions?'

'As to the origins of the tobacco, I concluded that the filler and the wrapper for both cigars were grown outside of the United States. Most probably in Cuba.'

'And how did you come to that conclusion?'

'Process of elimination. To understand,' he says, 'you have to go back to Castro's takeover of the country. In the early nineteen-sixties when Castro was consolidating power, nationalizing industries, one of the things he did was to seize all the plantations. Many of the owners fled the country. Some of them took with them their Cuban tobacco seeds. A few came to the United States. Some went to Honduras. Others to the Dominican Republic. They set up and started growing, using the Cuban seed.'

'So what you're telling us is that the tobacco in the samples I sent you could be from Cuban seed cigars.'

'The tobacco in all the samples is definitely Cuban in origin. But I don't think it's what you would call Cuban seed. Certainly not grown in the United States.'

'How do you know that?'

'There aren't any traces of blue smut mold on the tobacco from any of the samples. Blue smut mold is a leaf mold very common in the United States. It comes up out of Mexico each year and contaminates the domestic tobacco crop. You would find traces of it in virtually every cigar from tobacco grown in this country. But it's not known to exist in Cuba.'

'Can you tell us, Doctor, besides the fact that the tobacco

for both cigars was grown outside the United States, were there any other points of similarity between the samples taken from the complete and unsmoked cigar in the one bag, and the crushed-out partially smoked cigar in the other?'

'Oh, yes. The samples of the wrapper from each are quite distinctive. They have an oily composition that is unique to wrappers grown in Cuba. Nowhere else are these quite the same, the Dominican Republic, Honduras. The wrapper is definitely Cuban grown in both samples.'

'And would you say it's the same kind of wrapper.'

'It's the same generic leaf,' says Bowler.

'And that would be something consistent, that a manufacturer of fine cigars would strive for?' says Ryan. 'Uniformity in the wrapper?'

'Absolutely.'

'Dr Bowler, by examining either the samples sent to you or the cigars themselves were you able to form any kind of scientific opinion as to whether the two cigars in question are of the same manufacture, the same brand?'

'Yes. In my opinion, they are. The same brand,' he says.

'Have you formed any opinion, or conclusion as to the identity of that brand?'

'I think so. Not from the samples themselves, but from the cigars. The distinctive torpedo shape, the oily texture of the wrapper, particularly on the unsmoked cigar, but also on the remnant . . .'

'You're talking about the cigar stub? The one found at the crime scene?'

'Yes. There's also a characteristic aroma that comes from storing these particular cigars in a cedarwood box. It's stronger on the full cigar, but still detectable on the remnant.

I would say that they are both the same. Premium cigars. Perhaps the best in the world. There's no doubt in my mind,' says Bowler. 'They're Montecristo A's. Both of them.'

CHAPTER
TWENTY-THREE

'It could be worse,' says Harry. 'They could have DNA from Jonah's saliva on the stub.'

It's not that I don't have faith in my client's protests of innocence, but the thought has crossed my mind more than once. The gods of forensics may have favored us at least a little. The business end of the smoked cigar was contaminated by the victim's blood at the scene, enough that they couldn't do DNA.

We are also guessing that one of the paramedics early on the scene may have stepped on it before the techs got there. Ryan has been unable to produce evidence of teeth impressions, though he tried. The crime lab looked and came back with nothing definitive. One of their theories is that the killer stepped on it to put it out.

'Doesn't make sense,' says Harry. 'That means the killer tracked in the blood. Nobody's gonna do that on purpose. Not to put out a cigar.'

'That assumes the blood was there at the time.'

Harry looks at me.

'She may have been bleeding. Maybe the pool hadn't caught up with the cigar when he dropped it.'

'You think she was still alive?'

'It's a possibility.'

Harry says the DNA could have been exculpatory, showing that somebody else smoked the cigar.

'Or a train wreck,' I say. There's no telling what a jury will do with evidence of probabilities on the scale of DNA. Glaze their eyes over for three days with the science of the helix, and you may find them flipping coins in the jury room.

The strain of the trial is beginning to show on Jonah. The first few days, when the state's case stumbled, fits and starts, he seemed to take refuge. Then Ryan got back on track with the evidence of the cigars. The resilience ran out of Jonah like a bucket with a hole in the bottom. Tonight he is showing more than his age.

We have called in the doctor. Jonah telling us there's nothing wrong, but his hands occasionally clutching gently at his chest, rubbing his left shoulder, are telling us something else.

Harry's worried about him. The doctor has assured us they'll hold him for observation overnight in the county's hospital prison ward where they can monitor and control his medications.

Right now Harry and I have other problems. Jason Crow didn't show up at the courthouse today. By seven-thirty, Harry and I are doing the honors. He drives. I navigate. Up the hill toward Crow's apartment.

'I thought he might do this. Parolee, par for the course,' I tell Harry. It's why Harry prepared the subpoena a week ahead of our case. To give us time to run him down in case he rabbited. Now if we're lucky we have time to find him, instill the fear of God, even if His chief archangel, Murphy, isn't with us. I tried to call Murph, had him paged, but no luck.

When we get to Crow's apartment I have Harry drive around the block, checking the lights, what I remember to be Crow's flat, side and back. It looks like it's dark, though a faint light can be seen coming from a small window a little higher than the others on the wall; I'm guessing a bathroom.

'If that's his apartment, looks like he's out,' says Harry.

'If he is, he's either on foot or somebody else is driving.'

Harry looks at me.

'The gray Datsun back there. On the left. It's Crow's car. Murphy traced the plates to find him.'

I have Harry park the car in the front, a space at the curb where we have a good view of the front porch and the door, Crow's car down the street. From here Harry can see and not be seen, not from Crow's apartment upstairs anyway.

'I want you to stay here.'

'Why?'

'To watch his car, and the front door. I'll ring the bell, slip around the back. If he's there, my guess is that's where he's gonna come out. On the run,' I tell him. 'Especially after the way Murphy nailed him the other day. He'll head for his car.'

I'm not about to try to jump him, get into it with him à la Murphy. I leave that to the process servers and PIs.

'If he gets to his car, you pick me up out on the street. There.' I point to a place where I'll be. 'Keep your lights out. We'll follow him to see where he goes. Once he settles we'll get a bench warrant, let the cops pick him up.' Crow has already violated the subpoena. I'm pretty sure I can convince Peltro to have him held pending his testimony. He's a key witness for our case, with a considerable record.

Harry sits tight. I head for the front door. Up the stairs. I don't have to hunt for the right button. I see the clean piece of paper with his name on it and press the button next to it. The sound of the buzzer upstairs. I hit it twice quickly and back down the stairs, along the other side of his building away from his windows.

There's a walkway leading to the backyard, broken concrete with weeds growing up out of the cracks. A few seconds and I'm in the backyard. Here there are some bushes struggling for survival among the weeds, shadows thrown by a good-sized avocado tree. I step back into the darkness and wait. I can see Crow's apartment, at least the back window. Still no lights. The stairs on this side of the house are wood in need of repair, leaning slightly, what used to be white, now a kind of peeling gray.

If Crow comes this way, in a hurry, he's gonna make a lot of noise. Plenty of time for me to get out front to Harry and the car.

I wait, look at my watch. Thirty seconds since I hit the buzzer, and nothing.

There's no way he could have seen me. I step out of the darkness, head down the walkway toward the front. A few feet past the fence, through a low three-foot gate, and Harry sees me. He's a silhouette in the car. He shrugs his shoulders, shakes his head. No action out front.

I know the front door is locked, so I head toward the back

312

stairs. I climb them quietly, two at a time, taking the wooden railing, avoiding the splinters, both hands, to the landing at the top. There's no light here, just a weather-beaten wooden door, single pane of glass on top. Inside through the glass I can see the corridor dimly lit, one door on the right, an apartment belonging to somebody else on the other side.

I try the outside door. It's unlocked. I step inside, close it behind me. Never having come this way, I'm not exactly sure where the door to Crow's room is. I'm thinking down the hall and around the corner to the left. I tiptoe, lightly as I can, not letting my heels hit the threadbare carpet.

Sounds of a television waft up from somewhere in the distance, muted by walls and closed doors, game show noise, banter and applause, nothing I can make out. Then I realize the channel's in Spanish.

I make my way to the corner and peek around the edge of the wall. Crow's door is about fifteen feet down the hall. I'm wondering whether I should just knock. There's no way out, unless he decides to take a window, use some sheets, or has one of those rope ladders they use for fires, which I doubt. The last time I was here he wasn't prepared for much of anything, least of all Murphy.

If he comes out another way Harry's gonna see him, though it would take me a few seconds to get to the street.

I work my way to the door, stop and put an ear to it. The noise from the television somewhere downstairs is making it difficult to hear.

¡Muy Fantastico! Excelente! Applause and tinny music, a brass horn picks up the beat.

I press my head a little closer to the door, and as I do my shoulder rubs against it. There's a click, and the door opens,

313

not a crack or a sliver, but slowly, everything but squeaking hinges. It rolls with gravity to the lowest point, until I find myself standing, centered in the open frame, backlit by the light in the hall. It's too late to move. All I can do is hope Crow isn't inside with a gun pointed in my direction.

There's no movement inside, the room shielded in darkness, and no sound.

It looks as though Crow took a stroll. Probably ran to get beer, and didn't catch the latch on the way out.

I can't see much of the apartment, only with the light from the hall and what is directly in front of the door. I step inside and close it.

Now the only light is what filters in from one of the windows, a streetlamp half a block down, and a splinter of illumination from under a door off to my left. I'm guessing a night-light in the bathroom, what I could see from the small window outside.

I don't have a flashlight, and I don't dare turn on the lights. If Crow's out walking and comes back, he'll see the windows lit up and disappear.

I check the door, to make sure it's locked behind me. It's a tricky latch, what you get in a flophouse. I have to jiggle the knob a bit to get it to snap into place. I can feel with my hands the twist of a deadbolt above the knob. For some reason, Crow didn't use it. I have a feeling he didn't go far.

I turn a hundred and eighty degrees, shuffle away from the door, hands out in front of me, blind man, trying to give my eyes time to adjust. Part of the room I can make out. The folding card table under the window. I kick something on the floor. It skids across the uncarpeted surface. The tinny

314

sound as it hits the card-table leg gives it away; an empty beer can. For a moment I just stand in one place, trying to get my bearings.

Off to my right would be the sleeper sofa, opened out so that it takes up a good part of the room. I can't see this, just make out one edge, the bottom corner of the bed, what looks like a rumpled blanket in the shadows. I take a wide berth to my left to avoid tripping over the bed.

My best shot is the bathroom door. If I open it, the night-light inside should give me enough to see. I shuffle toward the shaft of dim light escaping from under the crack. Kick a cardboard plate from a TV dinner. Finally I reach the door, find the knob and turn it, and open the door.

Inside it's not brightly lit, but I can see. A shower curtain is drawn around the tub, pushed out at the tap end by something inside, dark, pushing out the curtain in this area.

I study it for a second, small dark form, size of a cat, dark shadows through the translucent curtain.

I step inside, take the curtain, throw it back sliding on its rings.

Jason Crow is stretched out in the tub, his unblinking eyes looking straight at me, not moving when I do. His feet still wrapped in their Reeboks are propped up on the tap-end edge of the tub, heels down, toes up. His head is against the other.

Crow's right hand is drawn across his upper body reaching for something, but not quite making it. A syringe stuck in his left forearm, plunger fully depressed, a short bungee cord, hooks on each end, lying in the bottom of the tub, just beneath his left arm.

I move to the head of the tub, try his neck, the pumped-out

315

trail of the carotid below his left ear. The few random hairs of a beard still on his chin. There's no pulse, and the skin is cool.

I rise up slowly, standing straight, staring down at the lifeless form in the tub. There is no doubt that Jason Crow was part of this world's underbelly. From everything I'd seen and read, he'd drifted in that direction most of his adult life. Nothing in his sorry existence could be said to be a part of any design, certainly not his own. Still, I can't help but wonder that only hours earlier he had stumbled out of his bed, looked out the window, taking in the sunshine beyond the salt-filmed pane of glass as his day began, never entertaining a clue that this would be his last.

I turn from the tub and catch my own face in the mirror over the sink. It is tired, looking like it belongs to someone I don't know. I am long past a five o'clock shadow. Dark hair mussed, and eyes with pouches under them, abysses of stress and sleep deprivation.

Jonah's in the hospital, and I'm now back to square one. I no longer have a witness to connect Jessica to the Mexican drug dealer Ontaveroz. My theory of defense is evaporating like spit on a hot sidewalk.

There's a strong urge to splash a little water on my face as I lean over the sink, but I suppress it. This is now a crime scene, and my fingerprints are already far too prominent.

My first thought: Call Floyd Avery. Maybe he can cut some slack with the city PD. Otherwise I'm going to be answering questions all night, with a court call at nine in the morning.

I detach my gaze from the mirror, turn to leave the bathroom. That's when I see him. Shaft of light from the open door that was behind me. Sprawled on the foldout bed, staring open-eyed at the ceiling, the hilt and handle of a Bowie knife the size of a meat cleaver sticking out of his chest – Joaquin Murphy.

Crow could never have gotten the better of him, of that I am convinced. But I don't share this with the cops. I am sitting on a small wooden bench out on the front porch.

There are cops out front stringing yellow tape on sticks at the edge of the strip of lawn, mostly weeds, that border the sidewalk in front of the house.

A van, Channel 2, has just pulled up, getting their satellite antenna up.

Avery and Harry standing close by along with some detective from city homicide. They are crowded under one of the naked lightbulbs on the front porch, close enough to converse with me, but give me some distance.

'This was a friend? This guy Murphy?' says the detective.

'He was an investigator. We hired him a couple of months ago,' says Harry.

'In what capacity? What was the nature of the work?'

'That's privileged,' I cut in.

The cop finally turns to look at me, sitting on the bench.

'And what brought you over here?' He's got his notebook open, looking at me.

When I don't answer. 'Is that privileged too?'

Avery whispers in his ear, the guy comes back to me. 'You the lawyer in the Suade thing? Saw it on TV,' he says. 'Is that what this was about?'

'I can only tell you we had Crow under subpoena. He was a possible witness, that's all.'

317

'When's the last time you talked to this investigator, Murphy?'

'Two days ago.'

'What did you talk about?'

I give him eyebrows and a smirk.

'I tried to call him a couple of times today but couldn't reach him, earlier in the day.'

'We know. We saw his pager. Your number on it,' says Avery. 'It was still on his belt upstairs.'

This gives me pause to think. Who else has seen this?

'Let's get back to what brought you over here,' says city homicide.

'I told you. Three times. Jason Crow was supposed to be in court this morning. He was under subpoena. He never showed up. I came over to find out why.'

'And you let yourself into his apartment?'

'The back door wasn't locked. The door to his apartment was locked, but the catch didn't work.'

'Convenient.'

'Maybe, but that's what happened.'

'I could take you in for breaking and entering,' he says.

'And by tomorrow I'd be out. And Lieutenant Avery there would be in front of Judge Peltro downtown explaining why I'm not in court in the morning.'

Avery gives him a look as if this might not be wise.

'Let's go over it once more,' says the detective.

I roll my eyes. 'As I said, I rang the doorbell. Nobody answered. I tried the back stairs. The door was unlocked. The latch on Crow's door didn't catch. When I touched it, the door opened.'

'How did you touch it?'

318

'I was listening at the door.'

'What were you listening for?'

'To see if he was inside. If I heard voices. I don't know. Maybe he was asleep, didn't hear the bell.'

'I heard the buzzer,' he says. 'Nobody's gonna sleep through that – unless he's dead.'

'You think I knew they were inside?'

'I don't know. Did you?'

'This is getting nowhere.'

'I still haven't heard what your investigator was doing here,' he says. 'You already served Crow, you say?'

'Right. Two days ago.'

'Then why come back?'

'Because he didn't show up in court.'

'You knew that?'

'Right.'

'But your investigator didn't. Was he in court today?'

Harry and I exchange looks. Avery watching. He knows.

'No.'

'Then how could he know the witness failed to appear?'

'I don't know.'

'So you don't know why he was here?'

'No.'

'Tell me again how you got inside the apartment?'

'I told you. I had my ear pressed to the door. I touched it accidentally with my shoulder, and it opened.'

'Just like that?'

'You don't believe me, have your forensics people check it.'

'Okay. Then what?'

'I went in. I found the bodies. I called Lieutenant Avery

because I had his number. He called you. I went outside, sat in the car and waited. You showed up. That's everything I know.'

He looks at his notes. 'You say Crow was served two days ago.'

'That's right?'

'And who did that? The serving of process,' he says.

'Mr Murphy.'

'Were you with him?' He takes a stab in the dark. Gets lucky.

'Yes.'

His eyes light up. 'So you talked to Crow at that time?'

'Yes.'

'How long?'

'I don't know. Ten minutes maybe.'

'What did you talk about?'

'I think I'm gonna treat my partner like a client,' says Harry. 'I'm going to advise him not to say anything more.'

'You are?' says the cop. 'You were sitting out front in the car. Accessory to whatever we find here. I suppose you have to be in court in the morning as well?'

Harry nods, a little sheepish.

'Now, what did you talk about?' He turns back to me.

'Murphy handed him a subpoena, and we told him to be in court.'

'That took ten minutes?' he says.

'It was a slow conversation. It took Crow a while to understand the document,' I tell him.

The cop looks, smiles, his face flushed, fed with enough bullshit for one night. 'So now you're gonna tell me you were in there giving him legal advice?'

I nod. 'Yeah. He was on parole. Wanted to know what the effect was.'

'And what did you tell him?'

'I told him if he didn't show up, I'd call his parole officer.'

'Crow was gonna be a witness in the Hale case?'

'It was a possibility.' No doubt they've already found the subpoena with the caption on it. So this is no secret.

'What was he gonna testify about?'

Avery's all ears.

'You don't really expect me to tell you, do you? It's been a long day,' I tell the cop.

'It's likely to get longer.'

'I'm sorry, but I'm not going to be discussing Mr Crow's testimony.'

'If there's a coroner's inquest you may have to,' he says.

'We can talk about that if it happens.'

He fumes, a long exasperated sigh, studies me with eyes buried deep behind puffy cheeks, like he's deciding whether to haul my ass in or not.

'It's privileged information,' I tell him. 'It goes to a theory of defense. That's all you have to know. You know as well as I do that if you force the issue, you're only going to get slapped down by the trial judge.'

'We know Crow knew Jessica Hale,' says Avery. 'Does it have to do with their relationship? You can tell us that much?'

'No. I can't.'

The homicide detective's getting angry. Red face over a tie too tight around the neck. Avery takes him by the arm, leads him off to one side. They whisper for a few seconds. Nothing I can hear.

The problem is the state already has a good idea where we're trying to go with our defense. Our argument on the pretrial motion clued Ryan in as to the theory on Ontaveroz. The fear now is that if he finds out the details, discovers that Crow was my best evidence on this theory, he'll know my case is on the rocks. Ryan will race to the finish line, rest his case and turn to me, a sorry sight, a lawyer with nothing to say.

As I see it now, there are two possibilities. I can turn up the two federal agents, assuming that's who they were. On that score, my only link, Murphy, is now dead.

The second alternative would please Jonah much more. I can find Jessica, and with her, the little girl Amanda. Maybe I get Jessica to testify about her past, tell the jury about Ontaveroz in a persuasive way, which is not likely, short of applying implements of pain. Unless we can do one or the other, our case for an acquittal is about to hit a wall. It may be that our best chance is now a verdict on a reduced charge.

Over in the far corner the homicide dick gives up a big sigh, shrugs. Apparently whatever the argument, Avery's won it. They wander back over from the other side of the porch.

'We're not trying to make a problem here,' says the detective. 'What it looks like to me, your investigator was on the job. Came by at the wrong time. Caught Crow getting ready to put the needle in his arm. Crow panicked, they fought for the knife. Crow found a place to plant it. You could help us tie up the loose ends,' he says.

'That's how you see it?'

'Yeah.'

'You've got at least one problem,' I tell him.

'What's that?'

'The fact that Crow had no history shooting up heroin. Cocaine, maybe.'

'How do you know that?'

'Check his arms. Between his toes. I doubt you're going to find any needle tracks. Besides, he was on parole. He was probably being screened for drugs,' I tell him. 'I'll bet you a month's pay he never shot up heroin.'

'So who stuck the needle in his arm, your friend Murphy?'

'No.'

'You figure Crow killed him, though?'

I give him a shrug as if I'm not sure.

'So what do you think?' says Avery.

I look at my watch. I yawn. 'I think it's getting late.'

Before they can say another word, the screen door opens and one of the evidence techs steps out onto the porch. He takes a deep breath, two hands on the railing, leans over and barfs all over the lawn. The strobes from the TV camera catching it all. Must be a rookie.

The guy straightens up, out of breath, sucks in some air, and wipes his chin with the cuff of his jacket.

'Last thing you need, contaminate the scene,' he says. 'Smells like somebody up there killed a cat,' he says. 'Last month.'

'I'm told the man was not a neat housekeeper,' says Harry.

'So what did you find?' says the detective.

The tech still catching his breath. 'What's left from a piece of Black Tar.'

A piece is a street term. It's about twenty-five grams in this case Black Tar heroin. Going price to a buyer is about a thousand dollars. In this country the supply almost invariably comes out of Mexico.

'Just one question,' says Avery. He looks at me. 'Do you have any idea what Murphy was doing here?'

I shake my head, start to answer.

'Oh, we think we figured that one out,' says the tech. 'The other guy called him.'

'What are you talking about?' I say.

'We're checking phone records right now, see if we can place the time. We found this right by the phone.'

He holds up an evidence bag. Inside is a business card the one Murphy dropped on Crow the night we delivered the subpoena.

'We pressed redial,' says the tech. 'It was the last number dialed from the phone upstairs.'

CHAPTER
TWENTY-FOUR

V isions of Murphy on the bed, a slab of steel buried in his chest, dance in a dark web of restless dreams as the night wears on. I doze and wake, unable to find sound sleep, my head tossing on a rumpled pillow. Finally I reach over and move a pile of papers on the nightstand so that I can see the clock.

Susan is purring gently, sensuous little snores, her body curled up behind me, a spoon, one arm dangled loosely over my waist.

As gently as I can I move her arm, ease my legs out from under the sheets, and sit up at the side of the bed. It's three-thirty.

I'm wearing pajama bottoms. Susan's got the top, like a trophy.

As I stand up, the bed creaks. She is a light sleeper, so I turn to look. She stirs, adjusts her pillow. Just when I think she's going to drift back, her sleepy eyes open and look at me.

'Hmm.' She stretches long, languid legs under the covering sheet. 'What's wrong, you can't sleep? I can fix that.' She reaches over, takes me by the wrist and tugs me gently back toward the bed. Her hands are at the nape of my neck as I hit the sheets, bumping knees and naked thighs, one of my own drawn between hers as if by some invisible polar force. Her nipples are hardened like bullet points pressing against my chest.

Susan is good at this, mesmerizing acts of seduction, until you are no longer certain who is seducer and who is seduced. Like one of the giant predator cats she owns the darkness, the hours of the early morning.

Her lips are on mine, her tongue between them. Within seconds I can no longer control myself, pajama parts flung in the mêlée with the force of beasts in the brush. Susan likes to play rough. She has drawn blood on more than one occasion; her teeth now nibbling on my earlobe as I move within her. Her legs are locked around me. She grips me, rises up, arms around my neck. Balanced on the edge, her hands suddenly move, fingernails raking my back. Susan sends a jolt tingling down my spine until it washes over me, an instant of unsurmountable release.

Susan's not done. She spurs me on, her heels pressing, locked at the small of my back as she falls gently, a leaf in the wind, toward the sheets. The use of her muscles is a mystery to me. The small of her back arches up off the bed, her eyes shut tight, her upper teeth biting into her lower lip.

I move within her one more time before it dies. Susan issues a stifled scream, a rigid shudder passing through her body as she twists in the bedcovers beneath me. True to her word, she has fixed it. I have forgotten what it was that woke me.

We are both groggy in the morning, fallout from our adventures of the previous night. I stand looking in the mirror over the vanity in Susan's bathroom, running my hands through my hair.

'It seems I'm not the only one with a problem sleeping,' I tell her.

'What are you talking about?'

There are two little bottles of Ambien, prescription sleep medication, on the countertop. I pick one of them up and rattle the tiny white pills inside.

'Oh that. I take one once in a while. It's the job,' she says. 'Problems at work.'

'Maybe your inability to sleep is something else.'

'What do you mean?' Suddenly Susan sits up, image behind me in the mirror. There's a defensive edge to her voice, the sleepy tone gone, as if I've hit a raw nerve.

I turn to look at her. 'Maybe you're not used to living with somebody else. Strangers in your house,' I tell her. 'In your bed.'

'Oh, that!' She shifts gears. 'Don't be silly.'

'What did you think I meant?'

'Nothing,' she says. Her head's back down on the pillow. Patting the bed for me to return.

'Maybe Sarah and I should find someplace else?'

'No.' She props herself up on one arm. 'Not after what happened last night.'

'I'm not talking about going home. Maybe a hotel.'

'Sarah's not going to be comfortable in a hotel room.'

'You're right. I'll leave Sarah here.'

'She's not going to be happy without you,' she says.

'But she may be safer,' I tell her. 'I can't get the girl out of my mind.'

Susan looks at me, a budding question mark.

'Amanda. Jonah's granddaughter. You think they wouldn't do to her what they did to Murphy?'

'I'd almost forgotten about her,' says Susan.

'I haven't. Haven't been able to get her out of my mind since last night.'

'Why don't you go to the police?'

'No need to go to them. They've been coming to me pretty regularly.'

'You know what I mean. Tell them what's happening. Tell them about Ontaveroz.'

'Ryan already knows. More than he should. And I still have no evidence.'

'You've got two dead bodies,' she says.

'Yeah, but the cops have their own theory as to how they got that way. They're not going to believe me.'

'How do you know unless you try?'

'If it weren't for Jonah's trial, they might humor me,' I tell her. 'Provide some protection. At least watch the house. But with the trial, any action on their part that lends credence to the theory that the Mexican killed Crow and Murphy opens the door to arguments that he may have also killed Suade. No way Ryan will permit that.'

I'm looking out the window at her backyard. Sunlight filtered on the hard surface of the patio outside. Shadows of leaves, sharp edges dancing over the cracks in the stone pavers.

She gets up, comes over, nuzzles up behind me, hands around my waist. I can feel the warmth of her body against mine. We stand there, a swaying silhouette in front of the French doors.

'I'm worried that I'm putting you in danger,' I tell her. 'I saw what happened to Murphy. In the wrong place at the wrong time.'

'That wasn't your fault,' she says.

'I'm not talking guilt. I'm talking hard reality. What these people will do if they feel it's necessary to come after me. Right now they figure Crow's dead. They're in the clear. What happens if I get lucky? Turn over another rock? And I have to try.'

'Why?'

'Because otherwise the best I can do is a verdict on some diminished charge. Jonah's going to go to prison. Don't you understand? He'll probably die there.'

There's a deep sigh from Susan as she hugs me a little tighter. 'I'm sure if he did it, it was self-defense,' she says. 'Suade's gun.'

'Problem is he says he wasn't there.'

'So what are you going to do?'

'I have to try to find Jessica.'

'You think she'll help her father?'

'I don't know. But at least I can try to get the child back.' I turn to look at Susan, her arms still around me.

She's not looking at me. Instead she's gazing out at nothing, over my shoulder into the yard.

'I'll help you,' she says.

'No. I don't want you involved any more than you already are. If you'll take care of Sarah . . .'

'I'm already involved.'

'You mean Suade's gun? Ancient history,' I tell her. 'Another day or two in court, Ryan will forget where it came from.'

This doesn't seem to move her much.

'The child's in danger,' she says. 'We've got to find her.'

'You leave that to me.'

She doesn't respond. Instead ignores me, changes the subject.

'One thing puzzles me,' she says. 'How do you think they found this man Crow?'

'I've been thinking about that. It's possible they followed Murphy and me the night we served him. If so, Ontaveroz probably squeezed Crow to see if he knew where Jessica was. He would have found the subpoena and Murphy's business card.'

'You said Crow didn't know where Jessica was.'

'That's what he told us. Who knows what he might have told the Mexican? Anything to stay alive. If Ontaveroz found the subpoena, he would have known we were getting ready to put Crow on the stand. That could have put Ontaveroz on display in the middle of Jonah's trial. I doubt if he wanted the publicity.'

'That's why he killed Crow?'

'I think so.'

'It still doesn't make sense,' she says. 'Why would he kill Murphy?'

'If he thinks Crow told him something.'

'But he didn't.'

'Ontaveroz doesn't know that.'

I am thinking this was not a voluntary act on Crow's part, the phone call to Murph.

'They probably injected Crow after the call, put him in the tub, then sat and waited for Murphy to show up.'

I feel her body shiver against mine with this thought, her chin resting on my shoulder as she looks out through the glass.

'But if they think Crow told Murphy something. And they followed the two of you to Crow's apartment that night, then they must think you know something too.' She pulls her head away and finally looks up at me.

'That's why I can't stay here any longer,' I tell her.

This morning Ryan plows old ground, trying to get it right this time. His witness is a firearms and ballistics expert from the county crime lab, Kevin Sloan.

Blond and in his early thirties, he looks more like a cop than a lab technician.

They quickly go through the grain weight of each of the bullets, confirming that the rounds that killed Suade were a three-eighty caliber. After all the jostling with Dr Morris over this very point, Ryan for some reason is now comfortable with the caliber. In light of what we know about Suade's missing gun, Harry and I are left to wonder why.

Ryan gets into lands and grooves on the bullets, and the witness tells the jury that the firearm that killed Suade was a semiautomatic, based on the rimless cartridges found at the scene. According to Sloan the firearm isn't implicated in any other crimes, at least not according to the DOJ computer used to keep track of such things.

'Anything else you could determine from the cartridge

331

found at the scene, or the bullets taken from the victim's body?'

'There were ejector marks on the cartridge, indicating it was fired only one time. Whoever owned the gun was probably not what we would call a hobby shooter, someone sufficiently familiar with firearms that he would load his own ammunition.'

'Anything else?' says Ryan.

'The lands and grooves, the spiral for this particular pistol displayed a right-hand twist. That means the bullet as it traveled down the barrel of the pistol would have spun in a clockwise direction looking from the breech, the chambered end. As a general rule,' says Sloan, 'American-made firearms, semiautomatics, have a left-hand twist. The bullet spirals in a counterclockwise direction as it travels down the barrel. Colt, Browning, High Standard, Remington, most of these would be a left-hand twist. European-made weapons generally use a right-hand twist. Clockwise.'

'So the pistol in this instance was probably European-made?'

'That's what I would conclude. It's a popular caliber,' he says. 'There are a number of European manufacturers marketing semiautomatic pistols chambered in the three-eighty caliber.'

'So you're telling us it would be difficult to identify the specific make or manufacture of the gun used in this case, unless we found the weapon itself?'

'That's correct.'

Ryan's trying to head me off, undercut the significance of Suade's gun. Put it out of reach, so that without the pistol itself I can't prove the rounds came from her pistol. This leaves the jury in a world of conjecture. She owned a gun, but was it the murder weapon?

'That's all I have for this witness,' says Ryan.

I waste no time.

'Mr Sloan, are you familiar with a pistol known as a Walther PPK?'

'I am.'

'Is that a semiautomatic pistol?'

'It is.'

'And where is that particular pistol manufactured?'

'Orginally in Germany,' says Sloan. 'But, under license, some are made here in this country.'

'Do you know whether the Walther PPK is chambered in a three-eighty caliber?'

'It is.'

'Isn't it a fact that the Walther PPK three-eighty is often carried by police officers as a backup weapon?'

'I know officers who carry it,' says Sloan.

'Is that because of its compact size and weight?'

'Yes. I would say so.'

'Would it be accurate to characterize this semiautomatic, the Walther PPK three-eighty, as a "woman's weapon" because of its small size?'

'Objection. Calls for speculation. Assumes that there is such a thing as a "woman's weapon",' says Ryan.

'The witness is an expert,' I tell the court.

'No foundation,' says Ryan.

'Sustained,' says Peltro.

'Are there handguns that are more likely to be carried by women?'

'I don't know,' says Sloan.

'Isn't it a fact that women tend, as a general rule, to buy and use handguns with a smaller frame?'

Sloan thinks about this for a moment.

'As a general rule that's probably true.'

'Thank you. And isn't it a fact that the Walther PPK three-eighty is just such a firearm?'

'I suppose,' he says.

'So if a woman wanted to carry a gun, this would be a perfect gun to carry in her purse?'

'I guess, if she wanted to carry a gun.'

I get into the number of rounds the little Walther will hold, seven, eight if you put one in the chamber, and the fact that it produces a right-hand twist, just like the lands and grooves on the bullets taken out of Suade's body. I'm making good progress with the state's own witness, and for some reason, whether he's just putting on a face for the jury, Ryan appears unconcerned by this.

'Let's turn to the type of pistol we're talking about here, semiautomatic. Can you explain to the jury how a semiautomatic pistol operates?'

Ryan's sitting there. I can tell by the look, he's wondering whether he can make an objection, maybe beyond the scope. But he doesn't.

'That's quite complicated,' says Sloan.

'Just in layman's terms,' I tell him. 'A simple explanation.'

'Bullets generally load from a clip into the handle of a pistol. When the clip is properly seated, the top sits just behind the chamber. In order to chamber the first round, you have to pull the slide back and let the recoil spring slam it forward. This will catch the first round from the clip, and seat it in the chamber closing and lock the ejection port at the same time. On weapons that have a hammer it will also cock the hammer in firing position. Then if the safety is off, all you have to do is pull the trigger. Each successive round then as it's fired activates the slide sending it backward, automatically chambering the next round and cocking the hammer.'

'So all you have to do after seating the first round is pull the trigger?'

'Yes. If the safety's off,' says Sloan.

'And the gun will fire as fast as you pull the trigger?'

'That's right.'

'Are you familiar with the concept of trigger pull?' I ask. 'The amount of pressure necessary to fire any particular weapon?'

'Yes.'

'I'm going to object,' says Ryan. 'This is beyond the scope of direct.'

'Your Honor, counsel raised the question as to the type of weapon being semiautomatic. I think I have a right to inquire into how such a weapon works.'

'I'll allow the question.' Peltro from the bench.

'Just in general terms, isn't it a fact that trigger pull is measured in terms of pounds of pressure necessary to pull any trigger to its release or firing point?'

'As a general concept that's correct.'

'Now I'm going to set up a hypothetical question for you. You're an expert on firearms, right?'

'Yes.'

'Let's assume you're comparing a revolver, what is known as a double-action revolver. You know what that is don't you?'

'Yes.'

'Explain to the jury?'

'A double-action revolver would be one for which you don't have to manually cock the hammer to fire it. You can merely pull the trigger and this will rotate the cylinder, line up the next round with the barrel, bring the hammer back and fire it.'

'Let's assume you're comparing a double-action revolver and a semiautomatic pistol. Let's further assume that we're only dealing with the question of how many pounds of pressure are necessary to fire a second shot. Let's assume that both the double-action revolver and the semiautomatic pistol are being fired only by pulling the trigger after each has fired a first shot. Do you understand?'

He nods.

'You have to speak for the record.'

'Yes.'

'In that hypothetical, isn't it a fact that it would take considerably less trigger pull to fire the semiautomatic pistol than the revolver?'

'You're Honor, what's the relevance?' says Ryan.

'The witness has testified that there were two shots fired, two bullets taken from the victim's body. I think the defense has a right to inquire as to the amount of pull required on the trigger to fire the second round.'

Peltro nodding. 'Overruled.'

'You can answer the question,' I tell Sloan.

'It would generally take less pull to fire a semiautomatic pistol than a double-action revolver.'

'A lot less?'

'Yes.'

'Would you say that the semiautomatic would be closer to a hair trigger? A very light pull might set it off?'

'Depends on the firearm,' he says.

'Let's assume as a hypothetical that two people were struggling over a small semiautomatic pistol.'

I can see Ryan out of the corner of my eye as he shifts in his chair, uncomfortable with the mental images being painted.

'Let's assume further that one of them had his or her finger over the trigger and the other was trying to get the gun away. And let us assume that this pistol has a live round in the chamber, with the hammer already cocked and the safety off. Would it take much force on the trigger to fire that weapon?'

'As compared to what?'

'As compared to a double-action revolver, say?'

'It would take less.'

'Considerably less?'

'Possibly.'

'So slight pressure on the trigger could set the gun off?'

'It's possible.'

'And it would immediately recycle itself to fire again?'

'If it was functioning properly.'

'And the same amount of force, slight pressure on the trigger could set it off a second time?'

'The same amount of force, I don't know how slight. Would depend on the firearm in question.'

It's as good as it's going to get. Having climbed the wall, I go over the top.

'And let's assume, just for purposes of the hypothetical, that in struggling over the gun it got twisted around, and the first round struck the victim?'

'I don't understand?' says Sloan.

'If the weapon was in the victim's hand and got twisted around, could the impact of that bullet hitting her cause the weapon to fire a second time?'

'Objection!' Ryan's now out of his chair.

'Could the impact of that bullet cause her to pull the trigger a second time?'

'Assumes facts not in evidence. Beyond the scope of this witness. He is not a medical expert,' says Ryan.

'Sustained. Don't answer the question,' says Peltro. 'The jury will disregard the last question.'

'Nothing further of this witness, Your Honor.'

CHAPTER
TWENTY-FIVE

Ryan is operating on the notion that Jonah sat in the driver's seat and methodically pumped two rounds into Suade. This picture fits nicely with the theory that while Jonah may have been enraged, he took the time to go somewhere, get the gun, and then drive to Suade's, all the elements of premeditation and deliberation, malice aforethought.

Without evidence linking Ontaveroz, I am now being forced in midtrial to rethink the defense, not without risk.

Suade's gun is the key. I have considered the possibility of putting on my own medical expert, reconstructing the scene, the wounds, the powder residue, putting the weapon in Suade's hand. The image of whoever killed her, fighting for his life.

My problem is, Jonah says he wasn't there. What happens if I build this defense, and put him on the stand? *My client didn't do it, but whoever did was defending himself.* It becomes an open-ended defense of the world: everyone except my own client.

The alternative is not to put Jonah on at all. But if self-defense is the theory, the jury is left to wonder why a man who defends himself to the point of taking another life declines to take the stand to defend himself at trial. You can forget the instruction that the jury is not to infer anything from his silence.

I planted the seed with Ryan's firearms expert.

Peltro has done everything in his power to dig it up, including a session in chambers where he warns me, one more attempt like that and I'll be spending time in the bucket when the trial is over, paying some hefty fines by way of sanctions.

Harry and I spend the lunch hour with Jonah in one of the holding cells, a stainless-steel toilet against the wall and a matching single bunk bolted to the floor.

We're going over Ryan's witness list trying to cull the wheat from the chaff, people he might actually call.

Jonah does not seem well, sitting on the bunk looking pale and withered. The doctors are trying a different medication for his blood pressure, not having much success.

'The food is worse than in the army,' he tells us. He's looking at my sandwich, wondering why he got Jell-O and chicken soup.

'They put you on a restricted diet,' I tell him.

'Why don't they just kill me?'

'Give 'em time,' says Harry. 'They're trying.'

Jonah toys with the Jell-O, wiggling the little squares with the point of his spoon.

'Can you tell us about these people?' I ask him. 'The

former deckhand? Your gardener? The dentist. It would help if we could narrow them down.'

Ryan's put them all on the witness list. Every person the cops have questioned during their investigation. Without Murphy, Harry and I are now left to cull it down, split up the list and interview the ones we think might know something, that is, if they'll talk to us.

'Ed Condit and I fish together.' Jonah's talking about his dentist. Everybody he knows goes out on the boat. 'He doesn't know anything. What's to know?'

'You don't talk with him when he drills your teeth?' asks Harry.

'He's got his fingers in my mouth. How can I?'

'You never talked to him about Jessica? Never said anything about Suade?' I ask.

He shakes his head.

'So can we cross him off?'

'As far as I'm concerned.'

'What about this guy Jeffers?'

'Floyd? I don't know why they put him down there.' He's leaning over looking at the list in my hand as I sit on the cot next to him.

'I haven't seen him in two years,' he says. 'He used to work on the boat. Hung out on the docks. But I certainly never discussed anything personal with him.'

'Any reason why they might put him on the list?' I ask.

'No. I think they're just putting down names.'

That's a big part of it. Harry and I know it. Force us to waste resources preparing.

'You hired him as a deckhand?' says Harry.

'Right.' He shovels a square of Jell-O with the little teaspoon.

'Why did he quit?' says Harry. 'Did you have a falling out?' One of the things we would look for, disgruntled employee.

'No. No. Nothing like that. In fact, we had a drink the day he quit. Went to a tavern at the marina. Several people with us,' he says.

I'm sure Jonah was buying all the drinks.

'No he was fine. Left for a better job,' he says.

'Did you know he had a record?'

Jonah looks at Harry as soon as he says this.

'No, I didn't.'

'He does,' says Harry. 'Did eighteen months about ten years ago. Larceny rap,' says Harry.

Jonah looks at him like this doesn't compute.

'Theft,' I say.

'Ahh.'

This is something Ryan has to disclose, a convicted felon on the list. Jeffers could be subject to impeachment if he puts him on. Still, Jonah says that's not likely. According to him, there's nothing Floyd Jeffers could tell them.

We go down the list, maybe four or five live ones, people who might have bad things to say, a neighbor with a fence line dispute in the subdivision where Jonah lives, a woman who once cleaned house and who Mary thinks stole something. They fired her. Ryan has been busy digging up all the dirt.

In the afternoon Ryan puts on Victor Koblinski, 'Vic' to anyone who's ever met him, like me, that night outside Suade's office as they swept the scene for evidence.

342

Unfortunately, Koblinski's got a good memory for faces. He recognizes mine. Tells the court under gentle prodding from Ryan that I was there that night. This confirms what they've already heard from Brower. Not that any crime has been committed. Ryan may be working toward that.

Dark hair, parted on the left, the beginnings of a bald landing zone on top, Koblinski has saddlebags under both eyes, a face that looks like a beagle's, an expression you can't quite figure out, whether it's sad or just half asleep.

'Sergeant Koblinski. The night you saw Mr Madriani at the scene with Investigator Brower. Did you talk to him?'

'Not specifically.'

'Were you introduced?'

'No.'

'So you didn't know that he was a defense attorney working for Mr Hale, the defendant.'

'Objection. Mr Hale wasn't a defendant at that time. No charges had been brought.'

'Maybe I should rephrase the question,' says Ryan. 'You didn't know he was working for Mr Hale at that time?'

'No.'

'You were assigned to collect trace evidence at that scene, is that right?'

'Correct.'

'Can you tell the jury what's involved in the collection of trace evidence? Just generally,' he says.

'It's the gathering of very small items, sometimes hair or fibers, sometimes plant material, minerals, particles of sand, anything that can be examined by microscopy, put on a slide, viewed under a microscope, or analyzed in some other way.'

'And you've been trained in this field? What kind of training?'

'I hold a degree in police science, criminology. Eleven years on the job. Courses in Washington and Quantico, Virginia, through the FBI Crime Lab. Seminars annually, sometimes twice a year with the California Association of Criminalists. I've also taught courses on the collection of trace evidence at local community colleges.'

'Can you tell the jury what you observed when you arrived at the scene in Imperial City?'

'Ah. The victim was in a parking lot behind her office, lying upper torso on her back, lower torso twisted a little onto her left side. She was partially shielded from the street by the rear wheels and the back end of a large town car. We later came to learn that that particular vehicle belonged to the victim.'

'Did you inspect or examine the area immediately around the victim?'

'I did.'

'And what did you find?'

'There was a large pool of blood. Some footprints outside of it. We later determined that these matched the grid pattern on a sole of shoes worn by one of the paramedics first on the scene.'

'So paramedics had tried to resuscitate the victim before you arrived?'

'Yeah. But from what I heard she was already dead.'

'So they pronounced her dead at the scene?'

'Right.'

'What else did you find?'

'One spent cartridge casing. About eight feet from the

body. There was a smear of blood on the ground – from where the victim had been dragged.'

'Dragged?' says Ryan. He turns to look at the jury as he says this.

'Yes. It looked like she was either pushed or pulled from a vehicle after she was shot.'

'Then?'

'Then dragged on her back. One of the wounds was a bleeder. Lot of blood.'

'And this made a mark on the ground?'

'On the paving,' says Koblinski. 'Also we found little bits of gravel from the surface imbedded in her clothing, and abrasion on the cloth that would lead us to conclude that she had been dragged.'

'How far?' says Ryan.

'Maybe six, eight feet. No more. Just enough to allow the vehicle to pull away without hitting the body.'

'What else did you find? Besides the cartridge casing and the pool of blood?' Then Ryan holds his hand up. Stops him. 'Before we leave it,' he says. 'The cartridge's casing, did you determine the caliber?'

'Three-eighty,' says Koblinski.

'Thank you. What else did you find?'

'There was a cigar butt. Stubbed out.'

Ryan stops, shops at the evidence cart for a second, then hands one of the paper bags to the bailiff, who hands it to the witness.

Koblinski quickly identifies it as the one he found at the scene. 'Has my evidence tag on it,' he says.

'Did you show this cigar to anybody at the scene?'

'Yeah.'

'Who?'

'Him.' Koblinski points to me. 'And Brower.' He says Brower's name as if it's a four-letter word.

'Let the record reflect that the witness has identified the defense counsel, Mr Madriani.'

Ryan makes a mark on the piece of paper in front of him with a pencil, no doubt checking off a point he wants to be sure to cover.

'Was there anything on this cigar when you found it?'

'Some blood,' says Koblinski.

'Were you able to determine whose blood this was?'

'The victim's. Same type.'

'Were you able to determine how this blood came to be on this cigar butt?'

'Wasn't clear whether maybe it was kicked in there. Into the pooled blood, or if whoever dropped it, dropped it there and the pool caught up with it.'

'So you weren't able to do any DNA testing for saliva on the cigar?'

'No. Too much blood. We determined it would be contaminated.'

A couple of the jurors are looking more critically toward Jonah, just as he gives Harry a look, shrug of the shoulders, like he can't help that. Harry's expression is one to kill. A message to stop the body language.

'What else did you find at the scene?'

'Dusting of ash,' he says. 'Very fine. And two cigarette butts. One of them on top of the body. Both of them with lipstick on them.'

'Were you able to determine where these cigarettes came from?'

'They matched the brand we found in the victim's purse, which was also near the body. We analyzed the lipstick from the purse. It also matched what was on the cigarette butts.'

'Do you have any theory as to how the cigarettes got there, on top of the body? And the dusting of ash?'

'Yes. We believe that whoever killed her dragged the body away from the vehicle, and then probably dumped the ashtray from the vehicle on top of her.'

'What else did you find?'

'Fish scales,' says Koblinski.

'Fish scales?' says Ryan.

'Right. And traces of dried blood on the seat of her pants, under her legs.'

'So this would be blood from the victim's wounds?'

'No,' says Koblinski. 'What we found on the seat of her pants was not human blood. It was piscine.'

'Excuse me?'

'Fish blood,' says Koblinski. 'Serology determined this by analysis.'

'Laboratory blood analysis?'

'Right. It looked like some of this blood, partially coagulated, had adhered to the back of the upper right leg of the victim's pants. Upper thigh,' says Koblinski. 'She must have sat on it, not realizing, a small glob must have still been wet. Blood'll do that if it starts to coagulate. Then it smeared on her pants and dried there.'

'On the back of her pants.'

'Correct.'

'Can you tell us what drew your attention to this blood on the back of the victim's pants? I mean, the way you describe the body at the scene there was a considerable amount of blood.'

'That's true. But it was all on her upper torso, soaked into her clothes, this little bolero-type jacket and her blouse. There wasn't any blood on her pants except for this. We thought maybe we got lucky. That maybe there was some blood belonging to the assailant.'

'But this wasn't the case?'

'No. At least not directly,' says Koblinski.

'Now let's turn our attention to the fish scales. Were you able to analyze these?'

'We were.'

'Were you able to determine the type of fish these came from.'

'A marlin. A large game fish,' says Koblinski. 'Neon blue color. They're caught in the waters off the coast and south of here. A lot of people tag 'em, and let 'em go.'

But not Jonah. I know where he's going.

'In connection with your investigation did you have occasion to inspect the defendant's boat, the *Amanda*?'

'I did.'

'Before telling us what you found there, could you describe the boat in question?'

'It's a large sport fisher. Steel hull. Forty-two feet. Twin-engine diesels.'

'An expensive boat?' says Ryan.

'I wish I had one,' says Koblinski.

The jury laughs a little.

Jonah's smile is forced. He's not looking well.

'And what did you find on board?'

'Traces of blood. Lots of fish blood.'

'Is there any way of knowing if it was the same as the blood found on the victim's clothing?'

'I couldn't. Probably too much cross-contamination. Too many different kinds of fish.'

'What else did you find?'

'Fish scales.'

'This would be pretty common on a fishing boat?'

'Yeah.'

'Did you find any scales that matched the ones on the victim's clothing.'

'No. But I did find a picture.'

'Just a moment,' says Ryan. He whispers to one of his minions, an assistant at the table next to Avery. The younger lawyer scurries to the evidence cart and collects an envelope, hands it to the bailiff.

Koblinski gets it and opens the envelope.

'Do you recognize the picture?' says Ryan.

'Yep. It's the one I found on the boat.'

'Could you tell the jury what's in that picture?'

'It's a shot of the defendant, standing on the docks next to his boat. And a large fish,' says Koblinski. 'A blue marlin.'

'The same kind of scales you found on the victim's clothing?'

'Right.'

'Did you examine anything else belonging to the defendant either that day or shortly thereafter?'

'Yes.'

'What?'

'Some fishing overalls. Rubberized canvas,' says Koblinski.

'Where did you find these?'

'At the defendant's residence.'

'And did you find anything on them? Trace evidence?' says Ryan.

'A lot of fish blood on them. And organic traces.'

'Any fish scales?'

'All over them,' says Koblinski.

'Blue marlin scales?'

'Yes.'

'What else?'

'We impounded one of the defendant's vehicles, a nineteen ninety-six green Ford Explorer. We had it towed to the yard.'

'This would be the city's impound lot?'

'Right.'

'Did you inspect this vehicle?'

'We did.'

'And what did you find?'

'More of the same,' says Koblinski. 'Dried fish blood on the canvas seat covers, front and rear.'

'Driver and passenger side?'

'Right.'

'And what else?'

'We found a considerable amount of trace evidence on the seat covers, fish scales, a variety,' he says. 'But there was a concentration of blue marlin scales on the driver's seat and the front passenger seat.'

'Could you describe these covers?'

'Canvas,' says Koblinski. 'They look like they might have been used for something else originally. Boat dodgers, maybe an old bimini top. They were green, cut into large squares and laid over the seats.'

'And these marlin scales, the trace evidence that you found, they were just lying on them?'

'No. The scales are spiny. Sharp pointed edges when you look at them under the microscope. These would tend to adhere to fabric. The tiny spines would become embedded in the woven threads.'

'Is that how you found them on the victim's clothing as well? Embedded in the weave of the fabric?'

'Some of them.'

'Did you collect samples of the dried fish blood and the scales from the defendant's seat covers?'

'We did.'

'And you took samples from the victim's clothing?'

'Yes.'

'Did you discover anything else in your search of the defendant's vehicle? The green Ford Explorer?'

'Yes. We found a tag, what appeared to be a claim check from a taxidermy shop in the south bay. It was old, dated four months earlier. But we took a chance.'

'What do you mean?'

'We went to Sal's Taxidermy. The place that issued the claim check.'

'What did you find?'

'The claim ticket in question had been issued to the defendant several months earlier. According to the shop's records, it was for preparation of a large sea bass.'

'Preparation?'

'Stuffing and mounting,' says Koblinski. 'But we also discovered that a much larger fish had been delivered to the shop three days earlier, not by the defendant, but by one of his deckhand—'

'Objection. Hearsay.'

'Sustained,' says Peltro.

'Did you have occasion to see another fish while you were at Sal's taxidermy?'

'We did. In cold storage.'

'Could you describe that fish?'

'It was a large blue marlin, just under a thousand pounds. The weight was marked on the tag. It was a large fish for Southern California. They get bigger sometimes, off Kona in Hawaii and Australia. But a thousand pounds is big for the Pacific coast. Probably El Niño,' says Koblinski. 'Everything's pushed up from down south,' he says.

'You know something about marlin?'

'I've gone out for them on charter, a couple of times.'

'And this was a bigger fish than you'd ever seen?'

'Yeah.'

'You say you saw the tag. Was the name of the person who caught that fish displayed on the tag?'

'It was.'

'What was that name?'

'The defendant. Jonah Hale.' Koblinski looks at Jonah as he says it.

'Did you collect samples of blood and scales from this marlin, the one with the defendant's name on it at Sal's Taxidermy?'

'I did.'

'And did you examine the fish scales under a microscope?'

'Yes.'

'Did you form any conclusions, or opinions from your examination?'

'Yes. I concluded that the scales taken from the clothing of the victim, Zolanda Suade, under microscopic examination appeared to be consistent in size, color, and character with those collected from the seat covers of the defendant's vehicle. They also appeared to be consistent in size, color, and character with the scales collected from the marlin in cold storage at Sal's Taxidermy.'

'One final question. Did you collect samples of the dried blood from the victim's clothing as well as samples of blood from the marlin in cold storage and send them to another lab for testing?'

'I did. Along with tissue samples from the fish.'

'And where did you send those?'

'Genetics Incorporated in Berkeley, California.'

'Thank you, Mr Koblinski. Your witness,' says Ryan.

Ryan's getting up to speed, doing some damage now, though he's left a few items for me to chew on.

'Mr Koblinski. Is it Mister, or Officer?'

'Mister,' he says. Koblinski is not sworn law enforcement, but a lab technician.

'Let's start with your examination of Mr Hale's vehicle. The nineteen ninety-six Ford Explorer. You searched that vehicle, right?'

'That's correct.'

'How did you do that?'

'We vacuumed it,' he says. 'Special vacuum with filters. Marked each filter as to location and placed them in evidence bags.'

'This is how you collected the traces of dried fish blood and fish scales?'

'That and examination under magnifying glass. Collection with tweezers and forceps.'

'So your search was pretty thorough?'

'It was.'

'Did you find any spent bullet cartridges in Mr Hale's car?'

'No.'

'Did you find any evidence of human blood in the car?'

'It would have been impossible to distinguish. The car was too contaminated by other species. Fish,' he says.

'But you weren't able to find any human blood, right?'

'No.'

'Did you look?'

'Sure.'

'In your earlier testimony I think you described one of the wounds suffered by the victim as a "bleeder".'

'I'm gonna object,' says Ryan. 'The witness is not a medical expert.'

'His words,' I say.

'I'll overrule it.'

'Didn't you say one of the wounds was a "bleeder"?'

'I might have.'

'What did you mean by that?'

'The bullet probably hit a large artery.'

'So this would result in that wound producing a good quantity of blood? Isn't that what you described seeing on the ground. The blood smear?'

'Yeah.'

'And yet you didn't find any human blood in the defendant's car?'

'As I said, the vehicle was contaminated.'

'Mr Koblinski, have you ever examined fish scales previously, either in another case or while studying?'

354

'Sure.'

'Have you ever examined blue marlin scales?'

'No.'

'Isn't it a fact that samples or specimens of scales from one blue marlin might look very much like any other blue marlin under a microscope?'

'They might. But most people don't get that close to them to track the scales into their cars.'

Koblinski's smiling at me now, giving me the feeling I've stepped in it. I could drop it, but the jury's going to wonder why.

'You mean the average person doesn't catch a blue marlin?'

'No. That too,' he says. 'But most people who catch them tag and release them. Everybody I know,' he says. 'They don't haul them on board. Marlin is a sport fish. It's no good for eating. Most sport fishers are becoming conservationists,' says Koblinski. As he says this he looks at Jonah. So does half the jury.

I could get into it with him. This was a trophy fish. How many times do you catch a thousand pounder? Koblinski would no doubt draw images of harpooning a whale, Free Willie on a barbeque spit. I drop it as fast as I can. All the ways a sharp witness can kill you.

'Are you familiar with the theory of transference?' I ask him.

The jury's still seeing blood in the water. Not interested with what I'm saying at the moment.

'Sure.'

'And cross-transference?' I ask.

'Yes.'

'Could you tell the jury what these are?'

'It's where microscopic or macroscopic evidence clings to an object, say clothing. By static electricity or gets caught in the fabric, and transfers from one surface to another.'

'And cross transference?' I say.

'Other way around,' he says.

'For example, fibers from the victim's clothing found on a car seat cover. Or strands of the victim's hair on the back of a seat.'

He nods. 'Yeah.'

'Did you find any fibers from the victim's clothing on the seat covers in Mr Hale's green Ford Explorer?'

'No.'

'Do you know what kind of fabric the victim's clothing was made of?'

'It was wool. Pants and top. Kind of a toreador suit,' he says.

'Wouldn't you expect to find traces of fibers from this suit if she sat on these seat covers?'

'Not in this case,' he says. 'There was evidence that someone had cleaned out the vehicle recently. The ashtray was empty.' Like a land mine, I have stepped on it.

When I look over, Ryan's smirking from the counsel table, things finally going his way. The fact is not lost on the jury. How likely is it that a man who smokes cigars, enough to purchase them at a thousand dollars a box from a private back room, would happen to have a clean ashtray in his car on the day it's checked? Unless he had a reason.

'We think somebody probably shook the seat covers out, too,' says Koblinski.

'If she was dragged out of the car, wouldn't you expect

some of these fibers, fibers from her clothing to become abraded, left behind on the seat, maybe on the floor of the vehicle?'

'It's possible, but like I say, if the covers were shaken out, maybe not.'

'But you didn't find any in the defendant's car?'

'Fibers from the victim?'

'Yes.'

'No,' says Koblinski.

'Did you find any strands of the victim's hair on the headrest, or on the passenger seat?'

'No.'

'Did you find any traces of her hair anywhere in that vehicle?'

'No. It was pretty clean.'

'And you checked all your filters. The special forensic vacuum filters you used on that vehicle?'

'Yes.'

'And you found nothing?'

'We found fish blood and scales. They were stuck to the seat covers,' says the witness.

'You know what I'm talking about, Mr Koblinski. I'm talking about evidence of cross transference, hair and fibers belonging to the victim. Wouldn't you expect to find trace evidence of these if the victim had been seated in that car? Isn't it probable? Even if somebody shook out the seat covers? Isn't it likely that there would have been some trace evidence of the victim in that vehicle?'

'It's possible,' he says. 'I couldn't say.' All of this with a smile.

CHAPTER
TWENTY-SIX

R yan's on a roll. The next morning he comes right behind Koblinski with a clincher. It's what I'd feared earlier: DNA – not Suade's blood, but the fish.

Howard Sandler is a forensic serologist. A Ph.D. who, among other things, performs genetic fingerprinting, but with a twist. He works for a private lab in Berkeley, where their speciality is endangered species and poaching.

Ryan spends nearly half an hour qualifying the witness as an expert, going over Sandler's curriculum vitae before he gets to the issue – a DNA fingerprint.

'Is this something that you're asked to do on a regular basis?'

'Not usually,' says Sandler. 'Normally requests relate to fish stock identification, gene flow. What we could call population genetic structures, to help manage resources. It's unusual to get a request for specific genetic identification, but it does happen. Usually in cases of suspected poaching.'

'But it is possible to do what you were being asked to do in this case, to determine if a dried sample of blood came from a specific fish, a so-called genetic fingerprint?'

'That depends on the sample. Whether there's sufficient genetic material. But as a general principle, yes, it is possible.'

'Can you tell the jury what type of testing you used in this case?'

'The technique is called polymerase chain reaction. It's known by the acronym PCR.'

'And what exactly does this PCR process do?'

'All living organisms are composed of strands of genetic material known as chromosomes. They're arranged like beads on a thread. The order in which these chromosomes are arranged determines the genetic makeup of the organism. Whether it's going to be a cow, or a poppy in a field. If it's a cow, whether it's going to be light in color or dark. Whether it's going to be a Jersey or a Guernsey. The building blocks of the chromosomes are DNA molecules. These building blocks of DNA are arranged in a kind of coiled ladder called a double helix. And the precise manner in which the molecules of DNA are arranged is specific and unique to every individual living organism. This is what you might call the DNA fingerprint.'

'So by identifying this fingerprint you can determine whether a drop of blood from a crime scene came from that specific animal, or in this case a specific fish, as might be the case with the blue marlin in cold storage?'

'That's right.'

'Now this PCR process, can you tell us, just in layman's terms, how does it work?'

'The P stands for polymerase. These are enzymes used by the DNA molecule to assemble a new DNA strand in a proper sequence, consistent with the original or parent DNA strand. This would be necessary for cell division and growth, in order for the organism to continue living. In the polymerase chain reaction, small quantities of DNA or broken pieces of DNA from a crime scene, such as a small amount of dried blood, as opposed to DNA from a living cell, can be copied in a relatively short period of time, say a few hours. Once the DNA is copied, replicated, it can be analyzed by any number of methods of molecular biology in order to compare it with other known samples.'

'In this case, the samples of blood and tissue from the blue marlin in cold storage?' Ryan is good at this, bringing the witness back to the particulars of his case.

'That's right. The DNA strands will either be identical or they won't. There's no middle ground.'

'And what are the chances that two living organisms would have identical genetic fingerprints?'

'In this case?'

'Yes.'

'Infinitesimal,' says the witness. 'One chance in about fifteen billion.'

Ryan wrinkles his eyebrows, steps back from the podium. Puts on a display of incredulity for the jury.

It's as neat and clean a description of the process as I've ever heard.

'In short, you would have a much better chance of winning the lottery without a ticket. Is that what you're telling us?' Ryan looks at Jonah as he says it.

'Objection.'

361

'Sustained. The jury will disregard the question. Mr Ryan . . .' Peltro holding the gavel up like a school ruler about to rap knuckles. 'Get on with your case.'

'Dr Sandler, did you perform this PCR test on the samples of dried blood sent to you in this case by the crime lab?'

'I did.'

'And could you tell us what you learned as a result of this analysis?'

'The DNA sequencing, that is, the order of sequencing between the DNA strands from the dried blood on the victim's pants, and the sequencing of DNA strands from the marlin in cold storage were identical.'

'Were you able to form any factual conclusion as a result of this?'

'I was.'

'And what was that conclusion?'

'The three samples in question, the dried blood from the back of the victim's pants, came from the marlin in cold storage.'

'That specific marlin, to the exclusion of any other?'

'That's correct.'

The courtroom is motionless. A pivotal point. It is palpable. You can smell it, hear a pin drop, the scratching of paper by pencils in the front row as reporters try to get it down verbatim.

I look over and Jonah has his head in his hands, on the table. Mary seated behind him, beyond the railing. She seems shell-shocked, dazed. A stark, haunted expression on her face, as if occupied by a single thought, read her mind: is she married to a killer?

*　　*　　*

'Somebody must have put it there.' Jonah's talking about the dried blood on Suade's clothes. 'How else could it have gotten there?' he says.

'I don't know.'

He's looking at me as if I don't believe him. We're in a holding cell twenty feet from Peltro's courtroom, just Jonah and me. People milling in the hallway outside.

When Peltro stepped off the bench, headed for chambers, Ryan convened his own court. Surrounded by a gaggle of reporters, he was asked if the trial was over. Whether the DNA was the coup de grâce. I heard him tell them, in a voice loud enough to be heard halfway across the room, to stay tuned.

My cross-examination of Howard Sandler took all of three minutes. The only thing left to me was the chain of evidence. When I tried to get an edge into the collection of the samples, Ryan objected, and had me dead in the water, on grounds that this was beyond the scope of the witness.

Sandler could only say that once the samples were received at his own lab, they were properly handled and that no mistakes were made at that end.

The sole inference I tried to work toward was that maybe someone had made a mistake in labeling, mixing up the evidence from cold storage with the blood from the scene.

You can't always tell when a jury is buying something, but you can usually tell when they're not – and they weren't buying this.

'You did good getting Mary out of here,' says Jonah.

My only positive deed for the day. I had Harry take her home, run the press gauntlet, down the back stairs. There will be cops outside of Mary's home tonight to keep them away, the media horde.

We went to the house a few days ago, Harry and I. All the plants and shrubs across the front are now dead, trampled as if by wildebeest. There are ruts in Jonah's lawn from enterprising camera crews feeding the public's right to know, trying to catch any piece of film they can for their files – Mary taking out the garbage, Mary in the kitchen, Mary trying to pull the shades in her bedroom, all this with their thousand-foot zoom lenses. News copters fly over the house, morning, noon, and night, after dark they flash their lights in her backyard, cameramen hanging from the struts.

Two days ago she brought me a letter signed by the officers of their homeowners' association. They are asking Mary to move out, at least until the trial is over. Her neighbors can no longer deal with the invasion.

Jonah is looking at me, wondering where we go from here.

'There is another possibility,' I tell him. 'Self-defense.' We have talked about this before. 'Suade's gun.' I arch an eyebrow, look at him.

'You don't believe me,' he says.

'I don't know what I believe. I know the evidence is not favorable, and we're running out of time. We can't find Ontaveroz or any evidence of a connection. If we are going to shift defenses, I'm going to have to act soon.'

I pull him over, sit him down at the small stainless-steel table in the center of the holding cell, two chairs bolted to the floor on either side that cannot be moved.

'I have experts on my list,' I tell him. 'People I put there

364

just in case. Reconstruction experts. Medical witnesses, who are willing to testify that the wounds suffered by Suade are consistent with an altercation. They've looked at the evidence, the medical examiner's report, the wounds, the gun residue on Suade's hands. They are willing to testify that a struggle occurred in the car. A fight for the gun. We have the records of the purchase of the pistol, the one Suade bought. I think it was self-defense,' I tell him. 'She carried that pistol in her purse. I think she pulled it out that evening.'

'It could have happened that way,' says Jonah. 'But I don't know.'

'You don't know what?'

'I don't know what happened. I wasn't there.'

I offer up a deep sigh, look at the far wall over his shoulder.

Jonah hangs his head. 'You want me to tell them I was there, I will,' he says. 'I'll tell them I fought for the gun.'

I shake my head. 'Not unless it's the truth.' Besides the fact that it would be perjury, nothing could be more dangerous than Jonah on the stand concocting stories.

Then he shakes his head. 'Why can't you just put me on the stand and I can tell them I wasn't there?'

'Because they won't believe you. What are you going to say when Ryan asks you how that marlin's blood got all over Suade's clothes?'

'I don't know.'

'And when he confronts you with the threats you made in front of Brower? What will you say? That you were just kidding?'

'Maybe,' he says.

'So you weren't angry?'

'No, I was angry.'

'So you weren't kidding?'

'No, I was angry, but I wasn't going to kill her.'

'Then why did you say it?'

'People say things they don't mean all the time,' he says.

'Do you?'

Jonah doesn't answer. Instead he looks on, seeing the problem. Were you lying then, or are you lying now?

With all this, there is something gnawing at me that doesn't make sense. With all his evidence, the physical links tying Jonah to the scene, there are questions that Ryan hasn't answered: why would a woman who has met Jonah only once, and then in hostile circumstances, climb into the passenger seat of his car? What on earth could they find to talk about while she consumed not one, but two cigarettes? And perhaps more important, given the makeup of my jury, why would a woman, a natty dresser like Suade whose attire was meticulous even if bizarre, the tight little toreador costume, why would someone who took such care willingly jump on Jonah's blood-spattered, scale-covered seat covers? This last defies female logic, a messy question, and one that Ryan will have to deal with, or leave dangling for me in front of nine women on the jury.

CHAPTER
TWENTY-SEVEN

'The state calls Susan McKay.'

Ryan tries not to look at me as he says it, but in the end he can't resist a sniggering sideways glance. Satisfaction written on his face.

Until this moment, Harry and I had assumed that Ryan was keeping Susan out in the hallway under constant subpoena as a kind of penance. He has made her cool her heels for nearly a week, this for her help on Suade's gun, a detail we probably would have turned up in any event.

Jonah leans over. Harry and I have him sandwiched between us, trying to avoid a repeat of yesterday, the body English of defeat.

'I thought the two of you were friends.' He whispers a little too loud so that I am left to look at the jury, hoping that the ones in the front row don't have great hearing.

I cup a hand. 'Against her will. She's under subpoena,' I tell him.

'Oh.' He nods as if he understands. 'She's probably gonna

tell 'em what I did in her office. How I got mad and walked out 'n all.'

She might not have to if Jonah keeps talking. I put a hand on his forearm, finger to my lips to shut him up.

Even with the click of her high heels on the hard surface of the floor, I don't have to turn to look. I know Susan is in the room. I can feel the heat of her gaze on the back of my neck, like a laser shaving the fine hairs.

She had started to relax, accepting my nightly assurances that Ryan wouldn't call her. After all, Brower heard the death threats in my office. There's little Susan can add.

She may be a reluctant witness, but she walks with purpose through the gate in the bar, past the rostrum where she pivots. Standing near the witness box, she raises her hand. As she does this, her gaze is not on the clerk with his upraised hand and mantra . . . *Do you swear to tell the truth, the whole truth* . . . but on me. At the moment, I suspect it's not anger so much as the normal emotion that comes with surprise: fight or flight.

'Would you take a seat?' says Ryan. 'Give us your name. Spell the last name for the record, and your address.'

'Susan McKay.' I can tell she's scared. She spells her last name like she's spitting out the five letters, then gives her office address, not her home. Ryan doesn't seem to notice. The reporters in the front row will have a hard time hunting her down when she's done. Her home number is unlisted.

'Ms McKay, can you tell us what you do for a living?'

'I'm director of Children's Protective Services.'

'Is that a public agency?'

'Yes.'

'In the county or the city?' says Ryan.

'County,' she says.

'And what do you do there? What are your responsibilties as director?'

'I'm the chief administrative officer for the department.'

'So you run the agency?'

'Yes.'

'Are you responsible to anyone else?'

'The board of supervisors,' she says.

'You serve at their pleasure, is that right?' Ryan asks the question as if at the moment there is very little pleasure left with Susan in that place.

'That's correct.'

Ryan already knows all this. He's simply reminding Susan.

'Could you please tell the jury what your agency does?'

'We're charged with looking after the welfare of children. Abused. Neglected. We deal with allegations of child abuse and endangerment. We investigate charges. Take children into protective custody when it's necessary. We also file applications with the court for the appointment of guardians from time to time. The department makes recommendations as to if and when children should be made wards of the court.'

'You say you investigate cases of child abuse?' Ryan picks from this smorgasbord the one he wants.

'That's correct.'

'And in that regard did your agency have occasion to inquire into allegations of child abuse, specifically charges of molestation regarding a child by the name of Amanda Hale?'

369

'I'm going to object, Your Honor. Grounds of relevance,' I say.

'Goes to motive,' says Ryan.

'I'll allow it,' says Peltro. 'Overruled.'

'I don't do casework myself,' says Susan.

'Yes, but you do know about this case, don't you?'

'I know about the charges,' she says.

'Was an investigation conducted by your agency in regard to those charges?'

'An inquiry was made. I don't think it ever got to the level of a full investigation.'

'Can you tell the jury who lodged those charges with the county?'

'Objection, Your Honor. Can we approach?' I motion toward the bench.

Peltro waves us on. Ryan and I cozy up to the bench on the side away from Susan in the witness box. The court reporter with her computerized stenograph machine huddling in close to take it all down.

'You Honor, this is highly prejudicial.' I'm whispering now, cupping a hand, trying to keep it away from the jury and the front row with their scratching pencils and pens.

'No charges were ever brought against my client. All the evidence indicates that the events never occurred. There was never any evidence of molestation or incest.'

'The charges were made,' says Ryan. 'I'm not offering them to prove they were true. The fact is the allegations go directly to motive. The defendant knew these charges had been made. He was also aware that they were about to be renewed in the victim's press release. It may very well have been defamatory,' says Ryan. 'But that doesn'' justify murder. Mr Madriani knows that's our theory. It's been clear from the beginning. Our theory is his client killed the victim to silence her.'

'Your Honor, if you let this in, the jury runs the risk of convicting my client for all the wrong reasons.'

The judge is shaking his head, unwilling to cut the heart out of Ryan's case. It was a long-shot objection, and Peltro clearly sees it that way.

'Mr Madriani, you can cross-examine the witness later,' he says. 'You can make it clear at that time that the agency found no merit in the charges. But it does go to motive,' he says.

'I'm going to overrule the objection.' Peltro says it loud enough for the entire courtroom to hear. He sends Ryan back to the rostrum, me to my chair.

'Ms McKay. Can you tell us who lodged the charges in question, the allegations of child molestation involving the child Amanda Hale?'

'It was her mother.'

'That would be Jessica Hale?'

'Yes.'

'And who were the charges made against?'

'Jonah Hale.'

'The defendant?'

'Yes.'

'He was the child's grandfather.'

'Is,' says Susan. 'He is the child's grandfather.'

'Of course.' Ryan is well aware the child is gone, though his agency has done nothing to bring charges against Jessica.

'And you say you investigated these charges?'

'No. I said we made inquiries. It never got to the point of a formal investigation.'

'You made inquiries?'

'I didn't. My office did.'

'Fine,' says Ryan, finally getting her to the point. 'Who did they inquire with?'

'Neighbors. Other relatives. The child. The child's grandmother.'

'That would be Mary Hale?' Ryan points to Mary sitting in the front row right behind Harry.

'Yes.'

Ryan looks at Mary and smiles. He'd put her up next, on the stand, except for the spousal privilege that prevents it.

'And based on these inquiries, your agency decided there was no need for a formal investigation?'

'That's correct.'

'Did you make that decision, or did someone else in your office make it?'

'Someone else,' says Susan.

'Who was that?'

'I don't remember. I probably had to sign off on it. I'd have to look at the file,' she says.

Ryan doesn't pursue it. 'Now, I want to draw your attention,' he says, 'to the morning of April seventeenth. This year. Did you receive a phone call from Mr Madriani at that time?'

'I get a lot of phone calls,' she says. 'I can't remember all the dates.'

'No doubt you get a lot of phone calls from Mr Madriani.' Susan doesn't respond, except to look at me.

'Do you get a lot of phone calls from Mr Madriani?'

'Some,' she says.

'Isn't it a fact that the two of you are friends?'

Susan hesitates. Then says: 'Yes.'

'In fact, isn't it true that you are more than friends?'

'What do you mean?' says Susan.

'Isn't it a fact that the two of you are lovers?'

'Objection.' I'm on my feet.

'What's the relevance?' says Peltro.

'I'll withdraw the question,' says Ryan. He does it smiling at the jury.

'At the moment is it true that you are living with Mr Madriani? Or rather he is living with you?'

'Your Honor?' I'm out of my chair again.

Susan squirming in the witness box, looking at the judge.

'Mr Ryan,' says Peltro.

'Your Honor. Goes to bias.'

'He's trying to impeach his own witness.'

'I'm aware,' says the judge. 'She's stated they are friends,' says Peltro. 'One more question along those lines and you can get your wallet out,' he says. 'And go get your toothbrush. Now move on.'

Ryan nods, then picks up his place from his notes. It could be worse. Ryan is a little ham-handed on this. It's not so much the message, as the way it's conveyed. He delivers it like some sleazoid listening to heavy breathing on an audiotape.

'Let's go back to the seventeenth of April,' he says. 'That's the day the victim was killed. You do remember the day?'

373

'Yes.'

'Do you remember receiving a phone call from Mr Madriani that morning?'

'I'm not sure. I think so.'

'Would it help if we showed you a copy of his cellular phone records?' Ryan makes it sound as if I'm on trial, which at the moment I am.

'No. I remember,' she says.

'Do you remember the contents of that telephone conversation?'

'I don't know if I can remember all of it,' says Susan.

'Then tell us about the parts you can remember?'

'He wanted me to meet him at his office.'

'Mr Madriani?'

'Yes.'

'Did he say why?'

'He said it had to do with a client.'

'Did he say who the client was?'

'I don't know if he said at that time or not.'

'Did you later come to learn who this client was?'

'Yes.'

'Who was it?'

'Jonah Hale,' says Susan.

'The defendant?'

'Yes.'

'What else did Mr Madriani tell you on the phone?'

'I can't remember.'

'Did he tell you that he'd just come from a meeting with the victim, Zolanda Suade?'

'Objection. Counsel's leading his witness.'

'I just asked her if she can remember.'

'Yes,' says Susan.

'Don't answer the question when there's an objection pending,' says Peltro.

'Sorry,' she says.

'She knows the answer, Your Honor.' Ryan making the point.

'Go ahead,' says Peltro.

'I think he might have told me that.' Susan speaking before Ryan can restate the question.

'Did he tell you what they talked about, Mr Madriani and Ms Suade at this meeting?'

'No. Not on the phone.'

'He didn't tell you that it didn't go well?' Now Ryan is guessing.

'He might have said that.' Before I can object.

Ryan smiles.

'Did he tell you about a press release that Ms Suade had prepared regarding Mr Madriani's client?'

'Objection.'

'Sustained. Rephrase the question.'

'Did he tell you about anything else that transpired at this meeting with Ms Suade?'

'I can't remember if he told me about the press release then or after.'

'After?'

'I mean when I went to his office.'

'When did you go to Mr Madriani's office?'

'Later that same morning.'

'That's the morning of the seventeenth, the day Ms Suade was killed?'

'Yes.'

'And who was at this meeting?'

'Mr Brower . . .'

'That would be John Brower, your investigator?'

'That's right.'

'Why was he there?'

'I just thought it would be a good idea.'

'So you brought him along?'

'Yes.'

'Why did you bring him?'

'They were trying to find a child. Mr Hale's granddaughter . . .'

'So you knew who the client was before you got to the meeting? A moment ago you said you couldn't remember whether Mr Madriani told you the client's name on the phone or not.'

Susan looks perplexed, caught in her own confusion. 'I guess he did. I must have known.'

'I guess so,' says Ryan.

Susan is nervous. Not a good witness. She keeps talking with no question. 'I guess I'd been told at some point that she, the granddaughter, had been taken in violation of a court order by the mother . . .'

'At some point?' says Ryan. 'Did you have more than one conversation with Mr Madriani concerning Mr Hale and his granddaughter?'

'I believe so.'

Harry looks at me. I'm starting to sweat. Chapter and verse. Where and when?

'How many times did you talk to Mr Madriani, before this telephone call on the seventeenth?'

'He might have mentioned it to me once.'

'Do you remember where that conversation took place?'

I have visions of the jury looking on as Susan describes the scene on the chaise longue at my house with sunscreen on my hands, down the back of her bikini. This is a near-death experience.

'I can't remember.' She looks at me, a kind of guilty glance as she says it.

'Do you remember when this conversation took place?'

'No.'

'Do you remember why Mr Madriani discussed this with you?'

'The child. Mr Hale's granddaughter was missing. Taken in violation of a court order. I assumed he wanted my department's help to try to find her.'

'And you saw nothing inappropriate in this?'

'There *was* nothing inappropriate. You asked me why I brought Mr Brower to the meeting. That's why.' Susan recovers, puts him back a little, on his heels.

'Of course,' says Ryan.

'Isn't it a fact that you'd rather not talk about this? Isn't that true?'

'What?'

'This whole thing. Isn't it a fact that you'd rather not say anything that harms Mr Madriani or his client?'

'I'd rather not be testifying, if that's what you mean.'

'That's not what I mean,' says Ryan. 'Isn't it a fact that you'd rather help Mr Madriani than hurt him?'

'I've never thought about it.' Susan looks off to the side, away from the jury as if the question is beneath her, perhaps so they can't read her eyes, which at this moment are filled with fury.

'Who else was at this meeting besides yourself and Mr

Brower? The meeting on the seventeenth?' Ryan has not lost his place. Picks up without missing a beat.

'Mr Hinds.' Susan nods toward Harry at the table. 'And Mr Hale.'

'The defendant?'

'Yes.'

'Was that it?'

'And Mr Madriani,' she says.

'Oh, of course,' says Ryan. 'We can't forget Mr Madriani. Can you tell the jury what was discussed at this meeting?'

'Most of it was about Mr Hale's granddaughter.'

That and charges of scandal in the county, though Susan is not about to mention it. Neither is Ryan, unless I miss my bet.

'She was missing, and Mr Hale wanted to find her,' says Susan.

'That's all you talked about? How to find Mr Hale's granddaughter?'

'Mostly,' says Susan.

'What about the Suade press release?' Ryan reminds her about her testimony earlier, that I had mentioned the press release during our phone conversation earlier that morning.

'I remember.'

'Was the press release discussed during the meeting?'

'It might have been,' says Susan.

'Did you ever get a chance to see this press release?'

'Yes.'

'Did you read it?'

'I think I did.'

378

'Can you tell the jury what it said?'

'It was rambling,' says Susan. 'A lot of incoherent charges.'

'What kind of charges? Against who?'

'Against Mr Hale.' To listen to her, Susan has blocked out the allegations of scandal in the county.

'What did those charges say?'

'I can't remember the details.'

'Oh, come now, Ms McKay. Didn't you read the press release?'

'Yes.'

'These were pretty serious charges, weren't they?'

'I suppose.'

'Would you like me to get the press release to refresh your recollection?'

'That's not necessary,' she says. 'There were some ugly allegations of child molestation.'

'By whom?'

'You mean who made the allegations?'

'I mean who was alleged to have committed the acts?'

'Mr Hale.'

'The defendant?'

'Yes.'

'And you read this press release in his presence?'

'As I recall. Yes.'

'What else was alleged?'

Susan thinks for a moment. 'I can't remember how she couched it.'

'The victim, Ms Suade?'

'I assume she wrote it,' says Susan.

'Isn't that what Mr Madriani told you?'

'I think so.'

'Do you remember the other charge?'

'I think she alleged sexual assault.'

Ryan looks at the jury, arched eyebrows. 'By whom?'

'By Mr Hale.'

'Who were the alleged victims of these acts?'

There is nothing I can do to prevent this. Ryan is arguing it goes to Jonah's motivation for the murder. The fact is, it's poisoning the jury.

'Mr Hale's daughter and granddaughter.'

'They were the alleged victims.'

'Yes.'

'Did Mr Hale see this press release at the meeting in Madriani's office?'

'He might have been given a copy. I can't remember.'

'And what was his reaction to all of this?'

'He wasn't happy,' says Susan.

Ryan laughs, bellicose, for the jury. He turns toward them. 'I can understand that,' he says. 'Was he angry?'

'You could say that,' says Susan.

'Was he furious?'

'I don't know if I'd go that far.'

'Did he make any statements?'

'I can't remember,' says Susan.

'He didn't say anything?'

'He said something, but I can't remember what.'

'Isn't it a fact, Ms McKay, that Mr Hale, after hearing about the information in this press release and during this meeting, made death threats against the victim, Zolanda Suade?'

Susan's eyes flash toward me, just for an instant, a signal for help.

I'm projecting my most practiced expression of indifference, the best I can do with our case vertical, and in flames.

'He might have.'

'Are you in the habit of hearing people make death threats against others? I mean, is this a normal, everyday occurrence in your life such that you wouldn't remember it?'

'It happens,' she says. 'There're a lot of angry husbands out there.'

'So it's not likely you would remember this one? Is that what you're telling us?'

Susan doesn't answer. Instead she looks at Ryan as if maybe she is silently uttering death threats in her own mind at this moment.

'Is there something about the question you don't understand?' he says.

'No.'

'Then answer it.'

'I usually remember threats.'

'And what about this one?'

'Mr Hale probably made threats.'

'What did he say, when he *probably* made these threats?'

'He was frustrated that the law was unable to deal with Zolanda Suade and her activities.'

'Then he believed Suade was responsible for the disappearance of his granddaughter, is that correct?'

'She probably was.' Susan is now digging us in.

'That's not what I asked you. I asked you if Mr Hale believed Ms Suade was involved?'

She looks at Jonah. It gives her no pleasure to say it, but she does. 'Yes.'

'Did he say as much at the meeting?'

'Yes.'

'And you say he was frustrated that the law couldn't deal with Ms Suade?'

'That's right.'

'Did he ask you or your agency to do anything, specifically?' Ryan is doubling back on Brower's testimony, tying it all in a neat knot.

'He wanted us to go over and question her.'

'How? Did he say how he wanted you to question her?'

'I don't remember.'

'Isn't it a fact that he asked you to use force in questioning Ms Suade as to the whereabouts of his granddaughter?'

'He might have. As I said, he was very frustrated.'

'Did you tell him you were going to do anything?'

'There was nothing to do. We had no evidence of her involvement.'

'Did you tell Mr Hale this?'

'Yes.'

'And what did he say?'

'I can't remember his exact words.'

'As close as you can recall?' says Ryan.

'Something like "there ought to be ways to deal with her".'

'That's what he said?' Ryan's got something in front of him, numbered and lined pages I cannot read from this distance, but I'd be willing to bet it's a transcript of Brower's earlier testimony, checking it against Susan's recollections.

'I think so. As I said, I can't remember his exact words.'

'Would you say the defendant was angry when he said this?'

'I suppose.'

'You don't know if he was angry?'

'He was upset,' says Susan.

'Would you be surprised if I told you that your investigator, Mr Brower, said he was "ballistic" – his words? That Mr Hale was so angry he was "ballistic" after hearing Mr Madriani tell him that he, Mr Hale, was accused of raping his daughter and molesting his granddaughter in that press release? Would you be surprised by that?'

'John sometimes exaggerates,' she says.

'Is that right? Is that why you demoted him?'

'I didn't demote him.'

'What do you call it?'

'Mr Brower was assigned to other duties,' says Susan.

'Ahh.' Ryan now nodding for effect. 'This meeting in Mr Madriani's office. During this meeting, did you tell Mr Hale that your department had investigated Ms Suade and that you were unable to do anything, either to get an injunction to stop her activities or to bring criminal charges?'

'I might have.'

'Did you or didn't you?'

'I think I did.'

'And do you remember Mr Hale's response?'

'I don't remember.'

'Did Mr Hale ever suggest that your department go over to Ms Suade's office and employ force to find out what happened to his granddaughter?'

'I already said he might have done that.' Susan swallows hard. 'He might have. I can't remember.'

'Did Jonah Hale during that meeting ever threaten to kill Ms Suade?'

'He may have said some things . . .'

'Did he ever threaten to kill her?'

'He made a threat.'

'I'm going to ask you one more time, and remind you that you're under oath. Did Jonah Hale in your presence at this meeting in Mr Madriani's office threaten to kill Zolanda Suade?'

Susan's gaze suddenly drops toward the floor. Chin buried in her chest. She says something, but it's not audible beyond the clerk's desk.

'What did you say?'

'I said yes.'

'Thank you.' Ryan heaves a big sigh. He has now established two important points: the death threat, confirming Brower's earlier testimony, and more damaging, Susan's clear bias.

'When you left Mr Madriani's office that morning, following the conclusion of the meeting, did you leave alone?'

'No.'

'Who was with you?'

'Mr Hale.'

'The defendant?'

'That's right.'

'Where were you going, you and Mr Hale?'

'To my office.'

'To do what?'

'After we had talked to Mr Hale for a while at Paul's

office. Mr Madriani's,' she corrects herself, but the jury's already picked up on it. 'After the meeting,' she says. 'I thought that based on information he had given us . . .'

'Who?'

'Mr Hale. I thought we might have a chance to get a court order to compel Ms Suade to provide information as to the whereabouts of Amanda Hale.'

'Why did you believe you could get a court order then, when you'd failed previously?'

'Mr Hale told us that Ms Suade had appeared at his house a few weeks earlier, just days before the child disappeared and had made what he, Mr Hale, had called threats.'

'Suade had made threats?'

'That's what he said.'

'What kind of threats?'

'He said that Zolanda Suade warned him that unless he and his wife gave up legal custody of the child, they would lose her. And a few days later, that's exactly what happened. The mother came, took the child, and neither of them has been seen since. Mr Hale said that both he and his wife could swear to these facts. They were willing to sign affidavits.'

'But you never talked to his wife about this?'

'She wasn't there. We were going to call her. Bring her to the office.'

'Did you do that?'

'No.'

'Why not?' Ryan already knows the answer.

'Because he left.'

'Who?'

'Mr Hale.'

'Let me get this straight,' says Ryan. 'You offered to help Mr Hale, using legal means, and he just walked out of your office?'

'When we got to my office, the lawyers in the department indicated that they didn't feel the information Mr Hale gave would be sufficient for a court order.'

'And what did Mr Hale say to this?'

'He wasn't happy.'

'Was he angry?' Ryan is into this again, smiling at the jury this time. 'Come on,' says Ryan. 'Isn't it a fact, Ms McKay, that Jonah Hale lost his temper when he heard this news from your lawyers, and stormed out of your office?'

'He left,' says Susan.

'Isn't it a fact that he berated the lawyers in your department. Called one of them names that I will not mention here and stormed out of your office?'

'He was angry.'

'Angry enough to leave when he didn't have wheels. He didn't have his car there, did he?'

'No.'

'Do you know where his car was?'

'No.'

'Do you know how he got to Mr Madriani's office for the meeting that morning?'

'I believe Paul – Mr Madriani picked him up.'

'Where?'

'At his boat.'

'At Mr Hale's boat, at the docks at Spanish Landing?'

'Yes.'

'Thank you.' Ryan seems particularly pleased with this last piece of information. Apart from the fact that he couldn't get this short of putting me or Jonah on the stand, I'm left to wonder why he cares.

CHAPTER
TWENTY-EIGHT

'I don't like what I'm seeing.' Rahm Karashi is a medical resident student at the university. Six days a week he works at the county hospital. This morning his rounds include the county jail, which includes taking Jonah's vital signs, blood pressure, and pulse before he leaves for court, checking his medication regimen.

At the moment, Jonah is lying on a cot in a holding cell, waiting for the van to take him to court. He has a blood pressure cuff on his arm.

Dr Karashi is on a little rolling stool he's brought into the room. He tries it again, cup of the stethoscope pressed against the inside of Jonah's right elbow. The doctor is slowly turning the pressure valve attached to the cuff. He listens for a few moments, then shakes his head. It's the third time he's taken it since Harry and I have arrived, looking to see if it's the result of anxiety, morning jitters before another day of trial. Maybe it'll drop. It doesn't.

'I'm all right,' says Jonah. 'It's just the stress. It's always high when I know they're gonna take it.' He looks at me, as if I'm going to be angry if the trial is delayed for reasons of health. At the moment, the way things are going, it would be a blessing.

The physician takes the cuff off Jonah's arm. 'Relax for a moment,' he says, then taps on the door for the guard and motions for Harry and me to join him outside.

As soon as the solid door to the cell is closed, he speaks. 'I don't like it. Don't like it at all,' he says. 'The medication should have taken hold by now. He's been on it for a week. You're sure he's taking it? Sometimes they don't, you know. If they're depressed.'

'All I know is what they tell me. The staff says he takes it each night, before bed.'

'This is not good.' Dr Karashi looks at the blood pressure readings on the chart in the file. 'It is definitely up,' he says.

'How serious?' says Harry. Beyond life threatening, what Harry means is would they stop the trial?

'You want my opinion, I think it is sufficiently serious that he should be hospitalized. At least for observation.'

'That would mean at least suspending the trial.' Harry's smiling.

'I will of course have to inform the supervising physician at County,' he says. 'Recommend that he inform the court.'

'Maybe we should bring in Mr Hale's own physician?' I say.

'That would be a good idea. The prosecutors will want their own, of course.'

'You're not it?' says Harry.

'No.' Karashi smiles. 'They will want one of the senior staff physicians. Probably the head of cardiology from County to examine him.' Someone with whom Ryan can plead for a favorable prognosis is what Dr Karashi means. He has been around long enough to know how the game is played. The last thing Ryan wants at this stage is a defendant who is too ill to continue, after we've seen all his evidence, heard his witnesses. A mistrial at this point is Ryan's worst nightmare.

'You should get an EKG,' says Karashi.

'How soon?'

'I cannot tell the court that it's life threatening,' he says. 'But I would recommend perhaps tomorrow. In the afternoon. Court often ends early on Friday,' he says. 'I think I can schedule it.'

I thank him. Karashi puts his stethoscope back in his little black bag. 'If you can reduce the stress on him at all, I would recommend it,' he says.

'How do we do that?' says Harry.

Karashi gives him a look, a shrug. No answer.

We thank him, and he leaves.

I can see Jonah through the small square of inch-thick acrylic in the cell door. He is now sitting up at the side of the cot, looking twenty years older than he did on the day he walked into my office only a few months ago, to tell me about Amanda and her mother.

'What good is anything we do if he dies before a verdict?' says Harry. 'Maybe we should talk to the judge.'

'It won't do any good unless we've got a solid medical recommendation,' I say. 'Let's get his physician in. This evening if we have to, after court.'

* * *

W hat Ryan has in store for the morning is not something intended to reduce stress – Jonah's or mine.

He has Susan back on the stand, and Ryan is back in
her face.

I called her house last evening, to talk to Sarah. It was an
awkward moment when Susan answered the phone. 'We
can't talk,' I told her.

'I know. Not until I'm finished testifying,' she said. She
knew the rules, as if perhaps Ryan had already warned
her.

I could detect no bitterness or anger in her voice. Instead,
just an air of resignation.

'Where are you?' she asked.

'I'm calling from home.'

She said nothing, but I could tell she thought this was
foolish. It seems like another age since the Mexicans followed me from the jail that night. I checked the street in
front of my house, drove up and down several times. At this
point I am almost too tired to care. There were no unusual
cars that I could recognize, no heads silhouetted above the
backs of seats. I tried to remember what *Cyclops* might look
like with its lights out: an older-model Mercedes, limo. It
looked clear, so I parked the car, not in the driveway, but
in the garage.

I went inside and called Susan's. I spoke with Sarah,
said good night to her. She seemed confused, very quiet
as if maybe Susan might be in earshot. She asked me if
everything was all right, wondering why she was at Susan's,
and I was at our house. My daughter asked me if I'd had a
fight with Susan? She hasn't seen any of the activity in the
court, and Susan and I have taken great care not to discuss

matters in front of her. But children are perceptive. They can read tension in a relationship like vibrations before an earthquake.

I told her not to worry, that everything would be fine. That it was simply work, something I had to take care of. I'm not sure she accepted this. In my own mind, I'm not sure I do either.

Ryan is moving at the podium, using his hands. 'Later that same day, Ms McKay. I'm talking about the seventeenth of April,' says Ryan. 'Did you learn that the police had found Ms Suade's body at her place of employment?'

Today Susan looks more collected. In a dark power suit, blue pinstripes, pants and jacket, she's had a night to sleep on it, to get ready for whatever Ryan has to throw at her. Her natural competitive instincts now kicking in.

'I learned she was dead,' says Susan. 'I don't think I was told where her body was found. At least not on the phone.'

'Fine.' Ryan accepts this.

Ryan is looking down at a legal pad as he stands at the podium, penciled questions so that he doesn't miss anything. He looks up at Susan on the stand.

'Who told you about Zolanda Suade's death?' he says.

'As I recall, Mr Brower called me and told me that he'd heard something about it on the police scanner in his county car.'

'Do you know why he called you?'

'No.' Curt to the point.

'I mean this would not be something within the jurisdiction of your department, would it?'

'No.'

'Would it be fair to say that Mr Brower called you because

393

of Mr Hale's death threats made in your presence earlier that day?'

'It's possible.'

'So he must have thought this was significant?'

'Objection. Calls for speculation.'

'Sustained.'

'Did he mention Mr Hale's threats to you when he called you on the phone to tell you about Ms Suade's death?'

'He might have. I don't remember.'

'Other than those threats, the fact that both of you had heard them, can you think of any other reason why Mr Brower might call you with the information regarding Ms Suade's murder?'

'I don't think he said it was a murder at the time,' says Susan.

'Fine. Her death. Can you think of any other reason, other than the threats, why he might call you?' Susan thinks for a moment. Finally she shakes her head.

'You have to speak up for the record,' he says.

'No.'

'What did you do immediately after receiving this telephone call from Mr Brower?'

'I asked him to come into the office.'

'What time was this?'

'I don't know.'

'Wasn't it after the end of the business day?'

'It was probably late afternoon. I can't recall the exact time.'

'Would you disagree if I told you Mr Brower's cell phone records indicate the call was made after six o'clock in the evening?' says Ryan.

'Maybe it was early evening.' Susan concedes the point.

'But you had him come into the office anyway. Why?'

'I wanted to find out what he knew. What he'd heard.'

'Regarding Zolanda Suade's death?'

'Yes.'

'You could have talked to him on the phone about that couldn't you?'

'It was an open cell line.' Susan is quick on this. Apparently she's thought about it. 'It was official police business. Information Mr Brower had picked up on police bands. I didn't think it appropriate to discuss on the phone,' says Susan.

'I see.' Ryan smiles. 'But it wasn't anything involving your department?' Ryan knows precisely where he's going with this. Susan and Brower were both percipient witnesses, not to a murder, but to death threats made in my office. Why did Susan want to talk to Brower, the other witness, unless she had something devious on her mind?

'I simply wanted information,' she tells him.

'You were just curious?'

'There was the matter of Mr Hale's missing granddaughter. That was departmental business.'

'So you thought that somehow the issue of Mr Hale's missing granddaughter was involved in Zolanda Suade's death?' Ryan will more than settle for this.

'I didn't know.'

'I see. But you wanted to find out?' says Ryan.

'Yes.'

'So did Investigator Brower come into the office?' Suddenly it's gone from Mister to Investigator, cloaking Brower in his law-enforcement mantel.

395

'He came in,' says Susan.

'So he wasn't in the habit of declining requests from superiors even if he was off duty?' says Ryan.

'He was a professional investigator.' Without realizing she uses the past tense.

'You speak as if he's gone,' says Ryan.

'He is . . .' she stops herself. 'He's a professional investigator.'

'In fact he was a sworn peace officer, law enforcement, isn't that correct?'

'Yes.'

'That's why he had access to secure police bands on his radio, isn't that true?'

'Yes.'

'And what did you talk about, you and Investigator Brower when he got to your office?'

'He told me what he'd heard on the police bands.'

'What was that?'

'Not much beyond the fact that Ms Suade's body had been found and that the police were investigating.'

'Did you ask him anything in particular?'

Susan thinks for a moment. 'I might have asked him if he'd heard how it happened?'

Ryan raises an eyebrow.

'How Ms Suade was killed,' says Susan.

'I see. And did Investigator Brower have this information?'

'As I recall, he said something about the police saying she was shot. That paramedics responded, but that she was dead at the scene.'

'Did he tell you where this was? The scene?'

'Her office, I believe.'

'So he did tell you where the body was found?' Ryan jumps on it as if Susan may have misrepresented what she knew earlier.

'After he came into the office,' says Susan. 'That's when he told me the location. I don't think he ever told me on the phone.'

'What did you do then?'

'What do you mean?'

'I mean did you go home? After your meeting in the office with Investigator Brower? Did you go home?'

'No.' Moment of truth. Susan knew this was coming.

'Where did you go?'

'I went to the cineplex. South Area Mall,' she says.

'You went to see a movie?'

'No.'

'Then why did you go to the cineplex?'

'I went to see Mr Madriani.'

'Ah! Did he know you were going to join him at the show?'

'No. He was there with his daughter.'

'How did you know he was there if he didn't tell you?'

'I called his office. Found his partner.'

'That would be Mr Hinds?'

'That's right. And I was told that Mr Madriani had gone to the cineplex to see a movie.'

'With his daughter?'

'That's correct.'

'And why did you go to the cineplex if it wasn't to see the movie?'

'I wanted to tell him what had happened.'

'I see. About Zolanda Suade? The murder.'

'Yes.' Susan is no longer quibbling over the fact of whether she knew it was murder.

'Did you go to the cineplex alone?' Ryan already knows the answer. Brower has been thoroughly debriefed.

'I drove there by myself.' Susan's trying to evade the issue.

'Did you meet anyone else there, besides Mr Madriani?' says Ryan.

'Mr Brower,' she says.

Ryan's eyebrows are now halfway up to his balding crown as he looks at the jury. 'You had Mr Brower meet you at the cineplex?'

Susan doesn't answer immediately; instead, she takes a deep breath. 'I thought it would be best if Mr Madriani heard the details of what we knew directly from Mr Brower, since he was the one who heard the information on the police bands.'

'Let me get this straight,' says Ryan. 'You went to the cineplex to find Mr Madriani and you asked Mr Brower to meet you there in order to provide information to Mr Madriani regarding Zolanda Suade's death?'

'Well, he had been to see her that morning.'

'Who?' says Ryan.

'Mr Madriani.'

'Did you think he had something to do with her death?'

'No!' Susan nearly comes out of the chair.

Ryan is looking at me now, the jury following his gaze.

'Then what did all this have to do with Mr Madriani?'

Susan doesn't respond, so Ryan takes the opportunity to sharpen the point. 'Let's not even talk about why you did this,' he says. 'Let's talk about what you did next. Did you find Mr Madriani at the cineplex?'

'Yes.'

'And what did you tell him?'

'I told him about Ms Suade's death. What little I knew.'

'And did you have Mr Brower talk to him?'

'I think so.'

'You had him come all that way, but you can't remember if you had him talk to Mr Madriani? That's why you brought him isn't it?'

'Yes. I think Mr Brower spoke to him.'

Ryan smiling. 'And what happened next?'

'We talked for a while,' she says.

'And?'

'And I took Sarah Madriani home. Went in and finished watching the movie with her, and then took her to my house.'

'Where did Mr Madriani go?'

'He went to Ms Suade's office.'

'Where the body was?'

'I don't know if it was still there.'

'Of course. Did Mr Madriani go there alone. To your knowledge?'

'No.'

'Who went with him?'

'Mr Brower.'

Ryan pauses for effect, feigned surprise.

'Mr Brower? Who suggested that Mr Brower go with Mr Madriani?'

'I can't remember,' she says.

'Could it have been you?'

'It might have been.'

Ryan smiles at the jury. Susan's evasions are not looking good.

'And whose car did they go in, to the scene of the crime?' says Ryan.

'It was Mr Brower's.'

'His county vehicle? With county plates?'

'Yes.'

'Why did they use that car?'

'I don't know.'

'Could it have been to get through the police lines?'

'I don't know.'

'Let me get this straight,' says Ryan. 'You asked Investigator Brower to come into the office after you found out about the murder. You called Mr Madriani's partner to find out where he was because you didn't know. You went to the cineplex to find Mr Madriani, and you told Mr Brower to meet you there. And then you asked Mr Brower to take Mr Madriani to the scene of the crime in his county vehicle. Why did you do all of this?'

'I don't know.'

'You don't know! You don't know!' says Ryan.

Pencils in the front row are beginning to smoke, cutting grooves in paper. I can do nothing to stop Ryan from pounding on her.

'You heard Mr Hale make death threats against the victim earlier that day in Mr Madriani's office. You knew that Mr Madriani was Mr Hale's lawyer, didn't you?'

'Yes.'

'And yet you saw nothing inappropriate in asking a sworn law-enforcement officer, one of your own employees, to take Mr Madriani through the police line at the scene of an ongoing criminal investigation, one in which you knew that Mr Madriani's client might very well be involved?'

'Objection.' I'm out of my chair.

'Rephrase the question,' says Peltro.

It is all the more damning because of Susan's obvious motivation, to help a friend. I can object to the inference that somehow she knew Jonah was guilty, but the message to the jury is clear. Why else would she do all this?

'Didn't you think there might be something inappropriate in all of this?'

'I didn't think,' she says.

'You didn't think.' Ryan says it not as a question, but a statement of fact, nodding, turning toward the jury, pacing as far as the podium will allow.

'Let's turn our attention,' says Ryan, 'to events that occurred after April seventeenth. At some point after the events of that evening, did it come to your attention that Investigator Brower and Mr Madriani had been given a look at certain physical evidence at the scene that night?'

'Yes.'

'Can you tell the jury how you learned about this?'

'Mr Brower told me.'

'What did he tell you?'

'That one of the investigators at the scene showed them a bullet . . .'

'Bullet? You mean a spent bullet cartridge?'

'Yes.'

'What else?'

'Some cigarettes they found smoked at the scene.'

401

'What else?'

'A partly smoked cigar.'

Ryan stops her with his right index finger in the air like a pistol about to be fired. 'And do you remember on the morning of April seventeenth at the meeting in Mr Madriani's office the defendant Jonah Hale offering cigars to those in attendance?'

'Yes.'

'And how did you find out about this cigar being found at the scene?'

'Mr Brower told me he had seen it.'

'What else did he tell you? About the cigar?'

'Objection, hearsay.'

'Sustained.'

Ryan's trying to get at the question of whether Brower thought he recognized it as similar to the one Jonah had given him earlier in the day.

'Do you recall whether Mr Hale offered a cigar to Investigator Brower during the meeting at Mr Madriani's on the seventeenth?'

'I think he did.'

'You *think* he did?' Ryan is beginning to get angry.

'He gave him one,' says Susan.

'And did you ever talk to Mr Brower about that cigar, the one Mr Hale gave to Mr Brower after discovering that a similar cigar had been found at the scene?'

Susan looks at me.

'I'm going to object. Assumes facts not in evidence.'

'Your Honor, we have expert testimony on the cigars.'

'But we don't know the witness knew they were similar at the time.'

'That assumes Mr Brower didn't tell her they looked the same,' says Ryan.

'I'm gonna overrule the objection,' says Peltro.

'Did you ever talk to Mr Brower about the cigar he received from Mr Hale?'

'We had a conversation,' says Susan.

'A conversation. Ms McKay, isn't it a fact that you instructed Investigator Brower to turn that cigar over to you, and that he told you he'd already delivered it to the police? That you were angry with him for this?'

'I was his supervisor,' says Susan. 'He should have told me what he was doing before he got involved.'

'Why? You've already testified that this was not something within the jurisdiction of your department. This was an open homicide case. Why did you want that cigar, Ms McKay?'

When Susan doesn't answer, Ryan nails her. 'Was it that you craved a good smoke?' he says.

A couple of jurors actually laugh.

'Is that when you reassigned Investigator Brower?' says Ryan. 'He was good enough to take Mr Madriani to the crime scene for you, but he wouldn't turn over evidence, is that it?'

Susan is now looking at Ryan with all the fire she can muster. Molten steel shot with a gaze.

The inference is poisonous, that Susan, in league with the defense, wanted to destroy evidence. To this she has no answer.

CHAPTER
TWENTY-NINE

In the afternoon, Ryan puts on a taxi driver who testifies that he picked Jonah up on the street, two blocks from Susan's office on the day of the murder, and delivered him to the parking lot at Spanish Landing. All this before three in the afternoon.

Unfortunately no one saw Jonah on the boat, not that he was there long. Jonah has told Harry and me that he took his car and went driving in a daze of anger and frustration, he can't remember where, until the cops found him sitting in the sand along the Strand, his car parked illegally out on the highway.

The only bright spot is that Peltro had us in chambers over the noon hour to talk about Jonah's condition. Dr Karashi, as promised, called the judge and told him of his findings.

In response, Ryan has called Karashi's boss. The kid is now off the case. Judge Peltro is now forced to wait until more senior physicians can get in to see our client. Jonah's own doctor will not be in until tonight.

Jonah is looking worse by the hour. He spent noontime on his back on the cot in the holding cell. His color is flushed, and this morning Harry caught him in what appeared to be a breathless state. Jonah has denied this, saying he is feeling fine, as if it is a solemn duty to complete the trial.

Ryan, in an effort to mollify Peltro, has assured the court that he will call only one more witness. We can then recess for the weekend. According to Ryan, Jonah can rest, and get a thorough medical examination, a million electrodes, and if Ryan has anything to do with it, wires no doubt thrust up his kazoo.

'Mr Hale, how are you feeling?' Peltro looks down from the bench. 'If you want to take a break anytime,' he says, 'you just tell me.'

Jonah shakes his head. Waves him off. 'I'm feeling fine, Your Honor.' Certificate of health from my own client. He sees this as the fair thing to do. The state is trying to put him to death, and Jonah wants to be fair.

'Are you sure?' Harry's in his ear.

'No, I'm okay.' He says it loud enough now for everybody in the courtroom to hear, as if he is angry at Harry for asking, like a nagging wife.

Ryan looks at him. He would strap Jonah in his chair and prop his eyelids open, add a little heat if he had to, to keep the trial going. The last thing Ryan needs is a defendant too ill to continue, and a mistrial. Peltro himself is walking on eggs, trying to avoid it.

Ryan may be at the end of his case, but his last witness is troublesome. He calls Floyd Jeffers, the deckhand who worked on Jonah's boat, and who according to Jonah he hasn't seen for nearly two years.

Jeffers has that hint of the alcoholic about him: undernourished frame with a slightly bloated belly and bags under the eyes. It's a build that makes you suspect his liver is already corroded. His hair looks like somebody cut it with a dull pair of hedge clippers.

He's wearing a new pair of blue jeans, rolled up cuffs, something no doubt purchased by the county for the occasion, and a cotton flannel shirt, yellow plaid to match his color. The shirt is at least one size too big.

He's the kind of witness you don't dress in a suit. It would only look ridiculous.

Ryan has him spell his name for the record and give his address. I am only guessing, but I would bet that this is a halfway house, probably something connected to the county's detox center.

The worry here is why Ryan would call Jeffers, particularly as his last witness. It is a cardinal rule that you want to end on a high note, leave the jury mulling over your strongest piece of evidence and hope that they forget the weak spots.

'Mr Jeffers, I would ask you to look at the defendant, Mr Jonah Hale, and tell the jury whether you know him?'

Jeffers looks at Jonah, smiles, nods, he actually waves. What's worse, Jonah raises a hand and returns the gesture. 'That's him,' says Jeffers. Points with a finger

'So you're acquainted with Mr Hale?'

'Yep.'

'Can you tell us how you met him?' says Ryan.

'I worked for him.' Jeffers says it as if the entire room

should know this already. He has no doubt been going over it endlessly with Ryan and his staff.

'When was this? That you worked for him?'

'Worked for him for about six months. That would have been about two years ago.'

'And what did you do?'

'Deckhand,' he says. 'Worked on his boat. The *Amanda*.'

'And what were your duties working on the boat?'

'A little bit of everything,' says Jeffers.

And a lot of drinking, is my guess.

'Maintenance. Cleaned up after we went out,' he says. 'Handled bait lines on the water. Worked the gaff sometimes, if the fish were big.'

'Were you the only deckhand?'

'No. There were two of us. Sometimes three, depending on the weather. In the early going. When he first got the boat, Mr Hale that is. He'd bring on a skipper once in a while.'

'Did you get on pretty well with Mr Hale?'

'Oh, yeah. He was a good man. Good boss. Paid real well. Let me stay on the boat sometimes when I needed a place.'

'He allowed you to live on the boat?'

'Sure. For a few weeks in the summer. I needed a place,' says Jeffers. 'Didn't have any money. So he let me stay there. I sorta watched it for him.'

'When was this?'

'Oh.' Jeffers thinks now. He's not the rummy witness you might suspect. 'It was two summers ago. I was there for a few weeks is all. Till I could get up enough money for my own place.'

'When you lived on board, where did you sleep?'

'There's a salon, good sized, and V-berth up forward. That's where I slept.'

'So when you were there, you brought some of your . . . your personal belongings on board?' The way Ryan says it, emphasis on the words *personal belongings*, makes it sound like a kind of code.

'Yeah. That's when I brought the gun on board,' says Jeffers.

'Gun? What gun?' says Ryan.

'Your Honor, I object.' I'm out of my chair like a rocket. 'I'd like an opportunity to voir-dire this witness.'

'Your Honor, the witness was on the list,' says Ryan. 'The defense had every opportunity if they wanted to question him.'

'If the prosecutor has a gun, it should have been disclosed.'

'Do you have the firearm?' says Peltro.

Ryan shakes his head. 'No gun, Your Honor. But the witness can testify where it was, when he saw it.'

Like a torpedo from the fog on calm water, the details of Ryan's case suddenly come into focus, too late to avoid them. It's why he wanted Susan to explain to the jury that she drove Jonah to her office that day after our meeting; that Jonah's car was at the boat. Ryan's evidence, his theory is that the murder weapon was there as well. Now with the taxi driver's testimony, he puts Jonah back on the docks with plenty of time to drive to Suade's office and kill her.

'I'm gonna overrule the objection,' says Peltro. 'You can answer the question.'

'What about this gun?' says Ryan.

'It was a little semiautomatic.' Jeffers describes the pistol as if they've rehearsed it, which they no doubt have.

'Why did you bring this gun on board the boat?'

'We used it,' says Jeffers. 'For some of the bigger fish. One shark I can remember, about twelve feet long. We got it up near the side, still in the water. It was thrashing all around. So we got the gun and shot it before we brought it on board.'

'You say "we". Did Mr Hale know that this firearm was on board his boat?'

'Your Honor, I have to object.'

'Overruled,' says Peltro.

'Oh, yeah. I showed him where I kept it,' says Jeffers.

All this time I'm trying not to look at Jonah, though twelve sets of eyes from the jury box are burning holes through him.

'Do you remember what kind of pistol it was? Make or caliber?' says Ryan.

'Can't remember the make,' says Jeffers. 'But it was a three-eighty caliber.' The witness is nodding as if this is precisely what Ryan expects.

When I finally look over at Jonah, there is a burning emptiness deep in my stomach, caused not so much by what Jeffers is saying as by the expression on my client's face, like a veil of remembrance. *Oh yeah. That's right.*

'One final question,' says Ryan. 'Do you know what happened to this pistol?'

'Yeah. I left it on Mr Hale's boat when I quit.'

'Your witness,' says Ryan.

410

I can't wait to get at him. I arrive at the podium before Ryan can collect his papers.

'Mr Jeffers, do you have a record?'

'Excuse me?'

'Do you have a criminal record?' I ask.

Jeffers looks at Ryan. 'Do I have to answer that?'

Ryan nods.

'Yeah. I been arrested, if that's what you mean.'

'Isn't it a fact that you're a convicted felon? That you were sentenced to the state penitentiary at Folsom? That you did more than a year for embezzling money from a former employer?'

'That's true,' he says.

Harry and I had gone over Jeffers's criminal history, though we had never expected him to be called. Harry had even managed to get a copy of the arrest records so that we know some of the details surrounding his conviction.

'How did you acquire this handgun that you testified about?'

'I bought it from a friend,' says Jeffers.

'When?'

Jeffers has to think for a moment. Looks at the ceiling. 'Probably four or five months before I went to work for Mr Hale.'

'Who did you buy it from? What's your friend's name?'

'Maxwell Williams.' Jeffers doesn't hesitate with this, as if he was expecting it. Ryan has clearly prepared him.

'And how did you know this Maxwell Williams?'

'I met him in jail,' he says.

'And how did he get this gun?'

'I don't know.'

411

'How much did you pay for this pistol you testified about?'

'Two hundred dollars,' says Jeffers.

'How did you pay for it? Check or cash, or did your friend take a credit card?'

'It was cash,' says Jeffers.

'That's a lot of money for someone who can't even afford the price of a weekly motel room.'

'I needed the gun for protection,' he says.

'From who?'

'Living on the street,' he says. 'It can be dangerous.'

The problem with Jeffers is that everything he says has the ring of truth. I can see in his eyes that Jeffers can sense where I'm going. Why would a man who is broke, and who spends two hundred dollars buying a pistol, leave it on his employer's boat when he quits? So I don't go there.

'Mr Jeffers, do you know it's a violation of federal law for a convicted felon to possess a firearm?'

'Yeah, I know,' says Jeffers. 'I found that out. That's why I told Mr Hale when I quit, that I left the pistol on his boat.'

It's why you never want to jump at a witness.

'I forgot all about it.' Jonah says it to Harry out loud before we can stop him. 'I dumped it. Threw it over the side when Amanda started coming on the boat,' he says.

The courtroom is in a uproar. Peltro's hitting the gavel, nailing the wooden surface of the bench. Telling everybody to be quiet. 'Shut your client up, Mr Madriani.'

'I forgot.' Jonah still trying to convince Harry.

'Mr Hale, shut up,' says the judge.

These are the last distinguishable words I can remember

before Jonah's head hits the counsel table, dead weight, like a melon hitting a wooden wall.

CHAPTER
THIRTY

I can tell that Mary has been here before. She tells Harry and me about the other little room down the hall, the one with muted lamps on the side tables, large plush sofas against the walls, and blinds on the small glass window that looks out onto the hallway. That one is reserved as the family grieving room, the place where you do not want to be taken when the physician comes out with news.

'There was another lady when I was here last time,' she says. 'They took her down there.'

As to be expected, Mary is on edge. She is reading every message, looking for hope in the expressions of strangers as they scurry about their chores in the busy hospital. A young man in hospital greens goes by the open door at a clip. Mary takes solace in the fact that he is at least running. 'They wouldn't be running if he were dead,' she says.

There are probably two dozen patients in the ICU, and the kid in greens may have been called to clean out bedpans in another unit, but Harry and I don't say this.

For the moment we are in a small waiting room, next to the ICU, intensive care, bathed in antiseptic bright light from overhead fluorescents, waiting for some word.

I am told that Jonah never regained consciousness in the ambulance, but that there were vital signs: pulse and blood pressure. They had him on oxygen within minutes. Fortunately, a team of paramedics was just down the courthouse corridor, waiting to testify in their own defense, a civil case involving negligence that had spilled over from the Hall of Justice due to limited space.

Mary was not allowed to travel with him, so Harry whisked her to the hospital, nearly beating the ambulance.

For long moments we sit in silence until a woman joins us, a friend of Mary's, a neighbor, one of the few who didn't sign the petition asking her to move. She has heard the news on TV. Harry and I take the opportunity to leave them for a moment, and step out into the hallway.

'Did you see him when they brought him in?' I ask.

Harry shakes his head. 'They came in through the emergency entrance,' he says. 'Apparently they worked on him down in the ER for a while.'

It is possible to read something into the fact that they moved him to the ICU, though perhaps only to put him on life support.

I am looking over Harry's shoulder, down the long corridor, when I see Susan at the far end, rounding a corner, moving at a clip. There are three little shadows behind her, Sarah and Susan's two girls. The expression on Susan's face is one of angst.

She speaks before she reaches us. 'How is he?' Children in her wake, trailing behind.

416

'We don't know.'

'I heard it on the radio,' she says. 'I picked up the girls from school.'

Sarah snuggles in close up against my side for a hug. I give her a kiss on the top of her head, and she smiles. I have not seen my own daughter in nearly a week. I am feeling incredible guilt for this.

'I miss you,' she says.

Hugging my daughter is the best therapy I have had in weeks. It seems that all the misfortune, anxiety, and mistakes of the trial slip away in this single, simple act of holding the child I love.

As we talk, the hum of whispers, another figure is closing in on our small group.

The look in her eyes tells me she's not walking by. A physician, green cap on, green pants and top, an African-American woman, she looks me in the eye. 'Are you Mr Hale's family?'

'His wife is inside.' I nod toward Mary.

She's up off the sofa like a bullet, hands wringing, fingers suddenly interwoven as if in prayer.

'He is stable,' says the doctor. 'Out of danger.'

'Is he conscious?'

'Yes.'

'May I see him?' she says.

'In a moment. And just for a few seconds. He's had a heart attack. We don't know how much damage has been done at this point. But he's going to be in the hospital for a while.'

'Then he can't be in court on Monday?' says Harry.

'Absolutely not.' The physician turns on him as if Harry's asking for her blessing to take her patient back to court.

Instead Harry smiles, gives me an elbow. Time to talk to Peltro about a continuance. A mistrial could be in the offing. The judge is not going to be comfortable with a jury on the loose for any extended period, state's case in their mind with nothing to contest it, and publicity running wild. It is a prescription for appeal, and Peltro knows it. The question now is how long Jonah is going to be laid up.

With this on my mind, Susan leans up close and under her breath, in my ear, whispers, 'How about you and I go to Mexico?' she says.

Now is not the time. I give her a look, as if I'm chastising.

She cups a hand around the nape of my neck, presses her lips to the lobe of my ear, and whispers: 'We've found Jessica.'

CHAPTER
THIRTY-ONE

The drive in from the airport at Los Cabos seems to take longer than the flight from San Diego. The road is dusty and punctuated by potholes. The old GMC van, what passes for a taxi in these parts, has no springs left, and no air-conditioning.

Harry is watching Sarah, taking her to school and picking her up. Susan's former husband has her two girls.

'So you combing town here to fish?' The taxi driver has one hand on the wheel as he looks at us over the back of the front seat.

The windows are all open to give us some air. Susan and I are getting facefuls of heat like a million-watt hair dryer.

'No.' I have to shout above the roar of the wind.

'Bacation?' he says.

'You could call it that.' He can call it whatever he wants, as long as he watches the road and keeps one hand on the wheel.

'You're taking us to Cabo San Lucas, right?' says Susan.

'Oh, *sí*.'

'How much farther?'

'Ah. Little bit,' he says. 'Where you from?'

'Up north,' she tells him.

'Oh.' He gets the message: we're not in the mood for conversation.

He's doing seventy, bald tires sliding on the sandy surface of the road, showing us with his one free hand where the highway washed out in the last hurricane, as if the gully we just bounced over does not convey this. Every once in a while he hits the horn and waves to some other fool passing us at light speed in the other direction, another taxi with its load of *norteamericanos* headed for the airport. Speed in Cabo is a measure of machismo.

Ten minutes later we pull into the driveway leading to the Pueblo Bonita Blanca, one of the high-rises on the water looking out at Land's End.

The resort itself is composed of luxury condos, time-shares. At the airport, sales pitches for these are so aggressive that those who come here regularly call it 'running the gauntlet'. If you're not careful coming off a plane, you may think you ordered a taxi and instead find yourself hustled off to a time-share for a weekend with a salesman from hell. The condos are sold mostly to rich Americans and rented out to other tourists.

This resort has white stucco walls that rise several stories like the ramparts of some Moorish fortress, with blue-tiled domes every so often for architectural flair. The interior courtyard faces the beach and surrounds a free-form pool larger than a football field. This feeds down some stairs to the beach, where the ocean water is a deep blue, except near the shore where it has a copper patina, turned light by the crystalline white quartz of the sand.

Susan and I check into the room and punch on the air-conditioner. This requires the insertion of one of the room card-keys into the power box on the wall near the door.

The room is hot and stuffy. The resort is nearly empty. Summer on the Mexican Riviera is not the high season.

We leave my key in the power box to allow the room to cool and take Susan's while we head for the open-air restaurant down by the pool.

Here there are paddle fans on the ceiling, cool breezes off the water, and a roof to shade us. There are a number of yachts anchored off the beach, and a large naval vessel, what looks like a destroyer. The Navy no doubt is hanging out at the bars downtown. Cabo has been called one large tavern. There isn't much to do here except bake in the sun and drink.

I have been here only once before, with Nikki when we were first married. It is a place staked out by the ugly American. Though the Mexican government might disagree, the medium of exchange is the U.S. dollar. Everywhere there are American males edging on forty trying to repeat their adolescence, engaging in the same bravado and bullshit they did the first time around, letting down what little hair they have left, getting stone drunk in Cabo at night, staggering back to their resorts at three in the morning to wake up with headaches and dry heaves, bragging about how they got rolled and beat up in town. A real adventure. They hang around the pools by day bellowing to one another on the balconies like sated bulls, wearing their Rolexes and always with the obligatory bottle of Dos Equis in their hands.

There are American women in their twenties and thirties basting themselves in the sun with emollients and lotions, some of them with young children. It would not be difficult for Jessica Hale to lose herself in a place like this.

Susan has not said much since our meeting at the hospital. I have asked her how she found Jessica. She has avoided an answer, and given the whipping she has taken in court I have not felt free to press the issue. If Ryan were to discover that we were down here looking, he would no doubt try to reopen his case, put Susan back on the stand and turn her on the spit one more time.

My suspicion is that she has two reasons for involving herself further, the first being by far the most compelling. If she can do anything to extricate Jonah's grandchild from a bad situation, she will do it. The other is that Susan no longer has anything to lose. She hasn't stated it in so many words, but from her demeanor I am assuming she is finished with the county. Ryan and his boss will be working the board of supervisors relentlessly, the inference being that Susan tried to acquire Brower's cigar in order to destroy evidence, and that she was not forthcoming with Jonah's death threats. In their eyes she has demonstrated that she is not part of the law-enforcement team, but the enemy.

She orders a drink, some tequila to settle her nerves, a Margarita.

'So I take it we find Amanda today?' I say.

The waiter wants to know if I want something to drink. I wave him off. Right now I'm looking for answers from Susan.

'She is here in town?'

Susan nods. 'We'll need a car.'

'That can be arranged.'

'I have an address. We'll have to find it.'

'How did you get the address?'

'That I·can't tell you,' she says.

I am assuming that Susan is protecting her staff, that she may have used her authority one final time, probably to flog one of her investigators, put him on a plane and ship him south. Whoever it was got lucky, or else Jessica got careless. This latter gives me pause for concern.

'If you were able to find her, Ontaveroz can, too,' I tell her.

'We can't rush into this,' she says. 'We're only going to get one chance. If we lose her, we'll never find her again.'

It is Susan who settles me down. For someone who is taking the ultimate career plunge, cliff-dive onto the rocks, she is amazingly cool. She is all business. Strangely with all that has fallen on her, the roasting by Ryan on the stand, she does not seem to blame me for this. It is just that her actions are now more measured, less trusting. I think she sees herself as the unavoidable victim in all that has happened.

'She probably won't come back with us.' Susan is talking about Jessica Hale. 'Are you prepared to accept that?'

'I could use her testimony,' I tell her. Jessica could provide the vital link between Ontaveroz and Suade. The fact that Jessica knew him, had lived with him, might give me the evidence I need to satisfy Peltro and open up the defense.

'Our goal is the child,' says Susan. 'I think we have to start with the assumption that Jessica is not coming. She's here for a reason. She's running.'

'She's running because of the child.'

'Yes. And she may follow if we take Amanda back. But to try to take them both through the airport, through immigration and customs, would be a big mistake. If Jessica makes a scene, it's all for nothing.'

As much as I don't like it, Susan is right. The child we might be able to convince, keep her in check. An adult, especially someone as volatile as Jessica, there's no way.

'Agreed.'

'Good.' Susan's drink comes. She starts to sip through the thin straw.

'We're going to need some identification for the girl,' she says. 'That means a passport, something with a picture on it. It's possible that Suade provided some false identification. When we find the apartment, one of our tasks is going to be to find this. Search their luggage, look in drawers. We're going to need it to get out.'

I nod. I am amazed at how carefully she has thought this all out.

'If worse comes to worst, if all else fails, we take her to the American consulate in town. I've checked. There is one here,' she says. Susan opens her purse on the table. She removes an envelope and passes it to me. It's a certified copy of the court order of custody in Jonah and Mary's name.

'That and my county credentials,' she says, 'should at least cause them to slow down and hold the child for a while, until we can straighten it out. Get whatever authority we need to take Amanda back to the States.'

'When we find the place, one of us should go to the front door. Maybe that should be me,' she says. 'A woman would be less threatening.'

'And what are you going to tell her?'

'I don't know. Just occupy her time. Tell her something. That the landlord sent me to look at the place. That I'm getting ready to rent one just like it. Anything to get in the door.'

'And what am I supposed to do?'

'See if there's a back way in.' According to Susan this would prevent Jessica from running, and presumably it would allow us to keep the child between us.

'And what do we do with Jessica?'

'Leave that to me,' she says.

'What are you going to do?'

'If we have to, we subdue Jessica.' It is clear that Susan is prepared to go the whole nine yards, risk a Mexican jail if necessary.

'And what if there's someone else in the house?'

'I don't know. That's why I don't want to rush in. We should watch the place for a little while. Right after lunch,' she says.

We change to shorts, cooler clothes, dark glasses. I rent a small Wrangler, a Jeep, something I'm used to driving that can handle dirt roads and maneuver on narrow back streets.

In all our planning, there is one vast assumption: that the child will come with us willingly, that if we mention Jonah's name or Mary's, tell her that we are working for her grandparents, that Amanda Hale will walk out the door and get into the car.

According to Susan this would be preferable, but she tells me that in any event, Amanda will be leaving with us, even if we have to use force.

We stop at a market off the main drag downtown. I sit in the parking lot as Susan goes inside. Five minutes later she comes out carrying a single plastic bag. She climbs into the passenger seat and closes the door. Inside the bag is a fifty-foot coil of quarter-inch cotton rope, the kind you might use for a clothesline, and a roll of duct tape.

'One more stop. Lady inside says it's just up the hill.'

I drive and Susan looks for signs. Two blocks up she finds it. The pharmacia. This time it takes her less than two minutes, and when she comes out she carrying a pint-sized metal can with a screw-on lid. She gets in.

'What's that?'

'Ether.'

It's now clear how Susan is planning on dealing with Jessica: some sleeping juice on a rag, tie her up and tape her mouth. By the time they find her, we'll be in San Diego or L.A. or wherever the next plane for the States out of Los Cabos is bound.

We find the American consulate on a small tourist map. It is over near the harbor. We drive by it several times from different directions to get our bearings. The problem is that many of the streets are not only narrow, but one-way.

Within an hour we realize that our hotel doesn't work. It is too far from downtown. It also has the disadvantage that the police station is situated between us and the consulate should we have to retreat to the room with the child for any reason.

We spend an hour moving to another hotel, a place more centrally located. The Hotel Plaza Las Glorias backs up onto the marina, and is only two blocks from the consulate.

Several times, navigating from the passenger seat with a

map in her lap, Susan directs me past the tourist area of Cabo. We miss a turn and end up in front of our hotel across the street.

This part of town is mostly a strip of bars and T-shirt shops, discos and dives. It is a traffic nightmare, even in the off-season. The population swells with each cruise ship that pulls into the harbor. Two of them are sitting like floating hotels a mile out from the beach today. Motor launches ferry the passengers to the marina, where they clog the streets looking for deals from the vendors and wander in and out of the small shops.

It takes us ten minutes to find our way back out.

Susan takes another shot at the map, new directions. We backtrack, and this time we get it right, the main drag toward town, but we stay to the right when we get to the light in front of the market.

Here the street is one-way, narrowing as we head uphill, just enough room for two cars to travel side by side. Toward the top, Susan tells me to look for a place to park. Here some of the curbs are four feet high, with stairs to climb as you proceed up the sidewalk. The shops are thinning out, mostly small businesses. I find an opening and pull in.

Susan studies the map. The detail on it is not great, one of those tourist maps provided by the car-rental agency. The streets seem to disappear in the area where the hotel concierge told us the address was located.

'It should be two blocks up,' she says.

We get out and climb, first up the sidewalk, then the stairs. To the left and down the hill are the tourist hangouts and nightspots, Cabo Wabo, the Giggling Marlin, and Squid Row.

Up the hill ahead should be the plaza. There are fewer tourists here. We cross the street, what appears to be the last busy intersection, one-way traffic down into town, then climb stairs into what is the city square, an open area with a few trees. It covers a small block.

Susan and I look like two tourists. She's wearing a large straw hat, something to keep the sun off her head and out of her eyes. She's left the rope, the tape, and the ether back in the car, under the seat. For the moment, we are just trying to find the place.

We locate the mission, the Catholic church on the map. The Mexican customs office is next door, and farther down is an antique shop, a two-story building with a veranda reaching out over the sidewalk.

Susan heads in that direction, and I follow her.

We cross the street, pass the storefront, MAMMA ELIS'S ORIGINAL CURIOUS SHOP, antiques and knickknacks. In the cool shade under the overhanging veranda we hug the building and come to the end of the block. As we step around the corner, Susan suddenly stops. Up the street no more than a hundred feet away is a set of wrought-iron gates where the street dead-ends. The gates open onto a driveway, and overhead is a large wooden sign, LAS VENTANAS DE CABO.

Susan takes a deep breath. 'That's it.'

We step back into the shade of the veranda. The condos are nestled into the terraced hillside with a steep driveway that disappears around a turn. From the street it is clear, we're not going to be able to see much. The units are carved into the hillside high above us. It looks as if there may be ten or twelve separate units.

'Do we know which one she's in?'

Susan shakes her head. 'I just have the name of the place.'

'Let's hope the information is correct. Otherwise we've made a long trip for nothing,' I tell her.

I start up the hill.

'Where are you going?'

'See if there's an office.'

'You can't just go barging in.'

'Why not? Jessica doesn't know us. We tell whoever's up there we're looking for a rental. Check it out.'

Susan comes out of the shadows of the veranda, adjusts her hat, one hand on top of her head to hold it on as she cranes her neck to look up at the units on the hillside. I begin trudging up the hill, Susan following me.

Once through the gates we climb steeply to the left until we find ourselves in front of several garage units, a series of overhead doors with a set of narrow steps leading up the hillside through gardens planted between the units. There is no sign telling us where the office is, or whether there is one.

The heat of the afternoon sun is withering, taking its toll on both of us. My dark glasses are beginning to fog up. I stop on the steps to wipe them, take in the lay of the land. Small paths branch off from the steps in different directions, winding through landscaped gardens toward the condos nestled into the hillside.

'Can I help you?' A woman's voice comes from behind on a lower level.

As I turn to look I notice, for the first time, a good-sized lap pool built into the hillside, over the garage units, a patio with a railing around it and a commanding view of the town below.

'We were looking for the office.'

'You found it. I'm the manager,' she says.

Susan and I make our way toward the pool.

The woman is in her early thirties, wearing shorts with a tank top. She has on dark glasses and seems to be studying us with some interest, as if perhaps this far off the beaten path they don't get many visitors.

'Hello. My name's Paul. My wife, Susan. We saw your place from down below. It looks pretty nice. We're looking for a place that has privacy. We were wondering if you might have any vacancies?'

'At the moment we're full up,' she says. 'I could take your name, and a phone number.'

I remove my dark glasses. Offer her my best smile. A friend once told me that the key to conversation is not the mouth, but the eyes.

The woman doesn't reciprocate, still studying me from behind smoked glass.

'Are you looking for short-term or something longer?'

'Through the fall,' says Susan.

'Actually we might be interested in leasing for a year,' I tell her.

With this, the glasses come off. She smiles. 'I might have an opening at the end of the month.'

'Do you take children?' Susan with the sixty-four-thousand-dollar question.

'Usually I would say no. But we have one woman with a child right now.'

Bingo.

'Really. We weren't sure if we wanted to bring our daughter down here,' says Susan. 'She's eight . . .'

'Same age as the child who's here. Very quiet,' she says. 'Both mother and child. Not sure if it's a boy or a girl, to tell you the truth. Doesn't seem to ever come out. They're paid up to the end of next month. But it could be vacant any day now. She told me just this morning they would be leaving.'

'When?'

'She didn't say exactly. Sometime before the end of the month.'

Susan smiles, but I can sense some desperation in her expression as she looks at me. If it's Jessica and she gets away, we'll never find her again.

'As I said, if you want to leave a name and a phone number I could call you,' says the woman.

'Any chance we could see the unit?' I ask.

'I'm afraid not,' she says. 'I tried to show it last week, and she said no. The tenant likes her privacy.'

I nod as if I understand. I'm running out of questions.

'Does the unit have an ocean view?' Susan is good at this.

'I'm afraid not.' The woman's gaze travels up the hillside over my shoulder. Susan's eyes follow it. I turn and look.

'One of those up there?' says Susan.

'Unit three,' she says. 'The one on the right.'

'It looks very nice,' says Susan.

'You're sure we can't take a peek? We'd be very discreet. Very quiet.' Susan can be so sweet. *Just let us get our rope and ether.*

'I can't do that. I'm sorry.'

431

'How many rooms? Maybe you have a floor plan of the unit?' Susan is not missing a beat.

'Afraid I don't have any floor plans. There are two bedrooms, a kitchen, and living area. Two and a half baths. Some of them have a small den. I can't remember if that one does or not.'

'I suppose you have to come down here to get your car?' Susan looks down over the railing toward the driveway, and up toward the endless stairs.

'Actually there's a road that runs up behind,' she says. 'You can drive right up to the units and down into town.'

'Oh, really. That is convenient.' I can see Susan giving me a glance as she hears this, both of us thinking the same thing, wondering if this road shows up on our map.

CHAPTER
THIRTY-TWO

I check my watch. It's seven-fifteen. The sun has begun to set over Lovers' Beach, the bright orange ball of fire slowly descending behind the sandstone cliffs of Land's End.

After some searching, we managed to find the road that winds up the hill behind the condos. We have driven it twice, making U-turns up top and coming back down. There is a small parking area behind each of the units.

The one for unit three has no car, and we are left to wonder if anyone is home.

'Maybe she doesn't drive,' says Susan.

'Maybe we've got the wrong place,' I tell her.

'No.' Susan is certain of this. She is reading the instructions on the can of ether, trying to make sure we don't overdo it.

'Do you know how to use that stuff?'

'Put it on the cloth and hold it over her mouth and nose,' she says. Susan has purloined a small washcloth from the hotel for this purpose.

'All we want to do is put her out for a few seconds,' she says. 'Get her on the floor until we can tape her mouth, tie her hands and feet.'

'You better make sure you don't breathe while you're holding it on her face,' I tell her.

'I know.'

'And if she's smoking, forget it. That stuff will go up like a zeppelin.'

Like two moron outlaws, we're sitting in a rented car reading the instructions off the back of a can on how to kidnap somebody. I've seen others with similar streaks of brilliance, all long-time and repeat customers of various correctional institutions. 'One question.'

'What?' Susan says it with some irritation.

'What if it makes her sick? What if she throws up?'

This is something Susan hasn't thought about: Jessica drowning in her own vomit with tape over her mouth. She puts the can back in the large beach bag on the floor next to her purse, hiding it under the washcloth next to the rope and duct tape.

'Okay. We don't use the ether. We'll just have to talk our way through,' she says.

Despite her steely resolve, Susan is beginning to lose her nerve. 'If she puts up a fight, we'll just have to tape her mouth before she makes too much noise.'

'I'll hold her. You can tape her sharp, pointy little teeth,' I say.

Susan gives me a noxious smile. 'We can't afford to leave her free to call the cops. We'd never get to the airport.'

'I know.'

We have checked the flight schedules out of Los Cabos

There is nothing to San Diego, but there is a night flight to L.A. It departs a little after nine, which doesn't give us much time.

We have studied the pictures of Jessica and Amanda from the file, the ones Jonah showed me from his wallet that first time he came to my office.

If somehow we've got the wrong place, if it's not Jessica and Amanda, the plan is we are out of here in a heartbeat, offer some story about viewing the unit, and leave, but only after we've seen the child.

The condo units each have a single entrance, no back doors. The units are small, a lot of rooms in a compact space. On the back side, as you climb the steep incline of the hill, the property turns to rock: sandstone and desert brush.

An old concrete water tank is embedded into the hillside about halfway up the back road. Somebody has spray-painted graffiti in black letters across the front of it. We park just off the road in the shadows of this tank. I pull the lever on the side of my seat and recline while we wait.

It is almost seven twenty-nine when a light comes on in a window of one of the units.

'Is that it?'

'Yes.' I sit upright in the driver's seat.

'At least we know there's somebody home,' she says.

'Maybe. It could be a light on a timer.' I'm looking at my watch.

The illumination suddenly changes, subtle flashes on the window shade. Somebody's watching a television inside.

We leave the car where it is. Grinding gravel under the tires as we slowed down to park in the space behind the unit would only draw attention.

Susan grabs the beach bag and her purse, slings them both over her right shoulder. She is wearing shorts and sensible shoes: Nikes designed for running.

We start up the road. It's about a hundred yards from the water tank to the condos. We watch in silence the flashes of light dance on the window shade as we draw closer. When we reach the small leveled parking area behind unit three, we can hear the sound of the TV inside, the purple dramatic music of some Mexican soap, followed by the quick clip of Spanish as they try to sell something in a commercial. If it's her, Jessica has clearly picked up some Spanish in her stay. I try to get a glimpse through the window. Nothing. The shade is drawn tight.

We work our way around the building, toward the entrance at the front. From here we can see the pool below, and lights on in some of the other units, as well as the knee-high shafts of illumination from garden lamps along the path leading down.

'Let me knock on the door.' Susan whispers in my ear as we head down the narrowing path. I let her take the lead.

The door is painted Chinese red, and Susan taps on it with her knuckles. I can tell that it's too light. Whoever's inside didn't hear. Susan tries again, this time louder.

Suddenly the television goes mute. There are footsteps on the other side of the door. I expect it to open a crack, cautious eyes peering out from behind a security chain. Instead the door opens wide, and before we can say a word, the woman standing there turns her back and walks away. I don't even get a good look at her.

'You're early,' she says. 'I didn't expect you till eight.'

She says it as she walks with her back to us through the shadows of the dark living room, toward a door on the other side, a well-lit room.

She leaves us standing on the porch with the door wide open.

'I'm packed. Just one bag. That what you said, right?' She shouts from the other room.

'Right.' I look at Susan. She's as puzzled as I am. Still, we step instead and close the door behind us.

We follow the path the woman took through the living room. I'm in Susan's ear: 'Don't say anything.'

'I just have to write a check. Take me a minute,' says the woman.

We come through the doorway into the kitchen. She is leaning over the countertop, pen in hand, filling out a check. The small television, maybe thirteen inches, one like Susan used to own, is turned off. It's pushed under the overhead cabinets on a corner of the countertop for viewing from the kitchen table.

'Where did you park? I didn't hear your car.'

'Just down the hill,' I tell her.

'Take me a minute,' she says. 'You people really complicate things. Now I gotta pay the movers.' She looks up from the counter. The overhead fluorescents light up the features of her face. For the first time, I get a clear view.

'Are you sure we can't take my stuff with us? I just have the TV, a laptop, and some clothes.'

Her hair is dark, longer, not the pixie blonde from Jonah's photograph, and the clothes are different, more refined, a black pants outfit and low heels, but the face is similar, something about the eyes. She has Jessica's fine features,

437

thin nose, and high cheekbones. And the height looks about right. It could be her, but I'm not sure.

'Sorry. There's no room in the car,' I tell her. It seems to be what she's expecting, so I give it to her.

'Yeah. I know. Same old shit,' she says. 'Assholes are probably gonna steal all my stuff.' It's not clear whether she's talking about us, or the movers.

'You're gonna have to stop on the way out of town, though, so I can mail it.'

I don't say anything, so she looks at me again. I nod.

'Where's the child?' As soon as the words are out of my mouth Susan does a double-take, like she wasn't expecting me to be this direct.

It doesn't phase the gal with the checkbook. She keeps on writing.

'Sweetheart, come on out here. We're getting ready to go.'

As I turn I see a little boy in the doorway, slender shoulders, dark brown hair, a few freckles around the nose. He's wearing a pair of jeans and a T-shirt, high-top sport shoes like every kid I know, laced up only halfway with the baggy bottom of his pant legs caught on them.

The tension goes out of my body like an inverted hot-air balloon. I look over at Susan, wondering what the hell's going on, about to tell her it's time to leave.

When I do, Susan's not there. She's down on one knee.

'Honey. How are you?'

At first the child doesn't say anything. Then in a restrained, tiny voice: 'I'm okay.'

I look at the child again. When I do, I realize, it's not a

438

boy at all, but a little girl dressed up to look like a boy. The long hair is gone, and it's a different color, but the face, as I concentrate, is Amanda Hale's.

In that moment so much happens. Susan puts her arms around the child, lips to Amanda's ear and in a whisper that is barely audible to me three feet away. 'Your grandma and grandpa sent us.'

Amanda's eyes light up.

'Who are you? You get the hell out of here.' Jessica throws the checkbook at me. I catch it an inch from my face, ballplayer shagging a hot line drive.

She heads for Susan and the child, fingernails flaring, but I catch her from behind before she can get there, swing her around and pin her against the counter. She is wiry and strong for her size, flailing, trying to reach back over her head to scratch me, feet off the ground, kicking, calling me names, epithets I would not repeat.

Susan still has her purse and the beach bag over her shoulder. She reaches in the bag and comes out with the tape.

'Leave my mom alone.' Amanda's now hitting me in the behind, little overhand punches hardly perceptible, child's imitation of an eggbeater. Still, I feel like a thug.

Susan comes around the other side of the counter, the roll of tape in one hand. 'Hold her still.'

'No. Don't.' I stop her. Instead I snap Jessica around, do it quickly so that she can't get a free hand.

Now she's facing me. Spits at me. Dry mouth. She tries to knee me in the groin, but misses. I grab her by the arms just above the elbow and block her knees with my thigh.

439

'Let me tape her hands behind her,' says Susan.

'No.' Taping or tying Jessica, leaving her here is no longer an option.

I look her in the eye. 'Listen to me. I only have time to say this once. The people who are coming here are coming to kill you. Do you understand what I'm saying? They're going to kill you and whoever else happens to be around at the time.'

I glance down at Amanda, who has slid around me, and is now clinging to her mother's side.

'Who are you?'

'Never mind that.'

'You work for my father, don't you?' She's figured out that much.

'The only thing you need to know is that I don't work for Esteban Ontaveroz.'

'Esteban?'

'There's no time to talk,' I tell her.

'Why should I believe you? All you wanna do is take my child.'

'If that's all we wanted, you'd be on the floor gagged and bound,' says Susan.

'Why would Esteban want me? I didn't tell them anything.' She's talking about the authorities.

'It's what he thinks you might tell them that has him worried.'

'Stick around a few more minutes and we can all discuss it with him,' says Susan.

She has a point.

'How did he find me?'

'There's no time to talk about that now.'

'It couldn't be him,' she says. 'It was Suade's people who called me.'

'Suade is dead.' I feel a shiver go through her body. The expression on her face is like she has been sucker-punched, a dazed look.

'She was murdered nearly three months ago,' says Susan. 'It's been in all the papers up north. Don't you read?'

'I don't get the papers down here.'

She's no longer struggling. I loosen my grip on her arms. Step away, just a few inches. Amanda takes the opportunity, snuggles in closer to her mother.

'What about the TV?' I nod toward the set on the counter.

'The dish outside is broken. Spanish station's all I get.'

'The man who called you, did you recognize his voice?' says Susan.

Jessica shakes her head, looking around at the walls of the kitchen as if for answers.

'When did he call?' I ask.

'Late this morning,' she says.

'When?'

'I don't know. Maybe eleven. Just before noon.'

It's clear they couldn't have called from here in town. They would have been here by now.

'We don't have time to talk about it.' I grab Jessica by the arm, pushing her toward the door.

'Who killed Suade?' She stops, turns and looks at me, wanting to discuss this.

I don't tell her that her father is charged with the crime.

'Esteban?' she says.

'That would be my guess,' I tell her. 'Looking for you.'

'Oh, shit.' She looks at Amanda. 'We gotta go. Gotta get outta here.' She's finally getting it. Reality is setting in.

Absently, I pick up the checkbook that's fallen on the floor. I try to hand it to Jessica, but she's already out the door, pushing Amanda ahead of her.

'The car's down the back road.' I tell her.

Jessica grabs a purse hanging over the back of a chair in the living room. Susan's carrying the beach bag and her purse. Suddenly she realizes she's left the tape on the counter. She turns for it.

'Leave it.' I push her out of the kitchen ahead of me, as I take one last glimpse at my watch in the light. If Jessica was expecting them in half an hour, they're running late.

We race through the living room, out the front door, not bothering to close it behind us, and head up the path toward the parking area behind the condos. Susan's in the lead. Somehow she's gotten a hold of Amanda. The child is running full out, her little legs struggling to keep up. I position Jessica ahead of me, where I can watch her. She's having trouble in heels.

We've covered about twenty-five yards, a quarter of the distance down the dirt road to the concrete cistern and the Jeep, when a set of headlights suddenly veers onto the road below us. The dust kicked up by our feet hangs in the light like lasered smoke. Before we can move, the four of us are framed in the dual beams of light.

Whoever is driving hesitates. The car comes to a grinding halt. It just sits there, its engine idling, headlights staring at us. For a second I think maybe they're just nosing onto the road, making a U-turn.

Then suddenly the car lurches forward, wheels kicking up dust, throwing gravel.

Instinctively, we know. Susan is first; she turns and starts to run up the road pulling the child behind her. She stops, tries to pick up Amanda, but the child is too heavy. I grab Susan by the arm, push her in the direction of the condos, and scoop up the girl in my arms.

We run back toward the condos, Jessica falling behind, her heels not working on the dirt road.

By the time we reach the parking area, the car, a vintage dark Cadillac, has already passed the cistern and is racing up the road, Jessica a dozen steps behind us. I put Amanda down. Susan takes her by the hand, down the path toward the condos. I wait for Jessica. She catches up. We run down the path toward the condos. I've got her by the hand, retracing our steps. Without thinking, Jessica heads toward her condo.

'No. Not that way,' I tell her. 'There's no way out.'

Instead we run down the terraced path, jumping sections of steps, two and three at a time. Jessica falls in front of me. I nearly trip over her. She skins her knees but barely pauses. Hopping on one foot, then the other, she pulls off her high heels and tosses them into the shrubbery. She is now barefoot, more fleet. We make it to the level of the swimming pool, down the stairs to the garages, where we catch up with Susan and Amanda.

We stop for a second, try to catch our breath. Car doors slam shut above us on the hill. I count three. Then one more. There are at least four of them, men running, the sound of footfalls.

'Vámonos.'

They're coming down the path.

We start running, this time toward the street, under the wooden sign, LAS VENTANAS DE CABO. We race toward the antique shop on the corner, where Susan and I had first glimpsed the condos that morning. The lights are out. There is nothing open, no signs of life. The tourist area is still four blocks away. The nearest taxi stand is closer to eight.

We run under the veranda of the shop, around the front, down three steps into the street, and across toward the plaza.

Amanda is about to collapse. The child is out of breath, confused and scared. I grab her in my arms, throw her up over my shoulder, and we cut down the hill along the side of the plaza. Susan has now taken up the rear, beach bag and purse over her shoulder.

We cross the street below the plaza. Only two more blocks, all downhill. If we can make it, we can lose ourselves in the crowd of tourists.

I'm running, jogging with Amanda, her head bouncing on my shoulder, concentrating on the steep incline of the street, as it curves toward the right. The footing is treacherous, stone stairs loom up out of the dark. Like an obstacle course, the steps extend only two or three feet across a seven-foot-wide sidewalk. The rest is a sheer drop with no railing, and little light, a four-foot fall onto hard concrete if you're not looking.

I'm trying to watch the steps, so I don't look up until I reach the bottom. That's when I see them across the street, about a block down. The one on this side has just slammed the driver's-side door and is crossing the street. The other one is coming around the front of the car.

Trying to look like tourists, being casual, in dark suits and black shirts, just two studs out on the town, when one of them blows it. He makes eye contact with me.

Instantly he knows that I've made him. It's the driver, the man behind the wheel of Cyclops the night they followed me from the jail.

As soon as he realizes, they start to run, closing the distance between us. One of them reaches inside his coat. When his hand comes out, it's holding a pistol. I'm frozen in place. Jessica, then Susan come flying down the stairs, nearly piling into us.

Susan tries to keep going. I grab her arm, try to stop her for a second, then realize it's our only chance: the intersection to a small side street about twenty yards down. We run downhill toward the two men.

One of them stops, takes aim, pistol up in a two-handed stance.

'Get down.' I nearly drop Amanda on the sidewalk. We crouch down behind cars parked at the curb, lower our silhouettes and keep moving.

The gunman loses his target, doesn't shoot, finally lowers the gun and starts running toward us again.

We reach the intersection before they do. Now it's a full-out race, up the street. I'm lugging Amanda, her head over my shoulder.

Up ahead I can see tourists moving on the street. Neon signs, a walled courtyard, and iron gate leading to a restaurant. Music, the strains of 'Kokomo'.

Jessica is ahead of me. She starts to slow down, false

sense of safety. These men have been programmed to kill, and they're going to do it.

'Don't stop.' As I say it, a bullet ricochets off the building a foot from my head, followed by the crack of the shot like a muted firecracker a fraction of a second later. No one seems to notice. The crowds keep walking up ahead. People ambling in and out of shops.

We race across the street toward the restaurant, its courtyard and neon sign. There's a guy out front, wearing one of those traditional Mexican white cotton shirts, the kind they wear to weddings, greeting customers, working the courtyard gate from inside, watching us as we run toward him, wondering, I can tell, why we're working up a sweat on a warm summer night.

This thought coincides with the crack of air as the bullet passing my ear breaks the sound barrier. The guy's face at the gate assumes a vacant, quizzical expression. A perfectly round red circle appears with the suddenness of a fly landing, just above his right eye. An instant later a river of blood gushes over his face, turning it into a crimson mask. The report of the shot reaches us just as his knees buckle. He hits the stone pavers like a sack of dirt, his crumpled body blocking the closed gate.

A young woman sitting at one of the tables outside in the courtyard realizes what has happened. She screams, others turn. Panic sweeps the courtyard. Chairs are overturned as people run into tables. A large umbrella tips over and starts to roll.

I push hard against the gate, shoulder against wrought iron. Another shot. This time it hits stone over my head. I push harder, sliding the dead weight of the man's body

446

maybe eighteen inches until it jams up against the gate. I send Amanda through.

'Run,' I tell her.

Instead, she stands there looking at me, frozen in panic.

Susan and Jessica follow her through the gate. Susan grabs the child's hand, nearly jerking her off her feet, and hauls her toward the restaurant, Jessica grasping for Amanda's other hand trailing in their wake.

I step through, look down at the man on the ground. His eyes are wide open, death trance. There's nothing I can do, so I use his body. Close the gate and push him up against it. Another round whizzes by.

I move deeper into the courtyard, out of the line of fire. By now the yard is empty of people. I'm the last to retreat down a wide course of steps that seem to span thirty feet, like the mouth of some giant whale, hot salsa music erupting from the bowels. I find myself in a disco and bar, subterranean flashing lights.

Near the door the place is in a panic, people trying to crawl over one another to get away.

One of the bouncers is looking over from the bar that spans one side, wondering what the hell's going on. People are turning over tables, running for the exits.

Deeper inside, the panic spreads slowly, dampened by the noise. Couples on the dance floor are oblivious, their bodies gyrating to the music, timing their moves to the flashing colored lights that shoot up through the floor with each beat.

Susan topples a table and gets behind it with Amanda, Jessica on the floor behind them.

447

I'm watching the door, waiting. I join them, and suddenly realize there's no protection here.

One of the bouncers, cue ball for a head, standing at least six-four, two-eighty, heads for the entrance.

'No!' I shout at him above the music.

He gives me a look, like *Who the hell are you?* Whatever it is, he'll deal with it. He disappears up the stairs and two seconds later I hear shots, three or four, rapid fire, almost imperceptible above the percussion of the music. The man's body rolls back down the stairs. The dance floor empties. People disappear, vanish into the walls. The two bartenders are suddenly gone.

Jessica looks at me. 'They want me. Take Amanda and go,' she says.

'No.' Amanda's crying.

'Over behind the bar,' I tell them. It's a long serpentine affair running with the curve of the wall, the only place left to hide.

Jessica's not moving, but Susan grabs the child. Amanda's arm gets hung up in the beach bag on Susan's shoulder, so Susan takes a second and drops the bag. As she does, I see it.

'Go!' I'm not even paying attention to them any longer, my mind lost in thought.

Jessica tries to argue with me. I push her toward the bar.

She finally follows Susan, retreating on her hands and knees across the open floor.

I reach inside the beach bag, grab the small towel and can of ether. On the floor is a book of matches knocked out of one of the ashtrays as the tables went over. I pick them up and put them in my pocket

I try to turn the cap on the can. It won't budge, so I wrap the towel over it and try again. It comes loose. I unscrew it just one turn, then carefully keeping the towel over the can, I turn my face to avoid the fumes and scurry across the floor toward the stairs. I take a long sweeping arc, staying to one side to avoid becoming a target, and stop with my back against the wall, at one edge of a broad stairway.

There's a good thirty feet of open space across the base of the stairs. There are only four steps up to the level of the courtyard outside. One of the gunmen is centered in the opening above. I can see him backlit against the lights from the courtyard outside. Fortunately he's looking into a darker cavern with occasional flashes of light from the strobes under the dance floor, the music still blaring.

Now I'm committed. I unscrew the cap from the can and toss it, then turn and race across the opening, this time with the towel off the can, leaving a smoking stream of ether on the floor in my wake.

He takes a shot. It goes wide. Another shot. His friend has joined him. The bullet hits the floor where I'd been a stride earlier. What they're seeing is a moving picture, flashing strobes.

They fire one more time at the flickering image, but it's too late. I've made it to the other side, back against the wall, at the near end of the bar.

They work for an angle. I can hear their feet on the stone steps above. One of them puts three rounds into the wall above my head, plaster flying, covering fire, while his friend presses to the wall on my side and comes down two more steps. I can hear his breath around the corner.

Now there are voices outside in the courtyard. The second

gunman, the one up in the courtyard is talking to whoever is there. I realize their compatriots from up top have finally found us. That means there are now at least six of them. They're regrouping. Final assault.

I feel in my pocket for the matches. Shake the can. It has maybe an inch in the bottom still, the opening covered by the towel.

Down on one knee, I pour out the remaining contents, carefully forming a thin stream. Shaking the last few drops as I huddle behind the bar. I struggle to suppress a cough, the effects of the ether. I'm getting dizzy, going cloudy.

I hear footsteps on the stairs. Book of matches in one hand can in the other, I rise up on my knees and throw the can across the room. There's a hail of gunfire, flashes matching the strobes on the dance floor as two of the gunmen are silhouetted in the opening.

'Paul.' I hear Susan screaming, turn to look. Jessica's running across the open floor. Amanda's gone after her.

Jessica senses it, turns and stops. 'No!'

They fire again.

The flash of my match hits the stream of ether, just as the bullets rip through Jessica.

A devilish dancing blue flame streaks across the floor, igniting in a fireball, that sears my face as I am blown onto my back, behind the bar, by the blast.

Hideous screams as one of the gunmen twists and dances toward the opening at the end of the bar. As he comes into view he's a human torch. Flaming, he falls nearly on top of me. I crawl away from him like a crab on my back, feeling the oxygen as it's sucked from my lungs, out of the cavernous room.

I turn and scramble under darkening smoke to other end of the bar. By the time I get there, Susan has thrown her body across Amanda's, to protect her.

I hear the crack of gunfire outside, some of it automatic. I can't see a thing through the haze of smoke and flickering flames. The other gunman has joined his friend. His body lies smoldering in a heap at the foot of the stairs.

CHAPTER
THIRTY-THREE

I crawl across the floor toward Susan and the child. The heat over our heads is intense, the black smoke ominous. She and Amanda are shaken, but otherwise unharmed. The three of us crawl toward Jessica ten feet away. Her eyes are open, she is breathing, heavy labored gasps, frothing blood from her nose and the corner of her mouth. She looks at Amanda, smiles, and her eyes take on the trance of death.

I drag her toward the stairs under the ceiling of smoke. Susan follows on her knees, then tries to staunch blood from the wounds, alternately giving Jessica mouth-to-mouth, wiping blood from her own lips with the back of her hand as she does it. All the while Amanda is clinging to her mother's arm. It is a futile gesture from the inception. I think Susan and I both know it. But we can't quit, if for no other reason than Amanda.

It takes nearly ten minutes before someone opens a door somewhere in the back. The cross-ventilation begins driving the smoke from the dark cavern.

The music continues to blare, the strobes lighting up the smoke like sheet lightning in a hurricane. As Mexican police enter the building, they hold us at gunpoint while they search us for weapons, then quickly usher us from the building while they continue their sweep. I am left the heartless task of peeling Amanda from her mother's lifeless form.

Carrying the child up the stairs, I lose sight of Susan for an instant. When I turn to look, she is on her knees again, as if she has fallen over one of the bodies, the smoking corpse of one of the gunmen. She pushes herself away from it as if repulsed, then flees up the stairs as if trying to escape a nightmare.

The gunshots outside were the Mexican judicial police. Like the cavalry, they arrived in the nick of time. With them, are two more familiar faces: the agents that Murphy introduced me to that day at the restaurant in San Diego, Jack and Bob.

As we stand outside, watching smoke vent from the disco and crowds form behind police lines, it is Jack who tells me that they had been tracking Ontaveroz for days. They had followed him to Cabo, and were only moments behind when the ether-fueled fireball erupted from the mouth of the disco.

The agent wags a finger at me, tells me to follow him, so I do, toward a line of blanket-covered figures laid out on the ground like cordwood inside the wall of the courtyard.

The agent calling himself Bob reaches down and pulls back the blanket on one of the bodies sprawled on the ground. The dead man is lying on his back, hands at his sides.

'Meet Esteban Ontaveroz,' says the agent. 'Along with two of his enforcers. Not counting the ones you toasted inside.'

One of the shrouded bodies on the ground is Jessica Hale.

The fire department arrives and douses the last flames, some charred beams over the doorway, where the heat of the blast ignited the wood.

The Mexican authorities have already questioned Susan and me. We made no mention of our plan to kidnap the child, only to find her. They seem satisfied. Susan showed them the certified copy of the order of custody from her purse. With that, her credentials, and a good word from the DEA agents they released us to the custody of the American consul. For the Mexican police, though two of their own are dead, it is a law-enforcement fiesta. They have killed one of the most notorious drug kingpins in the country. The Mexican media will no doubt be eating it up.

Five hours later, we are back in San Diego, Amanda in tow. Mary meets us at the airport, and the scene that follows would dissolve a heart of stone.

Tuesday morning, I'm back in court. Jonah is still in the hospital, though his spirits seem to be carrying him toward recovery. With Amanda home, he now has something to live for. She has already visited him twice in the hospital, and yesterday he was sitting up.

Jonah has confirmed what he blurted out seconds before he collapsed that day in court; that he dropped Jeffers' pistol over the side months before Suade's murder. He'd gotten rid of it, he says, because he didn't want it on board, or at his house. Amanda was constantly having friends over, and

Jonah had begun to worry about accidents, kids and their curiosity.

Today Harry and I try taking the first step toward ending the nightmare of the trial. We make an offer of proof.

Ryan is furious, claiming that the evidence and my witnesses were never disclosed.

But Peltro allows the offer, relying on his earlier order that if I can show some connection to Ontaveroz I can use him in my defense. The offer of proof is in effect a motion to allow evidence, and can be conducted without the presence of the defendant. All the while Peltro is keeping the jurors locked up, sequestered in a hotel at night, and confined in the jury room during the day. How long he can do this is uncertain.

He asks me about Jonah's health. I tell him I don't know; I'll have to confer with the doctors.

Ryan has a serious problem. It is the evidence surrounding the unfolding events in Cabo. While Jessica may be dead, there is no denying that Ontaveroz was stalking her. The Drug Enforcement Administration will not allow either of its two undercover agents to testify. But they have produced a Mexican official, a member of a special unit, an untouchable of the federal Mexican judicial police, who has hunted Ontaveroz with dogged persistence for more than two years.

Lieutenant Ernesto Lopez Santez is an eighteen-year veteran of Mexico's drug wars. He is a tall, slender man, with a long narrow face, jet black hair, and intense dark eyes. He speaks very fast, Spanish tripping off his tongue while the interpreter struggles to keep up, before Lopez decides that his English, while not perfect, may be better for our purposes.

'Where did you learn your English, Lieutenant?'

'*Escuela*. School,' he says. 'In Jalisco.'

The purpose of the offer of proof is to determine whether the defense may produce evidence that Ontaveroz had both motive and an opportunity to kill Suade.

'Can you tell us where you were on Saturday evening, the eighteenth – that is, three days ago?'

'Your Honor,' says Ryan. 'This is irrelevant.'

'That's what we're here to decide,' says Peltro. 'Go ahead.' He motions to Lopez that he may answer.

'I was in Cabo San Lucas.'

'And were you on duty?'

'Jess.'

'Can you tell the court what happened that night?'

'There was a shootout, at a restaurant. Several drug dealers were killed,' he says. 'And two officers.'

'Can you tell us how many assailants, criminals, there were that evening?'

'Jess. Cin—' He corrects himself. 'Five of them,' he says. 'Maybe more.'

'Five of them were killed?'

'Jess. Dat is correct.'

'Did you identify one of these men, one of the ones who was killed as Esteban José Ontaveroz?'

'Jess.'

'And was he wanted in Mexico?'

He looks at me as if perhaps he doesn't understand something about the question.

'*¿Fugitivo?*' The interpreter helps him out.

'Oh, *sí*. Jess. Ontaveroz was a fugitive.'

'If I showed you a photograph of this man, Esteban Ontaveroz, would you recognize him?'

457

'Maybe,' he says.

On the podium in front of me I have a folder. Inside are several prints of the same photograph, made only hours before. I pass two of these to the bailiff, one for the witness and another for the judge, then hand one to Ryan, who begins to study it closely.

'This is an enlarged photograph,' I tell the witness.

He looks at it, and nods.

'Have you seen this photograph before?'

'No.'

'There are several people in the frame. I would ask you to concentrate on the man in the dark jacket in the background. The one with the mustache.'

'Where did you get this?' he asks me.

I ignore the question. 'Do you recognize that man?'

'Jess.' His eyebrows go up.

'Can you tell the court who he is?'

'It es Esteban Ontaveroz.'

'You're sure about that?'

'Jess.'

'Your Honor.' I look at Peltro. 'We have a witness who will testify that this photograph was taken on the docks at Spanish Landing here in San Diego on the morning of the day that Zolanda Suade was murdered.'

Jonah's drunk friend with the camera, the one who wanted one last shot with the fish, had taken perhaps the most important photograph of Jonah's life. I had seen prints when they came to Mary's house two days after Jonah was arrested. The police had subpoenaed these as evidence of the marlin and had introduced them into evidence. But I did not make the connection until I saw the bodies lined up in the patio outside the disco. I asked to see the body of Ontaveroz. I wanted to look at the man who had haunted my client and killed Joaquin Murphy.

It wasn't until I came back and looked at the photograph with a magnifying glass that I made the connection. Ontaveroz was indeed tracking Jonah, hoping Jessica would show up.

'Additionally . . .' I start to pass out other copies of the photograph; these are not enlarged or cropped, so that the entire frame is shown.

'Your Honor, you can see the defendant, Jonah Hale, standing near the marlin, the blood from which has already been introduced into evidence by the state. We have photographic experts who can testify,' I say, 'that Ontaveroz was no more than ten feet from the marlin when this shot was taken, and that the only way off that dock was past the fish, which took up almost the entire width of the dock.'

'Counsel's reaching,' says Ryan. 'Is there any blood on Ontaveroz in that picture?' He directs this to the court, but doesn't get an answer.

Whether this would be sufficient for the blood to get into the Mexican's car or not, Ryan now has a problem. Ontaveroz has been placed in proximity to the physical evidence. It is an explanation for the seemingly inexplicable, the stuff of which reasonable doubt is made.

The press is in the front row, taking it all down, jotting their notes, scratching on paper.

But I am not done. There is another, seemingly gratuitous piece of evidence, something that I could not have even hoped for a week ago.

'Lieutenant Lopez, did you or your men have an opportunity to search the dead assailants at the scene in Cabo San Lucas?'

He nods. 'Jess.'

'And what did you find?'

'Guns. Drugs. Mostly cocaine,' he says.

'Specifically with reference to one of the dead gunmen found inside the disco, besides firearms and drugs did you find anything else?'

'We found a cigar,' he says.

With this, there is a perceptible hum of anticipation from the courtroom.

'Do you have that cigar with you?' I ask him.

'Jess.' He reaches into the inside pocket of his coat, and when his hand comes out, it is holding a small silver metal cylinder, the same kind that held the cigar delivered to the cops by John Brower.

'Your Honor, we have a witness, an expert, who is prepared to testify that the cigar in that tube is a Montecristo A, and that the seal on the tube has never been removed. That cigar is identical to the partially smoked cigar stub found at the scene of Zolanda Suade's murder.'

With this the hum of voices in the courtroom turns into a roar.

'Your Honor. Your Honor.' Ryan trying to get the judge's attention. 'We demand an opportunity to test that cigar,' says Ryan.

Commotion in the courtroom, a tumult of voices. Peltro slams his gavel. He looks down at the witness. I have to read the judge's lips to comprehend what is being said because of the noise. 'You found this on the dead gunman in Cabo?'

I think this is what he has said, and the witness nods.

I'm not sure the court reporter has picked this up, but it doesn't matter.

'Counsel in my chambers,' says Peltro. 'The court is in recess.'

'Your Honor, they can't explain how that fish's blood got in their car.' Ryan is talking about the Mexican's vehicle. 'Do they have the car?'

'We don't need the car,' I tell him. 'What do you want, a picture of Ontaveroz shooting Suade?'

'I'll bet you could get me one in an hour,' he says.

'Are you questioning the authenticity of the photograph?' Peltro is looking at Ryan. The problem the prosecutor has is that the state has already made the photograph of the marlin hoisted on the dock a part of its case. The figure who is enhanced in the enlargement is clearly visible in the original.

'No,' says Ryan. 'There's still no evidence of blood on the man,' he adds.

'You couldn't walk on that dock without getting it on you,' I tell the judge.

Peltro holds up both hands, a motion for us both to shut up.

'We have a problem here,' he says. 'The defendant, at least for the moment, is unable to continue with the trial. The question is how long we should wait.' Peltro wants to sidestep the issues of evidence and get to more practical matters.

Ryan starts to see the handwriting on the wall. His case is now in shambles. Peltro is unwilling to hold the jury indefinitely, and the judge is looking for some middle ground.

'Even if I buy your argument on the blood,' says Peltro, 'what about the cigar?' he turns this on Ryan.

'We want to test that cigar,' says Ryan. As soon as he says it, he knows he shouldn't have.

'It's still sealed in its damned container,' says Peltro. He's got the cigar sitting on his desk in the center of the big green blotter where we can all see it. 'You really think you're gonna find it's not the same brand?'

In the face of such skepticism, Ryan has no answer.

'You can test the cigar, but I'm telling you right now that unless you've got conclusive evidence to the contrary, this is coming in,' he says. He taps the cigar in front of him. 'And as for the picture, that's already in.'

I sit in the chair across from Peltro's desk, smiling. If I could reach over and grab the little cylinder with Lopez's cigar in it right now, I might be tempted to take it out and light it up.

'That is,' says Peltro, 'unless you want me to declare a mistrial?' He is offering Ryan an alternative, something to save face.

I sit up straight in my chair, not expecting this.

'And you,' he says. He looks at me. 'Your client doesn't need the continuing stress of this trial, so don't give me any garbage about the need to clear his good name. Unless they changed the law since I got out of law school, you can't defame the dead, and that's what he's gonna be if you drag this out any longer.'

I don't say a word but settle back in my chair. Something tells me he is right. I can sandbag Ryan, probably kick the crap out of him if the trial goes forward, but Jonah might not live to see the end of it.

By morning the newspapers will be filled with it: the shooting in Mexico, another violent gun battle with the drug lords. Only this one will have a local angle, a connection to the murder of Zolanda Suade. Ryan's case is over, and he knows it.

'If we have a mistrial,' he says, 'it has to be predicated solely on the inability of the defendant to continue with the trial.' Ryan has already bought into it, scrambling for political cover. This way Jonah can't sue him, and he has a ready answer for the press. He didn't lose the case. In light of the evidence, he merely chose not to recharge it.

Peltro agrees. He looks at me. I would rather have an outright dismissal, but the judge cannot do that, and I know it.

'Then we're agreed,' he says. 'Let's go out and put it on the record.'

CHAPTER
THIRTY-FOUR

Tonight I am waiting for Susan at Casa Bandini in Old Town, sipping a margarita and listening to the strains of mariachi as they serenade a young couple across the courtyard, forty feet away.

The doctors have released Jonah from the hospital. They continue to monitor his condition, but it is believed that he has suffered only minor damage to some muscle tissue in the heart. He is home with Mary and Amanda, trying to put their lives back together.

The other night I sat with them for an hour and told them of the last moments in their daughter's life, the final glimpse of an existence that seemed so wasted. I watched Jonah's face as the tears washed down his cheeks, and explained to him that in the end it was an act of love that had cost his daughter her life.

The world may judge her for the thousand missteps of her youth, but that night in the disco she ran for a reason more primal than mere survival; she ran to put distance between death and her daughter. Jessica may have taken the child for reasons of spite, but in the end she surrendered her, and her own life, out of love.

The local papers are filled with the news of Ontaveroz. Jonah may be free as the result of a mistrial, but there is no way the state will ever retry him. The press has connected all the dots in its own inimitable fashion, some of them in the wrong places – the accepted assumption being that the Mexican not only killed Suade, but Murphy and Jason Crow as well. The cigar on the body of the gunman in the disco was the clincher – the cigar Susan dropped on him on the way out.

It took me a while to piece it together. A rare brand, the same cigar, it was too much of a coincidence, until I realized that the cops had never collected the one Jonah had given to her. I suspect that it was in the bottom of her purse, still in its little metal container, the way Jonah had handed it to her that day in my office.

In the urgency of the moment I had seen her fall over the smoldering body. I was wrong. Susan saw the opportunity to torpedo Ryan and his case, and she took it.

It is not something that, even if I wished to, I could prove. With all the fingers that have now handled the cigar container, Lopez, God knows how many Mexican cops, and Peltro, the chances of collecting anything that even resembles one of Susan's clear fingerprints would be on the order of a miracle.

What I do know is that without that cigar I might not have been able to convince Peltro to admit the evidence, or open the gate for a mistrial.

The cigar was Susan's way of giving Amanda her life

466

back, removing the cloud from Jonah's head. She was playing God. Jonah had given it to her, and now she was giving it back, in her own way. It was her path to redemption, because it was Susan in the car with Suade the night she was killed.

It has been a week since Peltro declared the mistrial. That afternoon, Ryan stood on the steps of the courthouse and announced that his office would not be recharging Jonah, that the interests of justice had been served.

It is perhaps the one point on which we agree. I am certain that Suade's death was a deed of preservation, an act of self-defense.

It wasn't until this evening that I finally pieced it all together. Changing to come here, I was going through the hamper, putting up a load of wash, when my fingers brushed against it: the hard, flat surface through the pocket of a soiled pair of Bermuda shorts. They were the ones I had worn that night in Cabo, still smelling of smoke.

In the back pocket I found the checkbook I had picked up from Jessica's kitchen floor, the one she'd thrown at me. In all the confusion I had slipped it into my pocket and forgotten it.

I opened it. The check, made out and signed in Jessica's hand, the one she had intended to mail to the movers, was still inside, connected at the perforations. The name on the signature was the same as the one printed at the top of the checks: the name of Susan McKay.

It came flooding back. The television set in the kitchen didn't just look like Susan's; it was Susan's. I'd wondered how Susan found them in Cabo when no one else could. The checkbook contained the answer. Jessica had used several

identities in Mexico, writing checks from other people'
accounts, and using stolen credit cards. She had writte
one other check from Susan's account. It was dated a wee
earlier. The carbon set was still in the book. It was a chec
for the last month's rent, written to Las Ventanas de Cabo

I suspect that Jessica figured no one would have time t
trace it. She was already on a fixed timetable, one that sh
and Suade had established when she first went south. Sh
would be gone, hustled by Suade back into the States with
new identity and a new life. That's what she thought. Wha
she didn't know was that Suade was dead.

Jessica and Jason Crow had broken into Susan's house, bu
it was no random act. They had taken her checkbook, credi
cards, her television, the small camera, and one other iten
the little laptop computer, the one Susan used for work.
am guessing that this is what Suade wanted, the reason sh
sent them to Susan's house in the first place, the quid pr
quo for Suade's help in snatching Amanda.

Whatever information was in that computer, couple
with the words of scandal in Suade's press release, it wa
sufficiently potent to send Susan to Suade's office tha
afternoon.

I see her coming across the courtyard, a broad smile, an
a swirling summer dress. I get up. She takes my hand an
leans across the table. I give her a peck on the cheek.

'Have you been waiting long?' she asks. Settles int
her chair.

'Just a few minutes,' I tell her.

She looks at my drink. 'I'll have to catch up,' she says.

The waiter comes and she tells him, 'I'll have one of those.
Before he can even leave our table, her expression suddenl

468

urns more somber. There is something she has to talk to me about. She tells me it is serious, that it affects *us*.

In this moment, the flash of an eye, I glimpse honesty, that Susan, after all that has gone before, is going to finally unburden herself: all the mysteries of that evening when Suade died.

Instead she says, 'I've taken a job in another city.'

I look at her, mystified, for the first time clearly confused by the woman I thought I had come to know.

'I know you're surprised,' she says. 'But I've thought about it for a long time. My career here is finished. There are people downtown who are never going to forget what I did.'

'What was that?'

'You know,' she says. 'Telling you about Suade's gun. Siding with you in the trial. Our escapade to Cabo.'

'They are saying good things about you in the paper. Calling you a hero,' I tell her.

She shakes her head. 'Publicly some of them are being forced to say that. But they have long memories for those who are not team players,' she says. She means politics being the low life-form that it is.

Her drink comes: tequila in a punch bowl. She takes the straw in her teeth.

I think she is waiting for me to ask the location of this new job, but I don't. Instead I reach into my coat pocket, take it out and place it gently on the table between us, blue plastic cover, just like a million others that the banks give out every year.

She looks at it sort of cockeyed, straw still between her teeth, before it dawns on her.

469

'Aw, God.' The expression on Susan's face is one of pain crossed with fear. She doesn't look up immediately, as if she can't bear to make eye contact.

'How long have you known?' The words seem to float from her as if from a daze.

'I found it this evening.'

A sigh escapes her, suddenly sapped, she sits and looks at me as if perhaps she is not sure what I am going to do now.

'I wanted to tell you,' she says. 'If you only knew how much I wanted to tell you.'

'Why didn't you?'

'My kids,' she says. 'I couldn't. They would have separated me from my children. I would have faced trial. They would have jailed me. It would have been easier,' she says, 'to take my own life.' She says it as if this thought has occurred to her more than once. 'I know what you're thinking. I let Jonah face it.'

It is the one thing for which I cannot forgive her.

'That's why I tried,' she says, 'to lead you in the right directions. Why I told you about Suade's gun.'

'What did you do with it?'

'That night, after it happened . . .' Her gaze trails off. 'I was scared, confused. I didn't even realize the gun was still in my car. I drove. I headed back toward Imperial Beach. When I saw it on the floor, on the passenger side, I didn't know what to do. So I parked in town and took a walk on the pier.'

Susan dropped the pistol off the end of the pier in Imperial Beach.

'When did you write the serial numbers down?'

470

'I didn't.' She looks hurt that I could even think that at such a moment of panic she would have the presence of mind. 'Obviously, I knew she had the pistol. I didn't know Jonah would be arrested. Afterward,' she says, 'I sent one of my investigators to check the federal sales registration records. I knew he would find it.'

'How did she die?'

'It was an accident,' she says.

'She pulled the gun on you?'

Susan nods, looks at me quizzically, not certain how I would know this. I've never told her about the business with Suade's hand in the bottom of her purse the day I visited her.

'You have to believe me,' she says.

'I do. Why did you go to see her?'

'She had information.'

'Your computer?'

She nods, tears beginning to form in her eyes. 'I'd helped her. I gave her information, on Davidson.'

The unbending marine had been beating his boy, and Susan knew it, but she was helpless to do anything about it. Even an out-of-county judge wasn't going to call a brother of the cloth an abuser, take away his joint custody. Susan's only recourse was Suade.

Susan provided critical information, stuff that wasn't public, from the messy divorce, so that Suade could help Davidson's former wife unload securities and clean out his bank accounts, gaining enough financial resources to go into hiding.

'Suade assumed she had an ally for life,' says Susan. 'When I told her I wouldn't help her on other cases, she sent Jessica to my house. She knew I wouldn't keep stuff like that, the information on Davidson's financial records, in my office.'

'Your laptop computer.' I say it matter of fact.

She nods. 'I downloaded information from court records,' she says. 'I had access.'

For a moment we just sit there. She looks at me, and then she says it. 'What are you going to do now?'

For the first time since broaching the issue, I smile at her. 'You should take your checkbook and put it back in your purse – before somebody steals it.'

The relief is written in her eyes. 'The job is in Colorado,' she tells me.

'You should like that.' I make no reference to myself. Somehow she knows that I will not be following her.